W9-DEE-706

JONATHAN JANZ

THE SORROWS

This is a **FLAME TREE PRESS** book

FLAME TREE PRESS
6 Melbray Mews, London, SW6 3NS, UK
flametreepress.com

Distribution and warehouse:
Baker & Taylor Publisher Services (BTPS)
30 Amberwood Parkway, Ashland, OH 44805
btpubservices.com

Thanks to the Flame Tree Press team, including:
Taylor Bentley, Frances Bodiam, Federica Ciaravella, Don D'Auria, Chris Herbert, Matteo Middlemiss, Josie Mitchell, Mike Spender, Cat Taylor, Maria Tissot, Nick Wells, Gillian Whitaker.

The cover is created by Flame Tree Studio with
thanks to Nik Keevil and Shutterstock.com.
The font families used are Avenir and Bembo.

Flame Tree Press is an imprint of Flame Tree Publishing Ltd
flametreepublishing.com

A copy of the CIP data for this book is available from the British Library and the Library of Congress.

HB ISBN: 978-1-78758-058-9
PB ISBN: 978-1-78758-056-5
ebook ISBN: 978-1-78758-059-6
Also available in FLAME TREE AUDIO

Printed in the US at Bookmasters, Ashland, Ohio

JONATHAN JANZ

THE SORROWS

FLAME TREE PRESS
London & New York

'Look about you, Clarke. You see the mountain, and hill following after hill, as wave on wave, you see the woods and orchard, the fields of ripe corn, and the meadows reaching to the reed-beds by the river. You see me standing here beside you, and hear my voice; but I tell you that all these things – yes, from that star that has just shone out in the sky to the solid ground beneath our feet – I say that all these are but dreams and shadows; the shadows that hide the real world from our eyes. There is a real world, but it is beyond this glamour and this vision, beyond these 'chases in Arras, dreams in a career,' beyond them all as beyond a veil. I do not know whether any human being has ever lifted that veil; but I do know, Clarke, that you and I shall see it lifted this very night from before another's eyes. You may think this all strange nonsense; it may be strange, but it is true, and the ancients knew what lifting the veil means. They called it seeing the god Pan.'

Arthur Machen

The Great God Pan

This book is for my grandmother, Martha Janz. I'd have never written this story or anything else without her love and constant support. Thanks for always believing, Grandma. I miss you every day.

PART ONE
BEN

CHAPTER ONE

On the way up the mountain, Ben Shadeland flirted with the idea of killing Eddie Blaze. The problem was, Ben could barely breathe.

"Good Lord," Eddie said. "You sound like an obscene phone caller back there."

Ben ignored him. Between ragged breaths, he asked, "We still on your dad's land?"

"Only a small part is residential. Sonoma County owns the rest."

Ben looked around. "So we're not supposed to be here?"

"Not after dark," Eddie answered, and in the moonlight Ben saw him grin.

Great, he thought. Trespassing on government land at one in the morning. Trekking around the wilderness was fine for hard-core fitness freaks, but for out-of-shape guys in their late thirties, this kind of hike was a surefire ticket to the ER. If a heart attack didn't get him, a broken leg would.

As if answering his thoughts, Eddie said, "Want me to carry you?"

"Go to hell."

When Ben risked a look ahead, the toe of his boot caught on something. He fell awkwardly, his outstretched palms pierced by thorns. He lay there a moment, riding out the pain but relishing the momentary rest.

"You still alive?"

Rather than answering, he rolled over and examined his torn palms. The blood dribbling out of his wounds looked black and oily in the starlight. He rubbed them on the belly of his shirt and pushed to his feet.

When they reached the cave Ben had to kneel for several moments to avoid passing out. This was the price he paid, his only physical activity lifting weights and chasing his three-year old son around the yard.

Of course, that was before the divorce. Now he only played with his son on weekends, and when he did he was haunted by the specter of returning Joshua to his ex-wife. The lump in his throat caught him off guard.

He spat and glanced up at the cave. "So what's the story?"

"It's a good one," Eddie answered.

"It better be."

"Come on," Eddie said and switched on a large black Maglite.

"You had that all along?"

Eddie started toward the cave.

"What, we're going in?"

"Don't you want to retrace Arthur Vaughan's steps?"

He stared at Eddie, whose face was barely visible within the cave. "You're kidding."

"I knew that'd get your attention."

Hell, he thought and cast a glance down the mountain. It wasn't too late to go back. He thought he remembered the way, though he'd been too busy trying not to break his neck to thoroughly memorize the terrain.

"This is perfect," Eddie was saying. "One of the most prolific serial killers in California history?"

"I'm not in the mood for a cannibal story right now."

"The deadline's in two months."

"I know when the deadline is."

"Then stop being a pussy and come on."

With a defeated sigh, he did.

Immediately, the dank smell of stagnant water coated his nostrils. As he advanced, he couldn't shake the sensation of sliding into some ancient creature's gullet, a voluntary repast for its monstrous appetite. The cave serpentined left and right, and several times branched into different tunnels. Ben was reminded of all the horror movies he'd seen with cave settings.

They never ended well.

At least the tunnel was large enough that he could stand erect. In addition to his fear of heights, sharks, and his ex-wife, he was deathly afraid of tight spaces. He remembered fighting off panic attacks whenever he ended up on the bottom of a football pile.

So why the hell was he going to a place where his claustrophobia could run amok?

Because they were desperate.

"Arthur's first two victims," Eddie said, "were a couple of teenagers named Shannon Williams and Jill Shelton. They were out here hiking and decided to explore the caves."

It was actually Shannon Shelton and Jill Williams, but Ben let it go. Eddie was a good storyteller as long as one didn't get too hung up on facts.

"Little did they know," Eddie said, "they'd wandered into the den of a beast."

Despite the fact that they'd mined for inspiration in eerie places several times, Ben felt the old thrill. Sometimes the tale inspired him, sometimes it was the setting. Often, the music didn't come until days later, when a specific memory triggered his imagination.

Lately, it didn't come at all.

"Who was murdered first?" Ben asked.

"Don't rush it," Eddie said. "I'm coming to that."

They moved up a curving incline that, to Ben's infinite dismay, narrowed gradually until he had to shuffle forward in a stooped position. When the tunnel opened up, he groaned.

The gap between where Eddie stood and where solid ground resumed couldn't have been more than five feet, but to Ben the space yawned, terrible and forbidding, an impassable expanse.

"This was where she fell," Eddie said, gesturing with the Maglite into the darkness. "Jill made it over, but Shannon ended up down there."

Ben stood next to Eddie and peered into the chasm. The flashlight's glow barely reached the bottom. He estimated the distance was sixty feet or more.

The image came unbidden, but once it settled in his mind, it dug in with the tenacity of a tick. He imagined the poor girl leaping and realizing halfway she wasn't going to make it. The hands scrabbling frantically on the grimy cave floor. The amplified scraping of her body as it slid downward. A fingernail or two snapping off. Then the endless, screaming tumble into the abyss.

He hoped it killed her. Goodness knew being eaten alive by Arthur Vaughan was a far worse fate.

"You ready?" Eddie asked.

"Hell yes," he answered. "Ready to go back."

Without another word, Eddie leaped over the expanse and landed with room to spare.

"Your turn," Eddie said.

"I'm not jumping."

"Scared?"

"I don't have a death wish."

"It's only a few feet."

"And a hundred more to the ground."

"Stop letting fear rule your life."

Classic Eddie. Put him in a bad situation and mock him for reacting sanely. Like last month, the double date that turned out to be a pair of hookers. *What's the difference?* Eddie had asked.

So Ben sat there listening to one girl's stories about her clients' sexual quirks while Eddie got it on with the other in a hot tub.

"Look," Eddie was saying. "I went first so you'd know it was safe."

Ben turned. "I'm going home."

The cave went black.

"Your choice," Eddie said. "Either jump a gap a child could clear with his eyes shut or take your chances alone in the dark."

Ben ground his teeth. Arguing with Eddie Blaze was like chasing a candy wrapper in a windstorm.

"Go ahead and leave," Eddie said. "You do remember your way, right?"

Ben sighed. Why fight it?

"All right, asshole, turn on the flashlight."

The tunnel lit up.

Ben backed up and took a deep breath. "You better not switch off that light."

"What kind of person you think I am?" Eddie asked. "I only want to scare you, not kill you."

Ben hesitated. "What?"

Soft laughter. "You do your best work when you're scared shitless."

He struggled to keep his voice even. "This is all a setup?"

"The night you were alone in that movie theater—"

"That was a fluke—"

"—the time your plane hit all that turbulence."

"Another coincidence," he said. "So this is some kind of elaborate scheme to frighten me into writing music?"

"I bet it works."

Clenching his jaw, Ben broke toward the gap. Sure that Eddie would go against his word, that the light would extinguish at the critical moment, Ben leaped for the other side, felt a vertiginous dread wash over him, and cried out when he tumbled onto the path.

He came up swinging, but just as his fist whooshed by Eddie's face, the cave went dark again. Ben stood panting and waiting for the light to come on so he could beat the shit out of his best friend.

He heard a metallic rattle, a tapping sound.

"Turn the flashlight on," Ben said.

"I'm trying," Eddie answered. "I dropped it when you freaked out."

The darkness of the cave surpassed any Ben had experienced. He remembered hiding in the closet as a kid, huddling under the covers. But even then there had been *some* light.

This was like being blind.

He fought the surge of panic. "Quit screwing around and—"

"I'm telling you the damn thing's broken."

He heard Eddie tapping on the Maglite.

"What now?" Ben asked.

"I don't know, I guess we feel our way out."

"Feel our way out?"

"What other choice do we have?"

"You get the flashlight to work, that's what."

"It isn't, so there's no use crying over it."

Eddie's voice was receding.

"*Hey*," Ben said and moved forward.

"What're you waiting for?" Eddie called, his voice farther yet.

Ben's heart hammered. Arms extended, he moved toward Eddie's voice. At any moment he knew he could plummet toward certain death. Or meet up with Arthur Vaughan, who was supposedly serving five consecutive life sentences but with Ben's luck had gotten a weekend furlough to relive the good old days in his cannibal home.

Ben groped forward and swallowed down the acid burning his throat. His stomach was churning, his whole body ached.

And this was supposed to inspire him.

He'd kill Eddie, the fucking moron.

The sweat was trickling down his forehead now, his eyes starting to sting.

"Eddie?" he said and the ground dropped away beneath him. He cried out, sure he was a goner, but his feet hit the ground and he went tumbling forward, spinning, somersaulting downward without a clue of how to land or how far he'd fallen. Amid the chaos he realized he could see a little and the farther he fell, the more light there was. Then he tumbled out of the cave and landed on his back.

Ben lay without moving. Distantly, he heard Eddie's voice uttering some nonsense, asking him if he could move his fingers, count to ten, give him some sign he was still alive.

Ben was inclined to let him wait.

A hand was on his shoulder, shaking him. He opened his eyes groggily and saw Eddie's concerned face gaping down at him. He even detected guilt in Eddie's eyes.

"Help me up," Ben whispered.

A sharp pain lanced his knee as he put his weight on it. A broken patella maybe. Or a torn ACL. Something pulsed in his mouth, and when he touched it and inspected his fingers they were slick with blood.

"Jesus," Eddie said. "That was some fall."

Ben stood, swaying on the soft grass, and waited for the dizziness to go away.

Eddie tapped his forehead with an open hand, said, "Shit, man, I just realized what the problem was."

Ben watched in dull rage as Eddie switched the flashlight on.

"You believe that?" Eddie said, relishing his dumb joke. "And here I thought the batteries had gone dead."

Ben punched him in the nose and Eddie went down. Suddenly, Ben felt a lot better.

Eddie fingered the corner of his mouth, frowned. "I think you knocked a tooth loose."

"You deserve worse."

Ben eased down beside him and reclined on his elbows. "This wasn't Arthur Vaughan's cave, was it?"

Eddie looked away, a sheepish grin on his face.

"You just wanted to scare me."

"Did you hear anything?"

"Nothing," Ben said and winced at the pain from his bloodied knee. "Not a damn thing."

Eddie got to his feet and helped him up.

"I've got one more card to play," Eddie said. "And if it doesn't work, nothing will."

Ben spat, tasted warm copper. "What is it, another cave?"

Eddie's face, for the first time that night, lost its sardonic mirth. "If I can arrange it, the place I'm thinking of is the Holy Grail for a guy like you."

Ben stared hopelessly down the mountain trail. They were miles from Eddie's car. From there, it was another two hours to home. If he was lucky, he'd be in bed by dawn.

"This place you're talking about," Ben said, "you ever been there?"

"No," Eddie said. "It's on an island."

CHAPTER TWO

Ben's ex-wife was waiting for him on the front lawn.

True, it had only been six months since Jenny'd divided the fabric of his existence with one merciless rip – the divorce papers served to him at the studio, of all places – yet his former home looked strangely unfamiliar, something belonging to another person, another life.

He stopped the Civic and cut the engine. He could see her peripherally, arms folded, hip jutting to one side, her body language making it plainer than any declaration, "You're not wanted here."

He took a deep breath, pocketed the keys.

If he wanted to see his son, he would see his son. No court order, no impersonally worded decree would keep him from Joshua.

She met him on the sidewalk. "I told you not to come."

He glanced at the house, hoping he'd catch sight of the boy peering through the window. If Joshua spotted him, he'd be out here in a heartbeat.

Unless she'd poisoned the child against him, a fear that had been growing ever since their last visit, an awkward question-and-answer session he never imagined could take place with the one person who truly understood him, even if Joshua was still just three.

"You can't see him until Friday," Jenny said.

"I'll only stay a minute."

She seemed to consider. "On second thought," she said, "maybe you should see him."

Distant alarms went off in his head. "What's going on?"

"We're moving."

"That's all right. I can—"

"We're moving back east."

Invisible fingers tightened on his throat. Deep down, he'd known this was a possibility, her returning to Indiana to be closer to her parents, but he'd never really thought it would happen.

"You can't do that."

Her mouth twisted into a hateful grin, the one that made her nostrils flare. "'In the case of joint custody where guardianship favors the mother—'"

"Don't start—"

"It's what a judge would say."

"A judge who doesn't know Joshua, who doesn't realize how much a boy needs his dad—"

"You're projecting again, Ben. That's your mania, not his."

"It's not a mania, dammit. There's a reason a child has two parents."

"Oh Christ," she said, "here we go with your childhood angst."

"It isn't—"

"Joshua will be fine. My father will visit—"

"He needs *his* father."

She paused, mouth opening wide. "You really think he needs you? Have you looked at yourself lately?"

God damn her, he wanted to grab her face and squeeze. Didn't she care that *she* was the one who'd done this to him, who'd put these purple hollows under his eyes?

He fought to control it. "You never have to see me again, if that's what you want."

"Thank God."

The pain in his chest grew, a dull ache spreading to his shoulder.

"I know that," he said. "But Joshua's a different story."

"The hell he is."

"He needs me."

"He has Ryan."

At the utterance of the unfamiliar name, the pain in his chest sharpened, bored deeper. All along he'd known there was another man, known Jenny was screwing around, the woman too insecure to throw one relationship away without another waiting in the wings.

With an effort, he said, "Whoever Ryan is, he isn't Joshua's dad."

"Not yet."

Ben stared at her.

"In a few months they'll be closer than you and Joshua ever were."

And now, oh Christ, the tears were close. He wanted more than anything to muster some rage, enough heat to equal Jenny's, but the feeling that his life was slipping away – that Joshua was slipping away – was nudging him toward panic.

"He's a pilot," she said. "He took us flying yesterday."

The thought of his baby boy in an airplane without him did it, stripped him of what composure remained. He turned and stared with blurring eyes down the empty street. He could feel Jenny's malice sweeping him away like a gale.

And he'd thought the nightmare couldn't grow worse.

Her eyes narrowed in mock appraisal. "You and Eddie bagged any starlets lately?"

He blew out air, shook his head, and noticed something he hadn't previously, two vehicles at the top of the driveway.

"Is that Kayla's Jeep?" he asked.

"That's right," Jenny said. "She moved back in."

"Why—"

"Because you're gone and Ryan doesn't lecture her the way you did."

More pain, the old regret at the stillborn relationship assailing him. The product of Jenny's teenaged pregnancy, born twelve years before Ben and her mother had even met, Kayla had made up her mind to hate Ben before they'd ever spoken. He hadn't been a perfect stepfather, but dammit, he'd never stopped trying either.

He said, "I'll come back Friday."

"We won't be here."

"What?"

"We're going to Europe for the summer. We leave tomorrow."

He swallowed. "You have to clear it with the court."

"File a complaint," she said. "By the time the judge gets around to it, we'll be back in New York."

Ben thought of Joshua in the city, the sweet little boy who loved to find worms and toads and hold them as they wriggled in his hands. Before Jenny could get the satisfaction of watching him break down completely, he turned and walked away.

He'd gotten halfway to the car when he heard a small voice say, "Why is Daddy here?"

Joshua stood beside his mother. The boy wore a red shirt and a sagging diaper. It was only noon, too early for his nap, which meant he was either wearing the same one he wore to bed the night before or he had regressed in his potty training. Kids, Ben remembered reading, often did that during times of trauma.

"Hey buddy," he said as he approached his son.

Joshua's large brown eyes flitted from his mother to Ben and back again.

Ben knelt and hugged the boy, but his little body felt wooden. He noted with something approaching despair how Joshua's hands remained on the tops of his shoulders rather than encircling his neck the way they used to when he came home from work.

He kissed the boy on the cheek and crouched before him. "How are you, pal?"

Instead of answering, Joshua glanced at his mom. *Is it okay to answer?*

Ben forced a smile. "Did you have fun in the airplane yesterday?"

Joshua frowned. "It's not a airplane, it's a sampiper."

"*Sand*piper," Jenny corrected.

Ben tried to swallow the lump in his throat. "I bet that was fun."

"Ryan let me fly."

As if cued by an unseen director, Ryan the Pilot appeared on the porch. The guy looked young but was probably Ben's age and simply in far better shape. Outlined clearly by the tight T-shirt, Ben could see the muscled torso, the tight midsection. Above that, the dimpled cheeks and stylish black hair gave Ryan the look of a fashion model. He watched Ben with the haughty demeanor of a cop preparing to hassle a homeless person.

"Ryan let me hold the wheel," Joshua said.

"That's good," Ben answered and did his best to pretend the man sleeping with his ex-wife wasn't smirking at him from the porch. He caressed Joshua's shoulder. "That's real fun, buddy."

"Ryan's going to live with us after we move."

The tears came then and Ben hugged the boy so he wouldn't see. He knew he was holding his son too roughly, but he no longer felt capable of bearing his own weight. A slight breeze wafted the scent of lilacs over them, and Ben was reminded of the time he'd planted the bushes as Joshua, not even a year old, watched him from the Pack 'n Play. Throat aching, he gripped his son tighter.

"Daddy?" Joshua asked.

He couldn't answer, could only hold on and wish he never had to let go.

"It hurts, Daddy."

Ben nodded, kissed his son on the side of the head. As he did, he breathed in the smell of the boy's hair. Sweat and oil. Three or more days without a bath.

"Ben," she said, a hand on his shoulder, looking for all the world like a prison guard breaking up an inmate's visit.

"Okay," he said, relaxing his grip on the boy. "Okay."

He sniffed, rubbed his nose with the back of his hand, and rose.

Joshua stared up at him wide-eyed. It wasn't fear exactly in the boy's eyes. A kind of awestruck fascination, perhaps. The sense that here was something new and terrible, something momentous – Daddy was bawling.

Ben cleared his throat. "I love you, buddy. I'll see you soon."

He went to the Civic and climbed in. Keying the engine, he stole one final glance at his baby boy. Ben raised a hand in goodbye, but his ex-wife was already ushering Joshua back to the house.

Ryan stood gazing from the porch, his feet wide, his arms folded. Without taking his eyes off Ben, the pilot reached out and ruffled Joshua's hair as he passed. Jenny patted Ryan's flat stomach. Ben's son and ex-wife disappeared into the house, but Ryan went on watching him, daring him to say something.

But he didn't. He drove away.

When he reached the coast road, his cell phone sounded. After several rings, he picked it up, looked at it.

Eddie.

"Yeah?" Ben said.

"What's wrong with you?"

Ben told him what happened.

Eddie was silent a moment. Then, "I'm sorry, man."

Ben stopped at a red light, a fresh spate of tears coming on. His eyes blurred as the light turned green.

Eddie said, "I know this isn't the best time, but primary shooting ends tomorrow."

"I know that."

"The music is due two months after they wrap."

Ben waited. He heard Eddie sigh, working up to something.

"Man…I know this is the last thing on your mind right now, but it's important. You weren't real enthusiastic about the island before, but now…"

"But what?"

"I mean…does this change anything? What you found out today about Jenny and…"

"Joshua," Ben finished.

"Right."

Ben pulled over and stared out at the ocean. The Pacific had taken on the hue of gunmetal; above that, the dreary, gray sky. Ben decided he would drink tonight. Drink until some of the pain faded.

"I tell you what," Ben said. "If you can get the island for a month and you're willing to pay for it…I'll go."

"Really?"

"Really," Ben answered. "I've got nothing better to do."

CHAPTER THREE

Fucking Warriors.

Beat hell out of the Spurs and Rockets, then turn around and lose to the Clippers?

Chris squeezed the remote and resisted an urge to chuck it at the television.

Curry caught the ball on the left wing.

"Shoot it," Chris said.

Curry faked a shot and fed Green in the post. The forward dribbled it off his foot.

Chris kicked the ottoman. Thirty-seven points Wednesday, forty-five on Friday, but the night Chris puts fifty grand on the Warriors to cover the spread, Curry pulls a disappearing act.

Tied at ninety with thirty seconds left.

Chris seized his whiskey and Coke and downed it in one furious swallow. He scrunched his nose at the watery taste of it. To use up some of his nervous energy, he rose and crossed to the bar, where he poured himself a double-shot of whiskey, to hell with the Coke. Drink in hand, he crouched, preparing to celebrate as Curry finally disregarded the goddamned offense and took it to the hole. The ball rattled in as the whistle blew.

Charging.

"*Bullshit!*" Chris roared and shattered his glass against the wall.

The announcers were saying it was bad news for the Warriors because – oh hell no – the foul was Curry's sixth.

He grabbed the bottle and drank, the seriousness of the moment finally taking hold. Fifty grand added to what, four hundred? Four-fifty?

Chris bowed his head and said a prayer to no one in particular. *Please let the Clippers miss. Please let it go into overtime.*

He jumped as the phone rang.

He exhaled a trembling breath. Probably the composer again. What was his name, Blades?

Blaze. Eddie Blaze.

Chris rolled his eyes thinking of the guy.

Fifty thousand for one month on the island, Blaze had said.

My father makes that in ten minutes, Chris had told him.

Take it or leave it, Blaze had answered.

Chris had left it.

Four seconds left. The Warriors were setting their defense. The ref handed a Clipper forward the ball. A rookie caught the inbounds pass, took a couple of dribbles, then drove hard toward the free-throw line. He pulled up and shot as the buzzer sounded.

Nothing but net.

This time Chris did aim for the TV. The bottle exploded and the screen went black.

For the first time that evening Chris allowed himself to think of Marvin. Was one of his men on the way over even now?

Marvin Irvin. Jesus, with a name like that you'd think he'd have a sense of humor. A year ago, when they'd met at a Vegas casino, Marvin had treated him like a Persian prince, his Very Special Guest. *Lost a thousand at roulette? No problem, Mr. Blackwood. It's on the house. Want an escort to the show later? She'll come to your room in an hour. You can attend the show or stay in, depending on your mood. Put away your wallet, Mr. Blackwood. It's on us.*

Then last month when they'd crossed paths at the Staples Center.

Haven't heard from you in a while, Mr. Blackwood.

Sorry about that, Marvin. I've been busy.

That's what I hear.

A beat, the little bookie watching him with hooded eyes. Spectators were milling around them, but they might as well have been the only people in the arena.

Oh yeah, Chris said, careful to keep his expression casual. About that, Marvin.

Please call me Mr. Irvin.

Chris's throat went dry. Right. About the money, Mr. Irvin. You know I'm good for it.

You're good for it, huh.

Chris's face flushing hot. Of course I'm good for it. My family's worth a billion dollars, for chrissakes.

Your family, Marvin said.

That's right.

Your family's your family. What about you?

I'm good for it.

I don't see any sign of that. All I see is you joining the high-interest club.

A knock on the door jolted Chris back to the present. He stared at the door, his chest throbbing. There was no way Marvin's men could have gotten here already. Not unless they'd been down the road listening to the game on the radio.

Actually, he wouldn't put it past them.

He'd heard stories.

On feet he couldn't feel, he walked slowly to the door. Something crunched under his slippers. Broken glass. One shard, sickle-shaped and razor sharp, lay on its side. Should he use it to defend himself in case Marvin and his thugs got tough?

He rejected the idea. A piece of glass would be no match for a gun. Or a blowtorch.

He'd heard stories.

Suddenly sure he was going to puke, Chris opened the door and saw the man standing in the shadows.

Granderson.

Thank Christ.

Chris crumpled to his knees, no longer caring how he looked. He'd go to his father tomorrow, tell him the whole thing. The old man would be angry as hell, and Chris figured he'd say *no* at first. But after a few hours and a few drinks, Stephen Blackwood would come to his senses, realize his son's life was worth a few hundred grand. Then Chris's leash would be a good deal tighter, his bank account drastically limited. But after a time it would all blow over, the way it always did. Like when he totaled the Ferrari. Or flunked out of Pepperdine. Or got that waitress pregnant.

Yes, Stephen would be pissed. Royally pissed. But he'd come through in the end.

He had to.

"I assume you watched the game."

Granderson's cool British accent grated on his already frazzled nerves.

"Just give me a minute."

"How much are you in the hole now?"

Chris pictured Granderson's iron jaw curved in a pitiless grin.

"Half a million?" Granderson asked.

"Not that much," Chris lied.

"More, I suspect."

When Chris rose, he saw Granderson fixing himself a vodka tonic, the man's close-cropped blond hair glinting in the overhead light.

"I'll take one of those," Chris said.

"From the look of this room, I'd say you've had enough."

"Jesus, I'll get it myself."

Drink in hand, Granderson passed him on the way to the door. "Will you be needing me tonight?"

Chris poured the vodka, but his hand shook. "I was thinking you could stay in the guest room."

Granderson smirked at him over his glass. "Anything wrong with my own quarters?"

Only that the guesthouse is an acre away.

Chris shrugged. "You never know with this kind of thing."

"You mean organized crime?"

Goose bumps rippled his arms. "I don't know I'd go that far." He cleared his throat. "It isn't like Marvin's some kind of killer."

Granderson watched him impassively. "If you say so."

Granderson turned to go.

Chris took an involuntary step forward. "You'll stay then?"

Granderson paused at the door. Without looking up, he said, "I forgot to tell you. The composer called again. He doubled his offer."

"A hundred thousand?"

Granderson waited.

"What did you tell him?"

"I told him I disapproved."

Chris took a breath. "Will you call him back and accept?"

Granderson's hand paused on the knob, his sinewy forearm tensed.

"You do know what would happen if your father found out, don't you?"

"He won't find out."

Granderson disappeared through the doorway.

Chris called after him, "When will you be back?"

A few moments later, he heard a door bang shut below.

★ ★ ★

He'd been sleeping he had no idea how long when he awoke, conscious of a furtive rustling somewhere in the bedroom. Chris remained absolutely motionless. He thought of his cell phone on the nightstand, yet he couldn't make his arm work, so quickly and completely had the fear paralysis gripped him. It was amazing, really, how the night and his imagination washed away the protective veneer of years and reduced him to the child who'd been afraid of the dark for as long as he could remember, especially after what'd happened on his fourteenth birthday, the time his parents took him to Castle Blackwood.

The memory of that terrible night brought him fully awake.

The only other person who knew the security code was Granderson, and if it was he in the bedroom, he was there for Chris's protection. Why else was his father paying the man?

Something was wrong in the house. He was certain of it. An astringent taste roiled in the back of his throat, reminding him of hung-over mornings during which he'd crunched aspirin to make it work faster.

Chris rolled onto his back and his breath caught. Beside the bed, framed in moonlight, stood a large figure.

"Granderson?" Chris whispered. When the figure didn't answer, he said, "Jim?" as though to humanize the man by invoking his first name.

The shadow shifted slightly, a slithery sound accompanying the movement, and Chris watched the figure – definitely not Granderson – peeling off a pair of gloves. The bare hands looked very large in the meager light filtering through the blinds. Rather than reaching for him, the hands went to the pocket of a Windbreaker. Something thin and silvery dangled at the figure's side.

"Sit up," a voice said.

The sound of it chilled him. Low. Raspy.

"Sit *up*," the voice commanded, and before he could obey, a viselike hand seized him by the throat. The silver object flashed, and Chris's hand exploded in an icy burst of pain. He cried out, already frantic for air, and grabbed the man's hand with both of his. Desperately, Chris shot out a knee and caught the intruder in the ribs. The throttling hand left his throat, but before he could relish the freedom of an unrestricted airway, a huge fist smashed down at his face. He turned but the blow caught him flush anyway, one side of his jaw a screaming web of agony.

The man mounted him, straddled his chest, and used his knees to pin Chris's arms. The man weighed a ton, and a cloud of aftershave made breathing even harder. Chris bucked to throw the man off, but the voice came again, its eerie calm making the threat infinitely more ominous. "Stop moving."

"Can't…breathe," he managed to say.

"Relax," the raspy voice said. "Relax."

He stared abjectly up at the man. He could make out features, but only vaguely. Short dark hair. A wide, pockmarked face. Deep-set eyes.

Where the hell was Granderson?

"Do you know who I am?" the man asked.

"I can pay you in—" Chris began, but the silver object silenced him.

He identified it and then, as he had done many times since that first awful night when he'd dropped a hundred grand on the Super Bowl, he wished this were all a bad dream from which he'd soon awaken.

The scalpel pressed into the soft flesh under his eye.

"Do you know who I am?" the man repeated.

Chris drew in a labored breath. "I know who sent you."

"Yeah?"

"Mr. Irvin."

The pressure on Chris's skin decreased. "That's right. So you know why I'm here."

"Yes."

The wide moon face spread into the parody of a smile. "Good boy."

Chris said, "I can pay you twenty thousand tonight. In a couple days I'll have a hundred more."

The man shook his head. "You're way short."

"No it's—"

The scalpel flicked down and shot a laser of white heat through his upper lip. Blood trickled into his mouth.

The man giggled. "Tough place for a wound, Chris. Put on a black Band-Aid, you could pass for Hitler."

Chris whimpered.

"After tonight's loss," the man said as he wiped the scalpel on the sheet, "you owe us three-quarters of a million dollars."

"It was five hundred," Chris said and shut his eyes as the scalpel flicked again. The blade cleaved a burning line between his eyes, the bridge of his nose separating. He wailed, the hot blood pooling in his eye sockets no matter how he thrashed. Then the man's weight was bearing down again. Crushing, suffocating.

The raspy voice at his ear, intimate as a lover's, "Don't contradict me."

Weeping freely, Chris nodded. Above him, the man shifted. There were more rustling sounds, the cool feel of the man's Windbreaker on his cheek.

By the time he realized what was happening, his left hand was tied to the bedpost.

"Wait," he said, "what are—"

The scalpel entered his left nostril, pierced the tender flesh within. Chris screamed, a high, gurgling, alien scream, but that drove the blade higher, deeper, the pain indescribable, and somewhere, beneath the strata of shock, he was aware he had soiled himself.

The scalpel went away. The voice, very close to Chris's face, "One more word and I'll make you a freak."

Chris stayed as still as he could, but his breath was thinning, his nose filling with blood.

"Don't move," the man said.

And though Chris wept with the pain and degradation of it all, he did not resist as the man tied his other hand to the bed frame. The man got up, and though Chris was grateful to be able to breathe again, the dismal sense that he was about to die grew stronger as his feet were bound to the posts.

Then, the bed shifted as the man sat beside him. "If you tell anyone – the police, your parents, *anyone* – I'll find out. You have no idea how much your body can hurt. There are so many places I can cut…"

A hand slipped inside Chris's boxer shorts, the scalpel tracing an almost delicate line down his penis, the sharp point pausing on the shriveled tip and grinding into the urethra.

Chris groaned, the voice rasping at his ear, "…so many places I can *dig*."

CHAPTER FOUR

Claire took a drink – she had no idea what it was – from the server's platter, and peered through the partygoers at the tall man standing outside on the deck, the tail of his sports jacket ruffled slightly by the breeze. Outlined by the red sunset and the dark Pacific, he looked drawn by an artist, rather than a man of flesh and blood. She had never been this close to him and now she memorized his profile, his strong nose, his broad shoulders slumped as he leaned over the wooden railing.

Ben Shadeland, she thought. She couldn't imagine what she'd say to him.

Eddie Blaze appeared at Ben's side and handed him a beer. Next to Ben, Eddie seemed a good deal shorter, even shorter than he'd appeared on last month's Oscar telecast.

Still, with his black hair and his square jaw, Eddie exuded a roguish charm. Though larger, Ben Shadeland looked a good deal more sensitive. He hadn't the confidence Eddie had, but Claire found him far more attractive. Ben turned and Claire caught a glimpse of his soulful blue eyes, his dimpled chin.

She moved the umbrella stirrer aside, took a sip and shivered, whatever tropical concoction she'd selected too strong by half. She considered leaving it on the bar, but then she'd have nothing to occupy her hands.

Ben said something to Eddie and walked away. Now was her chance.

She stepped out onto a deck twice as large as her entire apartment. As she neared Eddie it occurred to her she had no idea what to say.

Good evening, Mr. Blaze. Lovely party, isn't it? May I have a job?

An exotic-looking woman with shimmering black hair and wearing a black evening dress appeared out of nowhere and embraced Eddie. Claire stood dumbly in the middle of the walkway.

"I'm looking forward to tomorrow," the exotic woman said.

"Me too," Eddie replied. "How's Lee?"

The mention of Lee Stanley brought on a fresh wave of fear. The feeling grew in Claire that at any moment a team of men in black suits would descend on her and carry her out of the mansion. What the hell had she been thinking?

The woman gave Eddie's hand a squeeze and moved away.

He turned and smiled at Claire. "I don't think we've met." He gave her his name and offered his hand.

She shook it. "Claire Harden."

"Claire," he said, smile widening. The skin of her chest burned. She passed an unsteady hand over her throat. His eyes lowered and she thought of her hives, those angry red blotches that appeared at the worst times. Why on earth had she worn this dress?

"Nice party," she said lamely, and perhaps out of pity he nodded and told her that yes, the party was indeed nice.

As the silence between them thickened, she glanced dismally down at her flats. She should have worn heels. In her apartment the red flats seemed a good choice, but here, among the pretty people of San Francisco who could afford the right clothes and the right shoes for any occasion, they looked shabby and ill chosen.

"Are you an actress?" Eddie asked.

Claire searched his face for traces of irony, but if there were any, they were well concealed. Perhaps he meant she looked like some character actress, the plain-faced friend of the female lead.

Or maybe he was paying you a compliment.

"No," she said. "I could never be an actress."

"Me either," he said. "I clam up in front of the camera."

She looked around. "I've never been in a house this big."

Eddie glanced up at the twenty-foot wall of windows. "I call it 'The House That Blood Built'."

She followed his gaze to the upstairs balcony. "Is it new?"

"Basically. He commissioned it after he made *Hell House*."

Remade, she nearly corrected. Claire remembered the first version starring Roddy McDowell and bearing the dubious title, *The Legend of Hell House*. Despite the fact that Richard Matheson himself – one of her all-time favorites – had written the screenplay, the movie had failed to capture the novel's brooding atmosphere. The Lee Stanley version had been better – much better, in fact – though, as always, Stanley insisted on throwing in gratuitous sex and gore.

Claire thought of the exotic woman who'd spoken to Eddie earlier.

Had she been an actress, one of Lee's scream queens? For all Claire knew, she might have seen the woman naked before. She sure had the body for it.

She realized Eddie was staring at her.

"I'm sorry," she said. "I was just remembering the film."

"Very bloody," he said. "You a horror fan?"

"Of course."

"You have any favorites?"

"You name it," she said. "*Halloween. The Exorcist.* Cheesy stuff like *Evil Dead II.*"

He grinned broadly. "My kind of girl."

She felt herself relaxing. Amazingly, the hives seemed to be dissipating. For good measure, she kept her hand there in case he spotted them, mistook them for some rare disease, and fled on the off chance what she had might be communicable.

"I figured you'd be a horror fan," she said.

"Yeah, why is that?"

"To write scores for *Witching Hour Theatre* and *Blood Country,* you'd just about have to be."

He stared down at his drink, clearly pleased she knew his work.

"I do love scary things," he said. "Always have." Then, looking up at her. "Not many people have seen *Witching Hour Theatre*. I'm surprised you did."

"I saw it on DVD."

"That's the only way you could have. It was out of the theaters within two weeks of its release."

"I went out and bought the score the same night," she said. "It was one of the best pieces of suspense music I'd ever heard."

"Really?"

"Absolutely. The track called 'Longface' still gives me chills."

"Well, Claire, I'm very humbled by your praise."

She took a breath. "I have to be honest with you, Mr. Blaze. I—"

"Eddie."

"I have to be honest, Eddie. I came to this party to talk to you."

"Yeah?"

Had there been a subtle hesitation in his voice, a drawing back?

"Yes," she said, "I hadn't heard back from you since sending my information..."

His expression grew veiled, suspicious.

She plowed on, "I want you to know how much I respect you both. It's not just the score you wrote for *Witching Hour Theatre*, which is amazing…"

He was staring out at the bay.

"…but the way you spotted the music."

"What exactly did you admire about it?"

Claire willed her voice to remain calm. "I admired how the music lurked in the background."

When he didn't answer, she went on. "Rather than drawing attention to itself, the score mimicked the actions of the murderer. I loved how the buildup to the big scare in the middle of the movie developed in silence, the way the music stayed out of the way…I thought that made the scene more powerful. It was very bold of you."

He tossed back his drink, wiped his mouth. "What can I do for you, Ms. Harden?"

"You posted an opening for an intern. Someone to transcribe your music—"

"That's all changed."

"Aren't you scoring *House of Skin* right now?"

There was real heat in his look. "That's none of your business."

"I can take some of the load off you," she said. "I'm a good worker."

"We don't need distractions."

"You filled the position?"

He laughed. "Why am I explaining this to you? You crash Lee's party—"

"Did you read my portfolio, listen to my samples?"

"I listened to them."

"And?"

"I found them derivative."

It was as though the deck below her had dropped away.

He set his empty glass on the rail. "I don't have time for this shit."

The tears in her eyes appalled her. Could this have gone any worse?

He turned to go, but she stunned them both by grabbing his arm. He stared at her hand incredulously.

She released him. "Please," she said. "I just want to learn from you."

He studied her face, perhaps searching for signs of madness.

He said, "You're an accompanist, right?"

"First in my class at the conservatory."

"Your playing was better than your writing. Stick to that."

He might as well have slapped her.

She was almost to the sliding doors when she heard him say, "Hold on."

As he approached, his expression seemed to soften.

"You seem like a nice kid, but this really is the worst possible time."

"Then let me help."

Eddie shook his head, scratched the underside of his jaw. "We won't even be here."

"Why not?"

He looked away as though embarrassed. "It's normal for Ben to get writer's block – musician's block – whatever you call it…but never this close to our deadline. I mean, he always has some idea of what things will sound like by now…"

"You're trying to unblock him."

"I guess so," he said. "If going to the Sorrows doesn't do it—"

"The Sorrows?"

"Castle Blackwood," Eddie said. He paused, frowning. "Don't tell me you've never heard of it?"

She said she hadn't.

He shook his head. "And you a horror fan? I'm disappointed."

"What is it?"

"An island eighty miles off the coast of northern California," he said, "and the site of one of America's strangest unsolved mysteries."

"What happened?"

"No one really knows."

She waited for him to elaborate. When he didn't, she said, "And the two of you are going there?"

"Us and one other," Eddie said. "Lee Stanley's assistant."

"The woman you were just talking to?"

"That's right. Lee insisted we bring Eva along."

"For what?"

Eddie smiled ruefully. "To keep him abreast of our progress, I imagine."

Claire took a breath. "So I'll make an even four."

He cocked an eyebrow.

"Having me along will free you up," she said. "You and Ben can concentrate on the music. I'll stay in my room until you need me. Then, you can dictate to me and I can put things straight into the computer."

Eddie watched her.

She went on, "I can help cook too."

One corner of his mouth lifted in a grin. "I'll talk to Ben. If he's okay with it, you can come."

She fought an urge to jump up and down. Afraid he'd change his mind, she wrote her name and number and told him to call anytime. He surprised her by saying he'd let her know by morning since they were leaving tomorrow night.

Claire thanked him again and made her way to the restroom. When she finished, she peered outside to see if she could spot Eddie and Ben talking, but neither man was visible. Relax, she told herself. They'll call you if they want you.

Please let them want me.

Claire exited the deck and made her way along a winding stone path around the house. She'd parked her car down the road and was about to cut through a hedgerow when she heard someone say, "What's the big deal?"

Eddie Blaze.

"We don't have time for socializing," Ben Shadeland said.

She hid between a pair of low-hanging palm fronds. There, framed by green, she saw them on the front walk.

"She'll make an even four," Eddie said.

"I'm not looking to be set up."

"Then we'll use her as a maid."

Ben put his hands on his hips. "Come on."

Eddie laughed. "She volunteered, said she'd be happy to cook and clean."

A pause.

"What's she like?" Ben asked.

"You mean is she hot?"

"That's not what I meant."

"She's all right," Eddie said. "She's a seven. Seven-and-a-half, maybe."

Ben rolled his eyes.

Eddie added, "She's good-looking in a Renoir kind of way."

"What's that supposed to mean?"

"You know, the full-bodied type."

"What's wrong with that?" Ben asked, but Claire scarcely heard him. Her eyes burning, she veered away and set off through the hedgerow, not caring if they heard her, not caring if she tore her stupid red dress.

She shoved through the bushes, which scratched at her with disturbing eagerness, and nearly plunged into a manmade goldfish pond. She climbed up a sun-scorched verge and lacerated her palm on a piece of glass lying in the dirt. Nearing her car she saw that the backs of her arms had been lashed by branches. Somehow the wounds made her arms feel even flabbier than before. Claire reached her car and gritted her teeth at the way the window broadened her reflection.

Like she needed it.

She plopped down in her seat, started her Camry and drove toward a man opening his car door. It was Ben Shadeland, and though she didn't want to think about him or Eddie anymore, she found her foot easing off the gas as she neared. He watched her approach. Without knowing why she did it, she stopped next to him.

Ben's friendly, haunted face appeared in the passenger's window.

"Are you Claire?" he asked.

She mustered a smile and stuck out her hand. "It's great to finally meet you."

Seeing her bloody arm, his grin faded. "Are you okay?"

"I'm just clumsy."

"If you're sure," he said, though he didn't look convinced.

"Did you talk to your partner?" she asked, unwilling to utter Eddie's name.

He hesitated. "I did."

"And?"

When he didn't answer, she said, "Mr. Shadeland?"

He looked up at her.

"I think you're the most talented composer working today."

"Claire…"

"Please, I need someone to give me a chance."

He held her gaze a moment longer. Then he nodded. "I'll call you tomorrow morning and let you know where to meet us."

CHAPTER FIVE

"Not like that," Lee said, voice echoing through the master suite. "Like this."

Eva shifted her legs.

"Jesus Christ," he said. "Not that way…the fuck you doing?" Spreading her legs apart. "Like *this*."

She obeyed.

The black satin sheets slithered under her mostly naked body. In different circumstances the sensation might have been arousing.

If, for example, the man standing over her wasn't a monster.

"Now take your hand – not *that* one," he said, flinging Eva's hand away from her body. "This one." He licked his lips as he slid her hand over her belly. Eva studied herself in the giant mirror on the ceiling and suppressed an urge to laugh at the white bra and underwear he'd insisted she wear. Always white. Unless she got to play the villain, which almost never happened.

Lee usually got that part.

Right now he was Paul Carver, the protagonist of *House of Skin*. Early in the film Paul had been a decent guy. An alcoholic, but basically good. But now he was in the thrall of the vengeful but ravishing Annabel, the creature who brought out her victims' innermost desires, who made them do terrible things to the unsuspecting.

Right now, Eva was the unsuspecting.

Surprise splashed over her like ice water as Lee grabbed her mouth and squeezed her cheeks together. "Me, goddammit. Look at *me*, not your fucking reflection."

Eva waited for him to let go.

"*Do you understand me?*" he asked, clipping off the words as though she were a recalcitrant child. "Women do not admire themselves when Paul Carver is seducing them. They pay attention to him. They admire him, his physique. His rugged good looks."

Eva thought of Eric Kramer, the actor playing Paul Carver, who, unlike

Lee, did have a great physique and rugged good looks. She concentrated on Eric Kramer, on his ocean blue eyes, and Lee faded. His hairy, jiggling teats disappeared and Eric Kramer's muscular pecs took their place. Lee's eye-watering body odor – a funky miasma of unwashed armpits and portobello mushrooms – dissipated as well.

Lee noticed the change in her and nodded.

"That's right," he said. "You want me. You know the things I'm capable of, but you want me all the same. Getting fucked by me is worth the pain, worth dying even."

Eva let her eyes travel down Lee's corpulent midsection, her imagination transforming it into Eric's washboard stomach. God help her, she was actually growing aroused. A pleasant heat spread through her abdomen as she pictured Eric Kramer's erection, tumid and shiny and seeking her warmth.

"Uh-huh," Lee said. "Fuck yeah." Drawing down her waistband, his tongue lapping at her crotch like some alley cat slurping from a puddle.

But in Eva's mind it was Paul Carver's tongue, and regardless of whose tongue it was, it would all be over soon anyway, her manuscript finished and her editor at Rogue Books staring wide-eyed at the twisted behavior of one of the biggest directors in Hollywood, the amazing Lee Stanley, the King of Horror and the winner of numerous humanitarian awards, an outspoken advocate of women's rights and a dozen other noble causes.

Eva bit her lip as Lee entered her.

He pinned her arms to the bed and began thrusting. His weight was tremendous, smothering, like being mauled by a bear. Try as she might to hold on to it, the image of Eric Kramer faded and was replaced by Lee's flabby butt cheeks undulating like Jell-O in the overhead mirror. She shut her eyes against the picture, not out of revulsion, but because the sight made her giggle. Once he'd caught her laughing at him, and the beating he'd administered had blackened her eyes and made her ears ring for days.

"Uh-huh," Lee was saying. "Tell me how much you love it."

She told him how much she loved it, how sexy he was. How horny he made her feel. How wet.

His thrusts became feverish, and she intensified her dirty talk – with any luck he'd come soon. He grunted louder, and she felt his body tighten.

Then he was slumped over her. She patted his back and pretended she wasn't being crushed to death. Lee was sensitive about his weight.

After an eternity he rolled off and ambled to the bathroom. Eva regarded herself in the overhead mirror. Nude except for the white bra that he'd never bothered to remove, she watched in fascination as the bed rose slowly around her, Lee's huge imprint dissolving.

She swung her legs over the edge of the bed and stood. A wave of revulsion rolled through her body as she felt his seed trickle down her leg.

Eva got dressed, switched on the television, and waited for Lee to dismiss her. He emerged from the bathroom ten minutes later wearing a gleaming red robe. He looked like the world's worst boxer, twenty years past his prime.

Without looking at her, he went to the humidor on the dresser. "We shoot the police chief's death today," he said, taking out a cigar. "At least, the audience *thinks* it's his death. We leave it ambiguous like the novel did. You know, just in case there's a sequel."

Eva said nothing. On the television the hosts told a woman that her wardrobe was straight out of a nightmare. Eva read the woman's subtitled response – *But I like my clothes* – and waited for Lee to leave so she could turn on the sound.

He stood three feet from the screen, watching the show. "What a cow," he said, blowing smoke at the TV. "What'd look good on her is a tablecloth with a hole cut in the middle."

Eva imagined her editor reading about Lee Stanley making fun of a woman because of her weight.

"Jesus Christ," he said, gesturing with his cigar. "That dress makes her look even bigger."

Eva pretended to smile.

Lee sat down, getting into it now. "If I saw that fat-ass coming, I'd call the San Diego Zoo, tell 'em they lost one of their hippos."

As Lee continued, Eva reached into the pocket of her shorts and clicked on her tape recorder.

CHAPTER SIX

Eddie made sure he got the seat beside Eva. Ben and Claire sat behind them. Granderson flew the helicopter, Chris Blackwood sitting silently at his side.

They'd been in the air twenty minutes when Ben said, "There's no cell phone coverage on the island?"

"That's right," Eddie answered.

"No internet."

"Nope."

"How are we going to communicate, carrier pigeons?"

Eddie looked back at him. "I figured you'd be happy Lee couldn't get ahold of us."

Ben didn't answer.

Eddie thought back to when their agent had called with the news – Lee Stanley was ready to make another ghost story and believed the "unique stylings" of Shadeland and Blaze would be just the thing to lend the film the "necessary aura of darkness."

Then he remembered the phone conversation with Lee last week and felt his throat constrict.

The director asking, "How's the music for *House of Skin* coming along?"

Eddie grimaced. The title made him think of a dermatologist.

"You still there?" Lee asked.

"Sorry," Eddie replied. "It's coming along fine."

No answer, Lee waiting for him to elaborate.

"Ben's been writing some things," Eddie lied. "I'm trying different ways of shaping them."

"What does that mean?" Lee asked.

Who the hell knew? The truth was, there was nothing to shape, but he'd be damned if he'd tell Lee Stanley that. He could imagine how the news would go over. *Sorry, but Ben hasn't written a note. As a matter of fact, Mr. Stanley, the last time I mentioned* House of Skin *to him he said for you to take your precious movie and shove it up your ass.*

The helicopter began its descent.

For a moment, there was nothing but clouds, but when the blades tore a hole in the swirling, gray mist, Eddie's mouth opened and his breathing stopped. Larger than Eddie had pictured, the Sorrows was a stunning sight. There was a thin rim of trees ringing the island's eastern edge, and in the center of the island lay a large clearing that might have been a graveyard. The rest of the Sorrows appeared heavily wooded.

Inland a hundred yards or so, Castle Blackwood seemed the fortified remnant of some long-ago battle. The L-shaped castle was tall and thin, its upper stories populated by multiple turrets and corbels.

Granderson's voice took on the didactic tone of a history professor. "Robert Blackwood took a trip to Scotland in the summer of 1893. One of the sights that captured his imagination was Craigievar Castle, a sixteenth century—"

"Is that tower separate?" Eva asked. She leaned across Eddie to get a better view and one firm breast rubbed pleasingly against his arm.

"Yes," Granderson answered. "There's the main castle commissioned by Robert Blackwood to resemble Craigievar, and the tower – commonly referred to as the keep – which is the lone remnant of the original castle."

"I don't like it," Eva said.

Eddie said, "We'll only put you there if you misbehave."

"That's not what I meant," she said, frowning. "It looks like it's about to fall."

"It'll stand until someone takes it down," Granderson said. "Robert left the tower intact due to its privacy."

"Maybe he wanted to remember his father," Ben suggested.

Granderson grinned unpleasantly. "Robert Blackwood wasn't the sentimental sort."

As Eva leaned over him – Christ, she even smelled good, lush and peachy like his favorite Chardonnay – Eddie allowed himself a good look at her. Darker skin than he'd thought, the hair longer. Her eyes a surprising shade of green. His eyes crawled down her slender neck to the low-cut black dress and the perky breasts. Lower, to the smooth brown legs. She crossed them and cleared her throat. Eddie forced himself to look up.

Eva watched him with raised eyebrows.

He gave her a feeble grin.

Ben asked, "What do you think of the Clay incident?"

Eddie looked back and saw he'd been addressing Chris Blackwood. When Eddie turned to see Blackwood's reaction, he was stunned by the anger in the guy's face.

Blackwood said, "What do you mean 'what do I think of it'?"

But Ben seemed unabashed. Maybe he'd expected a rise out of their host.

"I only mean, do you know the story, and if you do, does it bother you?"

Blackwood swiveled completely around and looked at Ben as though he'd suggested they purposely crash the helicopter. "Of course I know the goddamn story." Blackwood glanced open-mouthed at Granderson. "Christ, you believe this guy?"

Granderson kept quiet but eyed Ben in the overhead mirror.

Blackwood shook his head and returned his gaze to the front of the chopper. Eddie glanced back at Ben, who shrugged and commenced staring out the side window.

After an interminable silence, Granderson said, "You should find the castle well furnished. I brought supplies earlier."

"Any liquor?" Eddie asked.

"The castle has a fully stocked wine cellar."

"I thought the island was abandoned in 1925," Ben said. "Does wine keep that long?"

For a moment no one said anything, but Eddie could see that this was another subject that made Chris Blackwood uncomfortable. His shaggy, blond hair dark around the edges, the guy was sweating like a teenager whose girlfriend was late for her period.

"The wine in the cellar is fifteen years old," Granderson said. "At that time Chris's parents renovated the castle with the notion of transforming it into a vacation retreat."

The helicopter banked right, heading for the castle lawn.

"I never heard about that," Ben said.

"You wouldn't be likely to unless you were one of the laborers or a member of the Blackwood family."

They descended.

"Claire?" Ben asked, and as Eddie craned his head around, he was amazed at the change in her. Upon takeoff she'd been quiet but composed. Her blonde hair had looked stylish, and though her makeup was minimal, the natural look suited her. All in all, Eddie felt he'd underestimated her the night before. Some might even call her pretty.

Now she looked like a plague victim.

Eyes glazed over, large beads of perspiration dotting her skin, her complexion had taken on a sallow hue.

Eddie scooted forward in case she puked.

The helicopter met solid ground. Chris Blackwood opened the door and hopped out of the chopper. Rather than helping them down, Blackwood moved off toward the woods.

Some host, Eddie thought.

He climbed out and reached up to help Eva. As he did so, he caught an exhilarating glimpse of sheer black underwear.

Naughty girl.

He wondered how long it would take to see the rest of her.

* * *

In the back seat of the helicopter, Claire sat still and willed her pulse to slow, her nausea to subside. The whirling blade, its whumping revolutions reminded her of that Poe story 'The Pit and the Pendulum.'

Ben was watching her, concerned.

Claire forced herself to smile, to ignore the huge, deadly cleavers swinging above their heads.

"Not a fan of helicopters?" he asked.

"I wasn't going to say anything," she said. "I didn't want you to think I was a wimp."

He helped her down, his hands strong yet gentle on her arms and back. Glad to be on firm ground, Claire watched Eva approach. The woman was, if anything, more exquisite than the night before at Lee Stanley's party. Claire almost convinced herself the sudden bitter tang in her mouth was from her fear of flying.

"You felt it too," the woman said.

Claire watched her uncertainly.

Eva put an arm around her. "You don't like this place, do you?"

The hand on her back was firm, protective.

"I don't like flying is all," Claire said. "I've always been that way."

Eva's hand lingered there a moment, then the woman released her and went to retrieve her suitcase, which Granderson had placed on the ground. As Eva moved away, Claire took in the glossy black hair, the supple brown skin and felt a wave of self-consciousness. With a creature like this along, would Ben even notice her?

Enough of that, she told herself. *You're here to learn your craft, not to hook up.*

"You want me to carry your case?" Ben asked.

"No thanks," she said. She pulled out the handle. "Mine rolls."

Ben nodded and shouldered his bag.

She stayed behind a moment and gazed up at the castle. Yes, she decided. There was an intelligence in its towering pallid contours. Something corrosive and upsettingly sly. It reminded her very much of another Poe story, 'The Fall of the House of Usher.'

Except this building did not look like it could fall. It looked like it would stand forever, far outliving its inhabitants.

Or claiming them.

Shivering a little, Claire followed the others inside.

CHAPTER SEVEN

Ben and the others followed Granderson into the foyer. There were doors on either side of the entry, and ahead he could see the great hall. The pleasing scents of old stone and burnished wood imbued the foyer with an intimate aura, despite the castle's prodigious size.

"Now," Granderson said to them, "a few items of note."

"You forgot your nametag," Eddie said.

"You'll be here a month," Granderson said, "I assume you'll want to know something of the place."

"I think we'll manage."

But Eva spoke up. "I'd like to hear it."

Granderson led them forward. "This room is a near replica of the great hall in Craigievar. To the right you'll find the dining hall, the kitchen, and the pantry."

Soon they came to a stone staircase. The stairs wound up and up, and when they finally reached the fifth story, Ben fought an embarrassing urge to lean against the wall to catch his breath.

"The studio is above us on the sixth floor. On this level there are four large bedrooms," Granderson said, gesturing at the open doors to the right.

Eva asked, "Which one's mine?"

"That's entirely up to you," Granderson said.

Eddie opened the first door and said, "I'll take this one."

Ben moved up and realized why Eddie had called the room. Though a few evergreens stood in the foreground, much of what he observed out the large windows was dark sea.

Ben took the next room, Claire the one after that.

"I guess that means Miss Rosales will be staying in the master suite," Granderson said and opened the heavy wooden door at the end of the hall.

"Oh man," Eddie said as they all went in.

Windowed on two sides, the room also contained a huge four-poster bed. To its right was a large sitting area with a brocade chair and a chaise lounge; to the left of the bed, French doors led to the master bath.

Eva winked at Eddie. "Thanks for giving me this room," she said.

"Stop gloating," he answered.

"Now," Granderson said as they left the master suite, "I trust you'll be able to acquaint yourselves with the rest of the castle." He turned to Eddie. "I believe you have something for me."

Eddie took out his wallet, handed Granderson a check.

As Granderson made to leave, Claire said, "What do we do if there's an emergency?"

Granderson gave her a dry smile. "Are you expecting one?"

Prick, Ben thought.

Claire said, "No...but what happens if one of us needs a doctor."

"I'd suggest you avoid getting sick," Granderson said and walked away.

"You've been a fun guide," Eddie called after him.

Granderson didn't answer, and within seconds, he was gone.

"Jackass," Eddie said.

"I think he's handsome," Eva said. "Kind of reminds me of James Bond. The blond one."

"You gotta be kidding me," Eddie said.

Eva cocked an eyebrow. "At least Granderson has learned something you haven't."

"What's that?"

"He's attractive without working at it. You try too hard."

Ben suppressed a grin.

But Eddie's smile never wavered. "I think you're trying to make me jealous."

"I don't have to try, Eddie. That's the difference between us."

CHAPTER EIGHT

"Congratulations," Granderson said as he fired up the helicopter, "here's the other half of your reprieve."

Chris took the check sullenly. He doubted it would do much good. How long until one of Marvin's thugs returned? How long before the bastard with the scalpel paid him another midnight visit?

He pocketed the check and closed his eyes as Granderson guided the chopper higher. His tongue was coated in a sour patina that reminded him of lukewarm coffee dregs. The base of his skull throbbed and he badly needed to a have a bowel movement.

He shifted in his seat, rode out the stomach cramps.

"Do you need me to land?" Granderson asked.

"It'll pass."

"You could have used the bathroom in the castle."

Sure, Chris thought. *I could've also visited the master suite so I could relive the night I witnessed my parents transform into monsters.*

"I'm fine."

He sensed Granderson's scrutiny, the pitiless blue eyes appraising him instead of concentrating on their ascent.

"You're frightened of this place," Granderson said.

"Just get us home."

A curt nod. Then, as they moved out over the water, "Have you thought of how you'll make up the rest of your debt?"

"Of course I've thought about it."

Granderson banked the helicopter and pointed it toward the mainland. "What have you come up with?"

"There's always Dad."

"I imagine your father is still unhappy about your arrest."

Goddammit, Chris thought, *that was almost a year ago, and I was barely above the legal limit.*

"I'm his only child. I doubt he'd like to see me murdered."

"Then you understand the gravity of the situation."

"Hell yes, I understand."

"And you realize this man Irvin can set whatever price he wants…raise the figure arbitrarily if he so chooses."

"He's already done that."

It reminded Chris of something. He turned. "Where were you the night Marvin's guy cut me up?"

"I told you," Granderson said, glancing incuriously out the side window. "I was in the guesthouse, where I always am."

"But I asked you to stay with me."

"That's right," Granderson said. "You asked."

"Tell me again why my father hired you?"

Granderson nodded, but there was an impish gleam in his eyes. As he often did, Chris had the feeling the man was toying with him, relishing some private joke. "Your father hired me to watch over you. I do what he asks, and I answer only to him."

The pain in Chris's bowels grew sharper.

"That's great. So if someone threatens to slice my dick off you're supposed to let it happen."

"Your father believes you have many character defects," Granderson said. "I happen to agree."

Chris folded his arms, sat back in his seat. "Go fuck yourself." He closed his eyes and resolved to call his father tomorrow. Surely the man would help him this once. Surely his father wouldn't let him die.

Chris thought of the scalpel touching his penis.

So many places I can dig.

Forget tomorrow.

He'd call Stephen Blackwood the moment they reached dry land.

CHAPTER NINE

At the knock on her door Claire almost wet her pants. Grasping the rim of her open suitcase, she gritted her teeth and waited for the adrenalin to subside. It did, slowly, and in its wake came anger. She hated being startled that way.

It reminded her of Bobby, her older brother, who never tired of scaring her senseless. Hiding behind closet doors to leap out bellowing. Planting rubber snakes and dead mice under her covers. Pouring freezing water over the shower curtain.

Still, part of her had always been skittish. Just born that way, she guessed.

Being in the castle didn't help.

The knock sounded again – she'd nearly forgotten about the person at the door – and she said, "Yes?" as evenly as possible.

No one answered.

"What do you want?" she asked, making no pretense of civility this time. The silence drew out. Sure now it was Eddie, she ripped open the door and gaped at the empty corridor.

Claire exhaled.

Movement to her left. Near the end of the hallway, where the stairs were, she was certain there'd been a subtle alteration of the shadows. She took a step that way and paused. Thirty feet away she perceived the leaded casement window, the pallid moonlight shining through.

Claire screwed up her eyes, told herself it was nothing.

Some trick of the light, some stupid, unfortunate trick, gave off the impression that a pair of hands rested on the windowsill, the wrists large and bony. The forearms of the figure gradually dwindled as they moved toward their possessor, though there was no one there of course, only the bunched darkness of the corridor, the shadows concentrated but by no means alive.

A hand fell on her shoulder.

Claire gasped, whirled, lashing out to ward off whatever evil resided in this place.

"Hey," a male voice said, laughing.

Eddie.

"What's wrong with you?" she demanded, the panic anger of her youth returning.

"I came down to see who you were talking to."

In the wan light sifting out of her room, she could see Eddie's expression, an infuriating mingling of humor and incredulity.

"You knocked," she said but he was already shaking his head. She headed him off, her years with Bobby instructing her in dealing with thoughtless pranks. "You knocked on my door, twice. Then you hid and snuck up on me."

Eddie was laughing now. "I was in my room when I heard you down here talking to someone."

His assured manner gave her pause. An inchoate fear had arisen in the back of her mind, though she strove to suppress it.

"Who would I be talking to?"

"I thought it was Ben," he answered. "It was a deep voice."

She had an urge to strike him. How dare he frighten her so? What possible good could come of planting such awful thoughts in her, and on their first night in the castle no less. Did he think by scaring her he could seduce her, send her scurrying into his room for protection? Too angry to speak, she brushed past him into her room.

Following, he asked, "Why are you so cold to me?"

"It doesn't matter," she said and returned to her unpacking.

"I'm sorry I called your samples derivative, if that's what you're so mad about. I was in a bad mood last night."

"I understand," she said. "You're too busy to waste your time on a seven."

Eddie's mouth dropped open.

"Or am I a seven-and-a-half?"

Claire folded her arms. "But at least Renoir would have found me attractive, right?"

Eddie's shoulders sagged. "I'm sorry, Claire. It was a rotten thing to say."

She waited.

"You've gotta understand, though…ever since the nomination and the article in *Premiere* we've been besieged by aspiring musicians, and frankly, most of them have been young women."

"And that gives you the right to lump everyone together, as though every girl wants you sexually?"

"That's not what I..." He trailed off and ran a hand through his hair. "After the party I went back and listened to your stuff."

"So?"

"So," he said, "your stuff is very good."

When she didn't respond he added, "It wasn't derivative of anybody, and I'm sorry I said it."

Despite herself, she felt some of her anger melt.

He went on, "It was a mistake, Claire. You were serious when you applied and you didn't deserve the way I treated you."

She studied his face for traces of irony, but the Eddie she'd come to expect seemed to have been replaced by a decent human being.

He said, "And seven-and-a-half was way too low."

A smile threatened to hijack her face. "Jerk."

He chuckled softly. "I was." He extended a hand. "Forgive me?"

She put her hands on his chest and shoved him toward the door. "Better not mess up again."

"I promise."

Claire shut the door, turned, and caught sight of her blushing face in the mirror. It was the anger that made her blush, she told herself. Or the fear she'd felt earlier.

It certainly wasn't Eddie Blaze and his smart-ass grin.

* * *

Ben was sitting in the first story parlor when he heard a voice ask, "Mind if I come in?"

He looked up and saw Eva watching him from the doorway. She wore tight blue shorts and a pin-striped baseball jersey. She looked like she was ready for a slumber party.

"Of course not," he answered. He gestured to the open book on the coffee table before him. "I'm just reading about the castle."

"Is it interesting?" she asked, moving next to his red velvet chair. She rested on the arm, her tawny skin agleam in the lamplight.

"Sort of," he said. "Not really. It's pretty dry actually."

The warm scent of her was delicious. He made himself concentrate on the open book.

"What's that?" she asked, pointing to a sketch.

He followed her pointing finger. "Let's see…" He tried to concentrate. "…right here it says 'Wine Cellar,' so I'm guessing this is the blueprint for the basement."

"Does that say 'Pit'?"

The open throat of her jersey showed a lot of cleavage, gave off more of her fragrance, some nice-smelling brand of soap.

He cleared his throat. "Yes, I think it does."

"Doesn't sound like a nice place."

Eddie came through the door. "What doesn't?"

Ben straightened nervously, but Eva didn't look up. Eddie stood on Ben's other side. "Blueprints?"

Ben said, "Uh-huh," and was angry at himself for wishing Eddie hadn't interrupted.

"So Eva," Eddie said, "what do you say to a little expedition?"

"What do you have in mind?"

"Ben and I are gonna explore the castle. Wanna come?"

Eva stood, stretched. "I'm exhausted," she said. "I'll look around tomorrow."

With a backward glance at Ben, she said, "Have fun," and left.

"Shame," Eddie said. "I hope I didn't come at a bad time."

"Of course not."

Following him into the hallway, Eddie said, "I kind of thought it would be you and Claire, you know? Eva's more my type."

"Your type," Ben said as they descended the stairs, "is anything with a pulse."

"It has to be female."

"I didn't realize you were that discriminating."

Ben opened a door on the left side of the foyer and saw more stairs leading down.

"That must lead to the pit," Eddie said.

Ben hesitated.

"Scared again, Shadeland?"

"No, but I'm not going down there without a flashlight."

"The switch is right here," Eddie flipped on the light. "See?"

"And according to the blueprints, the pit is lower than the basement."

"Good point."

They scoured the pantry for flashlights but came up empty until they checked under the kitchen sink, where they found several.

They returned to the basement.

The light above the staircase was a naked yellow bulb that kept winking like the jaundiced eye of some hoary old troll. Ben was damned glad he'd insisted on the flashlights. The first room they came to was the wine cellar. Ben didn't know wine and Eddie did, so Ben told him they'd skip it for now. The last thing he needed was another lecture on Merlot.

Continuing down the corridor, Eddie said, "Hey, I meant to ask you… why's this island called the Sorrows?"

"It's a symphony," Ben said. "Don't tell me you've never heard of it?"

"Robert Blackwood isn't exactly a household name."

"Robert didn't write it," Ben said. "His father did."

Farther down the hall and to the left they found a pair of double doors. Opening them, they were greeted with a generator the size of a nuclear reactor. Surprisingly, its deep hum wasn't terribly loud, which Ben took for a good sign.

Other than a couple of storage areas, that was it until they came to the next flight of steps. They paused at the top and shone their lights into the darkness. At the bottom of the stairs hulked a heavy wooden door, dark with age. It looked like something out of the Inquisition.

Eddie's voice was uncharacteristically tight. "I guess that's the pit, huh?"

"I'd imagine."

"Looks kind of spooky."

"That's one word for it."

Eddie said, "You wanna hold hands?"

Ben started down. The flashlight felt solid in his hand, but for some reason the beam it put out seemed diffuse and dim. It illuminated the door just fine, but the areas flanking it were shadow pools that made his skin crawl.

They came to the door and without hesitation, Eddie leaned on the rusty metal bar until it gave. With a puff of fetid air, the door creaked open.

Eddie held out an arm. "After you, Princess."

Ben made his way inside and was immediately sure they'd made a mistake. There was something corruptive here, a palpable sense of depravity. The pit was huge, the floor slimed with some viscous substance that made their shoes squelch with every step. The smell was even worse – a stinking olfactory casserole of animal den, landfill, and feces. His eyes began to water.

"Jesus," Eddie said and Ben was pleased to hear his best friend gagging in the near darkness.

"Seen enough yet?" Ben asked.

"Hell yes," Eddie said and made to go.

Following him out, Ben had a sudden premonition – the door ahead slamming closed, whatever horrible creature responsible for the riot of stench down here pouncing on them and rending them to pieces.

Eddie went through. Ben followed and did his best not to take the last few yards at a sprint.

They had gone a few steps up when Eddie stopped and asked, "Where are your manners?"

Ben watched as he went back and pulled the door shut.

Eddie was shaking his head. "You Midwesterners spend too much time humping livestock. Weren't you ever taught to close the door behind you?"

Ascending the stairs, Ben said, "The stench back there took away my ability to think."

"Worst thing I ever smelled," Eddie agreed.

They climbed the stairs under the flickering yellow bulb and emerged into the foyer. Ben shut the basement door but the noxious odor from the pit stayed in his nostrils. They went outside. The sea breeze felt good on Ben's face and the smell of brine went a long way toward cleansing his airway. They waded into the waving grass of the lawn and moved around the castle until they came to a weathered pair of sliding doors.

"What's in there?" Ben asked.

"I don't know," Eddie said. "Probably where they kept their servants."

Ben turned and glanced at the lone tower half a football field away.

Eddie said, "Wonder if it's unlocked."

"I doubt it," Ben said, but Eddie was already moving that way.

As they neared the tower door, Ben could make out the brass glint of a padlock. Eddie reached the door and tried it anyway, but the lock held fast.

Ben yawned, asked, "What now?"

"I don't know," Eddie said. "I guess we go looking for inspiration."

"My bed sounds more inspiring right now."

"You gonna put the moves on Eva?"

"I wouldn't dream of seducing your future wife."

"I hope to hell you come up with something soon."

"So do I."

Ben was nearing the castle door when Eddie added, "Some of us actually care about our reputations, you know."

Ben faced him. "What do you want me to say?"

"I want you to say 'Here's what I came up with, Eddie. Arrange it for me.'"

"The more you push," Ben said, "the more pressure I feel."

"Christ," Eddie said and raised his arms. "It's like some little kid who's afraid of going off the high dive. You stand there and stand there and refuse to jump, and all the time the clock is ticking on our careers."

Ben became aware of a twitch in his left forearm, the muscle there hopping erratically. Despite the coolness of the evening, he'd begun to sweat.

"I'm going up. Have fun out here."

"Sure thing," Eddie said. "While you're in bed feeling sorry for yourself, I'll be thinking of ways to get you to work."

CHAPTER TEN

Ben dreamed.

He recognized the setting immediately. Though Ben had only peeked inside earlier, the huge sixth-floor studio must have left an indelible imprint on his subconscious, for in his dream each detail of the forty-by-thirty room stood out vividly – the windows damasked with rich-green velvet curtains, the numerous bay window seats. The black Steinway. He could smell the crisp, salty sea breeze breathing through the windows in soothing draughts.

As he had earlier that night, Ben walked over to the grand piano, studied it a moment, and sat down. In his dream he played the sheet music that had been sitting on the tray God knew how long.

Though badly in need of a tune, the Steinway sounded magnificent. He recognized the melody – the final movement of The Sorrows. Ben was immersing himself in the music when his son appeared beside him.

"Hi, Daddy," Joshua said.

Ben's hands kept playing despite his overwhelming need to draw the boy closer, to hold him and rock him, to cover his sweet face in kisses even if Joshua sometimes recoiled at such displays of affection.

The boy tugged at his arm, trying to get his attention, but Ben's hands would not leave the keys.

I'm sorry, Joshua, he tried to say, but though his lips formed the words, no sound came. He was powerless to do anything save finish the song.

The heartbreak plain on his face, Joshua moved toward a window.

Facing the sheet music, which had fluttered automatically to the next page, he resolved to dash out the piece as quickly as possible. Then he would bolt across the room and enfold his son in an embrace that no one could tear asunder.

The music flipped again and Ben realized he'd made it to the final page. Only twelve more bars and he would be with Joshua again, and this time no Jenny nor court nor Ryan would stop what was natural, what was right. This child was part of him, the best part of him, and by God they belonged together.

His cheeks shining with tears of joy, Ben completed the song and glanced across the room.

The boy had cranked open the casement window, was straddling the sill.

No Joshua, Ben tried to say, but his voice wouldn't work. The boy gazed down at the lawn below, the stars outlining him in brilliant-white fire.

Ben advanced toward the child, sure at any moment he would frighten him into sudden movement, send him plummeting to his death.

He had halved the distance between them when Joshua said, "It's too late, Daddy, I've already gone."

Joshua's voice was the same – that husky, unassuming soprano that melted him – but the words themselves were too mature, too world-weary to be his son's.

Ben took another stride. If he could just reach out, grasp his sleeve…

But the boy said, "No, Daddy."

Ben lunged as Joshua fell backward out the window, his fingers just brushing one of the boy's shoes as he disappeared.

Then Ben awoke, harsh sobs wracking his sweat-soaked body.

After a time he glanced at the *Toy Story* watch Joshua had given him last Father's Day – he remembered how proud the boy had been for having chosen it – and saw by the faint green light between Buzz and Woody that it was only 11:38.

Ben did not sleep again that night.

* * *

When Eddie heard the girl's voice, he was sure it was Eva.

Sooner than expected, he thought.

In the shadows of his bedroom, Eddie pictured Eva's body and yearned to see her naked. He bet she tanned in the nude, her ass as brown and firm as the rest of her.

Was she even now drifting, wraithlike, through the inky darkness toward his bed?

Eddie propped himself on his elbows.

"I'm over here," he said.

Silence for a moment. Then, faintly, he heard the voice again. Female, yes, but it couldn't be Eva's. Not unless she was impersonating someone else. The voice was plaintive, immature. Nothing like Eva's low purr.

"Claire?" he asked.

Silence.

"All right," he said, "I'm going back to sleep. Whoever you are, you can forget about scaring me."

When no response came, Eddie closed his eyes and feigned sleep in the hope that sleep would come. He had no idea how long he'd lain there when he heard the voice again, louder this time, almost at his ear.

"What the hell—" he started to say, but the words clotted in his throat when he beheld the open door, the flutter of a white gown departing the room.

Eddie swung his legs over the edge of the mattress, furious with Claire. It had to be Claire, he realized now. The glimpse of leg was chalky and full. Nothing like Eva's lithe, brown calves.

So Claire was playing games. She'd said earlier she'd forgiven him, but Eddie knew how women could be. Climbing out of bed, Eddie thought of several girls he'd dated who stayed angry for days over some petty thing. That's what pissed him off most about women. It was the reason he'd never married. You had to walk on eggshells around them, pretend they were behaving rationally when rationality had nothing to with their behavior.

Eddie crossed to the door, craned his head around the corner.

The hallway was quiet. Here and there shadows shifted, the ocean wind worrying the trees. They threw thin, spidery images up and down the walls, giving the impression the corridor was acrawl with scuttling, secretive things that fled the daylight and lived for the darkness, now capering in their midnight riot, willing the unwary to enter their realm.

Jesus, he thought, smiling a little. *Relax already.*

Eddie strode into the corridor, the wood cold under his bare feet. He could see Eva's door at the end of the hall. Closed, of course. Next to hers, Claire's door was also fastened tight. He went to his door, preparing to lock himself in for the night, when he heard it.

Giggling, the voice high and girlish and far too familiar.

It came from the staircase. Eddie followed the sound, not wanting to meet the one responsible for producing it, but not wanting to stand there doing nothing either. The giggle came again, fainter now, the woman descending the steps.

Eddie followed it down and paused at the foot of the staircase. The great hall was steeped in a darkness nearly impenetrable. Only at its eastern edge, where it connected with the foyer, was there any light at all. His eyes adjusting to the gloom, he made out a figure. Silent, unmoving, it stood there facing him in the moonlight pouring through the foyer windows.

Eddie's lungs tightened, his mouth opening in horror. Warm copper flooded his mouth.

It can't be, he thought.

The figure turned and glided across the foyer. The door grated open, starshine streaming in, and Eddie glimpsed the long blonde hair, the tall, athletic body. The woman glanced over her shoulder, but before he could see her face Eddie bolted up the stairs, taking the steps three at a time, jerking at the handrail, barking his knees as he stumbled. He dashed down the corridor and ripped open his door. Hands shaking, he pushed it closed, shot the thick iron bolt, and backed away from it, sure at any moment it would fly inward.

Oh my God, he thought. *Oh my God.*

⋆ ⋆ ⋆

Claire frowned in the darkness. She knew there were a hundred valid reasons why Eddie would leave his room this late at night. Perhaps he wanted to explore the castle further, maybe he couldn't sleep. Whatever the reason, it was none of her business. But slamming the door at – she checked – 12:55 a.m.?

Footsteps sounded in the hall.

So she wasn't the only one Eddie had roused. Ben or Eva had awakened too. She heard the footfalls pause down the hall a ways, just outside Eddie's door. She expected a knock, Ben – it had to be Ben because the footsteps had come from that end of the hallway – inquiring after Eddie's well-being, or simply wanting to know why he felt the need to make such a ruckus in the middle of the night. But Ben didn't knock, only stayed outside the door, maybe listening for Eddie inside, making sure he was all right.

Claire yawned, waiting for the footsteps to recede down the hall. She waited a long time, lying on her side and staring at the rectangle of moonglow.

She waited, but the sound of departing footsteps never came.

CHAPTER ELEVEN

Lying in a ball between the bed and the dresser – he couldn't bring himself to sleep in his bed again – Chris allowed himself to go back to that night fifteen years ago.

★ ★ ★

When his parents told him what his fourteenth birthday present would be, his first impulse was to ask why.

Experience told him to bite his tongue. Once Stephen Blackwood gave you a present, you damned well better show your appreciation, or else the purse strings would draw even tighter.

Chris would have chosen a three-wheeler or a jet ski. Maybe a new pool table for the basement.

He guessed a trip to the Sorrows would have to do.

When his grandfather died, Chris didn't think about the island at all. He didn't think or feel anything at the man's passing, except that the viewing of the body, the funeral, the endless dinner that came after, were all about as fun as piano lessons with Mrs. Scheidt, a stern, gray-haired woman whose name reminded him of taking a dump. But the island was now his father's and soon after the inheritance, Chris received his birthday present.

It began with dinner, his father drinking too much, but that was nothing out of the ordinary. His mother hitting the bottle hard – that was most definitely *not* ordinary. And the way his father pawed at Rosa, the little Hispanic cook, right there in the open for his wife and son to see, that wasn't ordinary either. Sure, they all knew his father slept around. But to do it in front of his wife? Asking his son…

"You ever seen a tastier dish than this?"

Chris sipped his wine, grateful his parents allowed him to drink during vacations because it made them feel French or something.

Chris's father hugged little Rosa around the hips. "I think you're gorgeous, *comprende*?" He gave her a shake. "You understand what I mean?"

Rosa didn't say a word. The dining hall was dimly lit, but Chris could see the woman was uncomfortable.

He glanced at his mom, watched her swirling her dark-amber drink, her eyes fixed on the glass. As if her husband wasn't – holy crap – fondling one of Rosa's large breasts right there in front of her.

"May I be excused?" Chris asked.

When no one answered, he got up, lifted a corkscrew and a fresh bottle of wine from the serving table, and went out.

Instead of going to his bedroom, he entered the great hall.

This was their fourth night on the island, and this was the first time Chris had been in here alone. The entire castle gave him the heebie-jeebies, but no place more so than here. The sheer size of the room made Chris feel terribly insignificant.

Then again, his father had the same effect on him.

The large stone fireplace could accommodate a good-sized car. Above its burnished-wood mantel were posed two snarling lions. Their ferocious expressions made it plain that, if alive, they would tear each other apart.

Or tear Chris apart.

Stepping back from the fireplace he gazed up at the intricate designs adorning the ceiling. He supposed a more mature, better-trained eye would see order amidst the chaos of patterns, but to Chris it was an unattractive jumble.

In his periphery he spotted a dark smudge. Whirling, he faced a black statue of Cupid perched atop a white marble stand. He blew out a relieved breath, told himself to get a grip. His throat rasped like some desiccated husk. It reminded him of the bottle in his hand. A drink would help.

He shoved the point of the corkscrew in and began the job of getting the bottle open. While he did, he heard footsteps outside the great hall, his parents heading upstairs for the night. Chris removed the cork, cast aside the corkscrew and hunched his shoulders at the clatter it made on the hardwood floor.

According to his father, the renovation was 90 percent complete. Chris knew nothing of renovations, but to him it seemed they'd gone all out. Upgrading the plumbing and electricity. Refinishing the floors. Updating the kitchen and putting in one hell of a huge generator.

Still, he wondered if modernizing this place was such a good idea. He'd had bad dreams all week, nightmares such as he'd never experienced.

He glanced uneasily about the room, took in the deepening shadows that lay beyond the reach of the chandeliers.

He knew there was a great deal his parents weren't telling him, and he knew much of it had to do with his great-grandfather. He'd seen pictures of the first Robert Blackwood. A couple of them had been taken right here in this room.

Chris gazed up at the lions, wondered what terrible things they'd seen. He imagined them pivoting toward him, their soundless growls swelling into audibility. He shuddered. To take the edge off his fear, he tilted the bottle and took a gulp.

"A very good year," he said and wiped his mouth. He had no idea if the wine was any good or not, but it tasted fine to him. He drank from the bottle again and felt the pleasant warmth spreading throughout his body. He wondered idly if Rosa was in the dining hall cleaning up. She was many years older than him, but she was still very attractive. What would happen if he were to go in there and offer to help? He could carry dishes for her, offer her some wine. Then, who knew? If she was lonely enough, certain enough that one of her bosses wouldn't be down again that evening, maybe she would welcome a curious touch, a lingering kiss.

He hadn't gotten laid yet, but he knew all about such things. He'd fingered Carrie Lieberman at her birthday party a few months ago. Three or four girls had allowed him to slip a hand under their bras.

Chris took another drink.

A woman like Rosa wouldn't bother with such foreplay. He thought of her full breasts, her round butt. What would she do if he snuck up behind her, lifted her dress, said "what do we have here"? Would she smack him in the face? Tell his mommy on him?

Chris put the bottle to his lips, drank.

Only one way to find out.

He patted Cupid's glossy black head on the way by and sucked in a breath as his elbow grazed the tip of the little archer's arrow. He frowned at the dark pinprick of blood. Maybe, he thought as he exited the great hall, the accident was a good omen. Maybe Rosa would be pierced by Cupid's arrow too.

But she wasn't in the dining hall.

Nor was she in the kitchen or her own quarters. Chris knew the castle was large – twelve thousand square feet, according to his father – but it was now, he checked his watch, ten-thirty at night. He couldn't imagine where the woman could be.

More than a trifle drunk, the fruity flavor of the wine permeating his palate like some natural anesthetic, Chris wandered the echoing corridors. It was a little creepy, and he was glad to be drinking. He could never have walked the halls of Castle Blackwood sober and alone. Especially at night.

Yet now, emboldened by the booze, Chris drifted from room to room, from floor to floor, hunting for a woman more than twice his age whom he was now sure was hunting for him too, yearning for a pair of arms to warm her, aching for an eager young lover to take away some of her loneliness.

On the fifth floor Chris heard Rosa's laughter. At first he thought the sound came from his own room.

Holy shit, he thought. She was waiting for him.

A thickness in his throat, Chris opened the door of his bedroom and flipped on the light.

Empty.

The laughter echoed again, and Chris was amazed to find it coming from his parents' room. He told himself it had to be his mother laughing so. It couldn't be Rosa. Then he approached the door and felt his stomach lurch at the trio of voices.

Without thinking, he opened the door and there on the four-poster bed lay his mother, her knees spread apart, arms splayed as if crucified.

Between her legs Rosa's small head rose and fell, rose and fell.

In the corner stood his father, naked. Nearly blotted out by his overhanging belly, his hairy hand was stroking in rhythm with the movements of Rosa's plunging face.

No one seemed to notice Chris standing there. No one said anything to him as he wheeled and hurried away, sure he was going to spew hot wine and gastric juices all over the floor. Chris stumbled into his bedroom, tossed the bottle on the bed, and barely made it to the toilet before it all exploded in a scalding gush, the color of it a dull burgundy, except for a few bits of what looked like maggots but were actually rice, the only part of the meal Chris had touched. He vomited a long time, then hung there panting on the edge of the cool, white bowl. Through the ringing in his ears and the poisonous saliva dribbling from the corners of his mouth, he became aware of a new sensation, a tingling at the small of his back and a tightening of his sphincter.

Then he heard what his body had already reacted to – an ugly, enraged voice followed by a strident plea.

Confusion and terror at war in his mind, he pushed away from the toilet and navigated the sickly swaying bathroom. Halfway through his bedroom he heard his mother's laughter, and the afterimage of the Hispanic woman going down on her almost brought on another wave of vomiting. He managed to hold it together, to get his door open. Using the wall as a brace, he approached the master suite again.

With a superstitious dread, Chris approached the lurid crimson glow emanating from the doorway. He reached out to steady himself on the jamb and fancied the slick wood squirming under his fingers.

In the corner of the room, his father thrust his big hips into Rosa, whose back rested on the open windowsill. His father's expression was not of a man enjoying himself, but rather of one intent on inflicting pain. Even as Chris watched, his father's meaty fist shot out, bludgeoned Rosa in the nose. He could see how far his father had shoved the woman into the aperture, five stories from the ground below.

His dad reached out, still thrusting his hips, and began to choke Rosa.

Chris knew he should say something, somehow help her, but he felt himself mentally retreating, taking refuge in his dulled senses. He saw the three figures in a writhing, hellish tableau:

Christina Blackwood, sated and drowsing on the bed.

Stephen Blackwood's lips pulled back in a snarl, his eyes wild and feral.

Rosa's eyes huge and frightened, the tendons of her neck straining.

Chris's father said something unintelligible. Rosa's rear end passed over the outer rim of the sill, her body held there by the hand that strangled it. Her madly kicking legs slid outward another inch. Three more. If his father let go now, Rosa would plummet to her death. Chris opened his mouth to scream but it was his mother's voice that broke the trance.

"Go away, Chris," was all she said.

His father looked at him, and Chris took a step in that direction. Rosa's anguished face swiveled toward him, her eyes bulging with terror.

"*Help me*," she managed to whisper.

His father smiled, his eyes red-rimmed and empty.

Then he let the woman fall.

PART TWO
CLAIRE

CHAPTER ONE

Claire awakes and is immediately assailed by a sense of wrongness. For one thing, she is standing up rather than lying in bed as she should be. The fact that she's been sleepwalking barely registers in her wildly disordered thoughts, the far more urgent question being where the hell she'd sleepwalked *to*. The floor under her bare feet is startlingly cold, like standing in a field of newly fallen snow, but the knowledge does little to orient her – after all, the entire castle is uncarpeted. She could be in her room, the hallway, the great hall even. For all she knows she could be

(*in the pit*)

in Ben's room. Oh God, what possessed her body to choose this, of all times – her first night in the castle – to switch to autopilot?

A murmuring voice makes her freeze. Someone is in the room with her.

Okay, she tells herself, *okay. Nothing to freak out about, no reason to come unhinged.*

More words from her immediate right, nearly intelligible now, and though the voice itself is velvety and unthreatening, the ice-pick jag of her heartbeat accelerates with the sound.

Would you get it together? the voice in her head demands. *This is a good thing, right? It means you had the good fortune to choose, out of the dozens of rooms in this sprawling gothic nightmare, one of the three tenanted by your companions.*

"Hate you," a voice says clearly enough to make her jump. She slaps a palsied hand over her heart, backs away from the voice.

"They hate you, Gabriel," the voice moans. Then, even more plaintively, "Leave while you can. Before they…no…"

And though Claire now understands into whose room she has crept, can now make out the faint outline of the woman under the thin white sheet, this does nothing at all to allay her escalating dread. It's Eva all right, but her voice is different. Servile, fanatical. Not at all like her usual self-possession.

"They fear you," Eva moans, her voice loud enough to bring goose bumps to Claire's bare arms. "They're going to hurt you. They're going to—"

Claire claps her hands over her ears, backpedals to the door. Mercifully, she has left it open, and the noose of dread that's been tightening around her throat immediately goes slack. Striding swiftly down the hall, Claire realizes with a distant sense of amazement that she has shed her own gown before embarking on her somnambulistic adventure, that the only article of clothing she has on is a pair of old underwear, very comfortable but about as sexy as the flesh-toned pantyhose she sometimes wears to compress the flesh around her waist. She starts to jog now, realizes she's already missed her room, is continuing past Ben's and Eddie's, and the image she needs to banish is of Eva in bed, Eva's narrow, sinuous frame outlined in the sheet, her flawless form radiating sex and confidence, mocking Claire with its perfection. Down the steps now, looping around the spiral, a snapshot of Eva's bare shoulder pursuing her, the woman's smooth brown neck…

Claire cannot evade it, cannot escape the picture of Eva slumbering in bed, and beside Eva now is another form, a much larger, whiter one. It is Claire herself spilling over the sheet like a living sack of flour, her green granny underwear a farcical contrast to Eva's silky black negligee.

The vividness of the scene fills Claire's imagination, imprints itself on the dim corridor that leads her to the kitchen. The weird doubling continues as her clumsy cow's hooves slap the kitchen tiles. She sees her huge white twin – that other self who's somehow upstairs with Eva – reach across the woman's perfect shoulder and draw down the sheet. *No*, Claire thinks as she lurches toward the granite kitchen countertop, she doesn't want to see herself anymore, doesn't want to witness her arms groping for Eva and pawing at her like some desperately curious friend at a sleepover. But now she can see her hand reaching down, alabaster fingers closing over something lying on the sheet.

Claire leans over the kitchen sink and watches in horror as the Claire upstairs brings the carving knife to Eva's throat.

Standing nearly naked in the cold kitchen, Claire makes a tortured little humming sound in the back of her throat as the other Claire teases the flesh of Eva's neck with the tip of the huge knife. The pressure on the bronze skin increases, but Eva does not stir, and the sinister Claire smiles wickedly, emboldened by the depth of the other's sleep. In the kitchen Claire whimpers as the blade sheers through the dark silk of the negligee, the shimmering fabric parting neatly from armpit to thigh. What in God's name, she wanted to cry out, did the other Claire think she was doing? What would Eva do, what would Eva *say* to her when she awoke and saw the carving knife?

Stop it, she tells the other Claire, but her twin only grins wider, a ghastly clown's leer in the moonlit bedroom, and Claire watches in horror as her twin pinches what fat she can gather from Eva's exposed side – there isn't much to grab – and begins slicing into the flesh as though it were deli meat. The black runnels of blood gushing out of the growing wound are bad enough, but somehow worse than these are Eva's closed lids, the shockingly placid set of her mouth as the blade continues sawing, the blood blackening the fearsome knife as the blade sinks deeper and deeper into Eva's unresisting flesh—

(Claire!)

She hisses and thrusts herself away from the sink, the carving knife clattering against the steel basin. A flood of pain, so bright and overpowering that it makes her vision swim, rolls through her body. One bare heel slips on the trail of blood following her from the sink, and she just catches herself on the center island before she falls. It is dark in the kitchen, but not so dark she can't see the meaty flap of skin, the ugly wound in her midsection. She hasn't gotten as far as her twin had in the vision – she estimates the gash in her right side is less than an inch long – but it is bleeding plenty. The green granny underwear looks black on one side, and below that a half dozen rivulets are wending their way down her leg like newborn snakes.

Fully awake for perhaps the first time since she lay down for bed that evening, Claire opens island drawers until she finds a dishrag – clean, she hopes – and presses it to the wound. She has no idea what got into her, but she's damned glad she awakened when she did. She remembers her question to Granderson, only half-serious at the time – *What happens if one of us needs a doctor?*

Granderson's unsmiling blue eyes as he answered, *I suggest you avoid getting sick.*

Claire flips on the overhead light and suppresses a tide of revulsion at the blood slicking the floor. She wonders, *Does sawing the skin off one's side qualify as a sickness?*

Shuddering at the thought, Claire steels herself for the job of cleaning up the blood. Though the pain is an ugly, red buzzing, she will dress the wound later. She needs to get rid of this mess.

But then again…

What if one of the others, worst of all Ben, comes down here and sees her standing naked and bloody like the intended victim of a botched murder?

She brushes the thought away and tells herself it isn't anything so dramatic. She simply experienced an awful bout of sleepwalking, a macabre half-waking nightmare.

She increases the pressure of the dishrag on her wound. *Dang, it hurts.* She doesn't want to leave things the way they are down here, but she really doesn't want to be discovered in this embarrassing bloody underwear. The last thing she needs is for Ben to walk in on her now. *Yes, Mr. Shadeland*, she can hear herself explaining, *I do want to compose music with you someday. Just because I butcher myself in my sleep doesn't mean I'm not a steady worker.*

She pauses, eyes sweeping the kitchen scene one last time. Her gaze fixes on the smeared carving knife lying in the basin. For good measure, she hides it under the sink. Before she closes the bottom cabinet drawer, relief floods through her at the sight of the medicine kit. Bearing it under her left arm, she begins the long climb upstairs.

With luck, she thinks, she won't bleed to death on the way to her room.

CHAPTER TWO

The morning light warming her skin, Eva climbed out of bed and went to the window of the master suite. Though she had slept soundly, she had experienced the most vivid dream of her life. It had been feverish, erotic.

And, in the end, terrifying.

In her dream Eva found herself standing before the mirror. One hand languidly massaged her breasts, which were domed in an old-fashioned ivory corset. Beneath that she was nude.

The room darkened as a large shape appeared behind her. She moaned as a pair of rough hands untied the corset, peeled it off. She watched as the dusky figure drew nearer, nearer, its hot breath stirring the hairs on the back of her neck.

Without warning the hands seized her by the shoulders, pulled her against a pulsing, muscular body. It lifted her and impaled her. The figure clutched the undersides of her legs, its bulging muscles suspending her in the air and thrusting up into her, igniting her, bringing her within seconds to a dizzying climax.

Then it cradled her like a small child, carried her to the bed and laid her on her back. She spread her legs wide, offering herself to the dark figure, needing to feel its weight on her.

The creature – she could think of it in no other way – climbed onto her and began thrusting. She bit the flesh of its shoulder. The creature seemed to enjoy that. Its blood on her lips, she endeavored to pull away from it to better see its face. The smell of her lover, she now realized, reminded her of a caged animal; its wildness and its need stung her nostrils. A whiff of feces attended it, but this too amplified its primal aura. Its sounds were bestial – snarling, growling, eager to rend and devour. She told the creature to give her a moment, she needed to catch her breath. When its movements continued unabated, she raised her voice, demanded it set her free.

Then she heard the laughter.

Alarmed, she beat on the creature's shoulders. The pleasure she'd experienced earlier had subsided, and in its place bloomed a suffocating dread that canceled out all thought, all need, save escape. She pleaded with the monster, for she now knew it to be such, but it wouldn't listen. Desperately, she plunged her nails into the creature's ears, seeking the vulnerable organs within.

The monster jerked away and glowered down at her.

Eva screamed.

Then she was sitting bolt upright in bed, the sheets clutched to her heaving chest.

Now, gazing out the window, Eva searched her memory for the creature's face. Nothing came. Dimly, she remembered the merest intimation of staring, white eyes. A caprine brow.

Even now she could almost feel the creature tearing her insides, its hot breath searing her neck—

Someone knocked.

Breath quavering, she managed to say, "Just a second."

She made sure her robe was fastened securely, the soft cotton cinched snugly over her breasts. She opened the door and bumped into Eddie, whose eyes flitted down to her robe, lingered there a moment, then finally met her gaze.

"What?" she said.

"You naked under there?"

She made to shut the door.

Eddie stopped it with a hand. "Hey," he said, laughing, "I was only kidding around."

"What do you want?"

"Ben and Claire are going on a walk. I thought you might wanna walk with me."

"I run in the mornings."

"Then sit with me a little while."

"I really need to—"

"Twenty minutes," he said, still holding the door open. "Then you can run."

She eyed him a moment. Then she blew hair out of her eyes, said, "I suppose so. Give me a few minutes to put some clothes on."

"Need any help?"

She cocked an eyebrow at him, made to slam the door in his face, but he was already backing away, palms raised in a placating gesture. "Okay, okay," he said. "It was just a stupid joke. Arrested development, I guess."

As she shut the door on him, she smiled a little against her will. Even if he did act like an adolescent, he was very handsome. Probably good in bed too, though she doubted she'd find out. Something told her the only lover she'd couple with this month was the one she'd dreamt about last night.

CHAPTER THREE

From the Journal of Calvin Shepherd
June 6th, 1911
Were it not for the incredible events of the past twenty-four hours, events that have left me breathless with emotion and curiosity, I would not be scribbling by lamplight this evening.

Dear Diary – shall I address you thusly? When the very word conjures an adolescent girl confiding to a flower-covered book of blank pages?

Journal then.

Robert and I arrived at the mouth of the Greek forest around noon. The Mediterranean sun was fierce at that hour, and I must admit my eagerness to venture into the encompassing shade was not due to some fit of poetical fancy or rugged desire for exploration, but because my sensitive complexion was being roasted by the pitiless white sun overhead.

"No need to return today," Robert told the carriage driver. "We'll hike back to the village when we've finished."

At Robert's words my stomach plummeted. How on earth were we to make it all the way to the village if not in some sort of conveyance? Yes, the convulsive progress of the horses along the primitive mountain road made me ill, and I dreaded the prospect of the same abhorrent journey to bookend our day. But I still preferred riding to hiking.

The long-bearded driver stared down at Robert uncertainly. Then, the man glanced at me for confirmation of Robert's wishes. I was so taken aback at this abrupt inclusion in the decision-making process that I fear I made a sore job of appealing to the driver with my eyes, for any spoken desire contrary to my employer's would have resulted in a thorough thrashing.

The driver shrugged and snapped the reins.

Robert thumbed the shoulder straps of his backpack. "Don't look so forlorn, Calvin, the exercise will do you good." He pushed past me and climbed over the low rock wall that separated the road from the forest.

When I turned to watch him enter the woods I had an uncanny

premonition, a vague sense that a new chapter in our lives was about to begin. The nature of this new phase was unclear to me, yet when Robert disappeared under the overhanging boughs, I felt that some tie with the past had been severed.

I followed Robert clumsily into the woods, the rock wall giving me far more difficulty than it had given him.

The ghosts of all ages seemed to inhabit the gnarled old trees and the dank, curiously soft soil of the path we were following. I could almost hear the wood nymphs stealing behind us, ever watchful, ever just out of sight. Here and there, midst the enormous boulders that littered the forest and the brambles that occupied the gaps between their staring, ashen faces, I glimpsed tenebrous forms, leering white eyes, Arcadian demons flitting about in the shadows. My lungs burned as I trudged on, and though I knew we had only been at it for minutes, my legs were already howling a devil's chorus of fatigue.

I stumbled and fell, the odor of mouldering vegetation swimming over me in a repulsive cloud. When I looked up, Robert was gone. The forest had swallowed him whole.

As I sat panting, the phrase "heart attack" looming all too probably in my fancy, I became aware of someone or something lurking close by. Not Robert, of course. He had long quitted the vicinity. Not our driver, he of the long beard and the dull intellect.

No, the presence I felt was something totally unfamiliar, and even more disturbing, wholly unfriendly.

Forgetting my galloping heart and the raging conflagration in my lungs, I scrambled to my knees and peered about the ancient forest.

All seemed still. All seemed undisturbed. Yet the area's apparent virginity only enflamed my suspicions, lent an aura of collusion to the silent trees and rocks.

I became aware of a subtle movement to my left, the direction from which we had come. As I turned, I glimpsed an amorphous shadow hulking beside a huge cypress tree. I completed my turn, the ghastly tendrils of dread closing around my windpipe, strangling my nascent cry.

I beheld it, but only for an instant. It stirred, as if aware of being discovered, and then vanished into the undergrowth. I would like to write of the trail it left, the branches that snapped into place as the figure passed. But such a description would be fiction. The hulking black figure neither crashed away into the obscuring undergrowth nor clambered up a tree to evade detection.

Rather, like a wisp of smoke carried away by a breeze, it vanished.

I gazed into the shadows, frozen by an overpowering sense of awe.

Then, the trance broke.

In a panic I gained my feet and, ignoring the cacophony of protests issuing from my body, I set off after Robert, certain that if I failed to locate him straightaway, I should become a permanent fixture in this nightmarish landscape.

Panting, coughing, plunged into an ecstasy of terror, I emerged from the forest an eternity later to find Robert gazing serenely over the Mediterranean. Next to him in the long green grass sat a half-eaten ham sandwich.

"You could've waited for me," I said.

Without taking his eyes off the indigo waters below, he answered, "It's good for you, Calvin. Makes up for all those hours sequestered in your room."

My hermetic habits were a favorite source of his jibes. I bristled inwardly but said nothing.

"Anyway, this view should be enough to take your mind off it," he said, and although I was still fuming, I was forced to concede the point. Though a small part of me was eager to share my unsettling experience with the forest demon, the larger part, the part that knew what derision would arise from such a confession, prevailed. Stepping past him, I gazed out over the rocky bay. The sea was calm, almost reticent. So different from the churning Pacific, the white-capped tumult of the Sorrows.

"It's beautiful," I said.

"Beautiful doesn't begin to describe it," Robert answered. "One look at those waters ignites a blaze within me, Calvin. This is where I'll find my muse."

I was thankful he couldn't see my face. My grin would have infuriated him.

Oh, Journal, if you're ever found, I will be roundly dismissed. Robert's temper is unlike any I've encountered. A tempest. A maelstrom. Even our maintenance man, Henry Mullen, with his red-faced blustering and foul-mouthed taunts, fails to rival the thunderous rage that darkens the brow of my master when he is cross.

So let me say it, here and now in my inaugural entry, and by saying it consign myself to a future of nervous speculation regarding the secrecy of my musings.

Robert Blackwood is a talentless hack. A sham. The son of a rich father who inherited all but his father's musical ability. If the world knew his secret – that he has cannibalized his father's unpublished works – he would be jeered into oblivion. How many times I've been tempted to expose him! But first I must commit to paper today's events. They are too astonishing to delay.

The woods beyond looked, if anything, deeper and denser than any we had yet traversed, and I was suddenly certain I would be dead by day's end, a victim to the harsh Greek mountainside and the years of physical inertness of which I was guilty. I begged Robert to consider my asthma, my weak heart. I implored him to turn back. But he ignored me and announced we would continue up the mountain in ten minutes. I opened my mouth to protest but the words died on my lips. Robert held up a hand, but there was no need. He was gazing steadily at the forest beyond, his face a mask of intensity. I understood why, for I heard it too.

The music.

"Robert—" I began, but at that moment he set off into the forest to pursue the source. Enveloped with awe at the singular circumstances, I followed.

The forest beyond the clearing was darker and more forbidding than any we had yet encountered. The ground uneven, the path nonexistent, Robert nonetheless pounded on ahead of me, and had the hour been later, I fear one of us would have incurred a fatal injury in our mad flight. Yet the day was bright and the gaps in the towering trees just wide enough to illumine our way as we drew closer and closer to the intoxicating melody which beckoned us forth.

Robert was a man possessed. He leapt over crags, burst through tangles of underbrush. When I was sure he would either leave me behind or break his neck navigating the primordial terrain, he slowed to a trot as the woods opened once again. This time, though, we were not entering another sunny place. No, though the trees ahead did indeed open into a bowl-shaped clearing, the lonesome glade was plunged into a perpetual state of darkness by the density of the trees surrounding it.

Robert ascended a hill and took refuge behind a large gray stone. He was watching something in the dale below. I tiptoed up the rise and knelt beside my master.

"Robert," I whispered.

The answering look he gave me could have frozen whiskey. He peered into the grassy basin.

In the darkest part of the glen, his bare back reclined on a mossy stump, sat a young boy holding a primitive wooden flute.

Dissonant, lilting, the child's song spoke of lost years and heartbreak. I thought of the Sorrows. How perfectly attuned to the island this music was, how drearily lonesome. I felt the whole of my tormented being laid bare for the world.

"It's remarkable," Robert said, a tremor in his voice.

And it was. Though, as usual, Robert's powers of expression were insufficient tools, I had not the facility to embellish his description. Now, alone with my thoughts, how to better explain it?

When I was a mere slip of a boy – no older than four, I estimate – I recall a hiding I received for peeking under the lavatory door at one of the maids then employed by Robert's father. When my stepfather discovered me, he lifted me by a leg and hurled me onto the bed in the adjoining room. Before I could scramble away, he seized me and, removing my breeches with one barbarous tug, proceeded to administer a painful spanking. It was my first such punishment, and though it was far from the last, it was my introduction into an older, less sentimental mode of justice. Perhaps sensing my dismay at such unwonted violence, my mother hastened to comfort me. She gathered my aching body and rocked me tenderly in her arms. The song she sang, though sweet and soothing, expressed my mourning – the mourning of a now-past epoch in my life, the death of a more innocent time when such childish indiscretions brought only a gentle remonstrance and a grin.

The song I now heard from the boy's flute was unlike my mother's lullaby in melody and rhythm, but very much alike in the manner it affected me. I realized I was weeping, and before I could conceal my display of emotion, I espied Robert's downcast face and noted the tears streaming down his cheeks, as well. Much moved, we resumed our secret vigil, *feeling* the boy's lugubrious lament as much as hearing it. When the child finished his song, neither of us could move. The boy lowered his flute, appeared to examine it a moment, and as he did, I was able to get my first real look at him.

Dark eyes, skin a light brown with the faintest suggestion of olive. His russet-colored lips were parted, revealing small white teeth. His cheekbones were slightly protuberant, reminding me of the Indians I had pretended to shoot in childhood games. The eyebrows were jet black, the hair framing the boy's face black and wavy. Large ears poked out from the nest of hair. Most remarkable of all were the boy's large, staring eyes. More than any other trait, they gave him the aspect of a somewhat sinister woodland creature.

I put the boy at six or seven years old.

Setting the flute atop the mossy stump, the boy stood, and I was shocked to see that he wore no clothing. The boy turned in our direction, and though his face did not change dramatically, a faint tinge of amusement did seem to pervade his countenance.

Carefully, Robert rose and addressed the boy, who did not, as I had anticipated, bolt into the forest like a frightened fawn. He spoke soothingly to the child who all the while watched us with his head cocked slightly, an expression of sardonic good will in his handsome face. Robert offered the boy a remnant of his sandwich, and soon the child was willingly accompanying us back through the forest.

It is now midnight at the inn, and in the adjoining room the child is sleeping on a cot at the foot of Robert's bed.

Just before retiring for the night, Robert fed the child a bountiful meal and gave him a bath. After tucking the boy in, Robert looked up at me, his eyes fraught with emotion. "I know what I shall name him," Robert said. "Since he is obviously an angel, I shall call him Gabriel."

CHAPTER FOUR

Eddie took Eva to the stone balcony outside the second-story parlor, where they sat in the morning shade. He liked the black, strapless dress she was wearing. It seemed a bit too formal for the time of day, only half-past ten, which could mean she was trying to impress him. Or that she liked the way she looked in it.

Eddie sure as hell liked how she looked in it.

He gave her "the smile". Not seeming to notice, she sipped water from a transparent, green sports bottle. Her lips were full and naturally pouty and, when she set the bottle on the squat stone table between them, there were tiny beads of moisture on her bottom lip which she wiped off unselfconsciously. He could still detect a hint of her peachy Chardonnay smell, but now it was infused with the balmy scent of heated flesh. The combination made his breath quicken.

"Where'd you eat breakfast?" he asked her.

"In my room," she said. "Before my run."

"I run sometimes."

She didn't answer, instead stared out at the wild grass, the mossy stones barely visible within. Then, a tall rim of evergreen trees and beyond that, the Pacific. Eddie wondered if he could convince her to go skinny-dipping.

"Was your childhood satisfying?" she asked.

Great, Eddie thought, *the psychoanalysis thing.*

Eva was staring at him, chin in palm.

Go ahead and humor her. It could pay dividends.

"Sure, I'll talk about my childhood." He smiled. "But you've gotta share too."

"Tell me about your dad."

Where the hell had that come from? "He made a lot of money," Eddie said. "He still does."

"What kind of father was he?"

"Huh?"

"Was he attentive?"

This time Eddie couldn't swallow the laughter. What was this girl's problem?

Eva waited.

He said, "My dad's attentive to anything blonde."

Her gaze didn't waver. "You do that a lot, you know."

"What?"

"Crack jokes when you don't know what to say. Only it's rarely funny."

He laughed again, sat back and folded his hands behind his head. "With your whole student-of-psychology schtick, I'm a little disappointed. I mean, that's all you could come up with? That I kid around as a defense mechanism?"

Her mouth relaxed into a languid grin. It bothered him, made his fingers itch to strike her, to punch her beautiful, stupid mouth. *The goddamn—*

Eddie blinked. *Where the hell had that come from?* Granted, she had annoyed him, but wanting to hit her? He hadn't wanted to hit a woman since—

"You're easy," she said.

"I've heard that before," he answered, but his feeling of disquiet was growing.

"My question made you uncomfortable."

He chuckled again, but this time it came out badly, like a sitcom laugh track. She sipped from her water bottle and it made Eddie wish he had something to occupy his hands. They were perched tensely on the armrests of the wrought-iron chair; he imagined his posture gave him the appearance of a nervous flier just before takeoff.

Which is exactly what she's shooting for, a voice spoke up in his head. *She wants you off balance. She wants to humiliate you.*

Eddie grasped the armrests harder so his hands couldn't ball into fists.

"Eddie?" she asked. "Did I say something that troubled you?"

He shrugged. "I hardly know you. Why should I talk about private stuff?"

"You invited me in," she said. "But you thought you were getting a chance to cast yourself in a positive light. To brag a little. You didn't really think I'd be asking about the things that hurt you."

Hurt? the voice spoke up again. *You wanna talk about hurt? Just keep running that fucking mouth of yours, you wanna learn something about hurt.*

Eddie shut his mind against the voice, which sounded unsettlingly like Lee Stanley's, the director who might very well end their careers if they didn't get the hell in gear.

"Who said anything hurt me?" He laughed without humor. "For Christ's sakes."

"You didn't have to," Eva said. She picked up her water bottle and stood.

"Wait a minute."

She turned, a bored look in her eyes.

Eddie suppressed an urge to knock that smug expression off her face.

"You're supposed to share too," he said, his voice strained. "Why am I the only one getting interrogated?"

"I asked you a simple question—"

"I'd hardly call that simple."

"—and you got defensive."

"Who's defensive?"

"Listen to yourself, Eddie."

She turned toward the French doors. Eddie got up, fists clenched at his sides, the taste of raw meat boiling in his throat. "Where the hell are you going?"

"To do some writing."

"Oh yeah?" he asked and did his best to take the edge off his voice. "What kind of stuff you write?"

"Whatever's on my mind."

"Like how I refused to talk about my dad because of my deep emotional scars."

She said, "I only write about subjects that interest me," and left.

* * *

After looking around the castle awhile, Ben and Claire went outside. On the way to the forest she said, "I thought you and Eddie were going to write this morning."

He shrugged. "When I woke up I thought I had something, but it scurried away."

"Scurried," she said. "Is that how you think of it, like an animal you're chasing?"

"I don't know about an animal," he said. "A mythological creature, a siren maybe."

They took the first path they came to. The entrance was narrow, and as he let Claire pass him he noticed how cute she looked in her white tank top and beige shorts. He remembered his conversation with Eddie at the party, couldn't believe the way Eddie had sold her short.

When he caught up to her she asked, "I know you started out teaching… what was it?"

"Junior high band," Ben said.

"I forgot." She smiled, her teeth white and beautiful. A dazzling smile.

Easy, Trigger, he told himself. *You're only six months out of marriage. No need to get all starry-eyed so quickly.*

She said, "The article in *Premiere* said you and Eddie met at a party."

He nodded. "Jenny and I were out here visiting her sister, and Eddie was a friend of Jenny's brother-in-law. I told him I wrote music and he asked me to play him something. I did and the rest is history."

She moved to the side of the trail so he could walk next to her. It was a little narrow, walking that way, but he liked being able to see her face when she talked.

Not that there'd been anything wrong with the rear view. He put her at about five-ten, and her frame was just right.

He realized she'd asked him a question.

"Sorry," he said, "I was thinking of something else."

"I asked about your stepdaughter."

"Ahh," he said. "Kayla."

He fell quiet, wondering how in the world he could explain Kayla.

"You don't have to talk about it if you don't want to."

"That's okay," he said, groping for the words. They were approaching an impressive grove of redwoods. The sparse grass and enormous trees made him feel like they'd entered some national park. The smell of pine needles and spruce bark tinged the air.

"How old was Kayla when you married your ex-wife?"

"Thirteen," he said. "I think it was the worst possible age…it'd be hard on any kid."

"I take it you two aren't close?"

He laughed mirthlessly. "We're about as far apart as two people can be."

"Yikes."

He fell back a moment as they passed a nasty-looking thornbush. "I'll tell you something I've never told anyone, but you have to promise not to hold it against me."

She smiled. "I'll try not to."

"The truth is, I don't like Kayla very much. Does that make me a bad person?"

"It depends."

"Occasionally it would happen in the classroom. There'd be a kid who no matter how hard I tried, I couldn't like. I'd try to be patient and fair, but the kid wouldn't *let* me like him." He shook his head. "That's Kayla."

"You never got along?"

"I know how terrible it sounds, but…it's as if all Jenny's bad character traits – and there are plenty of them – were distilled in Kayla…all the meanness, the desire for attention…I don't know. Maybe I was too strict, I'm sure I made some mistakes. But I always tried to be good to her."

He stopped and glanced over at Claire, but she was gazing back the way they'd come.

"What?" he asked.

"Don't you feel it?"

He shook his head. "I don't—"

"Someone's watching us."

He was about to make a joke of it when he began to sense it too. A chill on the nape of his neck. A watchfulness in the woods.

"Let's keep going," she said.

He didn't argue.

A couple of minutes later she seemed to think something over, dismiss it. "Never mind," she said.

"You can't do that," he said, nudging her. "Ask your question."

"It's just that…" she shook her head, "…I don't see why you need Eddie."

"He's better at arranging than I am."

"You do all the composing, right?"

"So?"

"You're the one who makes the music, but he gets equal billing, the same pay—"

"Working with a partner, you can't let yourself think that way. If you did, you'd never get anything done."

"Does he resent you, the attention you get?"

Ben smiled. "He's the one who gets the fan mail, the women who think he's one of Hollywood's sexiest bachelors."

"Without you he'd be nothing."

"That's a little harsh."

"He puts a lot of pressure on you."

"That's the nature of the business. We're the last ones to do our job, and if we're late, we either get fired or the movie gets delayed."

"Have you ever missed a deadline?"

He remembered *Blood Country*, the executive producer calling them the night before the score was due. Threatening to sue them, make sure they never worked again. It had been Eddie who'd calmed the guy down and negotiated the one-week extension, which had proved to be enough. Barely.

"Look," he said, "Eddie isn't perfect...he's rash and profane and he goes through women like he's test driving cars. But he's stuck with me through all this. A guy could do a lot worse for a best friend."

Claire nodded.

They moved through the grove in silence and approached a rise. He moved ahead of her, pushed a stray branch out of the way.

"Ben?"

Claire had halted at the foot of the hill. He looked down at her. "Yeah?"

"You said Eddie was the one with all the fan mail."

"So?"

"I think you're a lot sexier than he is."

Ben stayed where he was, but staring into her pretty blue eyes, he felt some dead part of him stir.

And thought, *Here we go.*

CHAPTER FIVE

Eva glanced at the clock and made a pained face. It was nearing dinnertime, and she knew she should make an appearance, but all she wanted was sleep.

And her lover.

She thought of its brawny arms, its insatiable need…the sensation of its warm skin against her body, the way it had removed her corset and ravaged her…

Scary, yes.

But exciting too.

She found that with each passing hour she grew more excited at the prospect of another nightmare. She stretched her arms and brushed the edge of the red notebook.

A chill coursed through her.

Earlier, she'd been writing about Eddie and his feeble attempts to get in her pants when her mind had begun to drift. She didn't know what she'd been thinking about, but when she looked down at what she'd written, she discovered random phrases, names she'd never heard of.

The episode with the notebook left her uneasy.

Eva lowered to her knees, slid the notebook under the bed. She sat up, paused, then bent and pushed it farther into the enclosing shadows just in case someone happened to pass by and spot it lying there.

She stood and crossed to the full-length mirror, the one into which she'd been gazing when the figure had materialized behind her in her dream. Placing its hands on her. Entering her.

Eva blew out a shuddering breath. She tied her hair into a ponytail and surveyed herself. She was already dressed for the stupid dinner, and she needn't bother with makeup. Eddie would pursue her, makeup or not. He wouldn't care if she wore a burlap sack and slathered her face in green antiwrinkle cream. He was an erection with feet.

She walked over to the window and cranked it shut. If it rained, she didn't want the water to somehow pool on the floor, make its way to her notebook.

The notebook. God, she wished she could forego the meal, remain in here and curl up in bed with it. Gabriel was one of the names she'd written earlier, and for reasons she couldn't explain, she associated the name with her visitor.

She had another feeling too, one that wouldn't go away, no matter how ridiculous her mind told her it was. Eva's tongue pressed against her teeth, her breath quavering in her nostrils. She thought of her lover, of the soreness she'd experienced all day long.

She thought of Gabriel, of his muscular body, his dark complexion.

And wondered if it was a dream after all.

★ ★ ★

Claire stood in the kitchen chopping carrots for supper. Even though she'd washed and put away the carving knife after dressing her wound the night before, the knife in her hand was a grisly reminder of her injury and her bizarre vision. Why, she wondered, had she chosen Eva's room, of all places, to visit in her sleep? Thinking of Eva, Claire thought of how Eddie flirted with her, how he seemed unaware of Claire's presence.

Compressing her lips in annoyance, Claire lifted the cutting board and scraped the chopped carrots into the soup pot.

What if Ben was attracted to Eva too? Their walk today had been meaningful to Claire, but what if he'd just been passing the time until opportunity knocked with Eva? God, she envied the woman's beauty, her confidence.

Envy *is an apt word*, a voice in her head whispered. *You're so envious of her you dream of carving her up.*

No, she thought. *I didn't cut her. I cut myself.*

Because you hate your body, the voice agreed. *You hate being in your skin so much you sliced it open. What did you think? That you could shed your shell and find a smaller self within? A body more like Eva's?*

Claire grimaced at the savage ache in her side. To take her mind off it, she pulled out the celery and had begun chopping it when a voice behind her asked, "Need help?"

Ben stood in the doorway looking very handsome in an open-collared white shirt. His dark jeans revealed slightly bowed legs, but not unattractively so. More like a rancher than someone with a bad case of rickets. He'd styled his light-brown hair with more care than she'd ever seen it, and though the slightly feathered pseudo-seventies look might appear ridiculous on another man, on Ben the effect made her stomach flutter.

He was smiling at her. Her own smile flared intensely a moment before she remembered herself and toned it down. *Don't scare the poor guy away,* a voice reminded her. *Keep ogling him like that and he'll mistake you for an obsessed fan.*

Well, she answered the voice, *isn't that what I am?*

She pretended to study the chopping board, said, "No thanks, I think I'm okay."

Are you insane? The guy wants to hang out with you and you reject him?

"I mean," she said and gestured toward the water boiling on the stove, "I don't need help cooking, but you can keep me company."

She glanced up at him expectantly, afraid she'd swung too far again into adoration, but he looked pleased.

He moved up beside her and asked, "You want me to do the chopping so you can worry about the rest?"

Her hands shook. She nodded and turned away to get control of herself. *You spent three hours with him earlier today, for goodness sakes. It isn't as though he's scrutinizing you, waiting to pounce on the slightest misstep. Just pretend you're a normal human being and you might just avert disaster.*

She cleared her throat, began to peel a potato. "Did you cook when you were married?"

He shook his head. "Uh-uh, I was the clean-up guy. If I ever set foot in the kitchen, Jenny told me to get lost before I started a grease fire."

She dropped the peels into the large white bowl she'd set aside for waste. "What have you been eating since the divorce then? Microwave popcorn?"

"Sometimes," he said. "Mainly I get carryout."

"Not very good for you."

"Neither is my cooking."

She laughed at that and picked up another potato. Ben had moved on to a red onion. Her heart had decelerated to an almost-normal rate.

"There was something I meant to ask you," she said, "but I forgot to bring it up earlier."

Ben paused in his chopping. "It's not about my ex-wife is it? I think I'm at my daily capacity for discussing her."

"It's about the island," Claire said. "It's funny, but I never even asked you about the Clay incident, the question you asked Chris Blackwood in the helicopter."

"Ahh," Ben said with relish, "that."

Claire waited while Ben finished the onion, the withering smell of it stinging her eyes. Then he deposited the knife on the cutting board and hopped onto the counter. She wondered how she'd look to him from his perch – alluring and delectable or harsh and unattractive. For the first time since he'd entered, she remembered the silly green apron she'd decided to wear after finding it hanging in the pantry.

So much for alluring, she thought. *I probably remind him of his grandmother.*

"It's shrouded in mystery," Ben said and leaned back until his shoulders bumped the dark cherry cabinet. "Almost nothing is known of the Clay party, but whatever happened here, it wasn't good."

Claire added the chopped onion to the soup and covered it. "Tell me what you know," she said and hoisted herself onto the island opposite Ben.

His eyes lowered. "Green's your color."

"You're stalling," she said, but she reached back and untied the apron.

Ben leaned forward. "Richard Clay and his wife Linda – both of them anthropology professors at Stanford – wanted to know more about the Sorrows and what exactly happened here in 1925. So sometime in the late seventies they enlisted the help of a history professor named James Ryder, his wife Karen, and a spiritualist by the name of Pauline something…Kael, I think."

"Wasn't that a movie critic?"

Ben shook his head ruefully. "Damn, you're right. *Bale* was her name. Pauline Bale. I always get that wrong.

"Anyway," he went on, "I was talking about the expedition, or what's known of it at least. The one thing everyone agrees on is that James Ryder went crazy."

"The history professor?"

Ben nodded. "Ryder evidently had a sadistic streak. In the aftermath of what occurred, several of his students went public with run-ins they'd had with him in which he'd exhibited very little sympathy and more than a little vindictiveness. One girl – she was a grad student when this stuff took place – claimed that Ryder had accused her of being a 'conniving Jezebel' – his phrase – when all she'd done was ask him if there was any extra credit she could do to raise her grade in his course. He recommended her for expulsion."

"What a jerk."

"He was," Ben said, "but he was brilliant too. He'd published more than twenty books on topics ranging from Julius Caesar to the Tower of London. The guy was a genius, which makes what happened all the more puzzling."

"You said he went crazy?"

Ben nodded. "Pauline Bale was the only survivor of the expedition, so her version is the only one we have, and given the circumstances, most experts doubt her testimony."

"Why would they doubt her?"

Ben paused, a pained look on his face.

Claire said, "What?"

"I don't know," he said. "It's kind of…unsavory, I guess."

"I can take it."

Reluctantly, he went on, "The spiritualist—"

"What's a spiritualist?"

"You know," he said, "séances and all that stuff?"

"Gotcha."

"She was found floating on a raft several miles from the island. It was a miracle she was saved, but it turned out to be a short-lived miracle. After telling the story, she committed suicide. She claimed the creature was coming for her."

"Creature?"

Ben shrugged. "This is why most experts doubt her testimony. After hearing Pauline Bale's story, the Coast Guard and a couple Stanford officials traveled to the island. They didn't find a creature, nor did they find one shred of evidence that indicated the Clay expedition had ever reached the island. The whole thing was officially ruled a shipwreck."

Claire glanced at the timer – only five minutes left on the soup. "So what was Bale's version?"

"Incoherent raving, mostly, but the gist of it was that James Ryder murdered Richard Clay. And before Ryder could kill anyone else, he himself was dragged screaming into the forest by some kind of monster."

"The women saw it happen?"

"The spiritualist said they could barely make it out – she claimed it was terribly foggy that night – but the creature appeared somewhat human, though much larger and somehow bestial. According to Bale's account, the monster had horns and sharp talons."

"Sounds pretty crazy."

Ben shrugged. "That's what the authorities thought. The monster Bale described and the things it did were a lot harder to believe than the version they gave the public. The idea of a boat sinking in the Pacific made a lot more sense than a horned man-beast picking people off one by one."

"So that's what happened to the other women?"

"Bale claimed she and the two dead men's wives took refuge in the castle, but that the creature followed them inside. Said it got Clay's wife first, and as Bale and Karen Ryder were fleeing in the boat, the creature dove onboard."

Claire waited. "And then?"

Ben gave her an apologetic look. "Bale said the monster devoured Karen Ryder, then proceeded to destroy the boat."

"But Bale escaped?"

"So she said. The boat went up in flames as she paddled away on her raft. She said she hoped the creature burned and sank with the ship, but given her suicide note, she must have been convinced otherwise."

Claire let it sink in a moment. She asked, "Did the spiritualist say why James Ryder murdered Richard Clay?"

"Bale claimed the island had magnified Ryder's dark side. She said the spirits on the Sorrows amplified man's basest impulses. Greed, jealousy, sexual desire. Which is why, according to her, he murdered his best friend."

Which is why, a wintry voice murmured in her head, *you dreamed of cutting into Eva last night. Your basest impulses are growing stronger.*

Unconsciously, Claire touched the wound in her side.

CHAPTER SIX

They were clearing the dining room table when Ben said, "Maybe we should watch it again."

"We've seen it a hundred times," Eddie said.

"You mean you have the movie with you?" Claire asked.

"A very rough cut of it," Eddie said. "Much of it just dailies."

"Dailies?"

Ben explained, "Daily footage from the shoot, most of which is never used."

Claire said, "Let's watch it."

"Seriously?"

"Sure," she said. "I'd love to see Lee Stanley's new masterpiece."

Eva fixed her with an odd glance, but before Claire could interpret it, Eddie said, "I guess it couldn't hurt, maybe we'll notice something we haven't before."

They moved into a second-story living room. The large projection television took up nearly an entire wall. There were very few windows, and the soft-brown sectional couch reminded Claire of her parents' basement. She was pleased when Ben, after making sure the DVD was compatible with the older player, sat beside her. A few feet to Ben's right, Eddie lounged, looking half-asleep already. Eva sat on the floor.

A crude graphic proclaimed the film a rough cut of *House of Skin* and not intended for reproduction. Then the date, a black screen, and a slow fade into an aerial shot of a large forest. The camera pulled a slow zoom as it passed over the trees, until a clearing appeared below. The camera descended, revealing a small graveyard nestled within the tall trees. Now at ground level, the viewer passed between various gravestones, some of the markers ancient looking and festooned with moss, the inscriptions on a few of them still legible. The ones Claire could make out said 'Carver.'

Ahead, a huge black tombstone read 'ANNABEL CARVER, 1932-1996.' The camera drew slowly nearer, nearer, until the numerous designs on the stone became visible. So, too, did the scarred granite and the graffiti. Written in red spray paint, dripping like blood, were 'WHORE,' 'BURN IN HELL,' and other epithets Claire couldn't make out. The screen went black.

Eva glanced up at Ben. "You're going to score that, aren't you?"

"Of course," Eddie said, scowling.

A car appeared on screen, the voices within becoming audible.

"Fast-forward through all this," Eddie said.

Ben did, then they settled in and watched the rest.

Claire enjoyed the film. She could tell where scenes were still unfinished, where special effects hadn't been added. The experience of watching a movie without a score was surreal.

When it was over, Eva said, "That was certainly gruesome."

"Who played Annabel?" Claire asked.

"Wendy Malone," Eddie said. "Nice body, huh?"

"It was a brave performance."

Eddie snickered. "That's code for an actress who'll get naked for the camera."

"That's not what I meant."

"I know what you meant," Ben said. "I'm sure the role was a hard one to play."

"What about you?" Eddie said to Ben. "See anything inspiring? Other than Wendy Malone's bare ass, I mean."

Ben scratched the back of his head. "I don't know. Let me sleep on it."

Eddie's gaze was hard. "You do plan on writing something this month, right?"

"Of course."

"That was the point in our coming here."

Ben stared at him. "I know."

Eddie got up and stretched. "Just thought I'd remind you."

When Eddie and Eva had gone, Claire said, "You'll think of something soon, you just need to relax and let it come."

Without looking at her, Ben said, "I hope you're right."

CHAPTER SEVEN

Ben lay in bed, a dirty heat baking out of him. He seldom got sick, but when he did, it was swift and hard and nasty. His tongue became a drowning worm, bloated and tasting of brackish puddles. He recognized the signs and closed his eyes hoping to outrun the sickness into sleep. His eyelids ached, a dull throb pinching them with invisible fingers. He thought of Joshua and embraced the pain because it somehow brought him closer to his son…

★ ★ ★

Joshua on a tractor he got for his first birthday. A green-and-yellow John Deere tractor, Joshua's plump legs propelling him forward as he straddled its yellow foldout seat. Under the seat were clods of dirt the boy had collected, but now he was riding in the driveway Ben hadn't fixed, at a place where the asphalt dropped off only one or two inches, but enough to catch the front wheel and send Joshua jetting forward to face plant in the gravelly driveway, his sweet vulnerable forehead opening like a paper punched by a fist, jagged flaps of skin, white beneath, then filling red. Ben had been pulling weeds and that would haunt him, pulling weeds instead of watching his son on the tractor, Jesus Christ. Then the emergency room, Jenny accusing him with her dead stare and Joshua thinking it a game when they wrapped him like a mummy, twirling, before putting him on some kind of restraining board. Joshua screaming as the needle pierced his skin – no padding there, just skull bone – then the stitches, Joshua writhing as Ben held him and wept and told him Daddy was sorry for not watching closer.

★ ★ ★

Ben rolled over in bed to escape the memory. He buried his face in the pillow and thought of going back to the Midwest the summer before, taking Joshua to Wrigley Field for the first time.

★ ★ ★

Carrying the boy with his Cubs jersey between the milling Cubs and White Sox fans, a mutual antagonism in the beer smell and cigarette smoke. A rain delay, Joshua wanting to leave before the first pitch. The boy only two. Ben bribing him with Cracker Jacks, Dr. Pepper, anything to make him happy. The day warmed and the seats were too far from the field, but it was good. Joshua ready to leave. Let's just wait until 'Take Me out to the Ball Game.' The boy still wanting to leave. Desperate for a diversion, Ben took out Al the Alligator, a green hand puppet the boy liked. They made it through the top of the seventh inning, Sox up 3-1. Joshua pooping in his diaper. That's okay. The Sox had three outs to make, we'll make it back for the song. Ben rushing him to a tunnel to change him standing up as the song began, dirty wipes and a huge soiled diaper in Ben's hand. Picking the boy up, no pants on, and dashing to the mouth of the tunnel to sing the second half of the song. Boy smiling, crowd cheering. Finishing the change and somehow by the time they got back to their seats the Cubs had crushed two solo shots, and the game was tied. Pleading with the boy, can we please stay till the end? The boy asked for more Cracker Jacks. Okay, a huge cone of blue cotton candy too. Sticky everywhere but smiling. Bottom of the ninth, Ramirez jacks a hanging curve and it rockets over the ivy and the crowd explodes. Ben tossing his son in the air and everyone high-fiving Joshua like he'd won the game. The boy screaming "Yeah baby!" like Daddy. Finding a cab, the boy asleep in his lap before they'd gone two blocks. Ben holding Joshua thinking, Thank you, God, thank you so much. Thank you so much for this day. Thank you.

★ ★ ★

Ben lay in bed, drifting in and out of dreams, until well past midnight. Then, when his fever broke, he got up, urinated, and sat on the bed. He took the *Toy Story* watch from his nightstand and studied it, thinking, *Maybe the boy will hate it in New York, maybe he'll want to come back.*

Then, *What kind of garbage is that, wanting your son to be miserable?*

But was it so bad, when he believed – when he *knew* – he was the best person for Joshua? When Jenny, though she had her good moments, wasn't half as devoted to their son as he was?

Maybe the thing with Ryan wouldn't work and they would return to California. Then Ben could see Joshua every weekend. Before, it had seemed like a death sentence, only seeing the kid weekends, but now he would kill for that much time.

No, Ben told himself, *not kill. Don't even use that word.*

Why not?

You know why not.

I miss him, goddammit, I miss my son.

If he misses you enough, you'll see him again.

But Jenny and Ryan…what if they brainwash him?

You can't brainwash love out of someone.

You can when he's too young to know any better.

Ben lay back, the watch still clutched in his hand. The boy was slipping away from him and there was nothing he could do, except become a kidnapping dad who gets caught anyway and jailed for thirty years.

Ben had passed the point of tiredness and was tumbling into a kind of weightless lucidity. He got up and peered out the window at the tall, waving lawn, the thin vale of forest beyond. The obsidian smudges between the trees were glimpses of the Pacific. Second night on the island and he hadn't yet explored the beach. He would tomorrow. Maybe take Claire.

He tottered over to the bed, recognizing the first real waves of drowsiness. He'd hardly slept since the night of the party, and now his fatigue was crashing down on him with numbing power. His last thought before sleeping was of the cave, the tumble into the grass. He wondered what would have happened had he landed wrong. How a broken neck would feel, how death would feel…

CHAPTER EIGHT

The next morning Eddie stormed into the great hall with Ben following. Claire looked up from her novel.

"Maybe if we watch the rough cut again," Ben was saying.

"I'm sick of the goddamn movie. What we need is for you to quit acting like a kid."

Claire glanced at Eva to give her the cue to leave, but Eva watched the pair intently, the ballpoint pen poised over her notebook.

"I shouldn't have said anything," Ben said.

"You have a nightmare and all of a sudden we can't use the studio," Eddie said. "Pretty soon the whole castle's going to be off limits."

"It's only one room."

"Which happens to have the best acoustics in the castle."

"Maybe if we go outside," Ben said.

Eddie shook his head, but he followed Ben toward the foyer.

When the two had gone, Claire stood. "You want to grab a bite? I'm starving."

"In a minute," Eva said, still writing.

Claire came closer, circling behind the chaise lounge on which Eva reclined. "Is that your report for Lee?"

"Hardly."

Claire stepped nearer. "You never told me what you do for him."

Eva pressed the notebook to her chest. "That's because it's none of your business."

Claire turned to leave.

But Eva said, "Wait."

Eva eyed her a moment before saying, "Let's talk over lunch."

⋆ ⋆ ⋆

"I do have sex with him," Eva said, "if that's what you're wondering."

Claire almost choked on her salad.

Eva shrugged. "I have everything I need."

Claire frowned. *Why not just put on stilettos and stand on a street corner?*

Eva studied her. "Let me guess...you've lost all respect for me."

Claire tried to smile. "What you do is your business."

"I'm writing a book," Eva said.

"What kind?"

"You can't tell either of the boys."

Claire sat forward. "You're not writing about all this?"

Eva sipped her water, her eyes never leaving Claire's.

"Does Lee know?"

"Of course not. He'd have me killed if he knew about the deal."

"You already have a publisher?"

"And a six figure advance."

"No way."

Eva took a bite of salad.

"Am I going to be in it?"

"That depends," Eva said around her food.

"On?"

Eva shrugged her slender shoulders. "On what happens here. So far all I've got is Ben and Eddie struggling with the score. Oh," she added, "and I've been having a weird dream."

Claire sipped her water. "Tell me about it."

For the first time since they'd met, Eva didn't look completely sure of herself. She took a drink of water, shook her head. "It starts out all right. Quite well, actually. There's someone in my room—"

"It's that kind of dream."

Eva nodded. "It's wonderful at first but everything changes. It gets..." She shuddered. "Why don't we go outside?"

They finished and went out. Just as they were stepping into the bright June day, Eddie appeared from the forest's edge.

"Did you throw him in the ocean?" Eva asked.

Eddie smiled, looking decidedly cheerier than he had earlier. "No need," he said. "In fact, I think he might be hearing something. He got this weird look on his face and told me he wanted to be alone. I didn't argue. If he is on to something, I don't want to screw it up."

"Scare the siren away," Claire said.

Eddie looked at her. "That's right."

Eva said, "I want to get some sun. There must be a beach somewhere."

"There is," Eddie answered. "We passed a nice stretch of sand on the way to the cave."

"The cave?" Claire asked.

"Uh-huh," Eddie said. "Ben's in there now."

★ ★ ★

Ben gazed into the shadows, listening. The sound was faint but definite. A low thrum, an intermittent tapping. It sounded like bony fingertips scuttling over a thin flap of sheet metal. He suspected the source was a natural spring hidden deep within the cave, perhaps even a low-lying spot where the ocean itself encroached through an underground network of tunnels.

The noise grew clearer. The bass hum grew and now he wasn't so sure what could be making it. The wind maybe, transforming, as it raced around the cave walls, from a soft whistle into a demon-throated howl. The tapping grew more pronounced, a staccato pulse that reminded him of gunfire.

He moved farther into the cave. The thrum increased with each footfall. Overlaying the continuous deep bray was the chaotic tapping, which grew louder the deeper he strode into the shadows. He risked a glance over his shoulder to make sure the beach, the ocean, most importantly the *daylight,* were still there. Satisfied, Ben moved forward, letting the damp cloak of cave air enclose him. A plangent squall made him stand rigidly, his nerve endings sizzling from the jolt. He turned and saw the eider flutter away, its chubby, brown body struggling to defeat gravity.

A hand on his chest, he advanced. At once the sea smell became unwholesome, closer to rotting fish than fresh saltwater, and the ground underfoot squelched with every step. The cave forked just ahead. He took a step to the right and heard the hum and tap diminish. Left then.

As soon as he shambled forward into the gloom he knew he'd chosen correctly, for the demon's howl had grown, its skeleton percussion rattling in triumph. The rank fish odor made his head hurt. Ben heard a violin in his head, its harsh melody reminding him of falling.

Ahead, the cave glowed with a sulphurous incandescence. He blinked, certain the green light was imaginary, but soon the glow increased, became spectral. Ben moved forward. The hell's chorus swelled, and ahead he spotted the source of the greenish light. From somewhere far above, sunlight poured through a hole in the ground. And when he beheld the green pool, heard the rush and trickle of water, the siren finally returned.

CHAPTER NINE

"You know," Eddie said to Eva, "the more you fight your feelings for me, the stronger they'll get."

The ice queen lay on her back, the white blanket she shared with Claire making her dark skin and black bikini look even darker. He was glad of the spot he'd chosen up here on the smooth ledge of rock. From where he lay on his stomach he could stare at them through his sunglasses, feel the sun warming his back, and not have to worry about either of them noticing his erection.

Eva sat up and took out a bottle of suntan lotion.

"Need help?" he asked.

She squeezed out the clear liquid, rubbed it on her arms. "You already offered, remember?"

"I said I'd put it on your back," he answered. "This offer's for the other side."

She didn't respond. She set to massaging it into her chest, her fingers a couple of times slipping under the cups of her black top. Torturing him, he suspected. It was a good sign. If she didn't have any interest, she wouldn't bother teasing him that way. Eddie could smell the lotion, hot and redolent of coconuts, as it merged with Eva's dark flesh.

She turned to Claire. "Want some?"

The pale girl visored her eyes with a flat hand, shook her head. "If I used that, I'd turn into a lobster."

You might anyway, Eddie thought and eyed her pinkish white arms. Of course, in order for her to burn she'd actually have to expose her skin. The girl's beige T-shirt covered all but her arms; her white capri pants were rolled up to her knees. He wondered how she'd look in a nun's habit.

He studied Claire's long body through the Ray-Bans. Eddie squinted to see the writing on the shirt but gave up after a moment. Probably something about composing music or playing the piano. The girl seldom talked about anything else. Auditioning constantly, laboring to impress them.

Claire looked beyond Eddie, said, "Those cliffs are pretty impressive."

"Those?" he said, peering down the beach to where the coast became wilder. "Forty feet or so, that's not very high."

"High enough," Claire answered. "I'm afraid of heights."

"Yeah?" he asked, pushing his shades up into his hair, "I'd have never guessed that, the way you were so calm in the helicopter."

She stuck out her tongue at him.

Eva said, "Why don't you jump off one?"

"Would you like it if I did?"

"Don't do it to impress me," she said. "I wouldn't want you to break your neck."

He stood, studied the cliffs. "I'll do it if you two come watch."

"I didn't mean—" Claire began, but Eva cut her off.

"Sure," she said. "We'd love it."

It took a couple of minutes to reach the place where the rock rose highest, a black dragon's head engulfed by a tapestry of azure. The coast was rocky, a roaring cauldron of foam and sound. In most places, the cliffs cowered back from the water's edge, but in one spot – a promontory at least fifty feet high, Eddie estimated – the calcified rock face poked its chin over the ocean.

Claire followed his gaze. "You're not jumping off that?"

He loved the uncertainty in her voice. Was there just a trace of curiosity too? He knew the type – the Rule-Follower, the kind of girl who couldn't bring herself to use the f-word or smoke pot because she'd been conditioned to believe either one would send her to hell.

"The water isn't deep enough," Eva said.

"I'll be able to tell before I jump."

Eva turned on him. "And how do you propose to get up there?"

"I climb all the time," he said. "The Cascades, Sierra Nevadas. I've been doing it since I was a kid."

"Don't you need equipment?"

"Just watch," he said.

Eddie reached down, unbuttoned the fly of his cargo shorts.

"What're you doing?" Claire asked.

"They're too bulky," he said. "I don't want to get snagged on a rock." He shed the shorts and handed them to Claire, noticing how she avoided looking at his boxer briefs.

But Eva was smiling.

"What?" he asked.

"Is this how you get women? By showing off?"

"You're the one who wanted to see me jump."

"You're playing the daredevil," Eva said. "You think we'll fall swooning at your feet when you're done."

"That's up to you," he said and headed for the wall. "I just want to cool off."

She didn't say anything to that. Eddie counted it a minor victory.

* * *

The rock face was perfect for climbing. From their perspective it looked like it rose sheer, but up close it had hand- and footholds galore. Halfway up the wall he glanced back at them, both women shielding their eyes from the sun.

God, it was perfect. He'd been lifting more than usual lately, with his legs especially, and now he was glad he'd spent so much time on the squat rack. From where they stood, the girls would see how muscular his calves were, the striations in his hamstrings.

Only eight more feet, ten at the most. He was sweating, but the cool glaze would only show off his muscles to greater effect.

Two more feet. Straining.

He made it.

Eddie swung his legs up and crouched a moment to catch his breath. Then he stood and drank it all in. The waiting women, the roaring breakers, the black water.

The farther he leapt, the better off he'd be. Eddie cast a glance over his shoulder, noted that the promontory was flat for a good fifteen feet before it devolved into a snarl of fissures and rocky excrescences. That was good. It gave him more than enough room.

Eva turned and said something to Claire, he was too far away to hear what. Maybe wondering if he'd lost his nerve.

You want nerve? he thought and gazed down at Eva's black bikini, her perfect body. *I'll show you nerve.*

Eddie measured his steps the way he'd done in the Bahamas. Big, long strides, simulating his takeoff sprint. You had to do that or else you'd hit it wrong, jump too soon. Or worse, miss your footing at the end and fall screaming like a goddamned clown.

Five, six, seven. He stopped, turned. Nothing ahead but a gray shelf of rock and a hazy horizon. Above, blue sky everywhere.

Now.

Eddie darted forward, elbows pumping, his eyes on the cliff edge. He strode out, pushed, and swung his arms to give him every bit of torque he could muster.

The jump was good, his body descending in a smooth, fluttery arc. The wind blasted his hair as he picked up speed, the black Pacific racing up to meet him.

Then the bottoms of his feet smacked painfully on the surface. The cold ocean enveloped him. He held his breath as his momentum pushed him lower. His only misgiving before jumping – that the water had concealed a sharp rock formation – had proved baseless. In fact, he thought as his descent slowed, the ocean was far deeper here than he ever would have guessed. As he spread his arms preparatory to ascending, he peered down through the murky water to see if he could spot the bottom.

Eddie frowned. There was something down there, something pale.

What the hell?

His legs kicking into motion, he began the rise to the clearer water, the sun sparkling on the surface. He shook off the image already fading from his retinas. Some trick of the light, nothing to worry about.

His air was good, more than enough to make it back up, and for no reason at all he glanced down again and saw the object rising toward him, gliding higher, moving faster than he was, and he thought, *Oh shit, a shark, of all things?*

Frantic, he flailed his legs, his arms useless and rubbery. His breath grew thin, uncomfortably tight, and something brushed the toes of his left foot. He screamed underwater and forgot all about conserving breath.

Impossibly high above him the water glittered, its dappled surface unreachable, and something hit his ankle hard. Eddie reached down to shield his leg from whatever it was, and as he punched through the fizzing commotion, his eyes shot wide at the tangle of blonde hair.

Horrified, Eddie pushed away. Through the bubbles and the screaming, a pair of human eyes stared unblinkingly, a zombie stare, and he shoved away from them, arms grasping up—

Sharp claws harrowed his feet.

His lungs filled with salt water, almost to the surface, *God, let me make it.* Something

(her, it was her)

seared his calf, and he shoved with both legs, fought the water, jaw upthrust, *please don't let me drown,* face breaking the surface, gasping for air, choking, thrashing to stay up.

Eddie heard muffled voices. He coughed, sipped in short breaths, his arms pulling him toward the voices, the dimly glimpsed forms standing knee-deep in the surf. *Gotta calm down now, you're fine, kicking, moving smoothly through the water, you did it and they won't know any diff—*

Powerful hands seized his ankles, dragged him out to sea.

Eddie shrieked in terror, rolled on his back and saw the floating mass of hair like yellow seaweed trawling through the water, his feet below the surface gripped tightly by

(her, oh Jesus)

walkingstick fingers, ragged nails, and he saw the hateful, staring eyes just under the surface stretched wide and glowering. Eddie rolled over with a frenzied cry, his legs snapping loose of her grasp, stroking madly toward shore, the adrenalin of terror propelling him, closing in on the girls, *oh please, Eva and Claire, please meet me halfway, I don't want those hands on me again—*

His fingers scraped bottom and he realized he'd reached the shallows, the girls. He thrashed closer, closer, heard their scared voices. He gained his footing, waded quickly forward. He split them, stumbling a little, one of them calling his name. Closing on the shore, he thought of the terrible, staring eyes, and he took the last few strides at a sprint. Totally enervated, he pitched forward on the hot sand.

Lungs ablaze, he rolled over and gazed up at the sky. The brilliance of the sun made him grimace, his shut lids purple with sun spots. *That was fine,* he thought. Anything was better than those dead eyes, those clawing fingers. He shuddered, struggled to rid his mind of the image.

He sensed someone standing over him, blocking the sunlight. Hesitantly, he opened his eyes. Both women were staring down at him.

Eva lowered to one knee, the smooth, dark line of a leg folded a few inches from his face.

Eddie hardly noticed.

"Are you okay?" she asked.

He grunted. "Wonderful."

Claire, crouching at his other side, "My God, your feet are bleeding. What happened out there?"

Eddie swallowed, his heartbeat an arrhythmic tattoo.

"Eddie?" Eva asked. She put a hand on his shoulder.

He kept his voice level. "I went deeper than I planned and hit bottom. I'm fine now."

Claire exhaled pent-up breath. "Had me scared."

He closed his eyes, swallowed.

Thought of the dead stare.

"Me too."

★ ★ ★

A shudder ran from Ben's shoulders to the small of his back. He felt a little disoriented, but there was a giddiness too.

He moved through the cave toward the hot sunlight. He remembered getting a check once for seventy thousand dollars. Driving to deposit the check, he was elated and unbelieving and frightened as hell that something bad would happen on the way there.

This was like that, only far more powerful. His excitement was bursting within him, but his fear of losing the weird, wonderful music was stronger. Ben emerged from the cave and began a brisk jog down the beach, his steps accelerating. He played it back in his mind, listened to the elegant, urgent string part. His fingers fluttered in rhythm to the tapping he heard. And beneath it all, the deep thrum vibrated in his memory.

Another minute brought him to the castle. He had no idea if Eddie was there, but he had to coax the music out of himself and into existence. He ran to the piano in the great hall. Shaking a little, he began to play. He cried out when his fingers hit the right keys; the violin part filled the room. It was strange, wild, unmistakably sinister. With his left hand he played a chord, grimaced when it sounded wrong, and chose another. *Yes.*

The right hand spun out the second part of the melody. His left hand found another chord, pounded. He toed the sustain pedal and the chord echoed through the hall, took on the quality of a high-tension electrical wire, the thrum he had heard.

Yes.

Ben played the chord again, his right hand still skittering over the keys, the violin part a convulsive, erratic orgy of terror. My God, it was happening, and he continued to play, his hands exploring, locked in now, making order of chaos, bringing the song to life. Later they would add the percussion, the winds. For now, hearing the notes was more than enough.

Vaguely he heard a door open, a female voice hushed by another. Their footfalls were dull whispers in the hall, and he allowed himself a moment's vanity. *Listen*, he thought. *Listen to me play.*

Like she'd heard him, Claire's eyes dropped to his agitated right hand, his flexing left. It was intimate, sensual. His entire body resonated with those sustained, bone-chilling bass notes, his forearms full of tendons, his neck corded and alive. Claire's big blue eyes traveled up his arms to his face, open admiration written on her features.

Eddie seemed to jump. Ben had forgotten he was there. As Ben watched, amused, Eddie snatched the notebook from Eva's hands and the pen from her ear.

She made a grab for the notebook, but Eddie was streaking black lines across the paper. He noticed Eddie's hand shaking as he made harsh black dots on the lines, not worrying about rhythm yet, just getting down the notes.

When he looked up, he was disappointed to see Claire gone. Then he realized where she was going, to get her laptop. She would record it all in there, and *now* they would have something for Lee Stanley.

Ben played. He chanced a look at Eva, but she was watching Eddie, biting her lower lip, not at all the dispassionate goddess he'd come to know.

What's in the notebook, Eva? he thought. *What don't you want us to see?*

CHAPTER TEN

From the Journal of Calvin Shepherd
December 21st, 1923
Why, Dear Journal, have I neglected you for so long?

If I am honest, I must admit it is a product of my soul-destroying shame.

I am only forty-seven, yet the female servants now in our employ – five in all – seem not to see me, as though I were a dusty vase, a bit of faded drapery. More cruel than this wilting apathy is the betrayal my body has visited upon me, for rather than diminishing with age, my concupiscent urges have doubled and even trebled over the past several years, so that I am left with nothing save a raging, foaming, yet *unrequited* desire to couple with the fairer sex.

It has been nearly a year since I have lain with a woman, and even that clumsy, abbreviated fiasco of grunts and pleas was procured with a sizable fee and a solemn pledge not to utter a word of the affair to another soul. The other party to which I now refer is still in Robert's employ as a scullery maid, and despite her unremarkable features and her tendency toward coarse language, she assumes a pose of aristocracy when I appear, as though mere eye contact with me would sully her person.

I blush to confess that I still beg her to lay with me. She says she will…for three months of my wages.

Oh the indignity of my plight!

And I have not yet come to the worst.

My cravenness has transformed me into an accomplice in Robert's exploitation of Gabriel.

His first theft was the very song we heard Gabriel play that first afternoon in Greece. The only element of the piece original to Robert was the title, 'Forest of the Faun.' Upon its debut, the song was an immediate success. Months later, when Robert caused a sensation in San Francisco by unveiling a plagiarized symphony cobbled together from Gabriel's works, I was sure his villainy could get no worse. If only that had been the truth.

Would that I could transport myself back to that fateful day eleven years ago and somehow prevent us from ever entering that ancient Grecian glade, perhaps we never would have found the child in the woods.

Oh, Journal, locked in your lightless trunk as you have been these eleven torturous years, you have not witnessed the meteoric rise of Robert Blackwood – the Shameful Imposter – to the zenith of the music world. Since he discovered Gabriel and transported him to our island like an exotic pet, Robert has produced three complete symphonies, eleven concertos, and numerous other works. The reception to this body of work has been ecstatic, adoring, his name now mentioned in the same breath as Vivaldi and Wagner. And though this farce has vexed me beyond description, tonight I hope that I will finally see some benefit from Robert's treachery.

The boy has not set foot on the mainland since Robert brought him here, and the only company he has kept has been Gregory and Becca Blackwood and Henry Mullen's two daughters Amarinda and Tassee. But now in his insatiable quest for further adulation, Robert has taken it into his mind to introduce Gabriel as his prodigy to a select crowd of adoring fans. Among those in attendance will be the one woman who sets my heart aflame, the widow of the well-known merchant and music aficionado Frederick Milledge, Angelica Sparks.

I, of course, refer to her by her maiden name, and though I do so in an attempt to forget that anyone else was ever her lord and master, in my defense Angelica has taken to using her maiden name as well.

Thus I go to bed tonight in high spirits.

Oh, Angelica, could you possibly be my salvation?

★ ★ ★

From the Journal of Calvin Shepherd
January 4th, 1924
Though it is now a new year, this bleak, cold day possesses the aura of an ending rather than a beginning. I noted in my last entry how stern, how abusive Robert has become in his methods of exploiting Gabriel's ability. Had I harbored any doubt as to his feelings for the boy, those doubts were obliterated New Year's Eve.

Gabriel appeared in the great hall at the appointed time to perform for Robert's guests. Without including myself and the other permanent tenants of Castle Blackwood, the party numbered forty-five – eighteen couples and nine singles, the lovely Angelica Sparks among the latter number.

I marked her reaction as Gabriel stood and bowed to the gathered crowd. Like the rest of the onlookers, she was obviously taken by his strapping appearance. Though he might never achieve the robustness of the mountainous Henry Mullen, at the age of seventeen Gabriel has already surpassed the six-foot mark. He is muscular of limb and torso, and has a face so handsome that the angelic name given to him eleven years ago now seems eerily prescient.

I shall now, to the best of my ability, recount Robert's unconscionable introduction and the resultant unraveling of the entire affair.

Robert made his way to a position just in front and to the left of the grand piano. Above him the chandeliers had dimmed and a stage light rigged by Henry Mullen brought the man into stark relief.

"Ladies and gentlemen," Robert began, "I reveal to you tonight a source of joy to which we here at Castle Blackwood have been privy for more than a decade."

Robert gestured for Gabriel to join him, which the boy did, looking quite dapper in his black suit coat and white bow tie. A hand on Gabriel's shoulder, Robert went on, "My biological son is named Gregory, which means 'vigilant,' or 'alert'."

Robert picked Gregory out of the crowd with his stony gaze. "Would we have known his true disposition, we would have chosen a name more apt...one that means 'dazed' or 'uninterested'."

I could not help but blanch at such cruel words so publicly spoken. From where I stood I could not see Gregory's reaction, but I certainly saw Gabriel's. His bland expression went steely, his large brown eyes lingering on Gregory.

Robert continued, "Though God deprived me of an heir who bears the innate proficiency with music that has passed through generations of Blackwoods, He was good enough to rectify His error by leading me to Gabriel. *This* young man has the ability to surpass even his late grandfather Joseph in composition and performance."

With that, Robert muttered something at Gabriel's ear and took a seat beside his wife. I noted that Gregory did not look up at his father as he sat, stared instead at Gabriel, who gazed intently back at him.

The crowd rustled uneasily as the boys watched one another. I do not believe in telepathy, but if one were searching for proof of its existence, I believe Gabriel and Gregory would be a good place to begin.

Robert, who had been nodding and receiving approbation from the guests behind him, turned and realized that Gabriel had not moved. Robert grew very still. The air of the great hall gravid with emotion, Gabriel broke his communion with Gregory and stared directly at Robert.

Then, without a word, the boy strode down the aisle and exited the hall.

For a moment no one spoke, even the guests who hardly knew Robert recognizing the deep humiliation and simmering rage now plaguing their host.

He stood, said, "Stage fright, I imagine," then followed Gabriel out of the hall, his measured steps revealing a poorly concealed haste.

A murmur arose, and I picked Angelica out of the crowd, wanting in some way to share the import of the moment with her. She returned my gaze and nodded toward the back of the hall, where the two primary actors in our mystifying little play had disappeared. I nodded, favoring her with a knowing glance. *Worry not,* I tried to communicate, *I shall make all right.*

She smiled, a smile such as I have not experienced in many, many years, and I went after them. As I clambered up the stairs, I knew full-well that I had no intention of interfering in the ugly scene about to be enacted, yet it felt exhilarating to be part of the thing, and what was more, to have Angelica believe that I, Calvin Shepherd, meekest of the meek, had the power to improve the situation.

Dearest Journal, I must now confess another secret. I do owe Robert Blackwood one debt for which I have never expressed my gratitude – nor will I ever verbalize my appreciation for – the peculiar architectural detail contained within Castle Blackwood, for Robert must never know that I'm aware of it. If he did learn of my awareness...I am loathe to imagine the consequences.

My life is not completely without occasional moments of excitement; the bulk of these moments are attributable to the secret network of tunnels Robert included in his design of Castle Blackwood. These tunnels are narrow things and quite dark. The only source of illumination present in these serpentining passageways is the dim light that passes through the mirrors into which people gaze, having no idea that they themselves are being watched. Robert made certain that this castle would be a voyeur's wonderland, and as far as I know, no one else has stumbled onto his secret. Many a night have I spent spying on Elizabeth Blackwood and her daughter Becca. I know no joy greater than gazing upon the stunning Amarinda Mullen, Henry's young daughter, as she explores her nubile body!

I slipped inside the master suite and entered the tunnel. As I made my way down the passage to Gabriel's room, the voices began to clarify.

"How dare you embarrass me?" Robert was shouting. I reached the mirror and peered through. I couldn't see Gabriel's face, but the boy's strong shoulders were heaving, either in fear or rage – I could not yet tell.

"You will march back into that chamber," Robert went on, "and you will perform the solo I selected for you."

Gabriel stood unmoving by the window.

"Answer me, damn you."

Robert's hands knotted into fists, evidently ready to abuse the boy, but Gabriel surprised him by asking, "Why are you cruel to Gregory?"

"He has nothing to do with this," Robert said.

Gabriel approached Robert and said, "You're a wretched father."

Robert slammed a fist into Gabriel's midsection. The boy bent in half, coughing, but he did not otherwise make a sound. When Gabriel straightened, he appeared somehow taller, broader than Robert.

The boy said nothing but moved to the door.

"You've come to your senses then," Robert said, but Gabriel did not answer.

I made my way as swiftly as possible back to the great hall, where the guests were already reacting to Gabriel's reappearance. Robert rejoined them. He gave Gregory a withering look, folded his arms, and turned to the piano, where Gabriel now sat.

Without delay, the boy reached out, plunked a single note in the middle of the keyboard. Then, he repeated the same note, index finger pointing down like a small child experimenting with the piano for the first time. He played the same note a third and fourth time, then paused and stared at Robert. All eyes were on the pair.

Still looking at Robert, Gabriel slammed all ten fingers on the keyboard, a bone-jarring, fiendish cacophony.

The crowd shifted uneasily. From Gabriel, a barely perceptible smile. Then the boy's fingertips dazzled over the keys, the song foreign to me and absolutely astounding. A sigh seemed to escape from the audience as the melody took shape, the dissonant, darkly beautiful melody. It was like nothing I had heard before, and from the look on Robert's face, I judged that he had never heard the piece either. Gregory and Elizabeth were spellbound, but Robert was sitting back in his chair, a hungry sort of scowl on his face. I did not, at that moment, understand what Robert was thinking, but I soon found out.

The boy finished to a thunderous ovation and a tide of ecstatic praise. With what I can only imagine was a Herculean act of will, Robert controlled himself until our guests departed the next morning.

Then he and Henry Mullen administered such a violent beating that Gabriel lay unconscious for the better part of three days.

PART THREE
EDDIE

CHAPTER ONE

On the tenth try, Granderson answered his phone.

"Do you have any idea what time it is?" Granderson asked.

Chris wished he had the guts – and the ability – to kick the man's pompous ass. "Do you have any idea how badly Marvin's guys will hurt me if they get inside?"

"Don't let them in," Granderson said.

Chris rolled his eyes. Fucking comedian.

"I didn't let them in last time," Chris said.

No response.

He clutched the phone tighter. "You said you'd stay and protect me."

A yawn. "And I've done so for the past three nights. You never said the arrangement was permanent."

"Jesus Christ, I didn't think I had to. I mean, they could be here already and I wouldn't know it."

"You'd know it."

"Thanks for your help."

Chris wanted to hang up, but he was too frightened. Having Granderson on the phone was better than nothing.

"Is that all then?" Granderson asked.

Chris pried open the Venetian blinds, peered down the valley at the guest house. "You're still down there, right?"

"It's night," Granderson said. "Where would I be?"

"Your house is dark."

"I don't make it a habit to sleep with the lights on."

"It's only nine. What are you, some kind of monk?"

Granderson didn't respond.

Chris dropped the blind, paced the dark guest bedroom.

"Good night," Granderson said.

"Wait."

A long pause. "What now?"

Chris bit the nail of an index finger, a childhood habit that had returned in the last few nights. "Did you talk to my father today?"

An even longer pause. "Yes, we spoke."

"Why is it you can get through when his own son can't?"

"Maybe you should be a better son."

Chris ground his teeth. "Did you at least ask him if he'd help me?"

"We didn't discuss it."

"You didn't bring it up?"

Silence.

Then a click.

Chris stared out the window that overlooked the driveway. It was one of the reasons he'd chosen this room, he'd at least see any car that pulled in.

He cried out as his cell phone shattered the silence. Furious with himself for forgetting to turn down the ring tone, he opened it and put it to his ear. "Look, Granderson, I know you'd rather stay in the guest house, but I think it's better if you..."

He trailed off, the small black phone a poisonous spider in his hand.

"Come downstairs," a raspy voice said. "Mr. Irvin is ready to see you."

CHAPTER TWO

Ben gaped at Claire's blue dress. "Was I supposed to wear something formal?" he asked.

When her face flushed, he added, "It's not you I'm worried about… you look fantastic."

That seemed to relax her. "I wear it for recitals," she said. "It shows a little more than I'd like."

Eva's door opened.

"Good gravy," Eddie said.

The dark-green strapless hugged Eva's sleek body all the way to her knees.

Eva took Claire by the hand and said, "That's more like it."

Claire fiddled with a shoulder strap. "It doesn't feel like me."

When they reached the sixth-floor studio, Eva went to the windows and began tying back the thick green curtains. Claire joined her, and soon they were all bathed in a warm roseate glow, the cool evening breeze ventilating the large room.

Ben let his gaze linger over Claire. She did have a classical beauty. She was lovely, the stuff of poetry. A Waterhouse painting come to life. Her perfume dowsed over him, the fragrance reminding him of white jasmine.

Eddie turned to Claire and asked, "Will you play for us?"

She looked at him in surprise. "I guess so. Any requests?"

Eddie nodded and opened the binder in the Steinway's tray.

"'Annabel's Theme'," Claire read.

"Ready to debut it?"

Claire gaped up at him. "Really? Don't you want to—"

"You'll do it more justice than I will." Eddie regarded the sheet music. "It'll be better once we have the violin playing the main theme. There'll be some winds, but not a lot…I don't want to mess with the purity of the theme, clutter things up."

Claire centered the binder in the tray, examined it a moment. She took a deep breath and began.

Notes from the upper register exploded in the silence of the studio. Claire's fingers raced, finding the notes with an accuracy and a rhythm that Ben could never have managed.

The song was magnificent.

Claire was possessed, her fingers working the keys in a controlled frenzy of virtuosity. He couldn't remember seeing a player so skilled. The song changed keys, soared, plunged into hellish uncertainty, then returned to the brawling main theme, which charged, bludgeoned, and ultimately lifted the listener to a dizzying height before abandoning him and letting him plummet to his doom.

When she finished, they all stood watching her. Ben half expected to see smoke rising from the piano.

Claire looked up at him and asked, "Was it all right?"

But it was Eddie who answered. "It's the best piece of suspense music I've ever heard."

CHAPTER THREE

The night grew darker. Claire helped Ben pull a couch to one of the bay windows so the seating area felt intimate despite the spaciousness of the studio. Outside, the red twilight had given way to intermittent clouds, and in the distance, the faint rumble of thunder.

Rather than cooling the air in the studio, the encroaching storm heated it and sheened Claire's skin with moisture. She sipped her wine, enjoying the lack of inhibition it brought on.

She sat on the edge of the window seat, the aroma of ozone wafting over her. Ben sat on the couch opposite, Eva beside him. At Claire's elbow were Eddie's bare feet. Reclined in the open window a hundred feet from the ground, he made her nervous, but maybe that's why he'd chosen to sit there, for the thrill of it.

Eddie said, "I think it's time for Eva to drop the Mona Lisa smile and let us know what's on her mind."

Eva looked amused. "Maybe you won't like what I tell you."

Eddie grinned, a drunken glimmer in his eyes. "I wanna know what you've been scrawling in that notebook of yours."

Claire glanced at Ben, who looked on with a contented smile. Since his creative burst earlier he'd seemed a different person, transformed from the tortured soul who put on a brave face to a confident artist secure in his work.

She was more attracted to him than ever.

Eva said, "I'll tell you a story if you'd like, but you have to promise not to ask questions afterward."

Eddie crossed his legs in the window seat. "Sounds like a doozy."

Eva said, "My mother wanted to be an actress. She was beautiful too. She spent her childhood in a Brazilian town called Sorriso. There wasn't much there, but the town did have a theater. My mother – Gabriela was her name – grew up watching Grace Kelly, Audrey Hepburn. Actresses like Doris Day and Marilyn Monroe. She idolized these women and wanted nothing else but to be a movie star."

Eva crossed her arms. "My mother didn't like scary movies, but when she moved from South America to Hollywood, those were the only parts available to women of her…kind."

"Voluptuous women," Ben said.

Eva glanced at him. "Yes. Soon my mother met a man and they conceived."

"But not…" Eddie began.

"They never married, no."

She reached up, arranged a lock of hair behind her ear. "So I was a setback to my mom's career. There weren't many parts for pregnant women who spoke broken English."

Claire sipped her wine, pictured Eva with a fuller figure.

Eva said, "My biological father cast us aside before my mother delivered me. She had trouble paying the bills. She worked all sorts of jobs…not all of them the kind she would have wanted me to know about."

Eva finished her glass, held it out for Eddie to refill. "By this time I was six or so. Mom had a roommate named Kathy, also a struggling actress. She could be grumpy, but that was because of the drugs.

"All this time my mom was auditioning for commercials, television, even theater. But she still wanted to be in movies."

Eva crossed her legs, looked up at the ceiling. "You'd think that kind of life would have taken its toll, but not on Gabriela Rosales. She was still young, and if anything she was prettier than she'd been when she came to America. She answered a casting call for a film about werewolves."

Ben said, "It wasn't *Death Howl* was it?"

Eva looked at him in surprise. "Yes, it was."

Eddie sat forward. "Holy shit, the Lee Stanley picture?"

"His third," Ben said. "The first two were about vampires."

Eva smiled, but there was no humor in it. "*Bathed in Blood I* and *II*," she said. "Cinematic masterpieces."

Eddie said, "The second one had some good parts."

Eva gave him a thin look.

"Well it did," Eddie said. "The last scene where they make the girl eat the dead guy's—"

"I assume your mother wasn't treated very well," Ben said.

Eva sighed. "My mother went to the call and was told she was a finalist for the lead role."

"Just like that?"

"She wasn't a finalist for anything."

Eva went on, each word tightening the tense coil in Claire's belly. "Even though he'd only been on the scene a few years, Lee Stanley was already getting a reputation for being a scary guy. In his personal life, I mean."

She regarded her drink. "One thing I forgot to mention was my mother's drug problem. I suppose she got caught up in that…lifestyle. She developed a heroin habit. Lee exploited it right away. He told her whatever actress played the lead role might have to do so without much compensation. What budget they had, he explained, had to go to special effects, costumes…"

"Fake blood," Eddie said.

"He paid my mother with heroin. She was already carrying a serious problem when she met Lee, but within a couple weeks she was a zombie, a real-life zombie. She ceased taking care of me…I didn't know what was going on, but I knew it was something very bad."

Eva took a drink and Claire saw her hand shake. "Lee kept himself in business by selling drugs and working with pornographers. My mother appeared in her first adult movie without knowing she'd been filmed."

Claire asked, "What about the werewolf movie?"

Eva cocked an eyebrow. "*Death Howl*? Gabriela never shot one scene in *Death Howl*. She was replaced by another actress, one who spoke better English.

"Eventually mom caught on to Lee's game, but by then she was too wasted to care. She made five adult films in the space of a month, but by that time the heroin was spoiling her looks. So Lee cut her off."

Eva took a drink and shrugged. "She begged him to give her another fix, but he told her she'd gotten ugly – those were his words. My mom told him she'd do anything, so he said come back at midnight."

A tear streamed down Eva's pretty face. "Lee had invited about fifteen of his buddies for a sex show. He gave my mom her fix and then had a servant bring in a Rottweiler."

"Oh hell," Eddie said.

"You can imagine what the intent was…they tried to get the animal to perform, but it wasn't happening the way Lee wanted. So he demanded my mom manipulate the dog, use her hand…"

She blew out a trembling breath. "After she came to, she locked herself in Lee's guest room and gave herself a huge dose of heroin. Lee hadn't seen her take the pistol out of his dresser beforehand. The stereo must have been loud enough they didn't hear the gunshot. Or maybe they just didn't care.

"When they found her the next morning she was dead. The suicide note said she deserved to die for her sins. There was a bucket placed on the floor under her hand to catch the blood. She'd shot herself in the palm, punishing herself for touching the dog. Part of her hand had been vaporized by the bullet, but the coroner said it must have taken hours for her to bleed to death."

CHAPTER FOUR

When Eva had finished, they lapsed into silence. After a time Eddie said, "The storm's almost here."

Ben watched as Claire crawled forward in the window seat and peered into the night. Eva's macabre tale had been like a temporary anesthesia, but as he studied Claire's body, her rear end pressing the silky blue material, a pleasant sensation returned.

Claire made a surprised sound and stared down at the window seat.

"What?" Eddie asked.

"Stand up a second," she said.

Claire got hold of the edge of the seat and lifted. A musty cedar scent puffed out of the darkness. The large storage area hidden beneath the window seat looked like an oversized coffin.

"You don't behave yourself," Eva said to Eddie, "we'll make you sleep in there."

"Do I get to choose who sleeps with me?"

She smiled.

The breeze grew stronger. It felt good on Ben's face, a mixture of salt and raw electricity. He swallowed the rest of his drink, stood, and touched Claire's shoulder. She glanced back at him, eyebrows raised.

"Would you dance with me?"

She nodded and followed him past the couch.

He heard Eddie say to Eva, "Guess that means you're stuck with the psychological train wreck."

Eva didn't answer, but she did follow him over to the stereo.

"You want another glass?" Ben asked, leading Claire to the crate of wine. He got the bottle open, poured.

"I think I'm getting a little drunk," she said.

"Excellent," he answered. "My plan was to get you good and liquored up."

At the stereo Eddie asked, "Any requests?"

Ben glanced at Claire, who was sipping her drink and watching him. Ben said, "Name some options."

Eddie whistled, flipped open the CD case. "Looks like Sinatra, *The Best of Fred Astaire*, Ella Fitzgerald—"

Eva said, "I'd like to hear 'Night and Day' if you have it."

Ben stared at Eva a moment as she stood at the window. Framed by churning storm clouds, wreathed by a penumbra of moonglow, she reminded him of an angry goddess. He imagined her spreading her arms and commanding the seas.

"Astaire it is," Eddie said and put in the disc.

When the music came on, Ben smiled and stepped closer to Claire. Eyes wide, she put her hand in his and followed his lead.

"I have no idea how to dance," she said.

"Me either," he answered. "I leaned against the wall at dances."

"I never went to dances," she said.

"You always snuck out with a boy?"

"Uh-uh. I was a homebody."

Laughter to their left. They turned and saw Eddie and Eva moving together, his arms about her waist.

"I thought she wanted to castrate him," Claire said.

He could almost taste her skin, sweet and fresh, her ear close enough to kiss. He said into it, "I don't care about them."

"You don't?"

"Not one bit."

Her hand slid from his shoulder to the back of his neck. He pulled away slightly, looked into her eyes a moment, and kissed her. The taste of her was incredible, as summery as the air teeming through the studio. Her tongue met his. She was running a hand through the hair on the back of his head – he loved that – and kissing him deeply. If he didn't get her alone soon—

"*Jesus Christ*," a terror-stricken voice cried out.

They pushed away convulsively. Ben had forgotten Eddie and Eva were still in the room, but he witnessed them now in a bizarre tableau – Eddie gazing at the bay window with huge, staring eyes; Eva staring at Eddie as though he'd gone mad.

"What's wrong?" Ben called, over Fred Astaire, who was now singing "Let's Face the Music and Dance."

"I have no idea," Eva said, half-disbelieving, half-furious. She brought a palsied hand to her mouth, pulled it away and looked at her fingers. "We were kissing when he freaked out. He…bit me." She ran her tongue over her bottom lip and Ben saw blood there.

"Eddie?" he asked, approaching his friend's unmoving form. "What's going on?"

But Eddie paid him no heed, only stared gape-mouthed at the window.

He drew even with Eddie, put a comforting hand on his shoulder. "Don't tell me you saw a sea monster?"

Eddie seemed not to hear, was shaking his head in disbelief.

Ben turned to Eva. "You see anything?"

"Just him going crazy and shoving me."

Claire moved in front of Eddie. "What did you see?"

Eddie shook his head.

Ben said, "I hope it wasn't a ghost."

Eddie turned on him, his face a hostile mask. "*Shut the fuck up*," he said and strode toward the stairs.

Too shocked to call after him, Ben could only watch as Eddie disappeared, his descending footfalls soon lost in the growing thunder.

CHAPTER FIVE

Her name was Lily.

Eddie lay in his room, the window closed despite the heat. He rolled onto his side and remembered how Lily looked that first day.

★ ★ ★

Climbing out of the red MG in the tight-fitting white shirt, the sleeves short and her arms dark. Muscled too, but not as much as her legs. God, they'd been terrific – long and toned and muscular and shiny with sweat. Her face was attractive, her long blonde hair too, but it had been those legs – Christ, like a thoroughbred's – that had convinced him.

He was Cal-Berkeley's number-one singles player, had been for two years, and a preseason All-American. It was a point of pride for him to bed every good-looking female athlete at Berkeley, and when he saw the tall blonde stride onto the court beside his, Eddie knew she would be his next lover.

She served – a good, hard serve – to an empty court. She plucked another ball from her basket, wound up and cracked another serve that was barely foul. It was hot that day and sunny, the girl already sweating. Eddie sat in a folding chair, waiting for his coach to show up, and watched the girl take another ball from the basket, bounce it a few times – hard bounces, full of frustration – and serve again. This time the ball landed four feet out of bounds, so she wrested another ball from the basket, bounced it once, hard, and grunted with the force of the serve. Eddie smiled as the ball sailed way long, almost to the opposite serving line. His smile grew as the girl slammed several more out of bounds, in her anger pushing harder, always harder, and never making an adjustment, never thinking about where she was going wrong. In the weeks to follow he would come to understand that those first few moments with Lily defined her completely.

It didn't take him long to get to her. He introduced himself as she was leaving practice. Being a local girl she knew who he was, and he knew then it would go much faster than he'd anticipated. His friends told him what she didn't divulge, filled in the blanks for him. A highly recruited incoming freshman, she had an obsessive father who scared most prospective college coaches away. Early on Eddie could tell her daddy had polluted her mind with all sorts of crap about her incredible talent, what a short journey it would be to the professional circuit. The usual garbage.

Eddie sensed the pampered daughter in her, as well as the athlete who'd been driven like a draft animal to achieve, achieve, achieve. To procure a college scholarship. To make a name for herself in the tennis world. Eddie liked hearing her talk about it, recapitulating her father's nonsense. He would listen to her and think, *I'm going to fuck it out of you. The bullshit, the devotion to your slave-driving daddy. All of it.*

After she lost her first match, he drove her to his apartment and listened to her cry. He soothed her, and when she'd calmed a little, he convinced her a massage would help.

She cried afterward.

Telling him she had been a virgin (not anymore!) and how she was risking pregnancy and was he sure he'd pulled out?

Of course he was sure, nothing to worry about.

The next time was better.

The third time they slept together, she got into it some, using those strong, thoroughbred legs to brace herself as Eddie banged her. Soon they were going through the different positions, Lily finding she liked being on top best. She could not climax yet – her fear of pregnancy precluded that – but she was getting closer. Eddie lay beneath her, fascinated, as she pumped her glorious hips, pistoned up and down, her tongue poking out the side of her mouth in concentration.

One night in September she was riding him when her expression changed, her eyes suddenly alert, almost bewildered. She paused a moment, then began again, pumping with a purpose now, something going on inside her. Eddie watched, delighted, as she made a face, her voice going higher and higher, pouty and tortured, and around him her body quivered, clenched, a tremendous shiver spinning through her. It felt so good he let loose inside her.

He broke up with her the next day.

She took it badly, like he knew she would. She even, *Christ almighty*, threatened to tell her daddy how mean Eddie was being.

You do that, honey, and see you around.

Lily didn't give up easily.

He figured she would be that way. Clingy. Scorned. What unnerved him was the *tenacity* with which she demanded he change his mind.

I'm sorry, Lily, we had some good times, but I'm graduating this spring.

I'll go with you. Eyes glassy, obsessive.

No, you'll go on with your tennis career and your education.

I don't want those things. Not anymore.

Come on, Lily.

I want you.

Please, Lily.

In October he began to grow frightened of her. She showed up outside a bar where he and some buddies were drinking. She wasn't old enough to come inside, just stood at the front window, one of his buddies spotting her first.

Dude.

What?

By the sign.

His stomach dropped.

Outside the bar, *What the hell's your problem?*

I called you last night.

And this morning. And this afternoon. Can't you take a fucking hint?

I need to talk to you.

He thought, *Don't tell me. No way, not that.*

Her eyes confirming it.

He swallowed. *How late are you?*

A week.

That's not so long. It—

I've never been late.

Two weeks after, she showed up at his management class. Walked right in during the lecture, his professor staring open-mouthed at the intrusion.

Under his breath, *Jesus, let's go outside.*

In the hallway, loud enough for everyone to hear, *I got the test back. It's definite.*

Eddie leading her, hand on her back, practically shoving her out the door. Turning on her. *What the hell do you want from me?*

You should marry me.

Are you insane?

You're the father of my baby.

Hands to his ears, *Jesus.*

You should do the honorable thing, Eddie.

Get the hell away from me. Jogging to his car, too frightened or sick to run.

He holed up for two weeks at his dad's house.

She found him on Halloween.

He'd managed to hook up with a pretty little waitress at the Chinese fast-food place in Santa Rosa. The girl named Mi Chi or Mai Tai, it didn't matter. They were in the pool; he'd gotten her top off, when the gate opened and there stood Lily.

He yelled, *Get out.*

Crossing her arms. *What are you doing, Eddie?* Like she'd caught him.

Get the fuck out of here, Lily.

I'll be waiting outside.

You wait then.

He went back to Mai Tai, but she was paddling away. The Asian girl's white ass bobbed in the white bikini as she retrieved her top, climbed out of the pool and left without a word.

He could have killed Lily.

Outside the pool gate. Eddie in a towel, Lily actually looking quite hot in the short skirt – too bad she was a psycho.

What do you want, money?

You know what I want.

You're crazy.

Because I want to be with you? Raise this child—

Just quit talking. Jesus.

Eddie.

Don't talk to me. Walking away.

A hand on his shoulder. Her voice soft, *Eddie.*

Whirling and screaming into her stupid, stubborn face, *I don't want you, can't you figure that out. You want money you can have it, just stop following me.*

Eddie, please. Both hands on his shoulders, her face full of lunatic adoration. *We belong together. You and me and the—*

He hit her. Hit her hard.

Her belly felt soft, and the sound she made as she doubled over reminded him of what was inside her and then he really did get scared, the coughing and the shrieking and his dad was out of town but what if the Robertsons down the road heard and then he saw, *oh no*, the shiny black stuff that wasn't black but looked that way in the dying evening sun as it dripped down her legs. He put a hand on her back, felt her tense. She'd seen it, touched one black streak with her middle finger, looked at it in slow-dawning horror, her eyes locking on his.

Lily.

My...my baby...

Lily.

Walking, staggering toward her car.

Lily, I didn't—

Something he couldn't quite make out.

Lily, please, just wait.

Pats of blood on the concrete.

He swallowed. *Let me help.*

She fell forward or he shoved her toward her MG, knees scuffing concrete, head denting the car door. An ugly, red splotch on her forehead where she hit, eyes dazed. Eddie thinking prison, execution, and he didn't know how his hands got on her throat but they were there and she didn't even struggle, though her eyes still recognized him and they rolled to white. He looked down, saw the black blood pooling between her legs, about to reach his toes. He hopped back, stared unbelieving at her body, propped there against the car like a huge doll.

Lily slumped. Dead.

He couldn't think, couldn't look at her face anymore, at her white eyes.

He dove in the pool. Under water for a moment wondering, *What if I stayed down here? Would I die or would it all go away?*

He returned to the driveway, dragging the hose, and cleaned the blood as well as he could.

He stared at it. Thought, it would have to do.

Put her in the passenger seat, shut the door. Started the MG. Drove down the lane, curved right, Bennett Valley Road three miles ahead. He drove them up without a glance in her direction.

Steep turn. Climbing, curving. The spot he was looking for. Stretch of road a hundred yards long without a guardrail. Rocks below. Sharp, spiked teeth. Please let there be fire. Please.

He parked and hauled her over to the driver's seat. Heavy before, nearly immoveable now she was dead.

An ugly, black stain on the passenger seat. Part of that death, his.

Hoarse, choked sobs. *Please.* Body shaking. *Please make fire.*

Eddie stood wondering. Should he get gasoline, light it before?

Looking around. No one there, but any minute. He'd been lucky so far, but it couldn't last. Have to do it. Can't think anymore.

MG into neutral, door open. Eddie walking it easily, crunching gravel. Reaching in, turning the wheel. Sheer drop, fifteen feet away. Crunching, like gunshots. Ten feet.

Hand on his arm.

Alive.

Eddie screamed, recoiled, *oh Jesus*, looking at him, blood trickling from her lips and saying

Eddie

No no no no, he whispered

Confusion in her face, then comprehension, then panic

Eddie

Slammed the door, her wrist crunching, bones grinding. He shoved her arm inside, staring out at him frantic-eyed, white palms pressing inside the window

Eddie

Five feet

Rolling with grade

Eddie, muffled now

Front end dipping, scraping, muffled howl of anguish

Eddie on all fours watching it fall

Red car tilting almost gracefully, falling

Impaled on steeple of rock

Then the *whump*, explosion

A second one

Yes

Pushing up and jogging back, must return before they come asking questions.

Thought of Mai Tai – Witness.

Daddy, her tennis friends, Eddie's own friends – Motive.

Pace yourself, you can make it. No one lives up here, though soon someone will see. Have at least an hour before they come, much more if they can't identify the plates right away.

Could still hear the crackleburn. Scorched thighs. Charred teeth.

Eyes goggling at him inside glass.

Eddie.

Slapping palms, tears.

Eddie.

Descending tire tracks, Bennett Valley Road ahead. Making great time. Block out the other.

Thinking of grim faces at the door. *Where were you tonight?*

Out for a run, had a fight with my ex-girlfriend.

Jogging, panic cooling away, Eddie began to smile. *Yes.* Don't deny anything. But be shocked when they tell you.

At approximately…Lily Stearns died in an automobile accident about four miles from here.

What? Say it like a wince. Hand on your mouth. Slow head shake.

You were the last one to see her alive. We have some questions. Will you come with us?

Of course, Officer.

Cooperate, but you better look shocked. It was the whole ball game.

He got home and showered, listening for the bell.

Got into bed, still listening.

They came around dawn.

He did well. They did not act suspicious but probably were.

Days and days of unpleasantness. Daddy especially wanted Eddie to fry.

The Blaze family attorney came through. So did Eddie, an epic performance.

No charges. No trial. Eddie went back and finished spring term and graduated after summer school. Her friends thought he did it, but never said so. *Fuck 'em.*

After Berkeley, Eddie never mentioned her again.

CHAPTER SIX

He thought of Lily, floating in the studio window like some goddamned vampire.

Eddie shut his eyes, threw an arm over them, but the memory pursued him, Lily's grotesque grin, blood dripping from her mouth the way it had that night on the cliff. Only this time she was working her tongue around her teeth, smearing the blood to show him she liked its taste.

Now he chanced a look at the window, which he'd covered with the drapes. The thick fabric was wine-colored, like the droplets that stippled Lily's sharp canines. He could hear the storm kicking up outside, but that shouldn't make the curtains rustle, should it? He imagined them coalescing into the shape of a woman, the wine-dark material reaching for him. Breath growing ragged, he cast a glance at the nightstand. He wanted the light from the bedside lamp, but he kept it off knowing it would mark him as awake.

Turning away from the window, he shut his eyes again and tried to remember the last time he'd been so paranoid. No, not even after Lily died, Daddy threatening to have him killed. He had to go back to early childhood, his nightlight a talisman too feeble to ward off the boogeyman.

The wine had given him a headache. He lay there and sweated and knew he should take off his clothes, but that would mean getting up and what if his shoulder brushed the drape or the movement of his body alerted whatever was out there of his presence?

Eddie wondered what the others were doing. If Eva was still awake. Or Ben.

Claire was just next door. She seemed kind enough to sit with him until he got drowsy.

No, he couldn't imagine getting up now. Couldn't imagine braving the walk to the door, the hallway churning with reflections of storm clouds.

Eddie jumped as wind battered the castle. Then a bone-jarring rattle as freshets of rain pelted his window.

To get his mind off the hallucination – it had to be that, something in the wine exhuming the long-buried guilt – he thought of Eva. She was very different from the image she'd constructed, the real Eva more vulnerable than he would have thought, more human. Yet something about this new Eva frightened him too.

Her story about Lee Stanley and her mother was ghastly, the stuff of one of Lee's movies. He couldn't imagine what kind of havoc it had wreaked on her psyche, but if her cold staring eyes and her lowered voice were any indication, Eva was a woman bent on revenge.

And what would Lee Stanley do when he found out? Eddie felt an abrupt chill thinking of Lee and the dog and the glassy-eyed crowd. What would he do to Eva when he learned who her mother was, what Eva hoped to do to him?

The sleep haze evaporating, Eddie sat up. He needed to go to her, tell her to reconsider. Help her if possible. She was muddled by rage, she had no idea who she was messing with. If she happened to appreciate his concern, demonstrate her gratitude…all the better. She probably liked it rough. They'd wrestle a little, maybe even exchange a slap or two. Then he'd force her to the floor, one hand around her throat, the other one ripping her underwear off. He'd bite her, make her bleed—

Eddie jolted. Where the hell had that come from? He shook his head, wondering why the hell he'd been thinking so many crazy thoughts.

You know why, a voice whispered in his head.

He scowled, rubbed his eyebrows with the heels of his hands. A nasty glaze of sweat had enveloped him, itching and cloying.

Eddie stood and a wave of dizziness almost felled him. He extended his arms as though navigating a tightrope. The vertigo dissipating, he padded to the door and paused. He pushed away the image fluttering at the edges of his mind – the maniacal eyes, the bloody slaver, her white dress billowing. Jesus, Lily had never even *worn* such a dress.

Eddie's lips formed a wry smile. Too many horror movies, too much *Dracula*. He opened the door and froze as an unearthly glow lit up the hallway.

Just lightning. Eddie stepped down the hall as a roll of thunder vibrated the passageway. He ignored the windows, there was nothing to see anyway. Like sitting in a car during a storm without the wipers on. Pelting rain and indistinct shapes.

He knocked on Eva's door. No answer, she was likely asleep. What time was it? Two in the morning? Three? He knocked again, harder.

When no sound came, he tried the knob. He remembered the taste of her kiss, the killer body in the green dress pliant against his, Eva ready for anything if only he hadn't seen…

He opened the door.

A small Tiffany lamp glowed dimly in the master suite. He saw a twist of bedding, rumpled sheets, but nothing large enough to conceal a human body, not even one as slim as hers. For good measure, he went to the bed and leaned over with probing fingers. No Eva.

The master bath. Eddie sidled around the four-poster bed and peered into the darkness. He couldn't see into the little room with the toilet, but she might be in there. She'd be enraged to find she had an audience. Eddie stood just outside the bathroom and listened for underwear whispering up legs, a flush, but no sound came.

Had she fallen asleep on the pot?

Grinning, he stepped into the master bath and peered into the toilet area.

Empty.

Then where the hell was she?

Not with Ben, he was too into Claire. He thought briefly of Eva wakening Claire, crawling under the covers with her, but shook off the image, a teenage fantasy.

So Eva was up in the studio getting a bird's eye view of the storm. He thought of her up there, a black negligee, warm flesh strobing in the magnesium flashes of lightning. She would turn as he approached, a salacious gleam in her eyes. *What took you so long?*

Then he'd see the black eyes gazing hungrily through the windowpane, the white dress billowing.

To hell with that.

Eddie made his way back to his room. A peal of thunder rattled the knob as he shut the door.

He had to piss. All things considered, he thought as he crossed to the bathroom, the accommodations were good. The wind whispered over his face, it felt nice, but…

Eddie turned and saw the fluttering curtains, the sill slick with rain.

He'd shut the window. He knew he had. Christ, had he been able, he would have nailed two-by-fours over it.

And now it was open.

With a helpless moan, Eddie took a step in that direction even though he knew he could not compel his arm to reach out and crank the windows shut. What if a long-fingered hand fell on his? What if she pulled him, screaming, through the window?

His socks felt cold, soaked through. Mouth open, he lowered his gaze and saw the rain puddled on the floor.

So what? he tried to protest. The wind was driving it through the open window, the whole room was probably drenched.

Yet the water trail was narrow, winding. He tracked it around the side of the bed, where it disappeared. Walked over to where he had lain on top of the covers. They were bunched now, tangled, and he was certain he hadn't twisted them that much.

Dread gripping him, Eddie drew back the covers, beheld the soaking-wet *S* where she had lain. Touched the damp pillow, freezing cold.

He sank to his knees, but his sounds were inarticulate.

Eddie wept and waited for Lily to visit him one last time.

CHAPTER SEVEN

Ben dreamed he was walking through his recently broken home, but the pictures on the walls, the doorways he passed, seemed somehow askew. The air in the house had an unhealthy, curdled odor that made him think of seedy nightclubs and violent sex. He was overcome with an inexorable, atavistic terror. He heard voices in pain.

Sliding into the dream, Ben's breathing grew uneven, his reason a feeble defense against the icy talons of nightmare. He realized why everything seemed askew. He was seeing the world from three feet lower, through a trusting, terrified set of eyes.

Joshua's eyes.

★ ★ ★

Abruptly the thought came. *Ryan and Mommy are making noises again.*

Ben ached at the boy's innocence, his heartbreaking lack of understanding. He reached into Joshua's mind, did all he could to coax the boy back to his room, but he kept walking, walking. Ben wanted to turn away as he and Joshua neared Mommy's room, but Joshua passed it, and Ben's despair gave way to bewilderment. Joshua padded toward the room at the end of the hall. Ben realized that Mommy was asleep in her room, her sound machine flooding her dreams with the susurrant rush of Waves on Beach and was therefore unaware of the noises in Kayla's room, the room Joshua was approaching.

The little fingers turned the knob, pushed the door open.

Ryan was on top of Kayla. They were both naked. Ryan was hurting Kayla

(*no he isn't, leave the room Joshua*)

they hadn't seen him and he should go but what about

(*Kayla moved home for a reason, now I see*)

her face so full of pain and Ryan's eyes squeezed shut

(*a monster oh Jesus Joshua get out before he sees you*)

he'll hurt Kayla he's crushing her get off

(*don't say it, Joshua*)

The innocent, high voice screaming, "*Get away from her!*"

Ryan freezing and glaring at him in a way he'd never seen. It made him retreat. He heard Ryan say "stay here" to Kayla, and then Joshua was running as fast as he could, but he tripped and Ryan jerked him to his feet and carried him on his shoulder toward the kitchen. He was thirsty, but they passed the sink and went out the back door; and his head bumped the doorway and he told Ryan it hurt, but Ryan's hand covered his mouth and it was hard to breathe; and they went down the path to the ravine and he got very scared and tried to move; but Ryan said a bad word and told him to look.

Joshua looked where Ryan was pointing. Ryan said, "Do you know what's down there?"

Joshua's throat was dry and he wanted his daddy.

The pointing hand grabbed him roughly by the mouth, Ryan's nice face scary and very close to his. "*Answer me.*"

Joshua had no idea what was down there in the branches and shadows and said so, but he was crying and the words didn't make sense even to himself. Ryan squeezed the sides of his mouth to make him stop crying but he couldn't help it.

"I'll tell you what's down there," Ryan said smiling but not a nice smile. "Dead children."

Through the ache in his mouth and the terror Joshua peered down the slope and saw the branches white in the moonlight. Like bones.

"That's right," Ryan said. "Dead little boys who tell things they shouldn't."

Joshua struggled but Ryan jerked his face and it hurt so much.

"Listen to me," Ryan said. "If you tell your mom or your dad or *anyone* what you saw, I will bury you down there."

Joshua watched Ryan with wide eyes.

"Get it?" Ryan asked.

Joshua was crying, he couldn't help it, but he moved his head up and down to show Ryan he understood. From the corners of his eyes he saw the bloodless branches reaching for him, yearning to enfold him.

Ryan dropped him and his butt hurt, his shoulder too.

"Get inside," Ryan said through his teeth. "Go straight to bed."

Joshua got up and dashed to the house and before he got inside he heard Ryan shout, "*I'll bury you!*"

* * *

Ben cried out, fully awake. He pushed to his feet, his boxer shorts drenched with sweat and clinging to his thighs as he paced around the bedroom.

He went to the mirror, braced himself on the dresser. His eyes were bloodshot, mad, but he knew beyond a doubt that what he'd seen was real. He had to go to Joshua, had to save his boy from that evil son of a bitch.

With a groan he thought of Kayla – rebellious, aloof Kayla, who never gave him a chance, who never trusted him. And now…the irony of it made him dizzy.

Is that Kayla's car? he'd asked.

That's right, his ex-wife triumphant. *She's moved back in.*

Ben shut his eyes.

Because you're gone and Ryan doesn't lecture her the way you did.

He collapsed on the edge of the bed, breathless with hurt and rage. The afterimage of Kayla spread eagle under the pilot would not go away.

Shaking, he sat up and thought of his son again, his aching regret cauterized by a boundless fury. He would tear Ryan apart, talking to Joshua like that, hurting his son. He'd murder the bastard with his bare hands. He'd—

Ben froze.

He was stuck on the island. There was no way to help Joshua.

He dragged a hand through his hair, thinking. They didn't even have a phone. No way to communicate with anyone. There were – he calculated – *more than three weeks* before Granderson returned to transport them to the mainland. What the hell would Joshua do till then? What if he said something, told Jenny about it, and Ryan found out? Would Jenny even believe him?

No, he thought, pacing again. She wouldn't. She was too in love or lust or whatever the hell passed for affection in that dragon's heart of hers to see the despair in her son's eyes. She would blame it on Joshua's loyalty to Ben, on his resentment of the man taking Ben's place.

And then what? When and if Jenny told Ryan what Joshua had said… would the evil bastard follow through on his threat?

A chill whispered down his spine.

The man was diseased enough to seduce a teenaged girl – *his fiancée's daughter for Christ's sakes!* – and he didn't bat an eyelash at threatening a toddler with murder…

Ben thought of Ryan's horrible grin as he told Joshua about the dead boys in the ravine. He thought of the hideous force with which he'd squeezed the child's tender flesh. Ben choked back a sob. He really did believe Ryan was capable. If there were some way to get word back to the police…

Ben saw his terrified face in the mirror.

No, goddammit. No! he thought. *You can't let him hurt Joshua. You* can *do something about this.*

He would wait until the helicopter came. When it did, he'd go back. Then he'd beat hell to get to his house and once there he would take Joshua away and go straight to the police. And if Ryan got in his way, he would throttle him unconscious. The son of a bitch deserved worse, but Ben wouldn't make the mistake of removing himself from Joshua's life in a moment of unstrung vengeance. However…

The face staring at him in the mirror changed into something he had never seen before. It was feral and absolutely godless.

That's fine, he thought, *let it be.*

Let it be the face Ryan saw right before Ben strangled his serpent's neck. Maybe he would stop before Ryan was dead.

Maybe.

CHAPTER EIGHT

From the Journal of Calvin Shepherd
March 7th, 1924
In his treatment of Gabriel, Robert has systematically cast off the last vestiges of his humanity. Were I not so hateful of the young man myself, I might have offered up some resistance to Robert's descent into brutality. However – and I shudder to own up to my true emotions – I must admit that I have reveled in some, though not all, of the ill treatment doled out by my master.

On one occasion, Gabriel made the mistake of calling the island by its well-known name, the Sorrows. Joseph Blackwood coined this title when his symphony of the same name became a worldwide sensation. Nevertheless, due to its origins – Joseph Blackwood's wife, Dorothy, died while giving birth to Robert, thus inspiring the heartbreaking music of the symphony – Robert long ago expressly forbade anyone from speaking the title, or even worse, playing the symphony. When Gabriel uttered the forbidden words at breakfast, Robert erupted. He threatened to cast the young man into the ocean and decreed that Gabriel would have nothing but bread and water for a week.

Soon after this Gabriel claimed to be too sick to *collaborate* on a new symphony. Robert slapped the young man across the bridge of the nose hard enough to knock him down. That old Mrs. Cadman, who tends to our sick, corroborated Gabriel's fever after touching his forehead only enraged Robert further, so rather than providing the ailing young man with the proper nutrition and rest, he pushed Gabriel even harder, forcing him to stay up working on the symphony's third movement until well past midnight.

Gabriel, though sick, made the mistake of composing something rather incredible that evening – incredible even by the lofty standards set by his earlier work. So astounding was this third movement that Robert demanded the young man go back and rewrite everything that had preceded it. As can be imagined, Gabriel's fever grew worse, his breathing labored. Yet the waning of his health worked in direct contrast to the quality of his writing, and by the third night of his compulsory vigil, the symphony was complete.

I will not dwell here on the methods my master employed to bring about such remarkable results; suffice it to say that the average beast of burden receives better treatment than did Gabriel. His flesh scored by wounds, his visage purpled and swollen, the young man completed the symphony just before falling into a swoon.

It took him a month to recover.

When Robert returned from San Francisco subsequent to unveiling his latest masterpiece, he did not immediately compel Gabriel back to work. Rather, he treated the young man with a modicum of kindness, even venturing so far as to thank him for his role in the symphony's creation.

His role!

Perhaps, you wonder why I don't put an end to this farce and somehow protect Gabriel from Robert. Allow me to explain the events to which I have been witness that belie the innocence of the young man.

We found the boy nearly twelve years ago in the Greek Isles, a land of heroes and gods. Were Odysseus, Apollo, or even his father Zeus alive in this age of motorized car and electric light, I cannot imagine any of them equaling the majesty of Gabriel Blackwood. Taller now than even Henry Mullen, Gabriel stands six foot five, has a black mane of hair as lustrous as polished obsidian, and possesses a body that would make Adonis weep. Robert refuses to let Gabriel off the island, and I cannot fault his reasoning. Would the women of San Francisco glimpse the damnably handsome youth, I've no doubt they would kill for the right to wed him.

And why, you might ask, do I paint the young man in such carnal-red colors?

For many years he seemed to have no interest in girls, though he did count Becca, Amarinda, and Tassee as his companions. Along with Gregory, the five were inseparable, and despite their closeness, I never witnessed any hint of physical desire between any members of the quintet.

Shortly after that terrible New Year's Eve, however, I witnessed something that changed my opinion.

I was setting down Gabriel's dinner when I bade him come eat. When I received no answer, I entered the bathroom and gasped at what I saw.

I mentioned that Mrs. Cadman attends to our medical needs here on the island. For the past year, a young woman named Anna, a red-headed waif of a girl hired as a servant, has accompanied Mrs. Cadman in her work. Anna now tended to Gabriel, but rather than feeding him or helping him ingest medicine, she was bathing him with a damp washcloth. The smells of soap and steam filled the air. Gabriel stood in the tub, his back to me, while Anna squeezed hot water over his buttocks.

Just beyond them sat Becca, watching.

Though I knew not why, a black anger gripped me and I demanded to know why Becca Blackwood, Gabriel's half *sister*, for God's sakes, was spectating as though she were at the theater.

Becca, who has always been the most taciturn of the girls, favored me with a languorous smile, but did not otherwise respond. Anna went on with her soapy ministrations, seemingly oblivious of my presence. So it was Gabriel who turned to answer.

"Please join us, Calvin," he said.

Head down, I said, "I will do no such thing. Now cover yourself and come eat your supper."

"I'm not in the mood to eat. Anna here is providing for me." At this he patted the serving girl on the shoulder like some obedient pet.

Raising my chin, I said to Becca, "I shall tell your father of this."

Gabriel answered, "Father won't believe you, Calvin. He knows how much you covet the young women of the island."

"I do not covet…" I started to say, but Becca's laughter robbed me of my resolve and sent me tromping angrily from the room.

I want him to bleed.

★ ★ ★

From the Journal of Calvin Shepherd
November, 26th 1924
Gabriel still refuses to write, God damn him. I feel as though he is pushing all of us toward some dire conclusion. He must know that Robert will not stand for this ridiculous insubordination, that the punishments will only grow more severe as each day passes and the men at the San Francisco Symphony grow ever more demanding. The contract that Robert once deemed his greatest achievement has become a blade at his throat.

As I pen this entry, Gabriel is spending his second night in the pit. I cannot imagine residing in that dark, ghastly demesne for even an hour. The fact that Gabriel has spent two full days there staggers the imagination.

Ah, but gone is the long-suffering child who was ripped from the womb of his motherland and exploited for monetary gain. In his place is a man I despise more than even Henry Mullen.

Yes, Dear Journal, I do hate Gabriel, and you will soon understand why.

As I noted before, he has been two days in the subterranean darkness. As usual, I have been the one selected to deliver Gabriel's meager rations of bread and water. But in addition to this task, I have also been assigned the nauseating responsibility of emptying his chamber pot.

During the evening of his first day of confinement, I arrived to perform my demeaning task. As I neared the door, I heard something that I at first credited to my overactive imagination.

Voices, moaning in passion. What was infinitely more disturbing, I recognized not only *his* voice but the other as well. Gabriel uttered a single word, continually, like a demon's litany, and listening at the door of the pit, I felt my soul recoil.

Dear Journal, I have not yet shared one salient point, and you might forgive me for withholding it due to the fact that it is such an excruciating source of pain and unutterable embarrassment.

Angelica made the trip to the island a few days ago with the shocking intention of seeing me. Can you fathom it? A woman of such loveliness, of such discernment showing interest in *me*?

And during her first couple of days on the island, I finally experienced a taste of the paradisiacal bliss that has so long eluded me. Though Angelica and I never did more than engage in two incredible kisses that will forever remain emblazoned on my soul, we did not otherwise explore the physical side of our relationship. Rather, we walked through the woods. We visited the graves of those whom we both knew. We sat by the seaside and luxuriated in the sunlight and the mutual affection that bound us together.

And this – damn him – was the reason why the word muttered from the other side of the door filled me with such consternation, for during one of my sweet rambles with Angelica, I gave her the name Butterfly, so lovely and carefree she seemed.

And yes, I now heard Gabriel muttering "*Butterfly*" repeatedly, his voice – or so I imagined it – curdled with contempt and derision.

I told myself it was impossible, that the joke was too cruel. I did not yet believe that I could be cuckolded by a teenager, though of course I held no real claim over Angelica.

On tottering legs I stepped to the door of the pit, lifted the bar, and opened it.

I saw them.

And fled.

CHAPTER NINE

Ben sleeps fitfully, but around 4 a.m. he sits up and stares out his window at the ivory mist skirling around the tall evergreens. The rain has ended but a muggy dampness lingers in the air. He imagines what Joshua would think if he could peer out this window, what the boy's limitless imagination would conjure in the mist.

Then Ben remembers Ryan. The son of a bitch. *Makes me wanna destroy something*, he thinks. *Makes me wanna rip the bastard apart.*

The thought burns away the vestiges of sleep. Throwing aside the sheet and climbing off the bed, Ben welcomes the chill of the old castle, then experiences a moment's disquiet at the faint odor beneath the cold, something wild and oily and oddly reminiscent of animal spoor. It drives him toward the window, where he sees something even more disquieting – the casement is open just a crack. Ben reaches out, lets the night breeze whisper over his fingertips, and his mind immediately slips into rationalization mode. He had forgotten to close the sash lock before going to bed that night. It is entirely possible, he had been plenty drunk. Was it that surprising he'd left the window open?

Except he hasn't even touched the window since his first night here. He frowns, remembering the novelty of lifting the sash lock, cranking the windows open, and leaning out over the green lawn below. In his mind's eye he also watches himself cranking the window shut, leaning hard on the lock because it hadn't been used in so long, the steel bar bruising his palm a little from pushing down on it so hard.

So someone else opened it, he thinks.

But this thought is ridiculous, he knows. No one has touched his window, no one has opened it. Without thinking about why, he cranks the casement open all the way and leans out into the frigid night where, unaccountably, the smell of animal shit is stronger. He feels suddenly exposed, standing like this, with his fingers gripping the scabrous concrete ledge, and he's about to duck back inside and make sure the damned thing doesn't open again when his eyes wander up to the head of the window frame. Nothing extraordinary about the wood, but just beyond it, scored into the concrete framing the window, are what look like claw marks. Like some enormous bird of prey battened onto the overhanging ledge and hung upside down to watch him in his sleep.

Ben realizes that he must still be sleeping because as he leans out farther into the night he can see more grooves in the damp concrete, shallow scars on the alabaster castle façade that remind him unmistakably – though the thought is preposterous – of hooves. He remembers the night he and Eddie hiked up the mountain, the night of the cave. Before sundown and well before they'd been plunged into an utter void within the cave, Eddie had commented on several marks just like these on the craggy boulders over which they'd climbed. *Mountain goats*, Eddie had said, but Ben had been too winded to pay much attention.

But these marks are exactly the same, and he is certain now that the twin grooves wending a diagonal path up the sheer concrete façade all the way to the squat rectangular blocks – he rummages through his memory for the term, and in moments he has it – the *merlons* that guard the crenellated castle roof have been made by a hoofed creature.

Ben pauses, engages in another feverish scan of memory, this one from earlier that evening. He pauses only a moment on his kiss with Claire – wonderful but in no way related to the issue at hand – and searches for the image he needs. Finding it, he leaves his bedroom without bothering with the window or his shoes or anything to cover his bare chest and legs, and jogs down the hall in his boxer shorts. Soon he is in the sixth-floor studio, where the tiny red power light on the stereo still glows like an infernal eye along the far wall. To Ben's immediate right is the recessed door, the one that can only lead to a closet or the roof. He opens the door and is both excited and chilled by the sight of the staircase leading up. Swallowing, Ben moves into the cavelike gloom of the landing and climbs the stairs. It is too dim to see well, but he can see that the steps abruptly terminate in a few more feet. He reaches up and out as he climbs and is rewarded with a smooth steel surface. Fumbling now – Ben is suddenly terrified of being half-naked and alone in the dark – he gropes for the knob, finds it and twists. The door swings out onto the square turret and its tiled roof, and for one fleeting moment Ben marvels at the attention to detail, the amount of time and money it must have taken to construct this rooftop, a feature few would ever see. Then his admiration gives way to bemusement, for twenty feet away, at a spot approximately above his bedroom, there is a tiny figure swaying on the crenellated roof border. In a flash he recognizes the skinny shoulders, the tousled, greasy hair, and he is running for his son, determined to prevent the fall this time, the one in his nightmare. As he runs, his bare feet slipping on the slick wet tiles, he recalls the image from a few hours before, Ryan's face looming great and terrifying over Joshua as the boy wept. Remembering it now, Ben really could kill himself for letting his son slip away, for letting him live with a monster.

Is that any different, a vicious voice in his head whispers, *from what happened with your mother?*

"Yes," Ben mutters. He needs to keep his head clear, his thoughts focused on Joshua.

It isn't, the voice insists. *You could've saved your mom from years of emotional abuse if you'd have done something about your father, rather than letting him—*

"I was a kid, dammit, I couldn't—"

(Afraid then and afraid now and your son is dying because of it)

No! he wants to scream, but he is closing in on Joshua; he can't worry—

(left him there to be hurt, just like your mom)

"No."

(hiding under your covers as your dad yelled at her)

"Stop."

(beat her)

Ben opens his mouth but the words coagulate, the thought of—

(Joshua just like your mother, Ryan just like your father)

his mom's tear-streaked face becoming Joshua's

(but you're the same old Ben, aren't you)

"*Enough*," he shouts.

He is not far from the boy, the little body leaning and yawing as though aboard a storm-tossed ship, and as he reaches out, actually calls his name, Joshua falls. Ben screams, knowing he is too late, but the mist beckons him on with ghostly fingers, assuring him there is still time. His legs continue dashing toward the edge of the roof. His mind looks on like an impassive spectator, yet his body seems to yearn for the six-story drop, almost welcoming the release his fall would bring.

With a strangled cry Ben tries to stop, but his body continues forward, the low crenellated border nearly underfoot. He dips his right shoulder, hoping to crash into the rectangular merlon, but he's too late and his upper arm skids agonizingly over the gritty surface. His hip cracks the hard border, one leg swinging unimpeded through a gap. His body continues over the edge, his bare chest scraping raw on the porous concrete, then his legs dangle out over nothing and he is hugging the edge of the roof for dear life. *Jesus Christ,* he thinks dimly. *How did I end up like this?* And despite the deadly plunge that now seems preordained, a gauzy veil of unreality still hangs over all like the impairing caul of mist. Despite the moisture his grip is good but it won't be forever, and there's no use casting a downward glance. He knows how high he is, just as he knows his grip is weakening.

Let go, a voice wheedles. It is a woman's voice, yet in the deepest recesses of his mind he knows the feminine lilt is manufactured, that the speaker is masculine, if not entirely human.

Let go! the voice repeats, and Ben is horrified to feel his bear hug on the concrete merlon loosening. He is too weak, too old, too useless, too defeated. Giving up will be cathartic. He does look down now and is not shocked to find that his impending fall will be unimpeded. A nice, clean drop followed by a split second of pain. Then his son will grow up not having to endure a custody battle, the awkward visits punctuated with silent recrimination.

That's right, the voice murmurs as his arms continue their release, *it will be better for everyone now, better for everyone…*

Buried under the smoky membrane of confusion another voice strains to break through. It doesn't matter though because his fingers have lost their hold on the wet concrete, his biceps and forearms raking sandpapery trails down the unforgiving surface, his legs leaden, his wind gone. *No,* this new voice says. *No, please—*

Over, the lilting voice declares, *it's over so you can leave your boy to a better—*

NO! his reason explodes.

It galvanizes him. With a spasmodic movement Ben thrusts out his hands and is just able to hook his fingertips over the edge of the border.

You're not giving up, the voice urges, *you are* not *consigning your son to a life of danger or dysfunction.*

He winces at the pain in his arms and fingers. Still, he is able to lift himself enough to bring his face even with the bottom of the border. He knows this momentary burst of strength will soon disappear, so without further debate he pulls. For one delirious moment nothing happens and he is certain he won't make it; the next, he is straining forward, dragging his aching body over the concrete toward safety. His head passes over the edge of the border, then his neck. His shoulders come next, then his raw chest is again scraping over the rough surface. Somehow he manages to tumble forward, where he lies panting and bleeding, the obscuring mist cool on his aching body.

Lured me, Ben thinks, chest heaving. *The horrible thing lured me up here, thought it could trick me into killing myself.*

The thought that an alien presence could invade his mind and control his thoughts – hell, control his *actions* – is appalling. But he knows this is what happened. Arms extended as though he's crossing a tightrope, Ben makes his halting way through the thickening mist back to the open door. In less than a minute he is in his bedroom. He thinks again – he can't help it – of the scars on the castle façade. He imagines the sort of creature that could leave such marks and then wishes he hadn't. It is huge, bestial, but the worst is its face. It is Ryan's face, the man who wants Joshua dead.

With the thought comes a ghastly certainty – whatever intelligence almost tricked him into suicide is still peering at him through the mist. Ben cranks shut the window, leans on the sash lock till it's tight. Then, cinching the curtains shut, he looks down at his belly and sees the crisscrossing scrapes and cuts. He needs to wash up and dress his wounds.

But first he double-checks his window to make sure it's locked.

CHAPTER TEN

Dawn. Eddie sensed the breaking day on his shut lids, but he was too frightened to open them. He hadn't even flirted with sleep after dragging the spare blanket from the closet and wrapping up in it on the floor. After discovering Lily's imprint on the bed, the cold dampness, he couldn't bring himself to sleep there. The others would be awakening soon. He knew what he had seen, yet he could never admit to having seen it. Thinking of their reactions, their derision, he got up and slid on his shorts. Not bothering with a shirt, he stepped into his sandals and went outside.

The breeze felt good on his chest. He regretted not wearing his running shoes. No matter, he could ditch the sandals and run on the beach. He headed for the path, grateful for something to take his mind off Lily.

God, he wished he'd never met her. If only she hadn't been so obsessed with him, so persistent.

You didn't have to kill her.

"Stop."

You didn't have to burn her alive.

"Please please stop oh God."

Her face staring out as the car went over

Eddie got moving to outrun the image, but rather than vanishing, another image, even more disturbing, took its place.

Lily at the window last night.

"No."

Lily in the ocean, reaching for you

He sprinted down the trail.

Soon, he reached the coast. He took off his sandals, dropped them by the edge of the woods. His cargo shorts weren't really made for exercise, but he desperately needed motion. Eddie began to jog, the lethargy of insomnia burning off as his footfalls came more rapidly. His calves ached and his stomach was a knot, but he was alive, dammit, and that was more than he could say for Lily.

Shaking off the thought of her, the name that repeated like an idiot refrain, he picked up his knees, stretching as he ran. His arms were responding to the movement, his legs finally waking a little. The moist sand felt nice on his toes. Up ahead he spotted the cave from which Ben had emerged with a masterpiece.

Movement at its entrance arrested his attention.

Eddie slowed to a walk, hot breath singeing his throat, and strained to see through the bluish morning air. He discerned a child's bare skin, a large pair of eyes, but it was the music that made his breath catch in his throat. Soft and melancholy. Heartbreaking.

He took an excited step in the child's direction, but the eyes widened and the boy disappeared into the darkness of the cave.

Eddie stood indecisively, about thirty feet from where the child had been sitting and blowing on something that resembled driftwood.

What the hell?

Eddie glanced back the way he'd come and debated what to do. If the boy was another ghost, he was preferable to Lily.

Eddie paused, listening. The music had resumed, softer now, but still audible. Rather than entering the cave, Eddie took a couple of tentative steps forward and listened to the little boy's song.

It played on, an elegiac melody. Lovely and haunting. When it ended, Eddie held his breath, hoping it would start again.

It did.

He stood there a long time, listening.

Eddie listened to it three times through before setting off the way he'd come, an exultant joy gripping him. He would play the song in the great hall, rouse them all from their slumber. *See what I came up with, guys? How's this for the opening shot? Can't you picture it? Zooming in on the huge gravestone… the elegy converging perfectly with the image?*

And watch them stare in disbelief.

CHAPTER ELEVEN

When Claire awoke, she thought she was dreaming.

Eva stood over her bed, watching her. The woman wore the same black bathing suit of the afternoon before, and like before, seemed supremely confident.

Claire sat up. "What's going on?"

"Sleep well?"

Claire became aware of her exposed breasts, her utter nakedness beneath the sheet. She'd been restless last night, her attraction to Ben demanding some outlet.

She cinched the sheet tighter.

"It's okay," Eva said and held out her hand. "I have to show you something."

Claire leaned on an elbow, careful to keep the sheet over her chest. "Can it wait?"

Eva rolled her eyes. "Wrap yourself up if you want, but come on."

Claire watched her uncertainly.

"I have something to show you," Eva said. "Believe me, it'll be worth it."

"Can't I get dressed first?"

"Only if you want to miss something wonderful."

A hot fluttering in her stomach, Claire drew the sheet around her torso and wiggled off the bed. For a moment, her nude lower half was exposed. She saw Eva's eyes flit there and quickly covered herself. Eva crossed to the door.

Claire said, "I can't go out there."

Eva opened the door, stepped into the hall. "It's okay, no one's here."

The fluttery feeling grew as they approached Eva's door.

"What's in—"

Eva put a finger to her lips, shushing her. Claire followed Eva into the bedroom, but Eva surprised her by tiptoeing to a wall sconce and grasping its translucent rim. Before Claire could ask what she was doing, the sconce tipped down and the bookcase next to it turned sideways. The blackness within didn't register at first, but when Claire glanced at Eva comprehension dawned.

Eva said, "What castle would be complete without a secret passageway?"

Claire laughed, put the hand that wasn't holding up the sheet to her mouth in amazement.

"How did you—"

"Gabriel."

"Who's that?"

"My visitor."

Claire frowned, "What are you—"

"I saw it in my dream." Eva took her hand. "I have a surprise for you. You'll thank me for it."

Claire followed her into the darkness and immediately detected the smells of wet metal and old dust.

"I found it late last night," Eva said, "and I've been walking the walls ever since."

The disorientation, the closeness of the walls, brought on a chill.

"We need a flashlight," Claire said.

"I had one, but the batteries went dead."

"Let's go down—"

"There's no time."

Feeling a little sick, Claire allowed the woman to lead her through the darkness. Eva slowed, and Claire could hear the woman's hands slithering along the walls, groping for something.

"It should be right…about…"

Claire spotted a rectangle of light about four inches high and a foot long. "What room is this?" she asked, peering into the light.

"Ben's."

"Wait," she said, but the woman stilled her with a hand on her shoulder.

"Listen."

Claire did and heard a muffled roar.

The shower.

"Come on," Eva said and dragged Claire down the narrow walkway. The roar grew louder as they neared the bathroom, here and there the pipes narrowing the passage further. The slightly metallic scent of hot water reached her nostrils.

Another rectangle appeared and Claire's mouth dropped open. They were staring at Ben's naked body.

Eva stood beside her. "You know why there are mirrors all over the place?"

"I do now," Claire said, her throat dry as sandpaper.

The woman's mouth was very close to her ear as she said, "Don't worry, he can't see us."

"This is wrong," Claire said, but she was looking anyway, staring at Ben's broad chest, his hard stomach with just a trace of hair around the navel. Below that…

"There are two-way mirrors in every room," Eva said. "I guess Robert Blackwood liked to watch."

"We can't just watch him."

"Here," Eva said, taking a step backward. She put a hand on Claire's hip and guided her to the center of the looking glass. The fingers pressing her skin through the sheet were firm, insistent. Claire's eyes were an inch from the glass, and though the steam rendered the image gauzy, she could see enough of Ben's nude body to bring back the feeling of earlier that night, in bed, her fingers caressing…

As if reading her thoughts, Eva said, "I watched you last night, you know."

The hand on her hip hadn't moved.

"I don't know what you mean," Claire said, feeling faint. The hot steam seeped into the tunnel, misting her lips, her chin. Her bare shoulders.

Eva spoke, her sleek, warm body pressing against hers, "I was so glad when you took your clothes off…"

Oh no, Claire thought.

"…so I could see your body…"

The hand on Claire's hip slid up and down, slowly.

"…but I was so disappointed when you got under the covers…"

Claire whispered, "Please don't."

"Okay," Eva whispered, her lips touching the base of Claire's neck. A sense of weightlessness passed through her as the lips kissed, the tongue tracing a wet path along a shoulder. Both hands were snaking around her now, clenching the sheet, parting the white fabric. The drowsy mist coated Claire's skin, her body naked from the stomach down.

"Don't," she whispered again, softer this time, and the hands massaged her belly, lower, the fingertips warm.

The showerhead shut off and Claire reached down and gathered the sheet around her. She heard Eva behind her, laughing softly.

"*Stop it*," she hissed, but the laughter swelled, and Claire was suddenly sure that Ben would hear and discover them, and without thinking she cinched the sheet around her and plunged down the passageway with Eva's laughter trailing after her.

CHAPTER TWELVE

From the Journal of Calvin Shepherd
April 16th, 1925
May God pardon my tortured soul and save me from eternal damnation. I have committed a sin so grievous that it has taken me three sleepless nights to work up the courage to put pen to paper. It is true that I hated him with a passion that surpassed every other emotion in this dusty, old body, but not in a million years did I believe I would do to him what I did three nights ago.

I will briefly summarize the events that preceded my treachery, though this summarization will in no way explain or account for my complicity in the blasphemous deed.

Robert returned from the mainland a week ago, and his saturnine countenance made clear that things had not gone well with the head of the symphony. My master had journeyed to San Francisco to obtain an extension for his, or rather Gabriel's, latest work, and not only was his request denied, he was flatly informed that if he did not have the entire piece completed by the predetermined date, he would be sued for breach of contract.

As can be imagined, Robert took out his wrath on Gabriel. After a sound beating administered by Robert and Henry Mullen – for now Robert could never best Gabriel in a physical contest without his mountainous cohort – Gabriel was cast again into the pit. After spending five days and nights without food—his longest period of deprivation to date – Gabriel was taken from the pit and given a paltry meal in his room.

Gabriel had barely the strength to eat or drink, but he did so with my help. He was not, of course, allowed to see any of the women of the island, though several of them railed against Robert's cruelty. When Gabriel had finished his pitiful meal, Robert and Henry joined us in Gabriel's room. The chamber was clotted with the cloying fumes of watery chicken broth and stagnant air.

"I expect you're ready to give up this ridiculous charade," Robert said as he stood over his malnourished son.

Gabriel made no answer.

"You do know how severe the consequences will be if I do not finish this piece on time," Robert said.

Gabriel nodded faintly.

"I must warn you of the severity of the consequences you shall face should I miss the deadline. There are far worse things than going without food or water."

Robert's words chilled me to the core, yet Gabriel showed no sign of relenting.

"So be it," Robert said. Then to Mullen, "Take him to the tower."

It happened so quickly that I hadn't time to fully comprehend the gravity of the situation. Like a mindless cur, I followed the trio to the tower. Henry led the way with Gabriel slung over his shoulder like a sack of meal. Robert followed close behind. And I, restive but above all curious, trailed Robert, a half-eaten crust of bread still clutched stupidly in my hand.

We ascended the spiral staircase and when we reached the zenith of the tower I beheld the ancient grand piano sitting alone in the middle of the circular keep, the wind moaning forlornly through the windows.

It was what had been added to the windows that caused my heart to race.

Bars.

Robert had transformed the tower into a prison.

We all four stood in the keep, a single candle atop the piano our sole source of illumination.

Robert gestured toward the piano. "Will you write?"

Without turning, Gabriel said, "Be damned."

Robert's nostrils flared. I blanched at the prospect of another beating, but rather than advancing on his son, Robert nodded at Henry Mullen, who tromped across the room to something I had not seen, something that had been blocked by the piano. I took a few steps and noticed the white sheet, which Mullen cast aside, and when I glimpsed what had been covered, I wanted to run screaming from the room.

There were six stacked pallets full of bricks.

I glanced at Gabriel and saw that he too realized their function.

"If you do not compose in the next two hours," Robert said, "I shall wall you up in this tower."

Gabriel stared at the pile of bricks, the trowels and buckets of mortar beside them.

"You should consider your position," Robert said. "You need only start the piece. We have the rest of the week to work. If you write something good, our contract will be honored, and you may return to your room in the castle and perhaps someday see your child."

Gabriel looked at Robert in dawning amazement.

"My child?"

"Yes," Robert said in a bored voice. "The servant Anna has conceived and has been sent away."

Gabriel's face grew hard. "Bring her back."

"Depending on what you—"

"Bring her back, God damn you. *I want that child.*"

"You have chosen this path," Robert said, "I am only reacting as any father would."

Gabriel's voice rose. "This is madness."

"You have brought us to this."

Gabriel shook his head wonderingly. "I was happy in the forest. I was happy for many, many years."

A chill coursed through me.

"You were naked and alone," Robert said impatiently. "Only a stupid child could find happiness in such a life."

A horrible smile darkened Gabriel's face. "You really believe I was a child?"

I couldn't move. Even Henry Mullen was watching Gabriel uncertainly. But Robert only shook his head dismissively. "You have two hours. At midnight, your time runs out."

Robert brushed past me and exited the keep. Henry Mullen and I stood there and said nothing. I longed to follow my master, to escape the tower, but my role seemed clear.

I checked my watch. Somehow, five minutes had already passed. I ached to speak reason to our prisoner, yet Mullen's hulking presence somehow forbade it. Gabriel returned to the barred window and gazed out.

So we waited. At one point I escaped the tower for a few moments so I could relieve my aching bladder, but when I finished I plodded unhappily up to resume my post. Ten minutes before midnight, Robert finally returned. Gabriel had not budged from his station by the window. Robert's earlier placidity had vanished, and in its place had sprung a frantic agitation.

"Am I to believe you will forfeit your life just to spite me?"

"I have no life," Gabriel answered. "I have been a prisoner since the day you took me from my home."

"You imbecile, you *had* no home. I saved your life. You would have died without me."

"No, Robert," Gabriel said, his voice barely audible. "It is you who have brought me death—"

"I've no more time—"

"—but you shall know much of horror before the year is through."

Robert regarded Gabriel in disbelief. "Are you threatening me? Are you so insolent that—"

Gabriel turned and walked to the piano. My heart leapt as he sat on the dusty black bench and extended his arms. Thank heavens, I thought with indescribable relief, thank heavens this insanity has finally come to an end.

But my joy vanished at the sound of the tune I had heard so long ago, the music Gabriel had played that day in the Greek forest.

Robert's mouth became a thin line.

In a voice we could scarcely hear above the music, Gabriel said, "It is midnight, Father. Our time is at an end."

Robert's chest heaved with emotion, and for a moment I held out hope that he would swerve from this diabolical course.

He looked at Henry, at me, then at Gabriel.

"Wall this creature up," he said.

Of the deed itself I cannot speak. Though with a workhorse like Henry Mullen the construction of the wall moved along relatively quickly, our toil seemed to last an eternity. Of the many things for which I am ashamed, I will here admit that the tears I shed as we fitted the final few bricks into place are not among them. Yes, I wept for Gabriel, but even more I wept for my own soul. For what Mullen and I performed that night was murder, cold and brutal, and no rationalization could justify it.

I've no doubt that Henry Mullen has slept peacefully in his bachelor's den these past few nights, but, Dear Journal, I have lain tormented and sick, haunted by the last thing we witnessed before we finished our task.

Per Robert's instructions, the wall was constructed within the outer edge of the doorframe, so that if Gabriel were to open his door inward, he would be faced with an unbroken arch of brick. By unspoken mutual consent – or perhaps Mullen never even thought about it – we left the door open while engaged in our work. Why we did this I had no idea, since it afforded us a constant view of our victim as we worked. Furthermore, the open doorway allowed Gabriel's piano playing to assault us in all its singular beauty during the entire three-hour period it took for us to finish.

When the final brick, which it fell to me to put into place, was ready to be fitted, a sudden desire to see Gabriel one final time possessed me. I don't know what I thought I could do, disabuse him of his fatal stance? Tell him I would try to change Robert's mind?

I do not know.

But when I peered through the small rectangular aperture, the sole connection between Gabriel and his gaolers, I beheld something that shall haunt me for the rest of my life.

I earlier stated that a single candle placed upon the lid of the grand piano provided the one source of illumination in the lonely tower keep. This lurid, guttering candlelight must have deceived me.

What I witnessed was Gabriel rising from the piano and approaching the door. But it wasn't Gabriel as I had known him these past thirteen years. He had shed his clothing, but the body now revealed was something alien and awe-inspiring.

His feet had become cloven hoofs. His magnificent body had, in several places, grown shaggy with hair. His face had elongated slightly, goatlike but still human, a devil's visage.

Sprouting from his head were two curving horns.

The beast that could not be Gabriel grinned at me, reached up, and closed the door.

And with a hand that quaked, I fitted the final brick into place.

PART FOUR
EVA

CHAPTER ONE

Claire said, "I've been thinking about the Clay incident. About those people getting murdered and the woman who took her life."

Ben didn't return her stare, but he said, "I used to think the story was crazy. Now I'm not sure."

She folded her legs on the blanket they'd brought with them to the graveyard and inhaled the rich scent of pine. The day was hazy and warm, the blanket a little damp from last night's downpour. Claire shifted and winced at the soreness between her legs. She thought of the nightmare…

"Remember James Ryder?" she said. "The history professor who murdered his best friend?"

"Of course I remember him," Ben said, "and I know what you're thinking."

"Do you blame me? The way Ryder changed on the island and the way Eddie's been acting. He has this tortured look in his eyes…he's angry with everyone…"

"Claire—"

"Don't tell me you don't see it."

He was quiet a long time. Finally, he said, "Let's just say I can't wait to get back to California."

"Glad I'm not the only one."

"But there's another reason why."

She waited for him to talk, but he looked away and uttered a humorless little laugh. Claire reached out and held his hand.

He said, "I feel stupid talking about it…"

She squeezed his hand. "Go ahead."

He averted his eyes. Claire had a fleeting moment of paranoia, suddenly sure that Ben had found out about her and Eva's spying.

"Do you believe in…" He shook his head, laughed. "I feel like an idiot saying it, but I think I was inside my son's head last night. I think something terrible is happening back in California."

She listened to his dream about Joshua and Ryan.

When it was over, Claire caressed his arm. "You don't think it was a dream."

Ben frowned. "It's crazy, isn't it? It was almost like…what's the name for it…astral projection."

"I don't know," Claire said and sat back on her palms. "I went to camp once…some Baptist camp where they fill your head with the terrible things that will happen if you don't accept Jesus." She gazed at a gravestone, remembering. "I've always been a believer, but that camp scared me to death. Rather than talking about love and forgiveness, all they talked about was burning in hell.

"Anyway, my parents came halfway through the week to pick me up. It surprised me but I didn't argue. I was dying to sleep in my own bed and to get away from all those pictures of Satan and the souls he was roasting. I'd been back a few days before I asked my dad why they'd taken me home early.

"He said, 'We came to get you because your mother was having bad dreams.'

"'About me?' I asked.

"He nodded.

"'What did she dream?' I asked.

"He frowned like he didn't think he should answer me, but I kept begging. You know how persistent kids can be."

Ben nodded.

"He said, 'She dreamed of screaming faces…she dreamed of fire. I told her they were just nightmares, worry over you being away at camp, but she wouldn't listen. She said she was seeing things in *your* mind. Feeling *your* fear.'"

Ben's smile had faded, his gaze intense.

Claire said, "I kept Dad's secret until I was in college. Then something, I don't remember what, made me think of it again. I asked mom about it, and even though she was a little irked at Dad for telling me such things at that age, she remembered the episode vividly. She told me the dreams were about the devil chasing me, telling me he was going to stab me with his pitchfork and roast me over his fire."

Claire looked at Ben. "She told me *exactly* what I had dreamed."

Ben said, "Maybe her parents sent her to the same camp."

"I doubt it," Claire answered. "I think our bond was so strong that she was able to feel what I was feeling, to see my thoughts."

Ben blew out a pent-up breath, gave her a wan smile. "To tell you the truth, I hope I wasn't seeing what Joshua was. If it was real…"

"You can go to him when Granderson comes."

He nodded. "I plan to."

"Then what?"

"Then…I suppose I'll get Joshua alone and ask him to tell me. If I know it was all in my head…my heartbreak over being separated…"

"And if he says there's something wrong?"

She watched his corded arms tighten. "If Ryan really did threaten my son, I'll beat the son of a bitch within an inch of his life."

"Promise me one thing," she said.

"What, don't kill him?"

She didn't answer.

"Don't worry, I won't do anything that'd stop me from getting Joshua back."

"What do you—"

"I want full custody. I let a judge decide and didn't really fight it because I didn't want to cause Joshua any more pain. The last few nights, I've realized that my ex-wife cares more about herself than she does our son. It'll be painful for Joshua, but I'd rather him go through that now than spend the rest of his childhood in a place where he isn't loved."

"She doesn't love him?"

Ben looked at her. "Not like I do. Not even close to the way I do."

CHAPTER TWO

Chris feigned politeness as the blonde secretary buzzed to see if Stephen Blackwood had a minute for his son. Chris imagined the man back there, maybe fifty feet away, hidden behind the mahogany door like the Great and Powerful Oz.

She hung up the phone, said, "Your father will see you in a few moments."

Too jittery to sit on any of the imitation-leather chairs in the waiting room, Chris went to the window overlooking downtown San Francisco and waited. His stomach growled. He knew he should have grabbed a bite before heading over here, but nothing had sounded good, and besides, the fear that at any moment one of Marvin's goons might pop out from behind a building and snatch him from the world of the living took away whatever appetite he might have had.

The burns began to ache. He remembered Marvin holding the lighter under the metal tip of the cane.

When are you gonna pay us, Chris?

I did pay you. Jesus Christ, gimme time.

No more time, Chris. You're out of time.

The glowing red tip, a satanic eye, gliding toward Chris's chest.

I'll have it tomorrow. I'll get it from my dad. Please.

You shoulda had it yesterday.

The red eye sizzling his nipple. Then the screaming and the blubbering and the hideous bacon smell. This morning Chris had tried to count the number of burns on his skin. He counted sixteen circles before he grew faint.

He sensed the pretty secretary watching him, sizing him up. Comparing him to his father maybe. She couldn't be older than Chris. Midtwenties maybe.

He said to the woman, "How long have you been with Blackwood Industries?" It gave him a kick to call the company by its official name, as if it actually produced anything other than interest on the money his father had inherited.

"Just over a year. You don't come here much."

"I don't suppose the old man minds."

"I wouldn't know. He's never mentioned you."

Pretty *and* vicious, he thought. Chris moved closer.

"Was the interview difficult?" he asked.

"No different from any other I've been in."

"How much did he hit on you?"

Her mouth drew into itself, the pretty lips puckering as if tasting something sour. "Why don't you take a seat?"

"Why don't you stop pretend—"

"Chris?"

He stood erect at his father's voice, regressing into the old patterns. "Hey, Dad."

The man stood there, smug and inimical, his navy-blue suit nicely tailored, but the rest of him sloppy, reminding Chris of a toddler whose parents had dressed him up for a picture, but who'd soiled his outfit before they could take it. His father's chin was nearly lost in the swollen puff of flesh bulging out of his collar, his hair the color of an old Brillo pad, rust and dull gray battling for supremacy. His round belly reminded Chris of a garden gnome.

"You wanted to see me?"

"Yeah," Chris answered. "I did."

They went to the office, Stephen sitting behind the desk, Chris taking the chair opposite. His father regarded him without warmth.

"Well?" Stephen asked.

"I need your help."

"I expected as much."

Chris ran his eyes over the plaques on the wall. There were dozens of them. Gold mostly, with some red, silver, and green mixed in. He couldn't imagine what his father could have done to deserve any of them.

"I'm in a bit of a bind," Chris said. "Financially, I mean."

Stephen nodded impatiently. *Of course you are.*

"But this time…" Chris made a pained face, "…it's not like the others."

"You mean no one is pregnant?"

Chris shifted in the big chair. His ass was sweating and his head hurt. Meanwhile his dad continued to watch him like something stuck to his shoe.

"No one's pregnant," Chris answered.

"You haven't run over anyone, I assume."

Shit. Referencing his crash. His Ferrari had clipped an SUV before vaulting the guardrail, and though the impact on the SUV's bumper hadn't been severe enough to even spill someone's coffee, the driver had sued them for a bundle. To Stephen Blackwood, the fact that Chris had escaped unscathed was little consolation for the money lost.

"No," Chris answered, "I didn't run over anyone."

"Go on."

"I bet on some games and lost."

Stephen tented his index fingers, touched them to his chin. "How much are you behind?"

"Who knows?" Chris glanced at the plaques. "These guys tend to make their own rules."

"How can I know how to help you if you can't even provide a figure?"

Impulsively, Chris said, "Let's just call it an even million," and immediately regretted it.

In the silence that followed he could hear the low hum of his father's computer. Stephen Blackwood chuckled softly, described a slow back and forth semicircle in his chair. When he looked at Chris, his face was absolutely cold.

"You should know better than to tell lies," he said. "I speak with Jim Granderson every day."

Granderson, Chris thought without surprise. *God damn him.*

Stephen Blackwood rose, faced the window behind his desk. "Had you asked for the six-fifty you still owed after turning our family's island into a resort, I would have turned you down flat, of course. But you still would have been part of this family."

Chris could feel a pulse throb in his temples. His feet had gone numb.

"But since you also tried to extort three-hundred-and-fifty thousand, however, I have no choice but to do what I have resisted for so long."

Stephen shook his head. "Surely, I told myself, *surely* he will grow out of this kind of behavior. Surely he will realize what an opportunity he has. A billion dollar empire, worth more every day, and all he has to do is stay out of trouble. Is that too much to ask?" He turned and regarded Chris. "Is it?"

Chris sat forward. "They'll kill me if I don't pay."

"You should have thought of that before you dishonored your family."

"Was it honorable when you murdered a woman?"

The color drained from his father's face.

Then, faster than Chris would have thought possible, Stephen Blackwood seized him by the throat and lifted him from the chair. "I oughta have you *killed,* you little son of a bitch," the man hissed, spit flying from his mouth. "How dare you say such a thing?"

Chris grabbed the man's wrists, struggled to disengage them.

"*You have no idea what happened that night!*" Stephen shouted.

Chris pumped a fist into his father's gut and stumbled away. Rubbing his throat, he glanced back at his father, on the phone now, pushing buttons.

"I want security up here," Stephen said. "*Now.*"

Chris grinned savagely, said, "You fucked her and then you killed her."

"*God damn you,*" Stephen said, dropping the phone and advancing on him.

"She went down on mom while you jacked off."

Stephen swung a haymaker, struck him a glancing blow on the ear. Chris went down. His father swung again, clouted him between the shoulder blades.

Chris jerked up an elbow and caught his father in the stomach. Stephen Blackwood doubled over, coughs racking his large frame.

"I want that money by the end of the day," Chris said and lurched toward the door. His hand on the knob, he paused. "On second thought," he said, "make it ten million."

"You're done," his father said.

"If the money's not in my account by five o'clock, I'm going to the *Chronicle.* I'm sure they'd love a story this juicy."

He raced for the stairs, his father roaring something unintelligible behind him. He made it down three flights, four. Though his wind was spent, he knew he couldn't let them catch him. There'd been murder in his father's eyes.

Moments later, he trotted down the street to his black Mercedes convertible. He climbed in, started it, and gunned into traffic. In his hip pocket his cell phone rang. He pulled it out and saw it was his father, calling to tell him what would be done to him if he went public with the murder.

Chris muted the phone and thought, *Stephen Blackwood, Ladies and Gentlemen. Your Father of the Year.*

He tossed the cell on the floor.

His hands shaking, he halted at a red light. He drummed his fingers, waited for the light to change. He thought fleetingly of turning left, heading to the *San Francisco Chronicle* after all, spilling his guts to some thunderstruck reporter, but he dismissed the thought as quickly as it had come.

How would he, in the end, benefit from such a course of action? There was no way his father would pay him then, and though he would enjoy seeing the bastard publicly raked over the coals, sent to prison for the rest of his life even, the ensuing litigation would be a nightmare.

Who would get the money? His mother, of course, but to whom would she leave it? Would she side with Chris?

Hell no, he realized, she stood to lose almost as much as his father if Chris went public. Unbidden, the image of his mother receiving cunnilingus from a Hispanic maid clogged his mind. He pushed it away, shivering.

Ahead, a billboard for an upcoming movie caught his eye. Absently, he read the title, the cheesy catchphrase. His hands tightened on the wheel.

Feverishly, he steered the convertible on to the shoulder, the traffic *whishing* by. He threw it into park. He leaned over, retrieved the cell phone. He found the number in his contacts, pushed Send.

A friendly female voice said, "Hey, Chris."

"Hey, Sandra," he said, thinking of the girl's toned body, naked save a skimpy pair of panties as she fled from a legion of zombies in one of Chris's favorite horror flicks.

"I've been thinking about you," she said, and Chris recalled an image of her naked in his pool.

"I've been thinking about you too," he said. "I'd like to get together some time."

"That would be nice."

"That's great," Chris said, ignoring the beep informing him of an incoming call. "Hey, Sandra. I was wondering if you could do me a favor."

"Shoot."

"I need you to get me a phone number."

"Sure thing," she said. "Who is it?"

"The man who launched your career with that zombie movie," Chris said. "Lee Stanley."

CHAPTER THREE

From the Journal of Calvin Shepherd
June 1st, 1925
I have not the strength to chronicle the phantasmagorical happenings of the past six weeks, nor would I dare to do so had I sufficient energy.

I will, however, for the sake of posterity, record here a few particulars of what has occurred since that awful night, the night I consigned my soul to damnation. That my future readers will find my claims fanciful or even worthy of scorn, I have no doubt. Yet I swear upon my mother's cold grave that the words written here are free of embellishment or subterfuge. I have no reason to spin yarns – indeed, I have every reason to conceal the truth.

For many days after Henry Mullen and I completed the task of walling Gabriel in the tower, I bade my master to reconsider, once even going so far as to threaten to tear the wall down myself.

A glancing blow to the face and a flurry of remonstrance shattered my resolve. Still, I wept for Gabriel, listened to the continual strains of music that drifted down from the tower, filling me with melancholy and robbing me of both appetite and sleep.

In truth, I deserved far worse.

But, Dear Journal, I must now explain why I fear I will indeed experience worse – why, despite the blackness of my plight, I am plagued by the conviction that all my guilt and self-loathing have been a mere prelude to the real horrors in store for me.

We heard the piano all that first week. This did not surprise me, nor did it increase my anxiety. Conversely, the music I heard emanating from the tower represented my sole source of hope. As long as Gabriel still plays, I told myself, there is still a chance that Robert will see the error of his ways and give the prisoner a reprieve. The vestiges of hope inspired by Gabriel's playing eventually, I confess, gave way to perplexity, and eventually, to a suffocating dread. For the music persisted through the second week of Gabriel's entombment.

How, I asked myself, could a man survive so long without food or water? I had heard of rare cases where individuals of uncanny stubbornness and superhuman vigor had lasted up to ten or eleven days without eating or drinking, yet Gabriel's playing resonated through the thirteenth, fourteenth, and fifteenth nights.

Around this time Robert set sail for the mainland, taking with him his grown children and Mullen's two bereaved daughters. Although my master never explained his motive for embarking on this unscheduled trip, I knew too well why he had gone.

Even a villain as soulless as Robert Blackwood has a breaking point, and I could see plainly that he had reached his. In those last few days and nights preceding his flight, my master had taken to long rambles in the forest, extended examinations of his wine cellar. Even a candlelit excursion to the pit.

Yet wherever he ventured on the island, he could not escape the reach of Gabriel's piano. The notes originating from the tower possessed a bizarre ability to penetrate wood and stone, to pursue an unwilling listener wherever he fled. I knew this because I too had tried many times in vain to evade the accusing melodies.

So Robert left me to suffer the aural evidence of our crime. During the fourth week of Gabriel's imprisonment, I asked Henry Mullen if we might at least tarry forth to the tower keep in an attempt to engage the inmate in conversation. I did not state my true reason for broaching the topic, for I feared the brute would mock me for it. And who could have blamed him? Even now, the suggestion that it might have been *Gabriel's spirit*, and not the man himself, producing the music elicits disbelief in my own breast. There was no telling how Mullen would have reacted.

As it was, he responded badly enough, branding me a sodomite and telling me to go to hell. When I informed him that he might join me in my eventual descent, he threatened to throw me in the ocean. Self-preservation took over, and I apologized.

The piano continued to play for a full month before ceasing, and even after that, I was sure I heard occasional notes whispering down from the tower.

Now it is nearing two in the morning, and because Robert and the younger members of his party are due back tomorrow, I want to record the events of earlier this evening before they return.

It was just before midnight when I stepped inside the tower and stole quietly up the stairs. I don't know what I thought I would find when

I reached the top. Maybe I expected the bricks to be damaged in some way, reduced to rubble by the relentless vibrations of Gabriel's piano. Perhaps I believed there would be some message written on the wall, some confirmation that Gabriel had indeed escaped his entombment and had departed the island to finally taste the freedom of the outside world.

But the wall was intact. The bricks and the mortar completely filled the entryway, so that no part of the door was visible. And though I can't explain why, this only added to my growing unease.

Sure at any moment the piano would explode into some ghastly song, I tiptoed toward the brick wall, the candleholder clutched in my sweaty palm juddering enough I feared it would extinguish just as I reached the dreaded spot and thus plunge me into stygian darkness. The bricks stared at me without pity, their accusatory faces heightening my unease.

I drew nearer. A foot from the wall, I stopped.

I listened.

Though there was a light breeze, I didn't hear it whispering in the tower. A silence deep and unceasing choked the night, and maybe because I was so uneasy, I spoke a single word to break it.

"Gabriel?" I called.

When no response came, I repeated the name, louder this time. Again there was only silence.

I reached out, my fingertips lightly brushing against the rough mortar, the smooth brick. Though I feared a fiendish hand would break through the wall and seize my hand, all remained still.

"I'm sorry, Gabriel," I said. "I'm sorry for what I've done."

I backed away from the wall, not daring to turn my back on it, and nearly tumbled down the staircase. Suddenly mad with fear, I raced down the steps and did not slow until my feet touched the soft grass at the tower's base.

Halfway to Castle Blackwood I turned and gazed up at the barred windows.

The same full moon now gleaming through my open window lay half-hidden behind the triangular turret roof of the tower. From where I stood, I could see each slate shingle. I could see the outline of the stones that formed a conical shell around our makeshift tomb.

I could see everything clearly, and though part of me longed to, I did not see Gabriel's face peering through the barred window.

At last, the music had fallen silent.

CHAPTER FOUR

Eddie felt them watching him, the silence of the great hall heavy as iron shackles on his wrists. He could smell his own breath, fetid and tasting of onions, though he hadn't eaten one in days. For something to do, he reached up, flattened the crisp white sheets of music against the black binder, and pored over the first few notes. The arrangement had taken him almost eight hours, and even now he wasn't sure he had written it all that well. It certainly wasn't the same music he'd heard coming from the cave. He couldn't quite capture the melody's darkling spell, the manner in which it acted on the listener. Played by the boy – Eddie didn't allow his thoughts to linger there long, for how else could the child be explained but by the supernatural? – the song contained a fateful acquiescence, like a wayfarer lost in a snowy mountain range who has decided, finally, to succumb to the pristine glamour of the snow, to accept an icy grave and a good long sleep.

Yes, Eddie's arrangement held some, but not all, of that brooding inevitability.

But they won't know that, he kept telling himself. *Just calm down and play the piece.*

He cast a sheepish grin back at them to show he hadn't forgotten why he'd called them all here. Fleetingly, he considered bringing them forward so they would flank the piano rather than watch from behind.

Stop, he told himself. *Play*.

Eddie played. The first section was the strongest, he knew. The initial notes were peaceful, entirely neutral. Then his fingers descended the scale and the piece took on a decidedly darker bent. He could almost feel Claire's mordant gaze, Claire who played the piano far better than he ever could. His fingers blundered, neglecting a crucial key change. Eddie cringed as he played a sharp that should have been a flat. The keys evaded his fingertips, taunting him, sabotaging what should be his moment of triumph.

Dammit. He imagined Claire's grin, the pasty-white bitch. He came to the weakest part of the song, the climax and the transition to the denouement. He'd spent many hours on it and had still not gotten it right. He slogged through it, such as it was, and returned to the main melody with vast relief, the final few bars spinning themselves out, the song ending.

He sat, breathing heavily, his oily hair clinging to his forehead. Soon he would take a shower, but first he would see their reactions. Judging from the silence, they were too overcome to comment, to applaud even, and a joy he had envied Ben these past four years flooded through him, the joy of the artist receiving the adulation he deserves.

Eddie turned and looked into their faces.

"So?" he asked, unable to contain the smile.

Claire looked at Ben, who was nodding faintly but was otherwise unresponsive. Eva was scribbling something in her notebook, damn her. Probably a grocery list for when she got back to the mainland.

Eddie shook her off and turned to Ben. "Could you picture it?"

Ben frowned. "Picture what?"

"The opening shot. The aerial tracking shot of the forest, the graveyard?"

When Ben only looked confused, Eddie said, "Come *on*. The beginning of the movie." Gesturing at the sheet music. "*That's* the song that begins the film."

Ben said, "Look, Eddie, I like it…"

A slow trickle of acid rose in Eddie's throat. "You're kidding, right?"

He noticed Claire watching them, relishing the discord. She said, "It's a lovely variation of 'Annabel's Theme.' I'm just not sure—"

He faced her. "*What?*"

Her stupid face flushed, the hives rashing her skin like lead poisoning. She put on a smile that Eddie considered, at best, disingenuous. At worst… was she mocking him?

"I…" she began, her hands fluttering like idiot moths. "What I meant was…"

"'Annabel's Theme'?" Eddie said. He tapped the music with an index finger. "This is original stuff. It has nothing to do with the other—"

"You do have to admit," Ben said, the mewling peacemaker, "the two pieces do have a kinship."

"What kinship?" Eddie asked, standing.

"Hey, relax," Ben said, leaning over and flipping through the sheet music, searching for something. "Right here," he said, touching a page near the beginning. "This is the main melody in 'Annabel's Theme.' And here…" Flipping a page, scanning, "…right here is the chord that follows the violin part." He looked at Eddie. "Remember?"

Eddie glared at him, at his falsely innocent expression. "Do I remember? I arranged the goddamn music. Do I remember…" He shook his head and glanced at Eva. He asked her, "You heard both songs Did they sound alike to you?"

She shrugged, setting her notebook aside. "A little."

He stared at her.

"I don't know," she added, "Ben's song was better."

Eddie thought of plunging the pencil into her eye.

"But they're both good," Claire said.

Eddie walked over to where she sat, stood over her. "If you weren't a scheming little whore, that might mean something to me."

"Hey," Ben said, grabbing his arm.

Eddie flailed, shoving him away. "I can't believe you don't see through her."

"What the hell is wrong with you?" Ben said, his big doe eyes turning Eddie's stomach.

He imitated Ben's stricken expression. "*What the hell is wrong with me?* Where do I start? How about the way she's driven a wedge between us and you sit back and let her."

Ben glanced at Claire, then at Eddie, his mouth growing firm. "You need to calm—"

"Or the way you act when I finally write my own stuff? Jesus, you'd think you could at least pretend to be excited."

Ben's expression softened. "Hey…look…I didn't mean to…"

Somehow his pity was worse than his anger. If Eddie didn't leave soon, he'd kill somebody. Eddie stepped closer, their faces inches apart. "And not only were you not supportive," he said, "you accuse me of *stealing* it from you?"

"I didn't say you stole it," Ben said. "I said there was a similarity."

Eddie tapped himself on the chest. "*I arranged it.* Don't you think I'd notice a similarity?"

"Not when you're blinded by jealousy."

Eddie's fist shot out, caught him in the gut. Ben made a *whoomping* sound and doubled over. Distantly, Eddie heard one of the girls cry out. He kneed Ben in the chest and shoved him into the piano. The bench clattered, stood precariously on two legs, then toppled over. Claire rushed over to Ben.

Eddie moved past the couch, Eva watching him uncertainly, and before she could react, he lunged for the notebook. She gasped and made a move to stop him, but he passed her, stalked toward the foyer.

"*You have no right,*" she called after him. He ignored her.

Now he'd see, he thought as he opened the door. Now he'd see how badly the teasing bitch wanted him. And if what he read wasn't what he wanted to read, God help her.

CHAPTER FIVE

A knock on the door, Claire hoping she'd locked it. She appraised herself in the mirror – eyes puffy, nose raw and shiny with snot. She hoped it wasn't Ben. She couldn't let him see her like this. Eva? Claire hadn't been able to look the woman in the eye since the incident in the tunnel. Eddie?

Frankly, she was scared of Eddie.

"Claire?" a voice asked.

Ben.

"Just a minute," she said, sniffing. She used a tissue to dry her nose and wipe away the slick of tears. The eyes…there was nothing to be done for them. He would have to witness them in all their puffy glory. "Come in," she said.

Ben entered and closed the door. He approached and stared down at her. "I'm sorry for what he said."

She looked away, tried to smile. "It's fine."

"No it's not," he said and lowered to his knees in front of her. He took her hands, which were resting limply on the bed, and caressed them.

He said, "I'm sorry I didn't stick up for you."

She glanced down at his face, just a few inches below hers. "You did stick up for me."

He shook his head, his mouth a thin line. "Not enough. I should have beaten the shit out of him."

It warmed her, Ben talking that way. She'd had very few boyfriends, and none had ever cared enough to defend her honor. She turned his face toward hers. "You've been amazing to me."

She kissed him. She kneaded his muscular shoulders, loving the feel of his lips, his tongue. He had a coarse growth of stubble on his cheeks that on any other man she'd have found unrefined. On Ben, though, it was the perfect counterpoint for his kind eyes, his endearing shyness. His hands had slipped behind her, pushing under her shirt and rubbing her back. As if she weighed nothing at all, he lifted her backward, centered her on the bed. Then, rather than lying on top of her, he slid up her shirt and kissed her belly.

At once she realized what was happening, and though she wasn't a virgin, she'd only slept with two other men, both musicians at the conservatory. Both just boys, really. Ben's lips grazed her flesh, sent quivers through her body. He climbed higher, raising her shirt as he went. She helped him by drawing her shirt over her head, tossing it aside, and then he peeled down the cups of her bra, his tongue teasing, tasting. He moved higher, his mouth on her throat, his strong hands working her breasts, her nipples painfully hard against his fingers. The smell of his body was exhilarating, sunlight and fresh water with an undercurrent of musk. He unbuttoned her shorts, and she raised her hips to help him tug them down.

Somehow he'd gotten his shorts and underwear off too, and in an instant he was on top of her, spreading her, penetrating her. He began to undulate, and she let her knees open wider, a bright spire of heat searing her. Soon she made a noise of exquisite pain, and as she cried out louder and louder she watched his straining neck, like some animal, heard him groan, and they rode it out together, both of them shuddering.

Slowing, her tongue found his and they kissed deeply. He slumped on top of her. She relished the weight of him, his strength. Claire kissed his mouth languidly. His cheeks, his eyes. She kissed his temple, and when he looked down at her, she kissed his lips again.

* * *

Eva watched until they'd finished, provided commentary into her Dictaphone for the fun of it, a play-by-play of their lovemaking. She eyed Ben dispassionately as he exited Claire and lay beside her. He had a nice body, she'd noticed that watching him shower earlier. Part of her envied Claire – the girl obviously had it bad for him. Coupling with Ben must have been the pinnacle of her sexual life.

Of course, Claire had never lain with Gabriel. Eva doubted the poor girl would survive it. Claire had no idea how much power existed in sex, how the act could be used to gain control, to alter lives. Eva, however, had learned those lessons long ago.

Gabriela Rosales had been her first teacher.

Eva shut her eyes against the wave of shame that always accompanied thoughts of her mother. Poor Gabriela. The woman had suspected the power inherent in sex, but she'd never mastered it. Had instead been mastered by it. Ultimately, it had killed her as much as the heroin and the gun.

Eva remembered losing her own virginity at age thirteen. Her mother's roommate, Kathy, with whom she had remained after her mother's suicide, had brought a pair of men home from the club. Eva wasn't forced into anything, but Kathy had made it clear it would help them pay the rent if Eva were to cooperate.

When it was over, Kathy took her out to celebrate. They spent most of the money on a limousine and a lavish dinner. The rent still unpaid, Kathy had asked the next morning if Eva would help her with another private party.

That was how it went, and by the time Kathy's looks were gone and Eva – still only nineteen – was their only source of income, they had traded their apartment for a nice townhouse near the ocean. Eva joined an escort service and began to make real money, though a cocaine habit kept her from being truly prosperous. Kathy died of an overdose, and for a few hours at least Eva had mourned her, but soon the drugs and the sex took her mind off Kathy. Eva's reputation grew, as did her skill in bed.

And all along she dreamed of getting even with Lee Stanley.

She picked up a couple of clients with ties to the movie industry, and she knew she was getting closer. By her twenty-fifth birthday, she had sobered up completely and counted among her clients two A-list actors, the lead singer of an all-girl rock band, and one Oscar-winning screenwriter.

But it was Lee she wanted.

Finally, she met him at a premiere. He fell for her right away, as she knew he would. That night he asked her how much she charged. She told him nothing, that she wanted to work for him full time, a legitimate job. He hired her, but soon he invited her over, showed her his bedroom, made it clear it was all part of her duties.

She vomited when they were done, but of course he had passed out by then. Over the next two years she insinuated herself further and further into his life, and now, though she was three months shy of her twenty-eighth birthday, she was in a position to cash in on Lee Stanley and ruin his reputation with her book.

God, it would be wonderful.

Smiling, she peered through the mirror and noted that Claire had risen from the bed. Her back to Eva, Claire slipped on her bra. The panties came next, pink ones, like a little girl.

Eva suppressed a grin. Claire really was a girl in most ways. She recalled the encounter in the tunnel and relished the girl's conflicted yearning. Too bad she'd ended it when things had begun to get interesting. Eva doubted they'd have that chance again.

Not after Eddie returned.

The memory of his audacity – ripping the notebook from her hands – rankled her. But more, it frightened her. There was no telling what he'd do when he read all the awful things she'd written about him.

About all of them.

She groped her way down the dark passage until she reached her room. Emerging into the light, she pitched the Dictaphone onto the bed and kicked off her sandals. She craved a run. Lord knew, she needed a way to defuse the tension that had been building in her since Eddie's thievery.

She opened the master suite's door and wavered there a moment. Ahead, the lovers were emerging from Claire's room, and Eva had no desire to make small talk. She prided herself on being a good liar, but she had just watched them having sex. Would they see it in her face?

For a moment she stood poised in the doorway, hoping they wouldn't spot her. Then, Claire turned and put a hand to her chest, startled.

Eva came forward. "Didn't mean to scare you."

Ben nodded, his expression sheepish.

Like they've been caught, Eva thought. *A couple of postcoital teenagers.*

"It's getting cloudy outside," Claire said. "I hope you don't get rained on."

"I don't mind," Eva said and moved past them. "I just hope I don't run into Eddie. He won't be happy after he reads what I wrote."

"Is it that harsh?" Ben asked.

"Nothing he didn't deserve," she said.

She jogged down the stairs, went out, and immediately detected the threat of rain in the air. It was hot out too, the atmosphere smoldering with humidity.

For the first time Eva really studied the exterior of Castle Blackwood. Such an odd design, she thought, attractive but somehow askew. The façade was still damp from last night's downfall, and as a result the upper, more elaborate parts of the castle were darker than the rest, a sloppy magenta color, as though the walls were bleeding.

The turret directly above Eva reminded her of a helmet belonging to some medieval knight, the conical roof tapering to a point. Below, twin sets of windows glowered out at the iron-colored day like the eyes of some grim warlord. One of the curtains rustled faintly, as if stirred by the wind. The window appeared closed, but maybe it was open a crack. A light misting of drizzle had begun to tickle her arms, and the sensation brought on the memory of the nightmare, the recurring nightmare she had welcomed – invited even – until she had woken this morning.

A sharp stab of fear got her moving. She set out toward the forest.

What amazed her about the island was the lack of animal life inhabiting its woods. Where there should have been squirrels, rabbits, snakes even, there were only stands of ancient oaks, wild thickets of thorns.

She trotted up a gradual incline. The woods were very dark, but at least the overhanging canopy of trees served as a shelter from the rain. She could hear another storm in the distance, a vague din on the Pacific.

Eva neared the freshwater creek and the rickety, old wooden bridge that traversed it. She slowed as she approached, not trusting it to support her weight. She'd passed this way twice already, but never had the bridge looked so untrustworthy. Whole sections, she now realized, were missing. The entire left side dipped in a kind of swale, the wood mossy and rotted through.

Standing at the edge of the bridge, the sweep of the water surprised her. A product of last night's rain, maybe, the runoff of the entire island emptying this way. She considered heading back, running on the beach after all, but that could bring her into contact with Eddie, who might be hiding there, lurking in the cave like some mad anchorite.

Eva grasped a rail, the wood sodden with rain. She tried to wiggle it but it held fast. Only slightly reassured by the handrail's solidity, she took a tentative step forward, the wooden plank soft but unmoving under her rubber sole. She ventured another step, then another. A few more paces and she had reached the middle of the old bridge. The water beneath her trickled cheerfully, sounded much more like a creek than a rushing river. She peered over the edge and recalled a fairy tale her mother had read her before the heroin, "Who's that trip-trapping on my bridge?"

Eva grinned, a delicious little shiver on her moist skin. She always imagined the troll in the fairy tale to be like a goat, but larger, darker. Like a hideous mythological beast.

The recollection faded, blurred, and in its place she perceived the face of the monster in her nightmare. The full force of its hateful lust fell on her, her breathing suddenly thin. She tried to suppress it, struggled to blot out the white, leering eyes, the taut, hairy skin, but it clawed through her defenses, ripping and growling as it approached. Its face pervaded her mind, its lewd, snarling mouth, its razor sharp talons, and without thinking Eva peeled the left leg of her shorts up, stared in sick wonder at the gauze she'd taped over her thigh to conceal the claw marks. If it was a dream, she asked herself, how could the creature harm her? But the only answers her reason could provide were the three bloody trenches ripped in her flesh, the sopping, red sheet under her midsection that looked for all the world like the residue from some violent menstruation.

But still…part of her wanted the beast to return.

Wanted Gabriel to return.

Eva let the shorts climb down over the bandage. She felt very vulnerable here on the bridge, very alone. Definitely time to head back.

She took a step in that direction as overhead, lightning chalked the sky. She waited for the thunder, and drew in a shocked breath as the bridge below her gave way. Her left leg plunged through the splintered board, wooden teeth furrowing her flesh. She caught herself before the rest of her body could tumble into the creek below. It would be a short fall, no more than ten feet to the surface, but she had no idea what lay below the frothing water. Her leg stuck in the ragged hole and the image of the beast arose in her mind. What if the creature, as the wounds on her thigh suggested, really had sprung to life, was now awaiting her under the bridge? A wave of revulsion propelled her out of the hole and onto her knees. She threw a cursory glance at her leg and saw how badly the fall had bloodied it. Careful not to make the same mistake again, she made her way on hands and knees toward the end of the bridge.

When her fingers scraped the moist soil of the trail, she lunged forward and lay panting on her stomach. She was filthy, and she didn't like the idea of facing Ben and Claire that way, but anything was preferable to remaining out here in the forest while her memory and her imagination tormented her in some fiendish collusion.

She got shakily to her feet and saw Eddie standing in the middle of the trail.

He was staring at her, his mouth curdled in a savage grin.

The red notebook hung limply at his side.

Eva managed a smile. "I hope you didn't take any of that stuff personally."

A jarring peal of thunder shook the forest, but Eddie remained silent.

"I know how it looks," she said, "but I write down everything. It doesn't mean I really feel that way."

When he spoke, his voice was disturbingly calm. "How did you know?"

The rain was pelting the trail now, breaking through the protecting trees.

She shook her head. "I don't—"

"Who told you about her?" he asked. "Who told you about Lily?"

She opened her mouth, shut it.

He seemed to draw back, something dawning in his face. "You're going to have this published, aren't you?"

"Of course not, I..." she trailed off, damned by her silence.

He took a step in her direction. "What if I stop you?"

She backed away, the bridge creaking beneath her. She gripped the handrail, tensed as lightning jagged the sky above them.

"What if I toss this in the ocean?" he asked. "Would that bother you?"

"Eddie..." she said, glancing at the notebook. She imagined it sinking to the bottom of the sea, all that work gone.

"Better yet," he said, closing on her. "What if I threw you in?"

For the first time she noticed the twitch in his temple, the way his free hand was balled into a fist. Her foot slipped, passing over the hole she'd made earlier. Shivering in the rain, she stepped over the chasm, glanced down to make sure she didn't slip again.

"I'll change those parts," she said, almost to the end of the bridge, but Eddie was too close now, no more than fifteen feet away.

His face spread in a ghastly grin. "I'll let you rewrite it," he said, shoving the notebook down the front of his shorts. "But first you have to come get it."

She felt solid earth. He neared the place where she'd fallen. She discerned the ugly glint in his eyes and hated him. He was a better-looking version of Lee Stanley, a monster like the rest of them.

He peeled off his shirt. "I liked the way you kissed me last night. How about we finish what we started?"

"Fuck you," she answered.

He bolted toward her. She turned to run, but not before she saw his body dip, the planks crumbling under his weight. She dashed ahead to put distance between them and chanced a look back at him. He had indeed fallen, but he was pulling himself out of the hole, his face a murderous mask.

The clouds had opened up, the rain assaulting the island now. Her tennis shoes slipped on the muddy trail, but in his sandals he wouldn't fare much better. Eva grinned, hitting her stride now. There was no way he would catch her.

She turned and glimpsed him bearing down on her, ten feet and closing.

With a cry she veered right and cast off into the woods. She had no idea where she was heading, but she was certain now, if he caught her, he would kill her. She leaped over a fallen tree, stumbled and nearly lost her balance. She split a pair of denuded thorn bushes and hurdled a protruding root.

Ahead she spotted an opening in the forest, the remnant of a trail maybe, and without thinking she took a hard left toward it. She grunted as her foot landed on a rock, her ankle twisting, and though she longed to curl into a ball and massage the pain away, she limped on grimly.

Eva moved through the forest, the rain pelting her face, her clothes clinging to her skin. Her eyes darted right and left, and she kept looking over her shoulder to make sure he didn't catch her from behind.

What the hell had gotten into him? Yes, she'd said some things she probably shouldn't have, but talk about overreactions…she couldn't remember being as frightened of anybody—

She looked back as Eddie appeared on the path behind her.

She dashed down the trail. She heard him laughing, coming for her. No diverging from the path now, she thought. No leaving things to chance. It would be a footrace to the castle. If she beat him, she would tell the others and who knew what would happen then. If he caught her—

He wouldn't catch her.

Eva pumped her elbows, lengthened her strides. The rain hammered the earth around her, the downpour so fierce she could hardly make out the trail. She knew Eddie was in good shape, but she was too, and she had the advantage of being terrified.

A few moments and the trees began to thin, the trail winding to an end. She knew he would be behind her, but if she stayed focused, she would make it. The trail wound right and in her periphery she distinguished a figure knifing through the woods, Eddie trying to cut her off.

She gritted her teeth, ran for dear life despite the stitch piercing her side. Eddie was almost to the edge of the forest, but so was she.

She whimpered as she watched him emerge, angling toward the mouth of the trail.

He would beat her there.

Ten feet from the edge of the woods Eva dashed off the path and sprinted toward where Eddie had left the woods.

She heard him shout something in surprise. Glancing that way, she saw him slip, land on his ass, the sandals too slick to gain purchase on the wet grass.

She broke for the castle. To her right stood the lone tower.

Fifty yards to go. She focused on the door, *Oh please, let me make it,* and Eddie appeared to her left. She was ahead of him, but not by much. He neared, his hands clutching for her. In midstride Eva whipped an elbow back and exulted in his cry of pain as it connected with his throat. Still sprinting, she saw him stumble, fall. Bellowing with rage, he gained his feet, but she was almost there. She would make it.

Hand slipping on the wet iron handle, she finally wrested the door open and lunged inside the castle. She wrenched the door shut behind her but screamed as Eddie wedged his body in the gap. She let go of the door and hurried toward the great hall, screaming for Ben and Claire, but before she could escape the foyer, he fell on her. His sweaty fetor was overwhelming. She scrabbled at the floor, frantic to escape, but he pinned her there, his weight too great to overcome.

Eva rolled over, struggling. A fist shot down and crushed her nose. She howled, the pain unlike anything she'd ever felt. Where the hell were the others?

She kneed him in the groin, cried out in triumph when his face contorted, and thrashed wildly to extricate herself.

Eva tumbled away and pushed to her feet. She darted for the great hall, but Eddie caught her from behind, lifted her. She screamed, kicked at his shins, clawed the forearms about her waist, but he would not relent. At first she thought he'd carry her back outside, but he was moving sideways across the foyer. Toward, she noted with dread, the basement door. He got it open, flipped on the overhead light, and slung her over his shoulder. He bolted the door, turned. They descended the stairs.

As they passed the wine cellar, her nostrils filled with the same dank odor she associated with her adolescence, Kathy taking her to live in a shitty apartment that was nevertheless better than the hellhole they'd been staying in. The basement of that apartment building smelled just like this. A dead mouse wedged in a pipe, its stinking guts wriggling with maggots.

The fulsome, nauseating smell worsened as they moved down a darkening hallway, headed for another flight of stairs. *The pit*, she remembered. Eva cried for help, but Eddie's grip on her legs was unbreakable. The basement grew darker, darker, the bare yellow bulb in the hall behind them growing dimmer as they advanced. She thought of the basement in that long-ago apartment building, the cobwebs and the damp.

Eva shut her eyes against it, redoubled her efforts to break free of Eddie's grasp. They moved down the murky stairs, came to another door. Eddie kicked it open, and before she could swipe at his eyes, blind him, he took a step and shoved her into the cold, black room. She landed on the back of her head, the rest of her body following. Dazed, she rolled over and watched his silhouette fill the doorway, his arms hulking at his sides, his face obscured by darkness.

"Please," she said.

"That's a good girl. Keep talking. It's better if you beg."

"*Please!*" she shrieked, praying the others would come, praying she'd hear footsteps clattering down the stairs.

"Poor baby," he said, his voice thick with lust.

He pinioned her arms to the floor, his lunatic face hovering inches above hers. Faintly, she could make out the whites of his eyes, the bleached shark's teeth. Eva shut her eyes.

"This is gonna be fun," he said. "Just pretend I'm Gabriel."

CHAPTER SIX

Ben looked up from the piano at the sound of Claire's voice. He met her at the top of the stairs. Her face was livid with worry.

"I heard screaming downstairs," she said. "It sounded like Eva."

He moved with her down the stairs. "Did she sound hurt?"

"I don't know," Claire answered. "I was in my room reading when I heard her. She sounded…I don't know. Terrified, I guess."

A vague but awful suspicion squirmed at the base of his skull. "Have you seen Eddie?"

She looked up at him as they rounded a landing. "You think he's hurting her?"

"I don't know what happened," Ben said. "It's like—"

He fell silent, not wanting to finish the thought.

Below them, a door crashed.

They reached the ground floor, moved across the foyer. An acrid trickle had begun in Ben's mouth.

"Eva?" he called.

They listened for a response. Faintly, they heard someone cry out below. He turned to Claire, who stared open-mouthed at the basement door.

Numbly, he jogged over, tried the door. Though it wouldn't open, he could hear the woman's muffled voice rising up to them.

Eva was screaming.

★ ★ ★

Eddie slapped her hard across the cheekbone, liking the way it made her whimper. Just how stupid did she think he was, writing it all down and expecting to get away with it?

"Please, Eddie," she said, crying, "please don't do this."

He reached down to free himself, but she lashed out, raked fiery lines across his brow, damned near got his eyes. He backhanded her, her nose crumpling beneath the blow, the blood spuming out over her perfect lips. She shielded her face and made pathetic keening noises. He loved the sound of it, her urgent pleading, still feeling sorry for herself. And God, the *smell* of her…salty perspiration and that delicious perfume…he inhaled another whiff of it and blew it out slowly, savoring the aroma in his nostrils. Taking his time now, he reached down, unbuttoned his shorts.

"*Please*," she gasped.

"If you insist," he said and bit her neck.

She howled, bucked beneath him, and then her fingernails were clawing at his ears, inside, *Jesus*, digging at his eardrums. He howled in pain, pulled away, then let her have it, *bam*, in the mouth. Her hands flew there, the blood bubbling over her teeth, through her fingers, and though his ears rang in agony, Eddie grappled with her. Almost…there…

Something moved in the darkness. Something in the shadows.

Eddie pushed himself up, sat on his knees. *What the hell?*

She was blubbering, making too much noise, calling his name, and he told her to shut the fuck up a second, let him listen. He heard it again, a deep animal sound, like growling only worse, like a rabid wolf snarling far back in its throat, blood lust and wrath and a desire to inflict pain.

Eva rolled onto her side, bringing her legs together and hugging them to her chest, but Eddie barely noticed. All his attention had been drawn to a spot about ten feet away, a shadow that loomed larger than the rest.

The shadow shifted and huge white eyes shuttered open.

"Oh Jesus," he said and scrambled away on feet he couldn't feel.

Let it get Eva, he thought, *please let it eat her so he could get the hell away*. Eddie lunged through the doorway and scampered up the stairs and down the hall, away from the pit. He heard pounding on the door above, but that didn't matter. What mattered was the thing behind him.

He paused as he reached the halfway point between the flights of stairs. The dull thuds of someone hammering on the locked door above made it difficult to hear the sounds coming from below, the sounds from the pit. Eddie faced the dark passageway he had just run through, listened.

Eva was crying out, screaming.

"Oh shit," he said.

He passed a hand through his hair, terrified and more than a little ill at the thought of the monstrous creature attacking her. Through Eva's cries and the pounding on the door, he heard another voice. A guttural sound in the pit.

He muttered into his fist, "Oh shit."

He walked on legs he couldn't feel, past the wine cellar. The pounding on the door was infrequent but louder, and he realized Ben was battering it with something, the boy scout coming to save the day.

He looked up, watched the door open, Ben tossing the steel wastebasket aside. Eddie started the climb, spotting Claire's stupid, shaken face behind Ben. Then the boy scout said something, he couldn't tell what. Eddie drew nearer.

"What did you do?" Ben asked.

He was blocking the doorway, Eddie now saw.

"Get out of my way."

"There's blood all over you," Ben said in a small voice. He took a step down. "Eddie, what did you do to her?"

"Get out of my way," Eddie repeated and made to move past, but Ben barred his way.

"You wanna see what happened to her?" Eddie said. "Go right ahead."

Ben stepped closer. "You're not leaving until I know what happened."

"Oh no?" Eddie said and swung an uppercut at his crotch. It got him. Jesus, what a pushover, but though Ben was doubled over, he grabbed Eddie's leg as he tried to pass.

He grasped Ben's hand and shook his leg to break away, but the stupid bastard wouldn't let go. Claire was baying like an idiot. Careful not to lose his balance – they were on the second-to-top stair – Eddie jabbed and caught Ben in the face, but rather than stopping him, Ben got both his arms on Eddie's legs and lifted, upended him. The back of his head cracked the top stair, and red spots bloomed in his vision. His head swam with the pain, but rather than taking advantage of the moment, Ben paused to gaze down the stairs. He was listening to the sounds below, Eddie realized. When Ben turned to look up at Claire in disbelief, Eddie saw his opportunity.

Before Ben could react, Eddie shot out both legs and drove him backward. For a moment, Ben's arms windmilled, but he couldn't catch himself in time to prevent the fall. Ben pitched backward, tumbled end over end down the unforgiving stone steps, Claire screaming, Ben coming to rest at the bottom of the stairs.

He lay face down, his body motionless.

* * *

Rather than throwing her down the stairs too, Eddie shoved past her and through the basement doorway. Claire hurried down the stairs and knelt over Ben. With an effort she rolled him onto his back. Her first thought was *broken neck* and that she'd been a fool for moving him, but he was still breathing, the rise and fall of his chest a sight so beautiful she allowed herself the luxury of hoping he'd live.

His eyes were shut as though he were sleeping peacefully. Examining him, she spotted an ugly crescent-shaped gash at his hairline, the blood trickling over his temple and pooling in his ear. With a palsied hand Claire tried to wipe it clean, but fresh blood flowed in its place. Worried he would die from all that blood loss, she pulled off her white top and wrapped it around his head in a makeshift turban, hoping it would staunch the flow.

She leaned over and put an ear to his chest. His heartbeat was fast but steady. She took one of his hands in hers and studied his face. She willed his eyes to open.

A sound from below choked her breath.

Eva. She'd almost forgotten about her. She could hear the woman down there wailing, and something else too. Something that made the hair stand up on the back of her neck.

Oh God, she thought. *What was it?*

She told herself she couldn't leave Ben here alone, but that was fear talking. She knew the real danger lurked in the pit. What had compelled Eva to go down—

Then she remembered.

Eddie.

Eddie had compelled her, had dragged her screaming, down through the musty old cellar to the pit. To have his way with her. To take from her what she wouldn't willingly give.

But he'd been frightened away by something. Had been, Claire remembered, frantic to escape what he'd seen.

And now Eva was alone with whatever horrible thing was making those sounds.

Claire stood on nerveless legs. She hated to leave Ben here, but what were the chances of getting him up the stairs by herself? He weighed over two hundred pounds, she would need Eva to help her. So there was really no choice at all. Besides, Eva was calling for help. Claire heard her voice clearly now. The wail coming in waves, muffled as though something were on top of her. As though…

Claire gave Ben a final backward glance as she moved past the wine cellar and stepped deeper and deeper into the darkness. No yellow bulbs down here, no light at all. The sound of Eva's voice and the other voice, a feral growl, grew louder. Eva's sobs were heartbreaking, the abject wail of the damned. The other voice, a spine-tingling combination of lust and sadistic laughter, brought a trembling hand to her throat.

Claire whimpered. She couldn't do it. She hadn't the strength to face whatever lay down there. But her feet kept shuffling forward despite the maelstrom of terror in her mind. Ahead she saw the stairs, barely discernible in the gloom. She thought of rats, of skulking, red-eyed creatures peering at her in the dark. The stairs themselves seemed to undulate like wriggling gray eels. She took a step down, Eva's cries pulsing up from the darkness like a malfunctioning police siren. The brutish male laughter, the rhythmic grunting, conjured images of rutting pigs, of a frat party gang rape.

When she reached the bottom of the stairs, she extended a hand and touched the cool iron door handle. The monstrous male voice grunted faster, louder, as though nearing its unspeakable climax. With a cry of disgust, Claire pushed open the door and sucked in air at the sight of the pair locked together on the floor, the light dim but more than enough to see by.

Eva was splayed out naked, her lean body shimmering with sweat or blood or both. The creature atop her looked like a mythological satyr, its enormous hands prying apart Eva's legs as though snapping a wishbone.

The creature turned and leered at Claire with huge white eyes. Its mouth was full of serrated teeth, the lolling tongue long and red. She covered her mouth, wanting to look away, but its face transfixed her, the face of the devil in her darkest nightmares. Protuberant brow, pointed chin. She thought she could even see curved horns jutting from its head.

Eva turned to Claire. "*Help me.*"

Claire took a step inside the pit but the creature sprang up immediately, bounding across the room like a monstrous panther. She staggered backward, arms upraised to fend the monster off, but rather than leaping on her, it grabbed the door and flung it closed with a bone-rattling *boom.*

Claire backed away from the door, hating herself for abandoning Eva, but knowing she was powerless to intercede. In that awful moment before the creature had slammed the door, Claire had seen its face, and in that moment she had experienced a terror so total and paralyzing that she could hardly summon the strength to breathe, much less escape.

The noises from the other side of the door began again, Eva's screams making Claire dig her palms into her ears, so hideous were the sounds. The monster chortled, its laughter a blasphemous dirge. Try though she might to block out the sound, it plagued her mind like lunatic blackbirds. On all fours Claire climbed the stairs, knowing she had forsaken Eva, knowing a hellish night of torture awaited the poor woman. Who knew how long Eva would be kept alive as the creature's plaything.

Weeping, Claire reached the top of the stairs and tottered down the basement hallway toward Ben's unmoving body.

CHAPTER SEVEN

The rain had let up a bit, though here on the beach it still whipped in stinging gusts. Naked, Eddie spread his arms and let the sea wind lash his body, the rain and salt spray lance his limbs, his genitals. The black clouds stretched on unabated as far as his sight would reach. It was late, but what sun there might have been at this hour had been smothered by the storm. Soon it would be full dark. Eddie closed his eyes, enjoying the tempest.

If Ben was still alive, Eddie would have to kill him. Tragic, yes, but all of them would need to die before the chopper came at month's end.

After all, allegations of attempted murder might hurt Eddie's career.

He wondered if Eva had survived whatever had happened in the pit. If she had, and if Ben did live, the three would soon begin fortifying the castle against him.

Eddie smiled. Just like medieval warfare – no guns, no help imminent.

The lone tower would be his headquarters. The padlock would be easy to break. He would spend the night there, make his plan tomorrow, then tomorrow night he'd find a way back inside the castle and pick them off, one by one.

And what about the creature? a voice in his mind asked.

Eddie dropped his arms, thinking. Whatever lurked in the pit had been pure evil, of that he was certain. He remembered its colossal size, how its horrible eyes leered at him. Eva was likely dead already. In fact, it was possible – probable even – that none of them had gotten out of the basement alive.

Eddie shivered, for the first time really feeling the cold. No matter what had already taken place, it was best to stay away from the castle until the beast was sated.

Then what about the here and now?

The tower appealed to him, yet it stood a mere thirty yards from the castle, far too close to the beast's home for Eddie's liking. There had to be some place safer, somewhere—

He turned and peered into the cave. It was the same cave in which he'd seen the child earlier.

Had there been a sound, faint but definite, coming from within?

Eddie pushed wet hair off his brow, approached cautiously. He feared seeing the child again, but he was also aching with curiosity. Yes, he could hear the sound now. Muffled, distorted.

He stepped closer, a new thought arising.

Could the child have been real? Was it possible the boy had washed ashore from some faraway shipwreck or plane crash? It was possible, wasn't it? But why would the boy live in a cave when there was a perfectly good castle in which to sleep?

The answer came immediately – the child *did* live in the castle but had fled when he'd seen visitors approaching.

The storm behind him had begun to lag, a brief respite in its relentless assault, and in the stiller atmosphere Eddie could better hear the tune playing deep within the cave. Though the song was different, its style was very much like the piece Eddie had arranged earlier and played for those unappreciative assholes in the great hall.

He closed his eyes, entranced by the music. Its lyrical, mystical lilt was more complex than the song of earlier that day. More seductive. A love song, an ode to a lady's beauty. A lightning flash followed closely by a rush of thunder propelled him deeper into the cave. The storm was about to worsen, but Eddie was safe in here. And though the cave was dark, it was not as dark as he'd expected. In fact…

Yes. He detected a faint source of light. And deep within the cave he heard the music growing stronger. Echoing, liquid. The light was also intensifying, a pale green effulgence that seemed to warm the very air of the cave. He crept forward, his bare feet padding on the cool sandy floor. Beneath the music he could hear the sound of a flowing fountain, some bubbling trickle within the cave.

He suddenly wanted – needed – to see the child, to watch him play his crude wooden flute. The memory of the boy's features rose in Eddie's mind, clarifying, until he could construct the small face, the large eyes, the dark hair. The boy, he realized, looked somewhat like him. With the thought rose a weird species of pride. Yes, there had definitely been a resemblance. Moving forward, he detected a hint of something putrescent, but it might have been his imagination.

His excitement growing, he ventured farther into the cave. The green light grew brighter, and when he rounded a corner, he beheld the thin green oval before him, the place where the cave opened up into a vast, echoing cavern. The song mesmerized him, a hymn of nature, of love. Spellbound, Eddie strode the final few steps into the cavern and realized that, yes, the child was here. He sat with his back to Eddie on the far side of a large green pool, a hidden spring of some sort that splashed and rippled under the continuous stream of water and light pouring through a gap in the center of the rock ceiling. Eddie frowned, wanting to hear the notes above the babble of the water. The stench had grown – definitely not imagination – but he knew how easily a fish could get stranded by the tide and end up bloating in some hidden grotto. He scrunched his nose and sidled around the green pool, his bare shoulder blades scraping the wall. Eddie moved carefully, worked to control his anxiousness, but several times he almost tumbled into the spring. In some spots the ledge was only five or six inches wide, and he had to curl his toes like some goddamned marsupial to grip the rock and avoid falling in.

Finally, panting with the effort, he made it around to a wider space, six or eight feet between the wall and the pool. The child was younger than he had estimated, just a toddler, really. The face was shadowed, but this close Eddie could see the bare back, and something about it made his heart thump erratically. There was something wrong with the skin, the shoulders…

Eddie took another step and felt his insides go cold.

The boy's skin was badly burned. Here and there the flesh of his little shoulders rose in crisp ridges, the roasted edges curling up in black strips. The putrid smell wafting up from the child reminded him of flyblown meat, but the worst was the cremated scent that crawled out of the blackened flesh. Sobbing, Eddie took a step back, but the boy turned and regarded him, his pink face misshapen and blistered. The lipless teeth grinned at him.

"*He's ours,*" a voice behind Eddie said, and he turned and saw her standing in the entryway. Her face was burned beyond recognition, even worse than the child's, but the voice was smooth and clear and unmistakably Lily's. She circled the pool the way Eddie had come, hemming him in.

He gasped as tiny hands pawed at his leg. He backed away from the extended arms, the horrible longing in the burned face. The child had no ears, just clotted black pits that oozed a noisome scarlet liquid. Eddie gagged and retreated, but his back scraped the low cave wall.

"*Eddie*," said a voice at his ear. He shrieked, whirling, and saw her reaching for him, *Jesus*, something dangling from the charred cleft between her legs. Maroon and yellow, it glistened, and then Eddie did vomit as he realized it was an umbilical cord.

The child bit him in the calf, the tiny teeth sinking in like serrated daggers, and Lily grabbed for him. Sobbing, Eddie dove sideways into the pool, but the child came with him, gnawing, feeding. Eddie kicked his legs but above him the surface of the pool shattered as Lily dropped on top of him, reaching.

Though out of breath he flailed to go deeper, to push away from the fiend sinking onto him, but he saw in her grin there was no escape. The child clambered up his body and met its mother at Eddie's stomach, where both began to feed.

CHAPTER EIGHT

From a vast distance Ben became aware of someone shouting, the feel of warm skin pressing his cheek. It was like climbing out of a deep well, the voice growing louder, his sense of touch returning. He was being jostled, and the voice reminded him of his mother. "*Please...please...*" the voice that wasn't his mother's was whispering. "*Please*," as though the woman didn't want to be overheard.

His eyes fluttered open. A face staring down at him. Claire's face. Her eyes were squeezed shut, tears streaming out of them. She hadn't seen he was awake yet, and he wasn't sure he wanted her to. His head ached like death and he was having trouble breathing, his chest hurt so badly. She pulled away and locked eyes with him, and her face crumpled into a grateful smile that almost made him forget how awful he felt.

"Oh thank God," she said. "We have to go Ben, we have to go now."

He couldn't imagine moving, so he closed his eyes, hoping she'd abandon the notion. But hell, she stood and hooked her arms under his. It killed his throbbing head, and using his legs made it even harder to breath, but he figured if he cooperated she might leave him alone afterward. Halfway to his feet, her strength seemed to fail, and it was just as well because a molten tide of vomit was elevatoring up his throat. He swiveled his head and puked, and was amazed she didn't drop him, instead bent him forward, supporting him as he retched again and again, despite the fact that there was nothing left to vomit. He lowered to the ground, held his left side, where it felt as if someone had punctured his lung with a railroad spike.

"We have to go, Ben," she said.

Dimly, he remembered coming from upstairs, Eva in trouble, something about Eddie. The pain grew worse. He fought back panic, but it was so hard to get air. She shook him.

"Ribs are busted," he told her. "Can't breathe."

Her terrified face appeared in front of his. "Listen," she said as if he were a child, "something has Eva. It's..." She shook her head, chin quivering. "It'll get us too if we don't get upstairs."

Upstairs, Ben thought, and raised his head enough to follow Claire's gaze up the interminable staircase. Impossible, he wanted to tell her, but she kept shaking him, and some of her urgency seemed to communicate itself to him, because he started to worry about whatever dwelled in the pit, whatever had Eva.

"Okay," he said, "okay...just hang on..."

He fought the disorientation, the burning sensation in his throat that threatened to trigger another bout of puking. A nasty pounding in his skull, he finally got to his feet, vision gauzy and full of swirling black dots. She put her arms around him, but that made his ribs scream, so he started up the staircase without her aid. The wooden handrail helped some, but the going remained slow. She stayed a step or two behind him to make sure he didn't fall.

He paused as a spate of nausea rolled through his body. God, even his toes hurt. Leaning on the handrail, his forehead resting on his hand, he became aware of a noise from below, one he hadn't noticed until now. Slowly, he pushed erect and gazed down the stairs. Then, he looked at Claire. Her mouth twisted as though she were fighting back tears. Or a scream.

"Is that what you were talking about?" he asked, knowing how dumb the question was.

She nodded, her eyes those of a child staring into a dark closet.

Ben nodded and tried not to imagine Eva down there. A shroud of guilt already haunting him, he moved with Claire up the steps.

CHAPTER NINE

From the Journal of Calvin Shepherd
July 29th, 1925
I have locked myself in my room. My reasons for doing so will unquestionably raise the eyebrows of my future readers when taken into consideration with my earlier characterizations of Gregory Blackwood.

Yes, I refer to Gregory Blackwood, the frail, androgynous creature whom I've ignored throughout his nineteen years on this earth. Alas, we have all – the adults, rather – been guilty of hardly noticing the young man up until now, and I must say that I seem to be the only one sensitive enough to note the changes in him. I have always regarded the boy with an indefinable sense of pity. Not that my soul has ever been touched by the emotion, but I can at least say that I have recognized how unhappy his life has been.

Gregory has changed.

To explain this transformation, subtle though it might be, I must first share the rather shortsighted plan concocted by Robert Blackwood and Henry Mullen to conceal our crime from the four surviving members of the youthful quintet. As scheduled, Gregory, Becca, Amarinda, and Tassee returned to the island on June the 2nd. Making no mention of the tower, Henry Mullen callously announced to Gabriel's little cult that their leader had finally been manumitted from his servitude and had been delivered safely to a seaport just north of Bodega Bay. They were outraged, of course, but the absence of their leader soon became obvious. Amarinda, the most outspoken of their band, forthwith conducted an exhaustive search of the castle and the forest. Even the caves. Robert and Henry had gambled that the youths would not include the tower in their search, and I was astounded when this gamble proved correct. Despite their determination to scour the island for their absent leader, the quartet's lifetime of conditioning to never, under any circumstance, set foot in the tower prevented them from entering.

Until this morning, that is.

As I have said, Gregory has undergone a subtle but very real alteration.

This alteration has been expressed only in the occasional offhand comment that, to the disinterested listener, would hardly be worthy of note. Perhaps you, Future Reader, will find in Gregory's comments nothing troubling. Perhaps you will conclude that I, in my heightened state of paranoia, am jumping at shadows. In any event, here are two snippets of conversation that have led me to believe that Gregory knows more than he is letting on.

At dinner last week, I was refilling Elizabeth Blackwood's water glass when I looked up and saw Gregory watching me. We regarded one another in silence for what seemed an eternity. Then, as if nothing were amiss, he nodded to his empty drinking glass.

I walked with as casual a gait as possible around the long table and endeavored to pour water into Gregory's glass. I fear my hand shook, and though it sounds idiotic, I could feel the malice rising from his gaunt body. When I had finished, I straightened and took a step toward the kitchen with the goal of refilling my pitcher, but was arrested by the following words:

"I should like some ice with my water."

Taking care to behave normally, I responded, "Of course."

Before I could escape, Gregory spoke again, "I believe you'll find it shut up in the freezer."

Ignoring the whisper of fear his choice of words conjured, I said, "Of course it is, Master Gregory, where else would it be?"

He eyed me meaningfully. "Any place tightly sealed, I should think."

I glanced from face to face to see if anyone else had taken note of this bizarre statement. Robert was staring distractedly out the window. Elizabeth, as usual, was picking at her food.

But Becca observed the exchange with an avidity that bordered on obsessive.

This incident alone would not have stretched my nerves to such a terrible pitch had it proven isolated. Yet that very night another conversation occurred that made me fear for my safety.

Robert and Elizabeth had embarked on a moonlit ramble, and I seized the opportunity to slip inside the hidden network of tunnels with the intention of eavesdropping on Gregory and the three young women. I found them in his room. Unlike they had when Gabriel was alive, the four youths remained fully clothed this time, and I must admit it was surreal watching them sitting together on the floor, talking rather than engaging in wanton behavior.

I had observed them for a goodly while without much of interest occurring when Tassee, the youngest, became very still.

Becca frowned at her. "What is it?"

"Shh," Tassee said. "Do you hear it?"

Becca shook her head and opened her mouth to answer when Gregory stilled her with a gesture. He and Amarinda had apparently heard whatever sound to which Tassee had alluded, and soon Becca seemed to hear it too. I also leaned forward to pick up the sound, but nothing at all came.

Becca was suddenly overcome with emotion. "Is it..."

"Yes," Gregory answered.

"It's true then," Amarinda said.

Though their cryptic utterances could have meant anything, I was certain they pertained to our crime.

Since that night there have been several other examples of mysterious glances and inscrutable speech, and their cumulative effect has led me to avoid human interaction except when absolutely unavoidable.

Daytime is now as menacing to me as night. It is barely noon now, and I can hardly bring myself to venture downstairs to assist in the serving of lunch. I dread Gregory's eyes. I dread his insinuating voice. This is why I have holed up in my room like some animal at bay, the feeble remnants of my—

Someone is shouting outside. I must go.

* * *

From the Journal of Calvin Shepherd
July 29th, 1925
Though I wrote to you earlier today, I feel as though an eternity has passed. Oh, Journal, when I heard the shouting voices on the castle lawn, I did what instinct bade and scampered down the stairs to see what all the commotion was about.

How was I to know what horrors my eyes would soon behold?

In the center of the lawn I perceived a host of people. I immediately made out Robert and Elizabeth, and the majority of my fellow servants. Present also was Henry Mullen, whose apelike form I couldn't mistake.

I could also see flames.

Gathered around the flickering blaze, the figures reminded me of devils in a Hieronymus Bosch canvas. As they gesticulated and shouted to make themselves heard above one another, I moved quietly into their midst. The smell of roasted meat hung in the air, and in moments I saw why.

There were four rabbits spitted on wooden stakes. The tapered ends of the pikes were poking forth from the dead creatures' mouths like swollen tongues. Someone had surrounded the macabre arrangement with tinder and what smelled like kerosene before setting the rabbits on fire.

Another voice penetrated the general din, and one by one the members of our party ceased bickering and glanced about to locate the speaker.

Because of the noonday sun, we were able to spot the culprits soon enough.

Perched atop the castle battlement, six stories in the air, was Gregory Blackwood. Becca stood to his left. On his right were Amarinda and Tassee. All four stood poised on the crenellated border of the roof. A stiff wind could have sent them tumbling to their deaths.

When Gregory spoke, I am certain my heart ceased to beat in my chest.

"*Robert, Henry, Calvin,*" he shouted. "*Your monstrous deed has brought a curse to this island.*"

His voice, once so timorous, boomed as resonant and authoritative as some military general. And though he spoke from such a dizzying height, the sound of his voice rang as clearly as if he were standing beside me on the lawn.

"*May madness here forever reign.*"

Robert Blackwood stepped forward, as if to prevent whatever terrible course of action the young people were about to take, when Gregory's voice called out one more time.

"*May the son of Hermes rise again!*"

I tried to look away as the four young people locked hands. I tried to say something even though I knew it was futile.

I watched in horror as they leapt from the battlement and fell like hailstones.

I will never forget the sound those bodies made when they hit the earth.

The rest was chaos. Robert Blackwood, normally an unfeeling pillar of callousness, sank to his knees and stared in silence at the women converging on the bodies. I did nothing, only looked on with an empty heart.

After a time, I heard a high-pitched wailing that I couldn't immediately identify. I turned and realized it was Henry Mullen, who after watching both his daughters commit suicide, was finally exhibiting a human emotion.

CHAPTER TEN

They got as far as the foyer before the pain forced him to his knees.

"Let's rest here," Ben managed to say.

But Claire was shaking him, her knitted brow unsympathetic to the monstrous pain in his side. He had never broken a rib before but knew that's what he'd done. His shortness of breath, that horrible saber piercing his innards…he just hoped a jagged shard of bone hadn't punctured his lung. If it had, he might be facing something much worse than a few weeks of primitive convalescence.

Claire shook him, oblivious to his agony.

His teeth clenched tight, he whispered, "There's no way I can make it to my room. Please…just let me—"

"I don't want to go upstairs," she said. "It's too dangerous."

He looked up at her. "Huh?"

Staring at the basement door, Claire's eyes widened. "We can't stay in the castle," she said.

"But that thing…" he said. "It didn't follow us…I don't think it can leave the basement."

"You wanna take that chance?"

He could hear the storm out there, battering the castle.

"We'll stay in the tower," Claire said.

"What?"

"The one separate from the castle," she said. "We'll break the lock." She ducked so he could wrap his arm about her neck.

But when they went out, the wind and the rain slapping their faces, Claire stopped walking.

"Oh thank God," she said, and Ben turned to see her staring up at something. His first thought was Eva, somehow escaped from whatever had gotten hold of her, and waving to them from one of the castle's windows. But when he followed Claire's gaze, he saw something that made him cry out in relief.

A helicopter, floating toward them over the forest.

Claire broke into a run as the chopper began its descent. Ben hobbled after her as fast as he could, and as he drew nearer he glimpsed something so unbelievable he was certain this was another dream. A wonderful dream, to be sure, but a dream all the same.

Joshua was peering at him through the cockpit window, his little fingers pressed against the glass.

Twenty feet ahead, Claire smiled over her shoulder at him. "He looks like you," she yelled through the rain.

Ben spoke his son's name, took a step forward, the tears of joy already welling in his eyes, when the chopper abruptly dipped, its whirring rotor tilting sickly toward the castle.

Claire froze. Then she was sprinting toward him, shouting for him to look out, but he rushed toward the helicopter, which was now veering sideways, its spinning rotor perpendicular to the ground. Ben stopped and screamed as the blade nicked the lawn, furrowed a muddy trench, then shattered in a deadly hail of shards. A section of broken blade longer than his arm came tumbling end over end at him. It whizzed by, a foot from his face. What remained of the chopper slammed, propeller first, into the castle's stone façade, the fuselage ripping apart, then it lay on its side writhing like an animal in its death throes.

"*Joshua!*" he bellowed.

And within the helicopter, the screaming began.

PART FIVE GABRIEL

CHAPTER ONE

From the Journal of Calvin Shepherd
October 13th, 1925
Tonight the music started again.

We were in the dining room when we heard it. Henry Mullen sat opposite Elizabeth, with Robert at the head of the table. I was leaning over, in the process of taking away Robert's uneaten salad, when those first unmistakable notes from Joseph Blackwood's *The Sorrows* shattered the stillness of the evening. The music turned me to stone, and when I glanced down and noticed Robert's furious expression, I was somewhat reassured it was all a distasteful joke, some servant – who would be lucky to escape the affront with her life – tinkling out the exact notes Gabriel had often played during that last terrible month of his life, the month of his imprisonment in the tower.

Discarding his napkin and throwing back his chair, Robert stalked from the room with Mullen close behind. Elizabeth had not moved, the laudanum to which she has grown addicted since the deaths of her children rendering her well-nigh catatonic. I left the salad bowl behind and followed the others out.

I had thought the music was coming from the great hall, but when I joined Robert and Mullen there, I realized the hall was untenanted. Mullen turned with the obvious intention of climbing the stairs when Robert stilled him with a whispered oath. Indeed, we all ceased moving – ceased breathing – as we traced the sound to its source.

Since the walling up of Gabriel and the suicides of Gregory and the girls, I had not experienced any real emotion save a black resignation. Whether I lived one more hour or thirty more years, I knew what the afterlife had in store for me, and I knew that no amount of penance could undo what evil I had committed.

But now, for the first time in months, I was gripped by a new emotion.

Sheer, unadulterated horror.

Going outside, we joined the remaining servants – the majority of them fled after the suicides of this summer – who were gathered on the castle lawn, staring fixedly up at the tower. This then was the point of origin, the impossible but undeniable birthplace of the ghastly melody.

Without thinking, I followed the two men up the spiral staircase. The music grew louder, louder, damning us with each note, threatening us with unspeakable retribution. When we reached the top, we saw the wall was still intact.

We knew already that the windows were barred, and what we now beheld made clear that there was no physical means in or out.

Yet it was from the keep that the music came.

"Which one of you is responsible for this?" Robert asked, glancing from me to Mullen with a venomous hatred.

"You know it wasn't us," Mullen said. "The wall's still here."

"Don't lie to me, you fool. The two of you tore it down and rebuilt it."

I finally found my voice. "We didn't touch—"

A blow to the face ended my protest.

"Sir," I heard Mullen say as I lay on the floor, "you have to see it can't—"

"I only see the two of you after my wealth," Robert hissed. "You think now that I am childless I will leave my fortune to you."

Thunder darkened Mullen's brow. "You'd be smart to watch your tongue, Mr. Blackwood."

"How dare you—" Robert started to say but stopped when the huge man seized and lifted him by the lapels. Robert slapped at Mullen's face, but the brute slammed him into the wall and held him there. I marveled at the sight of my master's shoes, which hung suspended three feet off the ground.

"I shall leave in the morning," Mullen growled, "and if you refuse to pay me the wages I have coming, I'll kill you before I go."

With that he dropped Robert, who collapsed in an ungainly heap, and tromped down the stairs. Red-faced with anger and humiliation, Robert soon rose and followed Mullen out. Terrified to find myself alone in the tower, I too escaped and took refuge in my quarters.

And through it all the music had not ceased.

CHAPTER TWO

Ben knew the voices were screaming, but he could barely hear them over the ringing in his ears. Blue flames had flashed briefly, but now the only sign of fire was a steady puff of smoke rising from the mangled fuselage.

Numbly, he made it to the twisted pile of metal and for a moment had no idea where to look. Beneath the acrid smoke scent he picked up melting plastic, scorched vinyl, and something he dared not linger on too long. Something that reminded him of childhood barbecues.

Through the high-pitched ring needling his ears and the crackle of smoldering wires, he made out a pair of male voices. Neither of them Joshua's. He climbed onto a torn sheet of metal and discerned a sooty face below.

"Get me out," Chris Blackwood said.

Ben ignored the extended hand and climbed down into the cockpit, where the pilot was slumped in his chair.

He peered through the smoke and saw that the man was dead. A flap of forehead hung loose over the pilot's eyes, the sparkle of shattered glass decorating his body like rhinestones.

Oh Jesus, Ben thought, *oh Jesus, where is Joshua*?

The smoke made his throat tickle and burn. He pressed an arm over his mouth, but it did little good. Something brushed his shoulder, and he turned to see Ryan's face peering at him from the shadows of the back seat. The man's face was stippled with either blood or oil. Ben's money was on the former.

"Is he back there?" Ben shouted.

Ryan gazed at him uncomprehendingly.

His heart in his throat, Ben climbed over the seat and saw a body on the floor. It was dark and there was too much smoke, so he reached down and put a hand on the figure to make sure it wasn't somehow his son. The figure stirred.

Lee Stanley.

"*Help me goddammit*," a hoarse voice demanded. Chris Blackwood again, pleading from the front of the chopper. Ben climbed over Lee's unconscious form and drew even with Ryan, who sat dazed against the wall.

Close by, Ben perceived another body. Kayla.

He put a hand on her shoulder. Distantly he noted how warm Kayla was, her steady breathing, but he had to find his Joshua. Had the boy been thrown clear of the crash? Had he been hit by the whirling propeller? Ben let out a harsh sob. *Oh Christ, if he—*

He froze at the sound of a faint moan. *Joshua.*

Sucking in air, Ben crawled over Kayla's body and stared over the back seat. There, like a discarded rag doll, lay his son. Joshua's legs were pressed against the seat back, the space in which he lay too small for even his tiny body. Ben pushed forward, a sparking wire scoring his arm, and grabbed hold of the boy's waist. Then, his ribs screaming in pain, Ben hauled Joshua out of the gap and cradled him. In the darkness he could see a gash in the boy's forehead, the hair matted and shiny. But Joshua was breathing, his head twisting from side to side as if he were having a nightmare.

Ben was rising from the seat, ducking under a piece of torn metal, when someone screamed. He turned and saw Ryan staring at something a few feet away. Keeping Joshua's unconscious form pressed tightly against his shoulder, Ben followed Ryan's gaze to the far corner of the mangled hull.

Oh no, he thought.

It was no wonder Ben hadn't seen his ex-wife before now. In the swirling chaos of the crash, she had somehow been trapped in a corner between the seat and the wall. When the chopper had crashed against the castle, she'd been pinned. He crept toward Jenny's unmoving form, careful not to jostle his son too much, and he was almost upon his ex-wife before he noticed the blood that had spilled down her front, the dark crimson stain on the seat between her legs.

Her chin lay on her chest as though she'd nodded off before the crash. Ben drew closer and lifted the pretty heart-shaped chin and felt his gorge rise. The crash had slammed a nasty shard of sheared metal the size of a boomerang into her throat, its sharp point embedded where her Adam's apple should have been. *Shrapnel* was the word that sprang to mind. She'd been slain by a whizzing piece of shrapnel. The wound was ragged, gory. Almost as though she'd wrestled to remove it from her ruined throat.

Ben looked away and whispered, "I'm sorry," into his son's hair. "I'm so sorry, Joshua."

Breath quavering in his nostrils, he stepped over the middle seat and heard Ryan say something, but Ben kept moving, determined to remove Joshua from this metal tomb before it caught fire.

"Where're you going?" Ryan asked.

"I'm getting Joshua inside," he said, "I'll be back for Kayla."

"*You can't leave me here*," Ryan said, a childish tremor in his voice.

"Just hold on."

It took a tremendous effort to navigate the sparking wires and the sharp metal edges, but he managed to lift his son through the hole where the side door had once been. The rain assaulted them both, and though he wished he could cover his son's face, he knew the wet would do him no harm. He laid Joshua out on what felt like a smooth part of the shell, then climbed out himself. Chris Blackwood's pleading voice rose again, but Ben ignored it. Swinging his legs over the edge of the wreck, he slid down, reached up and lowered Joshua into his arms. Then he staggered away from the crash, in the direction of Claire, who was alive and seemingly unharmed. She was holding her arm, but she was on her feet and moving in his direction.

"You okay?" he asked as they drew closer.

She nodded, but Ben could see the blood bubbling between her fingers. The gash in her arm must have been deep. She stared at Joshua, reached out to shield the boy's face from the stinging rain. Then her face was twisting, mistaking the boy's unconsciousness for death.

"Claire," he said.

She peered up at him, and though it was almost full dark on the island, he could still see the concern in her eyes.

Ben said, "He might be hurt…I don't know. But he's alive."

She shut her eyes in relief, then took a step toward the castle.

"Wait," he said. "We can't go in there."

"We have to," she said.

He searched her wet face, the truth of her statement sinking in.

She put a hand on his arm. "Come on."

He stopped. "There are others in there."

"Then we have to get them inside."

He squeezed the boy's frail body against his, thought of the laceration on his head, thought of Kayla, unconscious. And then there were Ryan, Chris Blackwood, Lee Stanley to think about. He and Claire would need water, light to work by. Medicine, if any could be found.

Claire shivered in the storm, the driving, nearly horizontal rain.

"Okay," he said. "We'll get you and Joshua inside. I'll come back for the others."

CHAPTER THREE

From the Journal of Calvin Shepherd
October 14th, 1925
We found Mullen's body this afternoon.

No one mentioned his absence at breakfast. After the meal I accompanied Robert to the docks to see if Mullen had made good on his promise to set sail for California, but the boat remained moored in its place. A cold drizzle had begun to fall, so I was appalled by Robert's demand that I remain posted by the dock in case Mullen should try to commandeer the vessel. When my master vanished into the forest, I climbed aboard the boat determined to at least remain warm while I awaited the coming of a man I suspected was dead.

How, you might ask, did I come to this conclusion? My answer is simple, though I don't expect anyone to accept it.

The music from the tower has continued unabated since its recommencement yesterday evening, and during that time I have experienced a growing desire to end my pathetic existence. The careful reader might note that I have never harbored suicidal thoughts. No, even in my blackest moments I have not toyed with the prospect of taking my own life, but since the recurrence of Gabriel's playing – for who else could it be? – I have experienced an overpowering desire to slip a noose around my neck, to retrieve Robert's pistol from his bureau drawer and shove the barrel in my mouth. Dear Journal, I have even daydreamed about following Gregory Blackwood's example and leaping from the battlement.

Thusly, it was no surprise when I returned from the docks to find all gathered outside Henry Mullen's quarters, ashen-faced and silent.

I pushed through the small crowd of women and beheld the ghastly sight.

The man's fingers were buried in what remained of his throat. He had clawed through his skin, through tendon and sinew, through his now-visible windpipe. And just as hideous as the sight of his mutilated throat was the look of absolute horror frozen on his face. His eyes were huge, terrified moons, his mouth stretched wide in a soundless shriek.

Will I be next?

CHAPTER FOUR

By the time Ben got everyone out of the wreck and into the great hall, Kayla was awake. She was crying – evidently someone had broken the news about Jenny – but she seemed physically intact.

Joshua was still unconscious.

Ben stroked the boy's forehead and whispered to him. Every few seconds he would kiss the boy, whose bottom lip was split, his throat peppered with dull, yellowish bruises. Ben kissed him again, crying now himself.

A voice behind him said, "Concussion."

Ben stared up at Ryan.

"Other than that, he doesn't seem injured," Ryan said. "His breathing's all right, anyway."

Ben rubbed one of Joshua's hands and examined the cut on his head. Claire had dabbed some of the blood away with a washcloth, but a red stain still tinged his hair.

"Do you know anything about medicine?" Ben asked.

"Some," Ryan answered. "I've taken first aid classes, read a lot about what to do in case of injury."

Ben glanced at the couch a few feet away, where Claire held his stepdaughter, and wondered how on earth he'd break the news to Joshua.

Ryan limped over to the couch where Kayla and Claire sat clutched together. The pilot put a hand on Kayla's shoulder and lowered his head. Ben felt no stirring of suspicion, experienced no hatred, when only a day ago he'd been ready to murder the man with his bare hands.

It was only a dream, he told himself. *Look at the guy now. He's heartbroken.*

Ben said, "Why did you come?"

Kayla gestured at Joshua. "It's his fault. He had to make sure you were all right."

Ben glanced at Ryan. "What's she talking about?"

Ryan shook his head. "He's been out of his mind since you left. It started the first night – he woke up screaming, and nothing we could say could convince him…"

Claire asked, "What did he think was wrong?"

Ryan eyed her in silence. "He claimed his dad was going to die."

Ben felt a mental chill.

"Did he say how?" Claire asked.

"What does that have—"

"*Please*," Claire said. "It's important."

Ryan shrugged impatiently. "I don't know…he kept saying the monster was going to get Daddy…some monster with horns."

Ben thought of Eva, of the creature Claire had described.

From across the hall, Chris Blackwood asked, "Where are the others?"

Ben glanced at Claire, who looked like she might be sick. The bandage around her arm was soaked through with blood.

"Hello?" Chris said. "Where are Blaze and the other girl…what's her name?"

"Eva," a voice said.

They all turned and saw that Lee Stanley was awake and lying on his side. He looked like hell, but like Kayla, he seemed to have survived the crash unscathed.

"Where is she?" Lee asked.

Ben opened his mouth, but Claire said, "She's in the basement."

"The basement," Lee said.

Claire told them the story. Ryan and Kayla listened nervously, but Lee was frowning. Chris Blackwood looked as though he might faint.

When she finished, Lee said, "You expect me to believe all that?"

"I don't care what you believe."

"If it didn't follow you out of the basement," Chris said, "maybe it can't leave…maybe it has to stay down there."

Claire nodded. "That's what we're hoping."

Lee laughed. "What a crock of shit."

"Why are you here?" Claire asked him. Not very kindly, Ben noticed.

Lee nodded at Chris. "Because I was dumb enough to listen to this moron. I wanted to see if you guys had anything for me yet, so I paid him twenty grand for a ride out here."

"He only charged us ten," Ryan said.

Lee glared at Chris. "What the fuck?"

"You didn't have to pay it," Chris said, but his face was sullen.

"That's right," Lee said, sitting up. "And the goddamn pilot you hired wasn't even smart enough to land the fucking chopper. I'm going to sue your ass for everything—"

"We ran out of fuel," Ryan said.

They all looked at him.

"The engine started to sputter as we neared the island," he said. "When we were about to touch down, it stopped altogether."

"The pilot some kinda moron?" Lee asked. "Who the hell forgets to fill a helicopter with gas?"

Ryan shook his head. "That's what happened."

Chris's mouth fell open and he uttered a pained moan.

Ben said, "What is it?"

Chris sat back, covered his face with his hands.

"What the hell?" Lee said. "Let us in on the secret."

Chris sat forward, slid shaking hands through his blond hair. "I don't believe it," he said. "That son of a bitch."

Lee threw up his arms. "Jesus Christ, would someone tell me what the—"

"Granderson," Chris said.

Lee shrugged. "Who the fuck is Granderson?"

Chris was staring at Ben now. "Granderson refused to fly the helicopter, but he said if I found a guy to fly it, he'd get it ready for us. I was right there when he told Robbie—"

"Robbie?" Ben asked.

"The pilot," Chris said. "A guy I knew. He didn't have a helicopter, but he agreed to take mine."

Lee waved a hand dismissively. "What a bunch of crap."

"Not really," Ryan answered. "When you're flying over the Pacific, there's nowhere to land. All this guy Granderson had to do was make sure there wasn't much gas in the tank. Then, we'd either die on the way here or the way back." Ryan laughed bitterly. "Actually, we were lucky. Had we run out five minutes earlier none of us would have lived."

For a fleeting moment, Ben perceived a glimmer of the dream Ryan, of the fiend who'd threatened to bury Joshua in the ravine. Then the man's mouth began to quiver, and he dissolved into tears.

Lee Stanley rose, leaned against the huge fireplace. "Why would this guy want you dead?"

"Why does anybody want anybody dead?" Chris asked. "He wants my money."

Lee's grin was vicious. "I thought you didn't have any money."

Chris didn't say anything to that.

Ben looked at Kayla, who listened to it all with a kind of quiet fascination. He said to her, "Maybe you should lie down."

She tilted her face, eyebrows raised. "Maybe you should leave me alone."

Same Kayla, he thought, but something in him ached.

Ryan put his arm around her. "Take it easy, he's just trying to help."

Despite the words, Ben's unease grew.

"It's his fault we're out here," Kayla said. "Him and his precious son. If it wasn't for them, Mom would still be alive."

He saw Claire watching Kayla. She glanced at Ben, and her eyes communicated the thought clearly. *She's worse than you said.*

For the first time in hours, Ben smiled.

Kayla sniffed and looked at Ryan. "We have to get Mom."

Ryan made a pained face. "Kayla..."

"She's right," Ben said.

He felt their eyes on him.

"I'll do it," he said, then turned to Claire. "Will you stay with Joshua?"

Before the words were out of his mouth, she rose and took his place. The pain in his side was returning, his breath coming in quick, insufficient gasps. He kissed Joshua on the cheek and rose with an effort. The boy's hair smelled heartbreakingly like a camp fire. On the way out of the room, he heard a voice say, "Wait."

He looked back and saw Ryan shuffling toward him, the pant leg that had been trapped under the seat a mess of bloody ribbons.

"I'll help you get her out," he said.

Ben nodded but refused to give the guy more than that. Maybe he wasn't what Ben had suspected. Maybe he was just someone Ben resented because he'd taken his place in his son's life.

But Ryan hadn't touched Joshua once while they were in the great hall. Only Kayla. Even after the girl had regained consciousness and showed she was well enough to shout at Ben, Ryan had stayed by her side, the caressing hand almost never leaving her shoulder.

While the three-year-old boy lay unconscious on the couch.

CHAPTER FIVE

Chris took a deep breath, the leather-bound journal in his hand feeling far heavier than it actually was. He knocked, and after a minute, Lee Stanley appeared in a silky, green smoking jacket. Chris didn't know men still wore smoking jackets. Maybe it was just directors.

"You really bent me over," Stanley said. "Twenty grand for a goddamn helicopter ride."

"We need to talk," Chris said, and when the man didn't step aside, he added, "It'll only take a minute."

Stanley sighed, but moved just enough to let him in. Shutting the door, Stanley said, "I better get a fucking refund, buddy. You gimme that and my lawyer might take it easy on you."

Chris sat in the chair next to the bed and raised the book so Lee could see it. "I read this journal, diary, whatever you call it, when I was fourteen. Something really bad had already happened…" He shook his head. "I don't really want to talk about that, but because of what happened, I was hiding from my folks. I ended up in one of the servant's rooms, the one where our…" He swallowed. "…our maid had been staying. I found this in a trunk under her bed." He tapped the leather cover.

Eyeing the journal, Stanley lit a cigar. The rich, spicy smell of it rolled over Chris's nostrils in a smothering wave.

Chris went on. "It's the true story about what happened here back in the twenties. It was written by the servant of my great-grandfather."

Stanley stepped forward, reached out.

Chris pulled it back. "If you decide to use it, make it into a movie, I want two million."

Stanley sucked on his cigar, gave him a twitchy nod. "I mean, we'll see, right? If it's good enough, you never know." He reached for the journal.

Chris held it against his chest. "The truth is, this was the real reason I called you yesterday."

Stanley put his hands on his hips. About to erupt, Chris could see.

Before he could, Chris said, "The other part was true…I did need the money, and you did want to hear the progress on your score, but—"

"I haven't heard shit," Stanley said around his cigar. "Eddie Blaze is MIA and Shadeland is too wrapped up in his kid to think about the movie."

"I know you're frustrated," Chris said, "but I'm telling you…once you've read this thing…" He tapped the cover. "*This* is going to be your next movie."

Stanley's eyes narrowed to slits. The man blew out smoke, went over to the window. "You never know, right? A movie needs a good setting, and sets cost a lot of money." He glanced back at Chris. "Now, if I could shoot a film on a location like this…"

"That's not a problem."

Stanley approached. "Lemme read it first, okay?"

Reluctantly, Chris handed him the journal.

Stanley eyed the brown-ridged cover. "It's old."

"The servant began writing it over a hundred years ago."

"No shit?"

"No shit."

Stanley nodded. He carried the journal over to his bed, reached down and picked up a pair of reading glasses. He looked up at Chris. "If you don't mind."

Chris rose and went out. On the way to his room he thought he heard a woman's voice, screaming in pain, but he told himself it was the wind. Unbidden, an image of Rosa, his family's ill-fated maid, impressed itself on his mind.

Ill-fated my ass, a voice muttered. *More like murdered in cold blood.*

He slipped into his room and gazed at the wainscoted wall. The whorled wood grain peered back at him in fathomless black hunger.

He'd begun to gnaw on a fingernail when he heard the woman's voice scream again.

It definitely wasn't the wind this time.

CHAPTER SIX

"There it is again," Claire said.

Ben nodded, wished he had a pair of earmuffs to put on Joshua, something to shelter him from the noise. The boy looked unconscious, but who knew what he really heard.

Again the scream sounded. If Eva was still in the pit, she was six stories below them; yet it sounded as if she were in the hall right outside their door wailing in agony, begging to be let in.

With every scream something in him grew, and though he knew it was crazy, he knew just as well that there was only one real course of action.

"Wait here a minute," he said.

Claire watched him get up, her expression miserable, but she didn't protest.

He said at the door, "Lock it when I leave."

She nodded and he went out.

He rushed down to Chris Blackwood's room and knocked. When no answer came, he knocked louder, banging until the side of his fist ached.

"Who is it?" Chris asked.

"Ben. Let me in."

"I'm turning in for the night."

"No you're not."

A pregnant pause, the guy debating. What a snake.

The door opened just enough for them to make eye contact. "Can it wait?" Chris asked. "It's been kind of a shitty day."

Ben resisted an urge to reach out and throttle him. He said, "My son lost his mother this evening, and he's still not responsive. I know how bad the day has been."

Chris hunched his shoulders as the scream erupted again. "Holy shit," he muttered.

"It's Eva," Ben said. "She needs help."

"What the hell happened to her?"

Ben forced down the geyser of fear threatening to douse his resolve.

"I didn't see it," he said. "Claire can tell you more."

Another scream, impossibly loud.

Chris swallowed. "I'm not going down there."

"I don't need you to—"

"Good night," Chris said and made to close the door.

Ben shouldered the door open and jerked Chris forward so they were nose to nose. "I need you to stay with Joshua and Claire while I'm gone."

Chris relaxed a little. "Oh, all right…I mean, if you need someone…"

"Come on." Ben dragged him into the hall.

When they were back in his room, Claire said, "You can't do this."

She hadn't left Joshua's side. It reassured him. Even if Chris was worthless as tits on a boar, Claire would protect his son.

Ben sat on a chair tying his shoes. He wished he had a pistol, but he'd never owned one, had never even fired anything more powerful than a pellet gun.

Chris said, "You taking Ryan with you?"

Ben shook his head. "I don't know if I can trust him." He got up, went over to his boy. He bent and kissed his cheek.

Claire said, "She's beyond help now, you need to stay here with—"

Eva's wailing cut her off.

When it dissipated, he said, "This could go on all night. Somebody's got to help her."

"What about Lee?" she asked.

Ben couldn't imagine Lee Stanley being much help, even if the man wanted to. Of course, if Stanley did get killed attempting to help Eva, Ben would be off the hook for the score.

"I'll go alone," he said.

At the door he looked back and saw Joshua and Claire on the bed. Chris was staring uselessly out the window. Ben thought of going to Claire, planting one on her lips, turning it into some kind of cheesy movie moment – the hero kissing the girl before venturing into harm's way.

The problem was, he didn't feel heroic. In fact, the more he thought about it, the more frightened he felt. He was impotent against whatever horror he was about to encounter and stupid for endangering himself when he was all Joshua had left. He shut the door before he could talk himself out of it.

In the kitchen he rummaged through drawers, scanned the knives and various implements for a weapon. Under the sink he found a carving knife with a rubber handle that felt good in his hand.

He regarded the knife a moment, what little courage he had flagging. A gun was too much to hope for, but he had to do better than this.

He flinched as another scream lanced his eardrums. The knife in his hand suddenly reminded him of a kid's toy, worthless against whatever he was about to face.

Then he remembered the storage area behind the castle. He jogged outside and found the wooden door, a rusty padlock barring entry. He scanned the ground with the flashlight and picked out a good-sized rock. He hefted it and bashed the padlock until the hasp popped open.

Sliding the door aside, he aimed the flashlight's beam at the wall opposite. Between a shovel and a rake hung a chainsaw. Below that and to the left, an axe. Ben had only used a chainsaw once, when he'd cut straight into the side of a tree and gotten the arm of the saw stuck. Then, trying to free the chain from the ruined arm, he'd sliced his knuckle to the bone. It'd required seven stitches, but at least, the doctor had said, the chainsaw hadn't been running when it happened.

Ben chose the axe.

The knife held in a belt loop of his jeans, his hands occupied by the flashlight and the axe, Ben went back inside and stood in the foyer, listening to the sounds coming from the basement. This close, he could hear not only Eva's shrieks of pain, but another voice as well. Deep, throaty. A merciless chortle that sent his pulse racing.

Ben tested the flashlight, eyed the axe blade.

Quit stalling.

He opened the basement door and descended the stairs.

⋆ ⋆ ⋆

Chris sat reading one of Ben's books. *Dark Gods* by T.E.D. Klein, Claire saw. Joshua's eyes had ceased rolling under his closed lids, and his breathing had grown steadier. Making sure she kept her voice low, Claire said, "Are you a horror fan?"

Without looking up, Chris said, "I'm not a big reader."

What a shock, she thought.

"That's one of my favorites," she said. "The author too, even though he only wrote a couple books."

Chris grunted noncommittally.

The silence was unbearable. "Which story are you reading?" she asked.

He glanced at the top of the page. "'Black Man with a Horn,'" he answered.

"I love that one," she said. "That and 'Petey.'"

He didn't answer.

She reached down, caressed Joshua's temple with the washcloth. The boy looked like a miniature version of his father. The chin, the nose, even the dark hollows under his eyes.

She gasped as Eva screamed again. As the scream drew out, she looked at Chris, whose face had paled even though he pretended to be engrossed in the book.

"Have you gotten to the part with the aliens yet?" she asked.

"Yeah."

"There aren't any aliens in that story."

He tossed the paperback aside and walked over to the window.

She said, "Joshua and I are okay here you know. Maybe you should go down and help Ben."

He laughed. "Not a chance."

"Would you go if I paid you twenty grand?"

He stiffened.

She combed the boy's hair with her fingers. "Of course," she went on, "you could do it because it's the right thing. It might be a nice change for you."

He turned and she realized that rather than being incensed at her words, he was on the verge of tears. He walked to the door and went out.

Alone with the sleeping boy, she regretted her sarcasm. Chris Blackwood wasn't much, but he was better than nothing.

★ ★ ★

Ben's bladder throbbed. He should have urinated outside because now he couldn't imagine laying down the axe long enough to relieve himself. He'd just have to wait. He glanced back at the wine cellar's door, the stairs leading up to the foyer. What was he doing here?

He almost dropped the axe as the scream exploded again. It sounded like Eva had already gone over to the spirit world. How else to explain the preternaturally loud noises erupting from her mouth?

And the other sound…oh man. He trailed a trembling wrist across his lips. It sounded like the devil himself.

He hadn't switched on the flashlight yet, a fear of dead batteries convincing him to use it judiciously. Ahead, the dank corridor darkened, the soot-colored walls slowly eaten away by shadow. He forced his legs to continue forward, though they seemed to have more sense than he did. He imagined his knees knocking together like some cartoon, but the vision did nothing to cheer him.

At the top of the final stairwell he threw another yearning glance at the yellow light that now seemed a mile away.

Please, he thought. *Please let me survive this. Please don't leave Joshua without a father.*

Please.

Ben went down on legs that wobbled. Halfway to the bottom he switched on the flashlight. He continued on, aiming the beam at the drab-gray door leading to the pit. Its hulking girth beckoned him forward, slyly insisting he'd be fine if he just stepped inside.

Eva cried out again, but this time Ben discerned a few words in her anguished screaming, "…please…away…no more…"

In answer Ben heard the satanic rumble, "*Lie still!*"

At the sound of the awful voice, Ben's whole body went limp. Dimly, he realized his bladder was close to giving way.

Some hero, he thought. *I'm here to rescue you, Eva. Too bad I forgot my diaper.*

Ben reached the landing. His shoes squeaked as he neared the door. He hoped the sound wouldn't give him away.

He reached for the handle, then paused when he realized he had no plan. He couldn't hold the flashlight, open the door, spot the creature, run forward and swing the axe all at the same time.

Ben shoved the flashlight down the front of his jeans. He lifted the axe and rested it on his shoulder, as if he were walking to the on-deck circle.

The demonic voice grunted, a questioning sound, and Ben realized whatever was in the pit was aware of his presence outside the door. As if to confirm this, there came a scuttling patter from within, the sound, Ben realized with new terror, of hooves on concrete. He stood debating, a long-forgotten smell wafting under the door to his nostrils. A neighboring family had owned several large dogs and had kept them in a small indoor kennel. This smelled like that kennel – pungent and eye-watering, the mingled odors of fur and fecal matter.

"Hello?" Eva called. "Is someone there?"

Ben shifted, and as he did, the head of the axe bumped the door.

Whatever composure had been contained in Eva's first questions vanished entirely. "*Oh please come help me, it's safe now he went away please!*"

His breathing shallow and weak, Ben grasped the handle and pulled the heavy door open. He shifted the axe to his right hand. The kennel smell assaulted him, made him cough. Sure at any moment the creature would slam him to the ground and plunge its talons into him, Ben removed the flashlight from his waistband and aimed it at the ground with a badly shaking hand. He picked out a bare leg, a hip drenched in blood, slid the beam up Eva's glistening body until he distinguished her face, staring hopelessly up at him from the floor.

"Help me," she said.

Ben moved forward, his entire body quaking, and placed the axe beside her. He bent and hoisted her onto his shoulder. Ignoring her anguished moans, he grasped the axe. He rushed forward, astonished the creature hadn't attacked yet. He was sure the door would close before he got there.

But the door did not close.

Eva's limp body bounced on his shoulder as he burst through the doorway, moaning now himself.

He made it halfway across the landing before he heard the voice say, "I want the boy."

Ben stood rigidly. He knew it was madness to do anything but dash up the stairs, but the wheedling cruelty in the voice, the obscene hunger forced him to turn, to rest the axe against his leg and raise the flashlight beam to the rectangle of darkness they had just escaped.

There, standing just inside the doorway, he saw the gaping white eyes, a face neither human nor animal, the dark hair cascading down muscled shoulders.

The curving goat horns.

Ben dropped the flashlight and fumbled for the axe.

The creature came for him, snarling, and Ben let Eva fall. Before he could raise the axe, the beast leapt through the darkness and smashed him against the stairs. The razor-like teeth snapped, clicking together, and Ben jerked his head to the side to avoid them. The keen blades of its talons harrowed his chest, the side of his neck. In desperation Ben shot a knee between its legs, heard the beast grunt in pain. He shoved out from under it. As he backed toward the door of the pit, he reached down, feeling for the axe handle, not allowing himself to look away from the creature even for a moment.

His fingers brushed the axe head. The creature leapt at him.

Ben ducked and sharp claws scored the middle of his back as the beast passed over him. The beast hit the doorframe and faced him on all fours, roaring in fury. Ben lifted the axe, cocked it, and swung just as he thought the beast was coming forward. But the creature sidestepped nimbly as the blade whistled by its chest, Ben going with it, thrown completely off balance by the force of his swing. He landed on top of the axe, and was just able to roll onto his back, the axe handle held before him to ward off the creature as it fell on him. The handle shoved against its throat, its strong jaws opened and closed, the hot slaver spattering Ben's face, the kennel smell overwhelming. Ben's arms were weakening, the creature's face snapping ever closer, and for an insane moment he could see the sharp cheekbones, the too-human expression in its caprine face. Ben jerked up a knee to slam the creature in the genitals again, but it shifted sideways and he only caught its thigh. The teeth lunged and Ben felt fire erupt in his ear. With a frantic shove, he got the beast off balance, thrashed from beneath its weight. He stood, clutching the axe, and heard the beast snarl. They were too close for Ben to get a full swing, but as it lunged for him he brought the axe around sideways in a short, swift arc and cried out in savage triumph as it crunched into the creature's side.

The demonic voice bellowed, the creature clutching the axe in its ribs. Ben dashed forward, gathered Eva in his arms, and hustled up the stairs. He didn't like the way her head flopped, but he didn't dare shift her to his shoulder, there wasn't time. As he ran he tried not to see how horribly she'd been assaulted, but as the light grew, more and more of the carnage revealed itself. Behind him he heard the axe clatter as the creature removed it. The clacking sounds that followed, he knew, were the hooves hammering the steps. Ben raced down the hall toward the final flight of stairs. Eva's body hung limply, the woman maybe unconscious, and she was growing heavy, so heavy in his arms. Ben mounted the steps and threw a feverish glance over his shoulder.

And wished he hadn't.

In the increased light the beast was even more hideous, and far more man than animal. Its hairy body was rippled with muscles, its grin a blasphemous marriage of virility and sadism.

If it got them, it wouldn't kill them quickly.

Ben looked up despairingly and realized how far they had to go before they reached the ground floor. An eternity of stairs. And behind them, the thing approaching fast. They'd never make it.

And he'd left the axe behind.

He gasped as the door above him opened, a frightened face squinting down at them.

Chris Blackwood.

"Help us," Ben called.

The man nodded, jogged down the steps.

Then went rigid when the beast laughed.

"*Please*," Ben said, his legs failing.

Chris shambled down the steps but kept his eyes on the landing Ben had just vacated. They met halfway.

Ben said, "Take her," and transferred Eva to Chris's shoulder.

"*You!*" the voice thundered.

Ben turned and beheld the creature staring up at Chris from the foot of the stairs. The recognition in its face chilled Ben to the core. Behind him Chris moaned.

"Go," Ben said.

When Chris just stood and gaped at the beast, Ben shoved him, "*Go!*"

Chris whirled and moved up the stairs, Eva's body jostling with every step. Ben followed, but he didn't dare take his eyes off the creature, which stood unmoving at the base of the stairs.

The large eyes never leaving Chris Blackwood's ascending form.

Ben sucked in breath as he bumped into something – Chris and Eva. "*Move*," he demanded. The creature was still watching from the landing, but Ben knew at any moment it could bound up after them and rip them to shreds.

God, he wished he still had—

The knife! He'd forgotten all about it.

He jerked it out of his waistband and kept backing up the stairs. Almost there now. He brandished the knife at the creature, but its eyes remained fixed on Chris Blackwood. Then the door opened and the pair above him stepped through.

The creature shifted his eyes to Ben, a cunning smile twisting its features.

Ben backed through the doorway and nearly tripped over Chris, who lay panting on the floor. Ben slammed the door and shot the bolt, knowing full-well it would never keep the creature in. The thing had the strength of five men.

He knelt over Eva, a wave of lightheadedness rolling through him.

Ruined, he thought. Though he hated the word, it would not go away.

Ruined. Eva was ruined.

Her naked body looked as though it had been mauled by a pack of wolves. Where once had been shapely breasts were now meaty divots. There were bite marks all over her body, though the patina of blood made it impossible to tell where she was injured and where she was unharmed. He glanced down at her belly, the area below. Like hamburger meat, raw and blood-soaked, her entire abdomen was slashed and torn beyond recognition. The first twinges of anger kindled deep within him, and though he knew he was no match for the beast, he longed to avenge this atrocity.

Chris sat with his elbows on his knees, his face a void. Ben touched his shoulder. Chris turned and stared at him.

"Thanks," Ben said.

Returning his attention to Eva, he put an ear to her chest and tried to ignore the way the blood squished against the side of his head. Faintly, he felt her heartbeat against his cheek.

When he sat up, Chris was looking at him.

"It got you good," Chris said.

Ben frowned at him a moment, then remembered his battle with the creature. He touched his ear but winced as his fingers met with raw flesh. His earlobe had been sheared off.

"What'll we do?" Chris asked.

"We need to get her upstairs. I don't think she'll live, but we can at least make her comfortable."

Chris looked at him doubtfully.

"And," Ben said, "I want to put as many floors as I can between us and that…whatever that was."

Lips parted, Chris glanced at the door.

Then he nodded.

CHAPTER SEVEN

Joshua opened his eyes just before midnight.

Claire had been standing at the door, agonizing between staying with the boy and rushing down the stairs to see if Ben was all right. Chris had abandoned them ten minutes ago, the coward, and the thought of Ben down there alone with the monster made her skin crawl.

When she looked over at the boy, he was staring at the ceiling.

Claire went to him, put a hand on his shoulder.

He blinked at her but didn't speak.

"You're safe now," she said. "Your daddy will be here in a minute."

I hope.

His brown eyes moved from side to side, examining his surroundings.

"You don't have to say anything, Joshua. Your daddy told me a lot about you, and I promise I'll stay with you until he gets back."

His mouth worked, but his voice came out a toneless croak.

She leaned closer as if she could understand him by proximity alone.

"…f…fersty," he said.

She frowned, shook her head, but when he repeated the same thing, she got it. "You're thirsty," she said.

He nodded.

Of course he's thirsty, you moron, she thought as she jogged into the bathroom. *He probably hasn't had a drop to drink since the helicopter took off, and what was that, five hours ago?*

She filled a glass and brought it to him. She inclined his head in the crook of her arm as he drank the water in violent gulps. She worried he'd make himself sick, but when she drew the cup away, he shook his head and said, "More." Smiling a little, she watched as he drank the rest. He sighed in satisfaction, then nodded to show he wanted to lie back down. She reached down and held his hand. He returned her gaze, seemed to really see her for the first time.

"Daddy's here?" he asked.

She nodded, opened her mouth, but a voice in the hallway silenced her.

Ben's voice.

Rather than stopping at their door, his footsteps progressed down the hall, and she remembered Eva, Ben's reason for going down there in the first place.

"Wait here a second," she said. Joshua's eyes grew frightened, so she kissed him on the forehead and whispered, "I have to tell your daddy to come in here. He doesn't know you're awake."

The boy seemed to relax slightly, but continued watching her as she went out. Down the hall she could see Eva's open door, a figure standing just inside. When she got there, she spotted Ben, and before she could throw her arms around him and tell him the good news, he came out and closed the door behind him.

"You don't want to go in there," he said.

She halted, frowning. "Who's with her?"

"Chris Blackwood. You believe it?"

She didn't, but now that her eyes were adjusting to the lightless corridor, she noticed how badly Ben was beaten up.

"Your ear," she said, putting a hand to her chest.

"I can't feel it," he said. "But I guess my modeling career's over."

She did hug him then.

Into her hair, he said, "How's Joshua?"

"Come see for yourself."

When they entered, the weariness vanished from his face. She turned in time to see Joshua rising up to walk on his knees across the bed. Ben wrapped the boy up, lifted him, and sobbed into his neck. Over his shoulder she could see Joshua's huge grin. They clung together that way for a long time, and she was just about to leave them when Joshua said, "Who's she?"

They were both looking at her, Ben's eyes wet with tears, Joshua's plainly curious.

"That's Daddy's good friend," he said. "Her name is Claire."

She smiled and gave Joshua a little wave.

"Was she nice to you?" Ben asked.

Joshua nodded.

Then he seemed to remember something. He searched the room with narrowed eyes, then turned to look at Ben.

"Where did Mommy go?" he asked.

CHAPTER EIGHT

Claire had just taken Ryan's place in the master suite when Eva moaned and rolled onto her side. Claire studied the once beautiful woman with an exhausted kind of sympathy. If Eva awoke during her shift, Claire had no idea what she would say. What was there to say? I'm sorry that thing destroyed you?

Ryan had told her before leaving that Eva's wounds were mostly topical, and that they alone would likely not kill her. Her blood loss, however, would almost certainly prove impossible to survive.

Only the woman's neck and head were exposed, and Claire could see how much tape and gauze Ryan had used to stem the bleeding. Even so, the bedding was soaked through, the bandages a dark red that reminded Claire of dying roses. Hard to believe this was the same woman who had tried to seduce her in the tunnel.

She slouched in a chair, laid her head against its wooden back. To have Ben with her now...she'd love to curl up in bed with him, protected by his strong arms.

But Joshua needed him far more than she did. She sighed, rubbed her eyelids. The poor kid, losing his mother. She couldn't imagine how he felt.

The wind gusted against her window. She thought of Eddie, out there somewhere – the wild-eyed maniac who'd attacked Eva, who'd almost killed Ben. If he did return, what would they do?

Her thoughts broke off when she realized Eva was staring at her. Claire stood and approached Eva, who lay on her side. She bent and reached out to touch the blood-caked hair, but Eva whispered, "Don't."

Claire pressed her lips together, wished she could somehow comfort her, but Eva stared at her as though forbidding any contact. The scent of sheared copper hung over her like a bright-scarlet shroud.

Claire made herself touch the blood-caked fingers. "Eva, I..."

"He should've killed me."

The words were spoken in a voice so flat and emotionless, Claire felt a chill. She tried to conjure a reassuring expression, but Eva said, "I wish it had killed me."

Claire took a step toward the bathroom to fetch her a glass of water, but the woman's eyes snapped wide. "Where are you going?"

"I was just—"

"*Don't leave me*," Eva pleaded, her face crumpling. "Please don't leave me, Claire."

Claire nodded, sat next to Eva's sobbing form. The woman edged toward her but froze as the pain racked her body. Eva closed her eyes, teeth clenching in agony. Claire looked at her helplessly, wanting to enfold her in a comforting embrace, but not wanting to cause more pain. She reached out, held the woman's quaking shoulder. "We're going to get you to a hospital. They're going to take care—"

"It won't let us leave," Eva whispered.

Claire pushed away the image of the monster, its gaping white eyes. "He can't...hurt you anymore. He's..." She trailed off because she knew there was no way to make things better.

So she held Eva until the woman cried herself to sleep.

CHAPTER NINE

Like he'd died and gone to heaven was something one of his suck-ass screenwriters would've come up with, but in this case, boy did it fit. And to think, Lee had nearly put the journal down after ten minutes or so – Christ, it bored him to tears even to skim it – when he happened upon the butler's description of the secret tunnels. At first he doubted they existed, but what harm was there in checking it out?

He went down to the second floor and searched until he found the library. Having no idea where the entrance to the secret passage was, he fumbled around like an idiot, pulling books and coughing from the dust until he spotted the bronze candleholders on the wall. No fucking way, he told himself, but the second candleholder he tried made one tall bookcase swing sideways.

And there it was.

In his excitement he went right in without thinking how dark it would be. After he'd looked through a pair of rectangular peepholes, he began to realize what this discovery really meant. The implications, so to speak. He broke out in a cold sweat as he went downstairs to find a flashlight.

Taking care no one would see him, he stole up to the library again and locked the door. He yanked the candleholder and slipped inside. He had to strain to pull the bookcase shut behind him, but with an effort he got it. Lee shone the beam around the back of the bookcase and noticed nothing to distinguish it from anything else in the dark, cramped tunnel. He reached in his pockets for something to drop on the floor by way of a marker, but other than a hairy tangle of lint and thread, they were empty. Lee considered a moment before unbuttoning his yellow silk shirt. What did it matter if he was shirtless? He wasn't about to run into anyone in here; he could get naked and no one would be the wiser.

Naked.

Lee licked his lips and set off through the tunnel. He still couldn't believe his luck. He recalled a conversation from his childhood, him and a few other boys talking about which super power they'd most like to have. Most wanted the ability to fly, but he argued for invisibility.

The topic had fascinated him all his life. Whenever he saw a good-looking woman go into a dressing room, he wondered what it'd be like to follow her, watch her get naked without her knowing. In high school he got laid a couple of times, but the ones he wanted most had no interest in a short kid who already had too much body hair. He'd stand outside the locker room pretending to read a book while his dick would throb at the thought of all those luscious honeys getting naked, their nubile tits white and wet in the shower spray.

Come to think of it, he thought as he groped through the darkness, this place smelled a little like a locker room. Wet like that, dank with the odor of sweaty bodies.

Nude, sweaty bodies.

He'd often considered making a movie about an invisible man, but it'd already been done several times, and not very well either. The first one had Kevin Bacon and the straight-to-video sequel starred Christian Slater. Both were crap, except for the parts with tits. Maybe someday he'd revisit the concept, and if he ever did, he could consider this research.

Because this was like being invisible. Only, he didn't have to go through some fucked-up genetic experiment to reap the benefits. Lee grinned in the dark and continued on.

He had no idea how the passages were laid out, but he assumed the network followed the same pattern the castle did. Yet when he got to the end of the tunnel, the damned thing dead-ended. He touched the wall, flummoxed as to how he should proceed. He pivoted, thinking to walk to the other end of the passage and try his luck there, when he happened to glance to his right.

Son of a bitch.

A ladder.

So that was how the tunnel went from one story to the next. A guy had to climb like a monkey. Disgusted, he switched off the flashlight and crammed it in his pocket.

The first few rungs were the toughest, Lee not at all used to climbing anything, not even as a child. He loathed that shit. Give him a television and a bag of cookies and he was golden. Let the other dumb shits climb trees.

He paused to rest on the third floor. Then he commenced climbing, his heart beginning to hammer. He had an important thing to do on the fifth floor, but that could wait. For now, he'd rather focus on something more agreeable.

Like Ben Shadeland's stepdaughter.

She was only eighteen, but he was sure she'd been fucked. And the mouth on her…he bet she liked it rough, calling her lovers dirty words as they put it to her.

There were…he calculated…five bedrooms on the fourth floor. The first one he had taken because it was the nicest. The second belonged to Chris Blackwood.

Lee reached Kayla's room and gazed in.

Ryan and the girl were sitting across from each other on the bed. Ryan was chewing his sandwich, but Kayla hadn't touched hers. Lee licked his lips. The girl wore skimpy pink pajamas. She stared quietly down at her plate like it was the goddamned Mona Lisa, and Ryan was watching her. Her hair was wet, which meant she'd already taken her shower.

Lee cursed his luck.

She said something, he couldn't tell what, and Ryan put out a hand. His open palm touched her cheek, and she seemed to crumble.

Christ, he thought. Just what he needed, more fucking theatrics. He'd half-turned to go when something made him stop. When Ryan's hand touched her cheek, she held it there, kissing his palm. Her tongue slipped out and glazed the tip of his middle finger.

What the hell?

Ryan crawled toward her, face buried in her neck, and her hands snaked around his waist.

Lee's eyes widened.

CHAPTER TEN

Chris switched on the flashlight. The night air was cool, but the rain had ceased. A warm haze hovered over the lawn, and when he shined the light on the ground, he couldn't see beyond his ankles.

He waded out into the haze, glad to be out of the castle. According to Ben there was a madman out here, but the thought of encountering Eddie Blaze didn't frighten him.

No human being could frighten him anymore. Not after tonight. Chris paused, considering. The creature – man, he sure as hell didn't want to think of those gaping white eyes – had paused at the threshold of the basement steps, like it could not pass beyond that point. If it had that ability, why hadn't it eaten them when it had gotten the chance? Yes, he thought, rounding a corner of the castle, they were probably safe up here.

Then again, arming himself might not be such a bad idea. He thought of the axe Ben had spoken of, but that was in the basement with the monster. The question was, where had Ben found…

He had it. Excited now, Chris made his way through the misty pool and spotted the open door of the enclosure built into the rear of the castle. He stopped a few feet from the opening, not yet trusting the murkiness within, and sought to penetrate it with the flashlight beam.

All kinds of tools. Hoes, a rake, different types of shovels. A pitchfork. He spotted the chainsaw and grinned. He took a step forward and made out a pair of loppers. A gas-powered edger. The scythe intrigued him. Garden shears. A hacksaw. Deeper in, a workbench.

Chris yelped as something brushed his face. Swinging the flashlight up, he spotted the dusty bulb, the frayed white pull string.

He blew out a quavering breath, not quite able to laugh.

Certain the bulb would be burned out or disconnected, he pulled and gasped when pale light flooded the storage room. He cast a quick glance over his shoulder, suddenly aware of how conspicuous he was here. For good measure he reached out and slid shut the door. If Eddie Blaze did happen by, at least Chris would have the squeak of the opening door to warn him.

He turned and studied the wall above the workbench, the various tools hanging from the pegboard. He dismissed most of the implements, which were far too small to be of any use. The hacksaw looked nasty, but that would only come in handy if he decided to divide a fallen enemy into sections. He recognized the large orange tool as a pair of bolt cutters, and though they looked solid and capable of inflicting pain, he couldn't imagine using them in a fight.

He was turning away when something on the workbench caught his eye. He moved over to it, forgetting all about Eddie Blaze, forgetting even about the monster in the basement.

He lifted the sledgehammer and thought about Calvin Shepherd.

What if Chris did what Calvin had longed to do if only the man had possessed the courage?

Chris shut off the light, went out, and gazed up at the tower. He thought of what he might find beyond the brick wall, what might still be sitting at the piano.

He grinned. Why not?

He'd never seen a skeleton before.

* * *

Claire asked her if she wanted something for the pain.

Eva nodded but the pressure in the base of her skull made her stop. What she really needed was a gun, she thought, something to put her out of her misery.

"I'll be back as soon as I can," Claire said and went out.

Eva closed her eyes and waited.

She had no idea how much time had passed when she heard the noise coming from her left. And even though part of her wanted to die, the idea of Gabriel finding her again made her throat constrict. She tried to sit up but her body rebelled. She turned and saw the bookcase swinging open.

Oh God. She shut her eyes.

She lay back and waited for Gabriel to sink his teeth into her once more.

Please let it be quick, she thought, please let her not suffer anymore.

A voice asked, "How you been, baby?"

She opened her eyes and saw Lee staring down at her.

She heaved a sigh. She never thought she'd be so happy to see the creepy son of a bitch. He might have even brought his gun with him; he rarely left his compound without it. A gun might stop Gabriel, and it would certainly keep her safe if Eddie Blaze returned. She opened her mouth to ask about it, but he put a quieting finger to her lips.

"Shh," he said. "Just relax and listen."

He sat on the edge of the bed, his weight creaking the box spring, and her whole body canted toward him. It brought on fresh waves of pain, and she wanted to tell him to get his ass off the bed. And God, he *stank*. The mushroom odor breathing out of his hairy, white folds was worse than ever. She wondered why he didn't have a shirt on. Certainly he didn't want her to…

"You looked surprised when you saw me," he said. "Didn't anybody tell you I came?"

She shook her head.

"They probably didn't want to upset you."

She started to say something, but the effort set off another bout of coughing. When she got control of herself, she gazed up at him.

His eyes crawled over her body and he shook his head. "Jesus, honey, you look like shit."

She fought back tears.

"Oh, I don't mean to upset you," he said, "but hey, I'm just stating the obvious, right?"

Eva put a fist to her mouth and bit her skin. She couldn't let him see her cry, she couldn't.

He gave her a wistful look. "You used to be a looker, no doubt about it." He made a humming sound. "I thought about putting you in one of my films, but I remembered what a burnout your mom was and thought better of it."

Eva stared at him, her throat going dry.

"That's right," he said. "I know all about you, honey. I know why you went to work for me, I know about that smear job you were gonna write." He licked his lips. "You didn't really think you'd get away with it, did you?"

She longed to cry out, to attract attention, but her throat was such a raw, pulsing wound, she doubted she could make herself heard. Eva glanced at the door. *Please come back, Claire. Please get here soon.*

"My people got the story on you right after you were hired," Lee said. "I hadn't screwed you yet, so I put off firing you." He giggled. "When we had sex I enjoyed it so much, I figured I'd savor it awhile. No sense throwing away a good thing, right?"

Her mind raced. She hadn't the strength to get out of bed, but if she tried she might reach the nightstand, grab something to smash him with. She didn't want to look that way, tip her hand, so she scanned her memory.

A washcloth. A lamp. And a glass of water.

Not much, but if she could reach the lamp or the glass, she might fight him off long enough for Claire to return.

Under the sheet her arm slid slowly upward.

"…and your book never would have seen the light of day," he was saying. "So I decided to wait until you got back to California before I killed you."

That got her attention.

"Oh yeah, honey, I planned on killing you. Usually I have someone do those things for me, but in this case, I figured you warranted personal attention."

She moved sideways, hoping he wouldn't see her arm edging higher, just under the rim of the sheet now. The lamp might be too heavy for her, but the glass…if she could seize it, bash it against his ugly face, she might buy herself enough time. And if she couldn't scream loud enough to bring help, maybe his screams would.

"So let me ask you something, all right?"

She nodded.

"All bullshit aside, what I wanna know is this. Are you really naïve enough to blame me for your mother's death?"

She fought to control her anger, to focus. The moment he looked away, she'd make a grab for the glass, roll her body, and smash his head with it.

"Seriously," he said, "a woman like that, jacked up on heroin all the time, selling her body for the stuff…you really think I'm the one to blame?"

Eva said, "You misled her, you told her—"

"Who gives a shit what I told her? If stupidity was a capital offense, your mom would have gotten the chair a long time before she shot her—"

Eva lunged for the glass. Her fingers closed around it just as the bed moved beside her, Lee reacting. She lifted the glass, swung it, but he caught her wrist, squeezed the wounds until the pain overwhelmed her. The glass thumped harmlessly on the mattress, Lee climbing on top of her. He had both her wrists now, pinning her to the bed. She screamed as loud as she could as his belly slithered over her, but even more sickening was the hardness beneath. *Oh God,* she thought, *the bastard's getting off on it, enjoying one of his fantasies, only this time it was real. Please Claire…Ben…anybody…*

But Lee's face filled her vision.

"You're too ugly for me to fuck anymore," he said, his sour breath clouding over her. "But I can sure as hell make sure you never fuck with me again."

He shoved her hands under the small of her back, then let his weight crush her. She couldn't breathe, the edges of her vision graying.

"You should hide your notebooks better, honey. I've been reading them for months."

She gasped for air, but his mouth hovered over hers.

He said into her mouth, "This is for making fun of my weight."

Then the pillow slid over her face.

CHAPTER ELEVEN

The sledge made short work of the padlock, but Chris began to lose his nerve the moment he stepped inside the tower.

Though he had always doubted the veracity of Calvin Shepherd's journal, deep down he suspected there were grains of truth beneath the fantastic events described. The graveyard confirmed the quadruple suicide, or at least that the four young people had died on the same day. Henry Mullen's gravestone also coincided with the date in the journal.

But that didn't mean the rest was true.

Did it?

The sledgehammer heavy on his shoulder, Chris started to move toward the staircase, wishing he'd downed a few shots of hard liquor beforehand. His skin chafed painfully where Marvin had branded him, his nipples most of all. If by some miracle he survived all this…if the beast in the basement didn't get him and if Granderson didn't show up to finish the job and if they somehow got off this godforsaken island in one piece…

He would hire someone to protect him, some bodyguard who would guard his body rather than seek to harm it. Then he and his own hired goon would return to his father and demand the ten million. If the man refused, Chris would go public with the Rosa story.

Three floors up now, his wind thinning. His heart stuttered and only partly because of the exertion. He was scared shitless, and he wished he were back in the castle. In fact, he might just turn around now, see if Lee Stanley was burning the midnight oil, the man already excited about making the journal into a movie.

Chris paused halfway to the fourth floor and gazed out a window. From here he could see Castle Blackwood, and though he couldn't see his bedroom from this vantage point, the bulk of the castle, its comforting solidity, seemed to beckon to him.

But if he didn't ascend the tower now, he suspected he never would.

Quit being a pussy.

He'd begun to take the next step when a mournful cry turned his legs to stone. He whirled and through an open window spied an owl sheltering in the turret cap.

Chris sighed. Clutching the sledgehammer with grim resolve, he started up again.

When he reached the landing he beheld the brick wall, just as Calvin had described it. Finding the description accurate did nothing to ease his jangling nerves. In fact, the sight accomplished the opposite. The brick arch seemed to whisper to him, to insinuate that the fantastical events in the journal were true. He could almost fancy a baleful murmuring from within.

No, he thought. Chris shook his head and jogged in place to scatter the fear enfolding him. With an effort, he drew in a deep breath.

The sledge was cocked and ready to swing when the music started to play. Legs gelatinous, Chris dropped the sledgehammer and backed away from the wall.

He recognized the piece. One of Joseph Blackwood's. *What the hell was it called…*

Of course, he thought. *The Sorrows.*

He turned and walked down the stairs, too terrified to run, too afraid he would trip and end up broken-legged and stuck in the goddamned tower. The music followed him to the lawn, all the way to the castle door. Even back in his room, the blankets thrown over his head like he was four-years-old again, he was sure he could hear the music calling to him from the tower.

★ ★ ★

Lee removed the pillow and stared into the glazed eyes, the chewed up face. Though Eva's mangled appearance made it easier to kill her, it was disappointing to find her so beaten up. The way he'd imagined it, they'd have sex first, and right after Lee shot his wad in her, he'd tell her everything. It would have been a risk, fucking her before he throttled her skinny neck, but that was the beauty of it. Besides, they couldn't do forensics on a corpse they never found. Lee figured he could weigh her down and toss her in the surf. They'd assume she'd drowned or killed herself. One less whore in the world.

But this…

For the first time he wondered what could have damaged her this badly. Shadeland and the girl weren't saying, and it wasn't like he cared enough to force it out of them. Logic dictated it must have been Eddie Blaze – the guy was hiding somewhere on the island, and people didn't go into hiding without a reason, right?

Still…he couldn't imagine Blaze going berserk enough to do this to Eva. He drew down the sheet and gazed at the carnage.

Holy shit. Good thing he hadn't eaten supper.

Lee sat up as footsteps sounded in the hall.

He jerked up her hair and shoved the pillow under her head. He spotted the glass lying on the bed, thought of returning it to the nightstand, but dammit there wasn't time.

He hurried to the open bookcase and jerked it shut behind him. He was tempted to wait and listen to the reaction of whoever came in, but decided it was too risky. He'd seen enough whodunits to know how important it was to come when the alarm was sounded. If everybody showed up in Eva's room but him, wouldn't it look a trifle suspicious?

Lee switched on the flashlight and walked briskly to the end of the tunnel. Within moments he made it down to the fourth floor. He took a few seconds to catch his breath – Christ, he hated climbing – then he descended the next flight. Hardly pausing – had he heard shouting from above? – he climbed the last set of rungs and found himself again on the second floor. He bent over, panting, as he got his story straight. After finding his yellow shirt and emerging from the tunnel, he'd exit the library and head back to his room. If he heard voices upstairs, he'd get up there as fast as he could and join the others in gawking at Eva's dead body. They wouldn't notice how sweaty he was, how out of breath, and if they did he'd just tell them he got that way from running up there to see what all the commotion was about.

He straightened, ready to give an Oscar-winning performance. He thought of what he'd say, the gestures he'd make. *Oh my God, Eva. Oh baby, I can't believe it. I'll kill whoever did this to you.*

Yeah. Lay it on thick. Maybe even muster a few tears. He could do that. He'd done it before. In front of producers, pleading for more funds.

He was scanning the ground for the yellow shirt when he first heard the growling. No one had said anything about owning a dog, but obviously, someone had brought one to the island. Or maybe it had been here before they came. Regardless of where it came from, the damn thing sounded mean as hell, and worse than that, Lee was certain the animal had somehow gotten inside the tunnel.

The first whispers of fear tingling his skin, Lee swept the flashlight beam ahead. Finding nothing, he shone the light behind him.

Nothing there either.

He took a couple of hesitant steps forward, wondering where in the hell his shirt was. It wasn't like the damned thing was camouflaged or something. It was bright fucking yellow. He couldn't miss it if he tried.

From ahead, low but growing louder, he heard the growl.

Shit. Lee threw a frightened glance over his shoulder and wondered if he should risk going back upstairs and escaping through Eva's door. He *thought* he'd heard a voice after leaving her room, but he couldn't be sure. What if it had been his imagination, his paranoia playing tricks on him? Lee stood agonizing, knowing with every second he wasted the others could already be hunting for Eva's killer.

While he stood here petrified by some phantom canine.

Angry with himself, he pressed forward, and a moment later, yes, he spotted the shirt. The reason he missed it before was because it lay bunched against the wall, hiding from him. He picked it up, pushed the wall, and stepped into the library. He reached out to close the bookcase and felt his skin break into goose bumps at the sound of snarling just inside the passage. The bookcase crashed shut, and he held it there for several moments, listening.

The noise went on, as though the animal was right on the other side.

Lee jumped as the barking erupted. Backing away, he heard the thing clawing, whining to be let through. He shook his head slowly, licked his lips.

Imagination, he thought. It had to be his imagination.

He exited the library and was nearing his room when someone shouted, "*Hey.*"

He froze. Turning, he saw Shadeland watching him from the end of the hallway.

Marlon Brando, he told himself. *Marlon fucking Brando. Be cool and carefree. Until he tells you about Eva. Then you can unleash the waterworks.*

"Where were you?" Shadeland asked.

Where is my score? he wanted to answer.

"I was checking out the island," he said.

"It's three in the morning."

"So what? Since I almost died tonight and I couldn't sleep, I figured I'd take a look at the island. That a crime?"

Shadeland stared at him. "Eva's dead."

Lee let it sink in, allowed himself a few moments to process the news. He shook his head uncomprehendingly. Shadeland watched him.

Lee put a hand to his mouth. "What are you talking about?"

"Claire found her a few minutes ago."

"Was it that…thing?"

Shadeland glanced at his feet. "I don't know. Ryan thinks she died of shock from all the blood she lost."

"Oh my God…" Lee said and felt the tears coming. An Oscar performance for sure.

"You said you were walking around the island?" Shadeland said.

Lee nodded absently, too overcome with emotion to speak.

"That why you're not wearing a shirt?"

Lee looked down at the shirt balled in his hand. As if seeing it for the first time, he said, "Oh yeah. I took it off because I was getting hot."

Lee shook out the shirt and began putting it on.

"What happened to it?" Shadeland asked.

"Huh?" Lee followed Shadeland's gaze to the shirt.

There were pieces missing. As though it had been slashed with a knife.

Or claws.

Lee waved dismissively. "It was getting caught on branches and stuff…I took it off so it wouldn't get ruined."

"I thought you took it off because you were hot."

Staring into the man's skeptical face, Lee welcomed the first rumblings of indignation.

"Listen," Lee said. "I've just lost a very dear friend, a girlfriend, if you want to know the truth. And you have the audacity to interrogate me like I'm some fucking criminal? I mean, where were *you* when she died?"

"In bed," Shadeland said, "with my son."

"Yeah? Maybe I should talk to the kid to see if your story checks out."

He really thought Shadeland might slug him then. The guy sure looked angry enough. Then, he shook his head and walked away.

Lee watched him go, a slow smile spreading on his face.

Then he touched the slashes in his shirt and felt his smile evaporate.

CHAPTER TWELVE

"You have a minute?" the girl asked.

Lee smiled and let her in. He watched her tight little ass shifting from side to side as she crossed the room to lean against the dresser.

"What can I do for you…" Shit, what was her name? Katie? Kara?

"Kayla," she finished for him.

"Ah, yes. Sorry."

"It's okay," she said, giving him a dazzling smile, "I know you're a busy man."

"Make yourself comfortable," he said. As she moved over to sit on the bed, he let his eyes crawl over her body. Bare feet. Good legs. Tight little jean shorts. Smallish breasts, but he wouldn't hold that against her. He'd seen them naked, and their shape more than made up for their lack of size.

She cocked her head. "I wondered if you had any advice for someone wanting to get into the industry."

Oh Christ, he thought. *You gotta be kiddin' me.*

He put on a sober expression. "It's all about perseverance and hard work. You've gotta be in it for the long haul if you want to make it."

"I'm totally serious," she said.

He moved over to the table, picked up the bourbon bottle and the glass. "Can I offer you a drink?" he asked.

"Sure," she said. Nonchalant, like she drank bourbon every morning at eleven. He brought her the glass and leaned on the dresser. She took a sip and shuddered, her whole body wiggling. She gave him an apologetic grin and he smiled too, to show her it was okay.

"So…hard work and staying with it," she said. "That's the only advice you have for me?"

He shrugged. "It doesn't hurt to know the right people."

Her eyes never leaving his, she took another drink. She shivered, but not as violently this time. Holding the glass against the tight front of her jean shorts, she said, "I really want to be an actress, Mr. Stanley."

He held her gaze a moment. "Really?" he asked.

Her eyes locked on his. "More than anything."

He nodded, walked over to the bed, and sat beside her.

"Call me Lee."

CHAPTER THIRTEEN

From the Journal of Calvin Shepherd
October 31st, 1925
It has been a fortnight since Gabriel returned from the dead. I know how incredible that sounds, but how else can the following events be explained?

Cloven hoof prints leading toward and away from the castle. Sightings of a huge beast reported by several different witnesses. A continuation of the ghastly recital from the tower. Had we any sense, Robert and I would have left the island days ago. Now, escape is impossible. Last night Elizabeth Blackwood, along with the six remaining servants in Robert's employ, stole down to the docks by cover of darkness and commandeered the last vessel, a sixteen-foot runabout that could scarcely have stayed afloat with so many aboard. In truth, I hope they sank before reaching the mainland.

When Robert and I learned of Elizabeth's treachery, we were understandably vexed. Yet as we have done for more than forty years, we went about the business of breakfast this morning at the regularly appointed hour. Of course, our bland expressions and our fluid movements were mere artifice; in truth, we were both haggard with sleep deprivation and unflagging dread. He sat alone at the head of the table, and I brought in a meager platter of cheese, dry bread, and sliced salami. I placed the platter before Robert, uncovered it, and prepared to leave him to his solitary meal when he said, "Wait, Calvin."

I stopped and folded my hands behind me, the trained animal, the obsequious clown. "Yes, sir?"

"I believe," he said, a magnanimous smile curling his lips, "that we should break with convention today."

"How so, sir?"

"Haven't you long desired to dine in this room?"

I dutifully examined the coffered ceiling, the wine-red curtains. "I would enjoy it, yes."

Robert motioned for me to sit. "Then by all means, Calvin, please join me."

I was too thunderstruck to do anything but comply. Even more surprised was I when Robert handed me his plate. I am embarrassed to say that I was overcome by his gesture, and though his treatment of me has engendered a hatred of him too powerful for words, at that moment I felt the adoration an abused pet must experience when it is thrown a few scraps from the dinner table.

I was bending to my food when Robert said, "Calvin."

The sandwich poised an inch from my mouth, I said, "Yes, sir?"

An ironic grin darkened his face. "I have no drink."

I tightened, but I deferred as always, placed my uneaten sandwich on the plate, and went to the kitchen.

So this, I realized as I poured his ice water, was why he had invited me to dine: so he could interrupt me and control me and thus demonstrate that he remained master of the island – master despite all that had taken place. Carrying the glass through the kitchen, I resolved to tell him that he was nothing now and that the true master of our island was a god once named Gabriel. I opened the door to the dining room and stood mutely. The glass shattered on the floor.

Robert was gone.

His chair had been overturned as if there had been a brief but violent struggle. Near the open window lay his crumpled white napkin, the only witness to the abduction.

Now, Dear Journal, I bring this record to a close. I know that Gabriel will soon claim me too, though even after all I have seen I still cling to the hope that he will leave me to dwell alone, a living ghost, in Castle Blackwood. Even now I wish to live, to experience any emotion, even sorrow.

Dear God. I hear something in the hallway.

CHAPTER FOURTEEN

The five of them stood in the cemetery staring down at the bodies under sheets. Ben had an arm around Claire, Ryan and Kayla stood a few feet away.

Every now and then Lee would glance at Kayla to see if she was thinking about earlier. He sure as hell was.

There were lays and there were *lays*, and Kayla had most definitely been the latter. He couldn't believe the energy the girl had, the twitchy enthusiasm. A lot of women were theatrical when they slept with him, but this kid acted like she was doing a floor routine at the Olympics.

Lee watched her. Kayla was gazing at the white sheet covering her mom. Had she looked over at him? He put on a solemn expression and pretended to care. He bit his upper lip, thinking of Shadeland stumbling through his ex-wife's eulogy, Kayla staring daggers at him the whole way through. Then it was Claire's turn, bullshitting about Eva.

Then the funniest part of all, everybody realizing they didn't have anything to say about Robbie, the dead helicopter pilot, because nobody knew a damned thing about him. The only one who did was Chris Blackwood, and he was in the nearby woods babysitting Shadeland's son. So they decided to give Robbie a moment of silence.

Apparently deciding they'd stood there pretending to be sad long enough, Ben said, "Let's bury the bodies."

Without asking Ryan or Lee to do it – thank God for small favors – Ben climbed down into Eva's grave and waited for them to lower her into his arms. Lee yearned for a pair of gloves, but he didn't complain. Eva's body felt heavy as hell, and he was relieved when they passed her off to Ben.

Jenny's corpse presented a new problem. Lee hadn't been out here when, an hour earlier, Ben and Ryan had carried the bodies to the graveyard, but now he wondered just how the hell they'd get the woman down to Ben, her head being barely attached and all. But somehow they managed it.

Robbie's body was the heaviest. It damn near gave him a hernia.

When the bodies were in the holes Ben, Ryan, and Chris had dug earlier

– about the time, Lee figured, he had been laying the pipe to Kayla – each of them took a shovel and began to fill in a grave. Ryan buried his erstwhile fiancé; Ben buried Eva. Somehow Lee got stuck with the biggest hole.

It pissed him off. His back already ached, yet he got stuck planting the guy nobody cared about. Lee threw an agitated glance back at the women, clinging together like they were caught in a hurricane, like it was their birthright to avoid menial labor. He shook his head, scooping a shovelful of dirt. Of all the ideas he disagreed with, chivalry had to be at the top of the list. *What bullshit. You're a woman so you don't have to work; let the men do that. You watch and hug each other. A bunch of crap.*

Muttering under his breath, Lee jabbed his shovel into the mountain of dirt, pivoted to throw it into the grave, when something caught his attention.

He reached down, used his shirt to rub sweat out of his eyes. He strained to see into the hole, to assure himself his vision hadn't deceived him, and yes…there it was…a foot away from the edge of the sheet, just beyond the pilot's left shoulder.

Human fingers. Poking out of the ragged dirt wall of the grave. Four of them, the thumb hidden by the dirt.

Lee threw a hurried glance over his shoulder to make sure the others hadn't noticed. The guys were still shoveling and the girls were still blubbering.

Lee rubbed his eyes to see the fingers more clearly, and as he did one of his earlier suspicions was confirmed. Two of the fingers were encircled by rings. What kind he couldn't tell, not from this far away, and even if he got closer he would still need to take them off and clean them to see if they were worth anything.

Taking his time, Lee pierced the mountainous pile with the shovel blade and tossed a smattering of dirt onto the white sheet.

⋆ ⋆ ⋆

Across the dining room table Ben studied Ryan and Kayla. At the gravesite he'd been too emotional to study the dynamic between them, but on the way back he understood it clearly. There was nothing paternal in Ryan's treatment of the girl. In fact, the more Ben thought about it, the more the pair acted like husband and wife.

Kayla said something to Ryan, Ben couldn't quite hear what, and stormed out. Ryan's face tightening, he placed his napkin on the table and followed her.

A few minutes later, Ben told Claire he needed some time alone with Joshua.

When they were back in his room, the boy lying on his side, Ben went to him and bent at the bedside. "Can Daddy talk to you a minute?"

Joshua rolled over, his back to Ben.

He thought of waiting, of dropping the subject for now. It was approaching Joshua's bedtime. The boy's mother had been buried earlier that day. Did he really need more stress?

Then Ben remembered the dream.

No. It had to be now.

"Honey," he said, climbing onto the bed behind Joshua, "I know how sad you are, and I know how hard all this is. But..."

Ben clasped his fingers, stared at them in his lap. "Joshua, you know that Daddy loves you and that he'd never hurt you on purpose."

The boy's little body remained still, the legs slightly bent. He wished he could see Joshua's face, but all he could tell from this angle was that he seemed to be listening.

"This isn't something I want to talk about," Ben went on, "but I feel like I have to. I need to ask you a question about Ryan."

Joshua did change then. The shoulders drawing in. The fingers curling into fists, as if for protection.

Ben said, "If I'm wrong about this, I hope you'll forgive me...but I have to know...is something going on between—"

Joshua faced him, a stricken look on his face, the tears already shimmering in his eyes. Ben gathered the boy to him as the sobs began to shake his little body, then Ben was crying too, rocking his son in his arms and telling him how sorry he was and how no one would hurt him again. Between sobs Joshua was saying, "...he'd bury me, Daddy...said he'd bury me if I told..."

Teeth bared, a bitter lump in his throat, Ben squeezed the boy.

"*Don't let him get me, Daddy*," Joshua pleaded, "*don't let him get me.*"

Ben rocked his son and let the hot tears ooze out. They lay clutched together on their sides, Ben whispering fiercely into the boy's ear.

"No one's going to hurt you," he said. "No one's ever going to hurt my baby."

CHAPTER FIFTEEN

Lee waited until sundown.

In the storage area he found the shovel where he'd hung it, and below that, something even better – a kerosene lantern. Hidden under a musty tarp, but full of fuel and perfectly functional.

He'd hoped Kayla might stop by his room for more fun, but when nine o'clock came and went without a sign of her, he figured it was time to see if he had guessed correctly about the fingers in the grave.

Walking through the forest, he thought about the corpse to whom the hand belonged. It probably wasn't a member of the family. The nearest gravestone to where Lee spotted the fingers was ten feet away, and that one belonged to someone named Amarinda Mullen. He suspected the real treasures lay beneath the markers that read BLACKWOOD, especially those of the female members of the family. If this expedition proved fruitful, he just might return tomorrow night to see if anyone else had been buried with her jewels.

That was, if he was still here tomorrow night. He doubted it.

Chris Blackwood could prattle on all he wanted about murder plots and crazed bodyguards, but Lee suspected the truth was far less exciting. The helicopter had run out of gas, plain and simple. Maybe Chris's bodyguard had told him the chopper was full, so what? Wasn't it possible the gauge was busted and the man had been as clueless about the malfunction as the rest of them? That the bodyguard would sacrifice seven people for money seemed highly improbable.

Of course, what did Lee know? Here he was, a multimillionaire whose current film would likely garner him his first Oscar nomination, stealing through the woods for a little moonlight grave robbing. How much sense did that make?

He eased the lantern onto the grass next to Robbie's grave and began to dig.

The job was a bitch. The smell was even worse, though it wasn't coming from the grave. For the first time he wondered about what kind of animals they had on the island. His forehead creasing, he plunged the shovel deeper.

He'd only dug a few minutes when his hands began to throb. And dammit he'd forgotten the gloves again. The blisters he'd developed earlier were screaming bloody murder, and the small of his back was tighter than a producer's wallet.

Thinking of his movie made things slightly more bearable.

House of Skin.

Man, what a title. He knew he'd make the picture the first time he heard his agent say those words. Fortunately, the novel had proved to be everything he'd hoped it would – violent, steamy, full of gore.

Like always, he knew he'd surpassed the source material with his direction. Even with a mindless slab of meat like Eric Kramer as his lead, Lee had managed to make a picture that was scary, erotic, and most of all, relevant. The subplot about the black servant wasn't in the novel, but Lee figured it would appeal to the bleeding hearts who voted for the Oscars. The Academy ate that shit up. Everyone told him a horror movie couldn't win Best Picture, but what about *Silence of the Lambs*? What about *No Country for Old Men*? If those weren't horror flicks, he didn't know what was.

Soon, they'd be adding *House of Skin* to the list. He even had an Oscar-nominated pair of composers working on the score.

Of course, one was currently missing.

The thought dampened his spirits. His hands throbbed. He held them up to the light and noticed how the blisters had split open, were oozing clear liquid all over the place. Maybe this wasn't such a great idea.

He leaned against the edge of the grave and stared up at the stars. It had gotten clearer. He couldn't believe how quiet it was here on the island. Maybe he'd shoot a picture here after all. Not the snoozer Chris Blackwood had brought him. A vampire film. Or something with zombies.

Yeah, he thought, digging again. Zombies. He hadn't explored them since *Shambler* back in '92, and many of his hard-core fans thought that was one of his best. He worked faster, liking the idea – zombies on an island. Fucking A.

He was thinking over the possibilities when his shovel tapped something firm. He pressed down on it, felt it give a little. Brushing aside dirt, he saw he was standing on Robbie's body.

A chill coursed through him. *Zombies*, his mind repeated.

He wondered what would happen if Robbie's cold hands seized his leg, if the stiff body began to wriggle beneath him. What a scene.

He'd long thought of writing his own screenplay. Yes, he always took liberties with his scripts, added or trimmed at his discretion. But to concoct an entire story from his own imagination?

Shaking with excitement, Lee knelt on top of Robbie's chest and began digging with his bare hands in the area he thought the protruding fingers had been.

Within moments something rubbery brushed his forearm.

He got to his feet, reached up and got hold of the lantern. Lowering it, he dusted off the fingers and spotted the pair of rings. He slid one off, tapped it in his palm to get rid of the dirt.

Lee swallowed. He couldn't be sure, but the diamond looked real enough. If it was, the damned thing was big enough to bring in fifty grand, more if it had any historical value.

Panting now, Lee slid off the other ring, smudged the surface.

A gold band. A wedding ring.

Was it possible this was one of the female Blackwoods? Could there have been a mistake, or could the bodies have been somehow moved?

Lee looked from the rings in his palm to the bare fingers. He wondered what else might be hidden in the graveyard soil. Might there be a pearl necklace around the corpse's neck? An antique broach? And what of the other hand, were there jewels on those fingers too?

Pocketing the rings, Lee picked up the shovel and jammed it into the wall of dirt.

★ ★ ★

Even if there wasn't a monster lurking in the basement, Chris would not have visited the wine cellar for a drink. He hadn't tasted wine since the night of Rosa's death. Just the odor of the stuff was enough to make him lightheaded.

He found what he needed in the pantry. "Come to Daddy," he said and took the bottle of Johnny Walker Red off the shelf. He peeled off the plastic around the cap, unscrewed it, and took a hearty swig. He wiped his mouth.

Chris tilted the bottle again, heard it glug like a water cooler before lowering it, his insides burning pleasantly. Pocketing the cap, he carried the bottle outside where the summer air kissed his skin. Chris drank again, spread his arms, and stared up at the blue-black sky. Stars everywhere. Beautiful. He felt that things had altered for the better. One of his schemes had to pan out, right? If his father refused to pay him off, he still had Lee Stanley as a backup. Maybe Chris could be an executive producer on the film.

Chris drank again, thinking of it. Yes, breaking into the movie business would suit him just fine.

Speaking of breaking into things. Chris sucked in a deep breath, rolled his shoulders as if preparing for a fight. The whiskey was already working its magic, thwarting his fear of what lay in the tower and leaving a weightless euphoria in its wake. Time to go up.

He approached the tower. He made it to the second floor before the music started, but he only paused a moment before continuing up. He recognized the song now, the final act of *The Sorrows*, 'A Father's Lament.'

He reached the keep landing and was not at all surprised to find the sledgehammer leaning against the wall rather than lying on the steps where he'd left it last night in his terrified escape.

The song played on, its frenzied notes echoing through the tower. Chris took it as an invitation.

Hands shaking, he picked up the sledgehammer.

★ ★ ★

The dirt above the protruding arm was tightly packed, but Lee managed to make a tunnel around it up to the elbow. No sign of a dress yet.

It worried him. Yeah, he supposed one of the Blackwood women could have been buried in a short-sleeved dress, but that didn't jive with the period films he'd seen. In movies like that, exercises in tedium that lasted three hours and contained maybe two scenes of honest-to-goodness action, women were always buried in flowing gowns that covered them from the neck down. Maybe this was a servant girl after all. He'd always read about dead bodies smelling like cinnamon, but the only scent he could pick up was the stench of wild animals, a crazed smell like whatever was out there in the woods had gone rabid.

Lee frowned. He squinted at the leathery skin a moment. He swung the lantern close and examined the arm. Those tiny dots wending their way up the mummified flesh...could they be anything other than needle marks?

Lee grabbed the arm about the wrist, turned it and gagged. Yanking his hand away he stifled a scream and backpedaled to the far corner of the grave.

Get a grip, he told himself. Yeah, the way the thumb and half the palm had been torn away was gruesome, but think a minute. The body's been underground for maybe a hundred years. Don't you think the bugs and animals would have feasted on it in all that time?

But the ragged wound…it was so localized. Why was the rest of the hand spared, and why hadn't the beetles or the snakes or whatever the fuck lived in the ground dined on those parts too? Why had they chosen the exact part of the hand that…

"Oh shit," Lee said aloud. He didn't want to go near the protruding arm again, but he needed the lantern. Half-expecting the fingers to batten onto his forearm, he snatched the lantern from the pilot's dead chest and situated it on the lip of the grave.

Under his feet, the body shifted.

Mouth opening, Lee studied the darkness around his ankles for signs of movement. The body lay still.

Of course it did. *Jesus Christ, Lee, get a grip.*

He looked up. Had there been a rustling sound? Some stealthy intruder coming to catch him in the act of stealing from the dead?

His escalating disquiet giving him added strength, he scrambled out of the open grave, picked up the lantern and set off through the graveyard.

He scanned the woods for the entrance of the trail, but so far the forest's edge appeared unbroken. He raised the lantern, wishing its glow was more precise, when a noise behind him sent goose bumps scurrying up his arms.

"Oh hell," he said, not wanting to see, but turning and looking anyway. He held out the lantern, peered into the darkness.

In the wan light he distinguished a huge shape poised on the rim of the open grave. Though Lee was some distance away, he could see well enough what it was.

A dog. An unnaturally large dog.

He'd taken a step backward, ready to run like hell, when he saw something that scared him even more. The dirt over Eva's grave was rippling, as if something was trying to claw its way out. Then, a few feet from the growling dog, he discerned a shadow emerging from Robbie's burial place almost as if…

Almost as if something was crawling out of the hole.

Lee did run then, not even bothering to keep the lantern steady. The kerosene sloshed and the glow danced on the markers, the grass, the trees beyond. Then ahead…yes. He spotted the trail.

He dropped the lantern and dashed into the forest. He had never been athletic, but he felt good as he climbed a curving rise and hurried down the hill. Dimly, he was aware of a dog's bark – a harsh, wolfish sound – but it sounded far away.

Jesus, this would make a great scene if he lived to shoot it. He was sure what he'd seen had been mostly imagination. There had definitely been a dog, but hadn't he already known that? So there were dogs on the island, big fucking deal. The stupid thing probably wanted food.

An immense relief flooded through him as, ahead, he made out the bridge, which meant he was halfway to the castle. Nearing it, he thought of the other things, the moving dirt and the shadow poking out of the grave. While troubling, they could be explained easily enough. There was a breeze tonight, and the cemetery was lined with trees. Obviously, the undulating branches and stirring leaves had fooled him into believing that Eva had returned from the dead, that her mother—

Stop it, he thought. *That was* not *her mother. Strike that bullshit from your head.* It made zero sense, and besides, Gabriela was buried somewhere in California, likely in some potter's grave.

He was picturing Gabriela's gun-blasted hand when the growling sounded in front of him.

He stopped, cursed himself for dropping the lantern. The growl grew stronger. On the far side of the bridge he spotted it now, the same hound of hell that had menaced him in the cemetery. The deranged smell of it made his balls shrivel.

Holy shit, it was huge. It had to be a trick of the shadows, a product of his poor vision. The damned thing looked like a grizzly bear on all fours.

Lee licked his lips, patted his pockets as if he might find a Milk-Bone.

His bowels began to churn as the dog stalked slowly toward him, and when it reached the middle of the bridge and entered a dazzling stretch of moonlight, Lee saw all too clearly the missing ear, the scar that began above its left eye and zigzagged all the way to its muzzle. He'd recognize that dog anywhere. After all, he'd owned it for five years. He'd named it in honor of one of his favorite movies, and the name fit perfectly, the glorious animal a diabolical force that destroyed its opponents, ripping them to shreds and winning Lee a hell of a lot of money. The dog never failed him, not until the night he brought it in to perform in a different way, the animal acting like it didn't know what to do, like sex was alien to it, like seizing an opponent's throat and tearing open its jugular was the only thing it understood.

The dog halted ten feet from the edge of the bridge and lowered its head.

Snarling. Eyes fraught with madness.

"Damien?" Lee asked. "Is that you?"

Its shoulders flexed, rippled, the muscles writhing like agitated vipers. Lee cast about for a weapon, anything to fend off the animal's imminent attack. *Jesus fucking Christ*, he thought. Damien had been his biggest dog, but this animal was freakish. No dog, not even a Rottweiler could grow to this size. He knew he was doomed if the animal went for him, but he sure as hell wasn't going to stand here and let it happen.

The bridge traversed a creek. He could hear its babble under the spine-tingling growl. If he could make it down the bank, wade out into the creek, maybe Damien wouldn't follow. Maybe it was deep enough Lee could swim for it. At any rate he couldn't stand here doing nothing. He took a step toward the corner of the bridge when something caressed the back of his neck.

Whirling, he beheld Eva.

He hardly noticed her nude body because he could not look away from her face. Restored to her former beauty – save the eyes, which were completely white – she reached for him and he backpedaled a moment before falling on his ass and tumbling in a ball down the steep bank.

He landed in time to hear something large splash into the creek. Dazed, he rolled over and stared into the turbid water as, above him, Eva began to glide down the embankment. He couldn't bear those horrible pupilless eyes, that ghastly grin, but when he turned back to the water he glimpsed the dog's huge head trawling through the water toward him. Lee stood and tottered under the bridge, thinking he could elude Eva and Damien by following the creek bank until he found a place to ascend.

When the third figure appeared, blocking his way, he sank to his knees in horror.

It was Gabriela, not as she had been at the end, but as she had looked when he'd first met her. Flowing black hair, her naked body the most voluptuous he'd ever seen.

Except the eyes. They were completely white, the same as Eva's.

"Don't hurt me," he whispered. "Please don't hurt me."

She approached, her face ravenous. She came closer, closer, and when she placed her delicate hands on his shoulders, he was certain she would tear his head from his body and bathe in his blood.

But she drew him forward, down, her touch almost loving. He found himself on all fours in front of her, like she was a goddess and he one of her followers. She knelt before him and wrapped her arms about his shoulder. He could feel her breasts on his bare skin, but the touch did not arouse him. Instead, every nerve ending roiled in revulsion.

Eva appeared to his right and followed her mother's lead.

The women's flesh was cold on his shoulders, the nipples hard and unyielding against his skin. For an insane moment Lee wondered if mother and daughter were about to ravage him the way the harpies had ravaged Jonathan Harker in Dracula's castle. Maybe drink his blood a little but allow him to live.

But then Lee heard the growling, remembered the monstrous dog, the one that looked exactly like Damien, the dog he'd slain with the axe the night it embarrassed him by failing to fuck Gabriela Rosales.

Soaking wet from the creek, its growl rumbling louder, the Rottweiler climbed on top of Lee's bare back, the razor claws flaying his skin as they tore through his shorts, his underwear.

Lee bellowed in agony as the women began to chew through the flesh of his shoulders. Then he let out a shrill cry as the dog's monstrous phallus split him wide open.

This time, Damien knew just what to do.

CHAPTER SIXTEEN

Ben paused outside Kayla's door.

Raised voices within. Ryan shouting, Kayla matching him in volume. He put his ear against the wood and listened, but it was still a furious garble, only the occasional word intelligible. Steeling himself, Ben knocked.

The voices quieted. He waited a few moments, then knocked again, louder this time. Still nothing. He raised his fist a third time when Ryan asked, "Who is it?"

"It's Ben," he said. "I need to talk to you."

The voice wary, "What for?"

Ben took a breath. "Open the door, Ryan."

"We're busy."

Ben tried the knob. Locked.

Kayla's voice, cold and biting as January sleet, "Go away."

Ben took a step back, thought of leaving it for now, but a flash of Joshua's terrified face flickered through his memory. *He said he'd bury me, Daddy. He said he'd bury me if I told.*

Ben cleared his throat. "I know about you two."

A long silence. Then Ryan's voice, tight and controlled, "You don't know anything."

"Kayla?" Ben asked.

Had Ryan whispered something to the girl, silencing her?

She made an annoyed sound, said, "Leave us alone, Ben."

He smiled grimly. "Forget how much you hate me a minute. We need to talk."

Ryan's voice, mocking, "What are you gonna do, break down the door?"

Ben said, "Kayla, I know this guy's got his hooks in you, but you need to know the truth about him." Then, though it pained him to form the words, "He threatened to kill Joshua."

Ben listened. Muffled voices. A sibilant whisper.

Then, Kayla's voice at the door, "You're lying."

Ben was about to respond when a familiar sound brought him to the hall window. He stared out in shock.

A helicopter was landing on the castle lawn.

The rotor had just begun to slow when Granderson stepped out of the pilot's seat and came around to open the passenger's door. A man Ben had never seen before climbed down and surveyed the castle. He wore blue jeans and an expensive-looking jacket. The man said something to Granderson, who nodded and joined him in studying the castle. And though the large man looked almost nothing like his son, Ben knew this was Stephen Blackwood.

The men turned and gazed up at something. The tower, Ben realized. Stephen Blackwood gestured toward the tower, a question. Granderson shook his head. *I don't know.* The men continued to gaze up at the tower and then Ben heard it too.

The music.

A rather dissonant piece, something in D minor. Though he barely heard it, the melody filled him with apprehension.

Below, Stephen Blackwood walked toward the tower, and Granderson approached the castle. It was then that Ben noticed the leather pilot's jacket, which would not have been incongruous at any other time of year. But this was June, and even at this late hour it was still warm.

Both of them wore jackets. As though concealing something.

When Granderson reached for the door handle, Ben strained his eyes to see if something bulged beneath the jacket. He couldn't see, but he knew he had to get Claire and Joshua hidden.

Ben sprinted upstairs.

★ ★ ★

Chris was a couple of sledgehammer blows from finishing when he heard the helicopter. He knew immediately it was Granderson, but when he gazed out he was startled to find his father had come along for the slaughter. Drawn by the music, Stephen Blackwood approached the tower.

Lifting the sledge, Chris pivoted and bashed a section of bricks. Rearing back, he swung again; this time a segment three feet high toppled onto the pile of rubble. He could see the doorknob now. Below, his father's footsteps echoed dully up the staircase. For a hideous moment Chris feared the door would be locked, but after resisting a moment, the knob turned in his hand, the years of rust squealing in protest. As the door swung inward the music fell silent.

He prepared to duck inside when an arctic chill blasted his body, immobilizing him. Vaguely, he was aware of the footsteps tromping up the stairs, but the unholy dread clutching him by the throat refused to let him go.

The footfalls sounded again, very close now, and self-preservation shattered his paralysis. Chris backed away from the cold room and squatted in the darkness of the landing, hoping his father's eyes wouldn't pick him out. The steps grew louder, louder, slowing until they had reached the top of the staircase.

A long, agonizing pause. Chris's breathing too loud in his own ears. Surely his father would hear him.

Stephen Blackwood burst onto the landing, the gun extended before him. The light pouring through the keep doorway illuminated him, but the rest of the landing remained in shadow. He pointed the gun left, right, jabbed it in all directions as if warding off invisible attackers. Chris sat as still as he could, sure at any moment his father would spot him and shoot him dead. Satisfied the landing was empty, Stephen Blackwood climbed over the remains of the wall and entered the keep.

His father screamed. The sound sent gooseflesh down Chris's arms. Then he heard something hard clatter on the floor.

The gun.

Chris rose and crossed the landing.

* * *

Coming through the door, Ben almost ran Claire over.

He opened his mouth to tell her about the helicopter, how they had to get somewhere safe right away, but she grabbed his shoulders, her blue eyes huge with fear.

"We have to do something about Ryan," she said.

Ben shook his head, overriding her. "Granderson and Blackwood's dad are here, they mean to kill us."

"So does Ryan."

He frowned at her. "What are you talking about? I just came from his—"

"The marks on Joshua's neck," she said.

"Huh?" He shook his head, struggling to focus. "We have to get out of this room. We'll be safer somewhere else, upstairs maybe..."

She squeezed his shoulders, spoke into his face. "He tried to strangle Joshua after the crash."

Her words finally broke through. He stared at her, appalled. "What are you—"

"He just told me," she said, hooking a thumb at Joshua. Ben noticed his son for the first time since entering the room. Joshua was huddled in a ball near the headboard, his face the only thing visible above the quilt.

Claire went on, "When the helicopter went down, Joshua somehow ended up in Ryan's lap. Ryan grabbed him by the throat and tried to choke him."

His mouth open in horror, Ben drifted to his son on legs he couldn't feel. He put his arms around Joshua, spoke into the boy's hair, breathed the sweet smell of him.

Then he remembered Granderson.

"We've gotta go," he said as he gathered Joshua into his arms.

"Where?" she asked.

"The studio," Ben said. "The storage compartments under the window seats. We'll hide you and Joshua in one of those."

"What about Ryan?" she asked on the way out of the room.

"I don't know yet," he said.

But he did.

CHAPTER SEVENTEEN

Chris went inside.

His father was a few paces inside the keep, on his knees as if praying at an imaginary altar. The gun lay on the ground beside him.

Chris picked it up and aimed it at his father, but the man made no move to stop him. Stephen's hands were clamped over his mouth, his eyes stretched wide in horror. Chris whirled and felt every hair on his body stand on end, every fiber of his being thrum with atavistic terror.

Robert Blackwood stared at them from the piano bench. Though Chris could only see the man's eyes, his forehead, his shiny black hair over the black piano tray, he knew beyond all doubt this was his great-grandfather. He had seen too many pictures of the man to mistake him.

Robert would be, his terrified mind calculated, more than one-hundred-and-thirty years old by now. The look in Robert's eyes was changing, transforming into something frantic, as if he were begging Chris for help. The music started again, but from the look in the man's eyes Chris was certain Robert Blackwood was playing against his will.

Forgetting his father for a moment, Chris edged around the piano and felt his legs turn to liquid. Yes, the man's eyes were terrible, but those were as nothing compared to this sight, the worst thing Chris had ever seen.

Robert had no mouth.

The skin where it should have been was perfectly smooth. Further, Chris realized the piano keys were playing without being touched, as if unseen fingers depressed them. Robert sat nude, "Forest of the Faun" playing ceaselessly before him, taunting him. Chris noted with dim horror that the man had no arms, yet this was only a fraction of the grotesque vision that lay before him.

Robert Blackwood had been transformed into a centaur of sorts, but a horse's haunches and hooves would have been infinitely better than what Chris now beheld.

Robert's body melted at the hips into two human figures who sat on hands and knees, supporting their master. And though Chris had never seen these men before, he knew they were Henry Mullen and Calvin Shepherd.

As they had in life, the two men occupied positions of subservience, but neither of them would ever move again, for where the men's hands and knees should have been, they were joined with the stone, as though they had fallen into the concrete before it dried and had been fixed permanently into place. Like their master, Henry Mullen and Calvin Shepherd wore anguished, pitiful expressions, but also like Robert Blackwood the two servants had no mouths with which to communicate their suffering.

Chris faced his father, who stared at the gun in amazement.

"Get up," Chris said.

Stephen did as he was told, but a contemptuous sneer began to darken his face.

"Over by the wall," Chris said.

"Why?" Stephen asked, and the truth was, Chris didn't know why.

"Go," he said, gesturing with the gun.

Stephen Blackwood did as he was told. Chris took a position where he could keep an eye on both his father and the apparitions at the piano. When he'd reached a spot three or four feet from the wall, his father halted and turned, a smug grin twisting his face.

"You shouldn't be smiling," Chris said.

"I can't help it," Stephen said, beginning to laugh.

Chris glanced down at the gun and wondered if the safety was on. Maybe that was why his father was laughing. Or maybe it was something else. The man's laughter grew intolerable.

"Shut your damned mouth," Chris said.

"You don't see it, do you?"

"I see a man who'd murder his own son."

"You're not my son," his father said. "You're a worthless piece of filth."

Chris's finger moved to the trigger.

"If you kill me," Stephen said, "Granderson will shoot you dead before you leave the tower."

Movement beyond his father lifted Chris's gaze. At sight of it, his trigger finger went numb. The wall behind his father was shifting. In moments a thin, wraithlike body materialized. Shadows and color bled into the figure, but rather than wearing an agonized expression like Robert and his servants, this face was a mask of rage. Chris recognized the figure from old pictures.

Gregory Blackwood.

Chris thought of the four young people joining hands and leaping to their deaths. He remembered Gregory's unwavering allegiance to Gabriel, a loyalty that amounted to worship. Chris glanced at his father, who hadn't yet seen the figure materializing behind him. Nor did Stephen Blackwood see the other figures emerging from the walls. There were a dozen of them, all of them dressed as they had in life.

"You're an embarrassment," his father was saying. "You blame me for Rosa's death, but you don't see the truth.

"What is the truth?" Chris said in a hollow voice.

"I had no control over what happened," Stephen said as he approached.

Gregory's form separated from the wall. He stepped forward and reached for Stephen Blackwood.

Chris couldn't move.

"And you," his father said, "have no right to judge."

Stephen reached for the gun just as Gregory seized him by the shoulders. His father screamed. Chris backed away and bumped into something cold and unyielding. He cried out when he saw the figure that had come loose of the wall behind him. It stared up at him with something like pity.

"Rosa," Chris whispered.

The figure closed its eyes softly, and when they opened again the face sharpened in rage. Chris weaved toward the door as his father's pleas devolved into an incoherent gibber. Gregory and the other figures held him in place as Rosa approached. A terrible comprehension shone in his father's eyes.

Chris wanted to look away but couldn't. His father bucked against the hands holding him. He thrashed his head as if fearing Rosa would tear out his eyes or sink her teeth into his throat.

He needn't have worried. The last thing Chris witnessed before stumbling out the doorway and vomiting was the shadowy figure of the maid kneeling and with one ferocious bite removing Stephen Blackwood's genitals.

As Chris puked up the last of the Johnny Walker Red, he heard the accursed song blaring from the keep as a dozen sets of teeth feasted on his father.

Stephen Blackwood's screams followed him down the stairs.

* * *

"Hello?" the British voice called. "Are you here, Chris? Mr. Shadeland? Mr. Blaze?"

Ben stood on the staircase three or four steps from the first-floor landing.

From the direction of Granderson's voice, he guessed the man was at the far end of the great hall. Ben glanced about the corridor and wished he had some kind of weapon. Of course, he didn't know for sure that Granderson and his boss meant to kill them. If the helicopter crash had been an accident, the men could deliver them to safety.

"Hello?" the voice called again, closer this time.

Ben stepped around the corner, said, "We're ready to go home."

Granderson stood in the great hall about thirty feet away. He smiled as though they were old friends. "Mr. Shadeland. Where are your companions?"

"Eva's dead," Ben replied. "Eddie's gone too. I don't know where."

"And the second party?" Granderson asked, moving nearer. "We saw the wreckage when we arrived."

Ben eyed the man's leather jacket but still couldn't see if anything was hidden beneath. "Your boss didn't look too sad," Ben said. "I'd have thought his only son's death would've impacted him more."

Granderson's gaze intensified. "Chris is dead?"

Ben nodded. "So is my son."

The ruthless son of a bitch nodded absently, as though that was to be expected, and if there had been any doubt before, he knew now.

A black cloud of fury enveloped him. He forced himself to remain focused. Granderson was now twenty feet away at most. If he fired on Ben he would almost certainly hit him.

"Were there any survivors?" Granderson asked.

Ben shook his head and studied the man's right hip, where the leather jacket bulged slightly.

Granderson raised his chin. "Then it must be the blonde woman we heard in the tower."

Ben looked at him uncertainly, then nodded. "Yes. Claire's up there."

The man's grin was glacial. "You're lying." Then, glancing at the staircase behind Ben, he asked, "Where are the others?"

"There's no one else."

Granderson bared his teeth. "Bring them to me."

The hand inching toward the right hip.

Ben lunged up the stairs. A shot exploded behind him, deafening in the stairwell. The second shot chipped the wall a foot from his shoulder. Ben rounded the landing, taking the steps three at a time.

Behind him he heard Granderson coming fast.

CHAPTER EIGHTEEN

Claire jolted as the shots sounded below. *No*, she thought. *Not Ben.*

Joshua's sweaty body trembled against hers. She lay behind the boy, her sweaty arm clutching him, their hiding place under the window seat suffocatingly hot. She listened for voices, more shots, anything.

"What happened?" Joshua asked.

"I don't know," she whispered. She clenched her teeth, agonized between staying here as Ben had instructed or going down the stairs to help.

But what help could she be? If Granderson had already killed Ben, she'd be killed too, and Joshua would be alone. If Ben was still alive, she might screw up whatever plan he had.

Claire compressed her lips. She couldn't wait any longer. She reached up, pushed the door slightly ajar.

"Where's Daddy?" Joshua asked in a whimper.

"*Shh*," she whispered into his hair. "Let me listen."

The boy grew still against her, though now and then his body would twitch, the fear an uncontrollable force. She heard footsteps, shouting. Ben was still alive, at least for the moment. She bit her lip, debating. She knew Ben wanted her to stay out of it, but what if she could sneak up on the man, knock him out with a blunt instrument?

She raised the lid, surveyed the studio. The wood floor swam with shadows, the tenebrous shapes rippling and darting like giant bats gripped by the hunt. Claire stared down the shadows until the panic ebbed.

"Stay here," she said to Joshua. "I'll be right back."

He grabbed her arm, gazed up at her abjectly.

"I promise I'll come back," she told him. "Just wait here and don't move a muscle until me or your daddy comes and gets you."

His bottom lip quivered, the eyes filling with tears, but he nodded. Claire bent and kissed his forehead. She closed the lid.

Her sandals made scraping noises that made her wince. Shedding them, she moved slowly along the wall toward the staircase. She heard running footsteps, but no voices and no gunshots. It sounded as though Ben were leading Granderson down the hallway below, away from the studio.

She glanced at the window. This one didn't have a window seat, was smaller than the one under which she and Joshua had hidden. She studied the pitted castle façade just beyond it. Claire could see the pale exterior reflecting the moonglow. She could have sworn she'd seen—

Claire gasped at gunshots, three of them this time. They came from directly below her. Her heart lurching, she took a step toward the staircase and screamed as the pane beside her exploded. The hail of glass floored her, her skin slashed in a dozen places. She rolled onto her back and looked in horror at the creature who had crashed through the window.

The monster from the pit.

It stood over her, its elongated face a rictus of cruelty and hunger. Its dark, muscled arms reached for her, but beyond it she saw something shift, *oh God*, the window seat rising. Joshua standing straight up in the gap and staring at what stood before him. The creature whirled and with a growl that chilled her blood, bounded toward Joshua on springy cloven hooves.

"*No!*" she screamed.

But the creature grabbed the boy and dove headfirst through the sixth-story window.

CHAPTER NINETEEN

The bullets whistled by as he ducked inside the master suite. He locked the door, a dead bolt, *thank God*, and glanced about for a weapon. He had only seconds, he knew, before Granderson blew the lock off the door and came in to finish the job.

He grabbed the Tiffany lamp off the nightstand. It wasn't great, but it would have to do. He heard footsteps outside the door, a clicking sound. Reloading, he assumed. He'd have to brain the man the moment he came through.

He was thinking this when the deadbolt disappeared in a haze of smoke. Ben rushed at the door as it swung open, its edge barely missing his face. Granderson had the gun up, but Ben caught him off guard. Avoiding the sweeping barrel, he whipped the lamp at the man's head. The gun went off a moment before the multicolored glass shattered on Granderson's blond pate. Ben staggered into the hallway as the bodyguard went to his knees. Ben spun, meaning to clout the man with the meager remains of the lamp, but Granderson brought the gun up, fired.

Heat seared Ben's hip and the lamp shattered on the floor.

He turned to run and heard voices, Ryan and Kayla attracted by the commotion. He dashed toward them shouting, "*Get down*," but they gaped at him, faces vapid with confusion. Rather than following his advice, they were actually approaching.

Looking back, Ben saw Granderson step into the hallway, the gun raised. Ben hit the floor and covered his head.

As the gunfire exploded in the corridor, Ryan seized Kayla by the shoulders and used her as a shield. Ben watched in shock as her body juddered with the bullets. Granderson popped off four, five, six shots, and on the last, a gout of blood splashed from Ryan's shoulder. He dropped Kayla's already lifeless body and limped toward the stairwell.

Ben got to his feet, and as he did he saw Granderson reloading. Ben whirled and barreled after Ryan. As the pilot disappeared into the stairwell, Claire appeared on the landing, a stricken look on her face.

"*Where's Joshua?*" he shouted as he heard behind him the clicking sound, Granderson preparing to fire.

"It got him," Claire said.

He grabbed her and pulled her around the corner. He squeezed her arms. "Where is he?"

She shook her head, and he knew in an instant what *it* was. "Come on," he said, leading her down the stairs. His hip screamed in protest, but he focused on his son to blot out the pain. She moved with him, but not fast enough. Above, he already heard Granderson's footfalls getting closer.

"Move, Claire. We don't have time."

"I'm so sorry," she said as they descended. "I'm so sorry, Ben."

Above, the footsteps were getting louder, Granderson gaining on them. Ben half-expected Ryan, the fucking coward, to appear out of nowhere and somehow get them killed too, but so far there was no sign of him.

When they reached the first floor, they sprinted through the great hall toward the foyer. Ben shouted, "*Closet,*" but Claire paused in the middle of the foyer and watched him irresolutely. He flung open the front door and said, "Open the closet door." Claire opened it and they crowded inside. Ben pulled it shut behind them just as Granderson's racing footfalls pounded through the foyer and straight out the open front door.

Ben held Claire in the darkness.

"That was smart," she said.

"Bought us a little time."

He felt her trembling body against his. "What do we do now?" she asked. "Wait till we know he's gone and go upstairs?"

He shook his head, thinking. "I have to get Joshua out of the pit."

"I don't think they're down there."

"What?" he said. "Claire, you smelled the base—"

"After it…" She hesitated.

"*Yeah?*"

She shivered. "It grabbed him and leaped through the window."

For a moment, he couldn't speak. His heart thundering, he said, "That's six stories up. It couldn't—"

"It did. It was dark so I couldn't see that well, but when I went to the window to look, I saw it…moving across the lawn with Joshua in its arms."

"Away from the castle?"

He felt her nod against his chest, as if he could see her in the darkness.

He swallowed. "We have to go out there then. We have to find them."

"But that's where Granderson is."

The thought of Granderson brought a searing wave of pain in his hip.

She said, "He'll be coming for us."

He nodded, trying desperately to clear his head.

"We could go out the other way," she said, and Ben nearly groaned aloud, it was so obvious.

"Okay," he said, and opened the door a crack. A few feet away the front doorway was still empty, but at any moment…

"Come on," he said and led Claire out of the closet. "Where's the back door?"

"This way," she said, leading him through the back hallway. He and Eddie had ventured down here that first night, but he didn't remember another exit.

They were moving past the parlor door, toward a bend in the corridor, when a voice behind them made Ben's heart skip a beat. Certain it was Granderson, he pulled Claire around the corner and perceived, several yards away, a short flight of steps leading to a plain wooden door. They were moving down the steps when the voice came again, and Ben turned this time to see Ryan coming around the corner. The pilot was grimacing and holding his shoulder. "I need help," he muttered. "That son of a bitch shot me."

"Go to hell," Ben said and opened the door.

But Ryan followed them out. "*Please.* You gotta help me."

In the forest Ben spotted a trail. He led Claire that way, but soon she was dragging him forward, Ben laboring to keep up.

"Hey!" Ryan called.

"*Would you shut up?*" Ben hissed over his shoulder.

"You can't leave me," the man said and turning back, Ben saw him stumble. They passed into the forest and moved down a muddy slope, the ground sloppy from last night's downpour.

"Where're we going?" Claire asked.

How the hell should I know? Ben wanted to shout. He glanced back and noticed Ryan still following. He scanned the forest and found what he was looking for fifteen yards away. They moved toward the fallen redwood and waded through a cold, wet thicket that tore at their clothes. As they hunkered down behind the fallen tree, Ryan joined them.

"Why's Granderson trying to kill us?" Ryan asked. "I thought it was Blackwood he wanted."

"He did kill Kayla," Ben said. "Thanks to you."

Ryan blanched, slid down the trunk beside them. "My shoulder's bleeding like a bastard."

"Good," Claire said.

"We've got to think," Ben said. "Exactly which way did that thing take Joshua?"

"To the left," she said.

Ben scoured his memory for the island's layout. He thought of the forest, the bridge, the graveyard. God, he'd been stupid. To think the creature couldn't leave the basement just because it hadn't followed them last night. He'd been programmed by too many scary movies, wrongly believing there were strict rules, the creature like some vampire or werewolf.

Think, the terrified voice in his head demanded. *Your son's life depends on it.*

The thing didn't take Joshua to the tower, and they hadn't gone straight ahead toward the coast…

Ben stopped, mouth opening.

"I know where they are," he said.

Claire waited, lips parted slightly.

He asked, "You remember our walk?"

She shook her head, brow furrowing. Then, comprehension dawned in her face. "The redwood grove."

Ben nodded, thinking of the feeling they both had there. As though something was watching them.

"I need to go back to the castle for something," he said.

Claire looked sick to her stomach. "You can't be serious."

He helped her to her feet. "I have to."

She gestured toward the castle. "But Granderson."

"It's dark," he answered. "He won't see me if I'm careful. You and Ryan wait here. I'll be back in a couple minutes."

Claire shook her head. "You're not leaving me here with this jerk. Not after what he did to Joshua."

"Hold on—" Ryan started.

"*Shut up*," Ben growled and seized him by the shirt. "You wait here until it's done. I don't trust you to help us, but if you're lucky we'll come back for you when it's over."

Ryan shook his head, started to argue. "Listen, whatever the kid said isn't true," Ryan began, but Ben's grip on the man's shirt tightened. He shook him, reveled in the way Ryan's head snapped back and forth, and in the deepest recesses of his mind Ben felt something squirming and red and murderous take hold of him. He pivoted, smashed Ryan against a tree, and then he was battering him, all the pent-up fury and frustration pouring into his pistoning arms, his cudgel fists. Claire fought to pull him away, but Ben brushed her off, swung, and felt a surge of black joy as his right fist crashed against Ryan's chin.

Dimly, he heard Claire shouting, "*Stop, Ben, please stop it*," but it didn't register until he remembered Joshua, who'd been kidnapped, Joshua who needed his help *right now*. He let Ryan fall, stood over him. Ryan whimpered something about being sorry, his mouth a smear of blood and saliva.

"You deserve to die for what you did to my boy," Ben said, "for *everything* you've done to him." He turned to Claire. "Come on, we've gotta find Joshua, but first we need to find something to kill that thing."

★ ★ ★

Claire and Ben surveyed the castle. No sign of Granderson.

"Wait here a minute," Ben said. "I don't want both of us getting shot."

She knew he was right. It was a one-person job. If he found weapons, he'd bring them. He surprised her by kissing her hard on the mouth.

"Right back," he said.

Claire watched him jog, head down, toward the weathered wooden door. In any other situation the tall man trying to keep such a low profile would have been comical. Now, though, the sight of Ben's six-four body hunched down to maybe five-ten made her anxious. If Granderson was hiding somewhere nearby, there's no way he'd miss Ben unless he had the world's worst vision.

The full moon bathed the castle lawn in a silvery glow, and though she was glad to be able to see Ben clearly, she knew it also increased his chances of being spotted by Granderson.

She jumped as a hand touched her shoulder.

Ryan.

She clapped a hand on her chest. "You scared me, dammit."

Ryan hunkered down next to her. "You shouldn't have left me alone."

"I don't suppose it matters that I wish you were dead."

He grinned. "You'll get over that."

Wonderful, she thought. An even cockier version of Eddie Blaze. But at least Eddie had possessed some semblance of a heart before going crazy, before whatever fell spirit possessed him. She wondered what Ryan would be like if the same thing happened to him.

What if it already had?

"He's been in there awhile," Ryan said.

Claire chided herself for allowing her mind to drift from Ben, who had yet again placed himself in harm's way to save someone. And it was largely her fault.

Tears threatened as she thought of the little boy in the clutches of the monster. God, she'd been a fool to leave him, even if she had only been a few feet away. She had failed Ben, failed Joshua, and now both of them would probably die because of her.

She looked away so Ryan wouldn't see her tears. All she could do now was hope Ben would return from the shed with a weapon with which she could atone.

"Here he comes."

She looked up at Ryan's words and glimpsed Ben, hunched over again, casting restive glances toward the tower. He carried a pair of long-handled objects in his right hand and another, curved object in his left.

When he spotted Ryan, his expression darkened. Kneeling next to them, Ben said, "I thought I told you to stay away from us."

"Three bodies are better than two," Ryan said. "Even if my shoulder feels like someone took a hacksaw to it."

Claire studied the scythe and pitchfork Ben had found. "Harvest time?"

He smiled wanly. "Best I could find."

She examined the third implement as Ben laid it on the ground. "What's that one?"

The tool was three feet long and had a wooden handle. Ben fingered one of the two forklike tines protruding from the end of it. "They call it a daisy grubber," he said. "My grandma used to have one."

Ryan looked at the tools skeptically. "You think those are gonna do any good?"

Anger flared in Ben's eyes. "They're better than nothing."

"Listen," Ryan said in a conspiratorial whisper, "we can get out of here right now. I've flown choppers before. If Granderson doesn't see us, we can take off before he knows what happened."

Ben said, "And leave my son here."

Ryan shrugged. "I'd rather three of us survive than none of us."

"Maybe we should kill him now," Claire said.

"Not yet," Ben answered. "We still need someone to fly us home."

CHAPTER TWENTY

When they neared the redwood grove, Claire whispered, "I think we should split up."

"Fuck that," Ryan said.

For once, Ben tended to agree with him. He glanced at Claire. "Tell me what you're thinking."

She gestured toward the legion of redwoods rising out of the glade. "If we divide the creature's attention, we have a better chance of hurting it. And," she added, "of getting to Joshua."

The rise surrounding the grove prohibited a view of the ground, but the feeling he'd experienced a few days ago had returned. He knew the beast was here. *Please God*, he thought, *let Joshua be here too, and let him be unharmed.* The odor from the pit was present too, routing the infinitely more pleasing scents of wet grass and pines.

"Listen," Ryan said in a voice Ben thought too loud by half.

Then Ben heard it too. The music was soft, strange, but very familiar. Then he had it—"Forest of the Faun."

"You stay here," Ben said to Claire. "I'll go left and Ryan'll go right."

Ryan clutched the pitchfork to his chest. "I don't think I can do this."

Ben eyed him over the scythe blade. "I thought pilots were supposed to be cool under pressure."

"In a plane," Ryan said. "Not against monsters."

The music grew louder.

Ben winked at Claire. "See you in a minute."

He turned and set off into the forest. He wondered if he should have given her the pitchfork rather than the daisy grubber. Neither one seemed very imposing in the face of the creature they were about to encounter, but then again, other than a Sherman tank, what would? When the axe blade had pierced its side, the creature had barely flinched.

His son's voice shattered his thoughts. Moaning, as if in pain.

He bounded through the underbrush knowing he'd be heard, but the hurt in Joshua's voice seared through his reason. When he thought he'd gone far enough, he climbed the hill and peered down into the grove.

His breath caught as he spotted them. Joshua lay motionless on the ground at the creature's cloven feet. The beast sat at the base of a redwood. Its knobby fingers floated over the woodwind's holes, its white eyes never leaving Joshua. It might have been serenading the boy.

Or eulogizing him.

Ben stepped into the clearing and said, "Give me my son."

The beast looked up and stared at him. Clutching the thick wooden handle of the scythe, Ben moved down the hill toward the creature, which rose and let the flute dangle at its side. Twenty feet away now and closing, Ben could see exactly how tall, how incredibly formed the beast was. Its chiseled body stood well over seven feet, its muscles striated and bulging. The talons were two or three inches long, the curving horns tawny and ancient-looking.

Ben thought back to his earlier battle with the creature and understood he might not survive this time. But Joshua's chest, he noted with a surge of hope, was still rising and falling sluggishly, as though the boy were in a deep sleep. Ben's stomach fluttered as the beast knelt over Joshua and traced the boy's jawline with one long fingernail. Ben neared, only a few feet away now.

"Get away from him," he demanded.

The creature's pupilless eyes gazed up at him, a malevolent grin stretching its face.

"*Mine*," it said.

Ben reared back and kicked the creature's grinning face as hard as he could. He heard the teeth click together, and when the eyes returned to Ben, its grin was gone.

With a bloodcurdling roar, it sprang forward, smashed Ben to the ground, the scythe skittering uselessly in the leaves. Its girth was suffocating. Its knees pinned his arms, its scimitar teeth dripping with slaver. Ben thrashed but could not rid himself of the beast's bulk.

With a swipe of its claws it tore through Ben's cheek, the blood spraying everywhere. Ben stared in dim fascination as its tongue slid out of its open mouth and licked at the droplets. It raised its huge right hand again, clearly intending to tear out Ben's throat, when its body suddenly jolted, a look of outrage contorting its face.

It whirled and with the back of its hand sent Claire flying through the air. As it stood, growling, Ben glimpsed the handle of the daisy grubber sticking out of its back. Halfway to Claire it stopped, reached for the implement with which she had stabbed it, and through a leafy copse of bushes Ben spied Ryan's gaping face, the son of a bitch too afraid or too selfish to help them.

Though his vision doubled as he pushed to his feet, Ben grabbed the scythe and staggered to where the beast towered over Claire. Numbly, he watched the beast toss the daisy grubber aside. It bent over, grasped the front of Claire's white tank top and ripped. Rage searing through his grogginess, Ben rushed forward and swung the scythe as hard as he could. The creature spun, got an arm up, but the blade cleaved through muscle and bone.

Ben stared in shock at the stump of the beast's arm, severed at the elbow and jetting blood straight into the air.

A look of depthless hatred twisted the beast's face, and before it could leap on him and tear him to shreds, Ben whipped the scythe again and bellowed in triumph as the curved blade disappeared into the pulsing tendons of its neck. It fell forward, shrieking in pain.

Apparently unhurt, Claire got up. They hurried toward Joshua, who still hadn't moved, and were kneeling over him when Claire said, "*No.*"

Ben followed her gaze and saw the creature wrench the scythe from its neck. Claire was shaking her head, saying they had to go, they had to go. Ben nodded, and as he gathered Joshua's body into his arms, he saw with a crawling sense of doom the creature's flesh knitting together where the scythe had been. It was on its feet already, striding over to retrieve its severed arm.

"*Run*," Ben said.

They did, moving as fast as their feet would carry them toward a gap in the woods ringing the hill. They had reached the top of the rise, Claire first, Ben and Joshua close behind, when he chanced a look over his shoulder and saw with alarm the empty glade, the beast no doubt disappearing into the forest to ambush them.

Claire uttered an inarticulate cry, and Ben was thinking the beast had found them when he beheld the man standing at the bottom of the hill, the gun trained on Claire's face.

"Lovely moon tonight," Granderson said.

CHAPTER TWENTY-ONE

Though her eyes were closed, Claire could feel the gun pressed to her temple. Granderson would kill them now, and in the vast scheme of things it didn't matter because there was no defeating the creature. At any moment she expected it to leap from the shadows and destroy them.

Granderson lowered the gun. "Over here," he said.

She opened her eyes and saw him gesturing to where Ryan lay facedown on the ground, his hands laced over the back of his head. She wanted to think Granderson was the reason Ryan had not helped them, but she knew better. He'd probably run at the first sign of the beast and had drawn Granderson to the glade.

Claire went over to where Ryan lay and on impulse kicked him in the side. He grunted, doubling up in agony, and behind her Granderson began to laugh. She turned in time to see Ben approaching with Joshua.

"That's close enough," Granderson said.

Ben nodded once and gave him a wider berth. He approached Claire, his gaze on her intense. She tried to discern his intentions but couldn't. He held Joshua out to her and she cradled the boy automatically. With a final look, he stepped away from where she and Joshua stood and moved to an open patch of the woods.

Granderson scowled, gestured with the gun. "I told you to go over there."

"Easy," Ben said. "You've got us."

As Ben stared at Granderson, a dark certainty arose in Claire's mind.

"I want you on your stomach," Granderson said. "Now."

Ben didn't move. "So you can shoot me in the back of the head?"

The ghost of a smile played on Granderson's lips.

"Okay then," Ben said, and Claire watched numbly as he broke straight at Granderson. The man's arm came up, the gun glittering. Ben lunged as Granderson fired. Claire screamed as Ben went down, and as Granderson spun to fire at her, she turned Joshua away so he would be shielded from death, at least for a moment.

The shot exploded. Claire waited for the impact but it didn't come.

She turned and saw Granderson on his knees, clutching his belly, blood flowing in torrents over his fingers. Chris Blackwood moved into the moonlight, the gun held out before him.

Granderson glared up at him. "God damn you—"

Then the words were lost in the thunder of gunfire, Chris shooting the man from three feet away, the side of Granderson's head shearing off, a hairy chunk of scalp twirling to the ground like a pinwheel.

Claire dashed over to Ben, placed Joshua gently on the ground beside him. She rolled Ben over, Chris Blackwood staring over her shoulder.

Ben's eyes were open, but he looked at her as though he'd never seen her before. She saw the blood seeping through his fingers, the bullet puncturing him in the left side just below the rib cage. *No*, she thought. It was too cruel a joke, surviving two battles with the creature only to be gutshot by a mercenary.

Ben's eyes shuttered wide as he sucked in breath.

She cradled his head, asked, "Can you move?"

He looked at her, recognizing her for sure this time.

She cast a nervous glance into the forest. "Ben, we have to get out of here. We have to go before…" she swallowed. "…before it comes back."

Ben winced. He opened his eyes and stared at Joshua next to him. He reached out a bloody hand and touched the boy's arm. In a barely audible voice, he asked, "Will he be all right?"

Chris reached down, got an arm under Ben's back. "He will if we get him out of here."

Claire joined in helping Ben to his feet. Ben leaned on them a moment, nodded and said, "I think I'm okay to walk."

Claire bent and swept Joshua into her arms.

Ryan said, "Oh Jesus no."

She'd forgotten about him, but she saw him next to Granderson's body, looking at something to their left. She turned and saw the creature standing atop the ridge, its arm reattached. Backlit by the moon's brilliance it looked more fearsome than ever, a mythological satyr come to life.

Chris turned to her, the gun poised in the air. "Get to the helicopter."

She started to move with Joshua, Ben and Ryan flanking her, but she looked back and realized that Chris had stayed behind, was aiming up at the beast. She raced to keep up with Ryan, Ben a few feet behind her staggering along. They didn't have far to go, but the things the creature could do, its unearthly powers…

A shudder rolled through her. There was no safe distance from it. And

Joshua was growing heavy, the steady incline they were climbing far too difficult with an extra thirty pounds in her arms. They had put fifty or sixty yards between them and the grove, and when Claire turned to see if Ben was keeping up, she saw Chris Blackwood fire at the creature from point-blank range. She halted, waiting for Ben, but also transfixed by the horrible scene playing out behind them. Ben reached out for his son but Claire said, "Your side. You can't carry—"

"One arm still works," he said and hoisted Joshua onto his shoulder. He turned, following her gaze. They watched in silence as Chris fired again. The creature's head jerked, the entry wound glistening in the bright moonglow. Then its arm shot out and knocked the gun from Chris's hand. Chris backpedaled a moment, then fell, the creature treading slowly toward him.

"We have to go," Ben said.

She saw Chris scramble to his feet and take a few frantic strides before falling again.

She could hear him whimpering in terror.

"*Claire,*" Ben said, his voice rising.

But she couldn't turn away as the creature stepped on Chris's crawling form. The cries grew louder. The beast reached down, rolled him over, then hauled him into the air, Chris's feet dangling a foot off the ground. Then, it drew him toward its fanged maw.

Chris's feet drummed the creature's thighs, his hands flailing to keep the deadly jaws at bay. He wailed as the white fangs punctured his throat. His voice dissolved in a hideous gurgle as the beast began to feed.

Ben seized her arm, dragged her up the incline. "If we don't get there fast, Ryan's not going to wait for us."

She looked into Ben's eyes and knew it was true. She lurched up the path next to him, sure now that Ryan would leave them. She imagined the chopper floating away, becoming a speck on the night sky as the creature hunted them down.

As they pounded around a curve and spotted, ahead, the mouth of the forest, her fear grew. Leaving them here to die would solve all Ryan's problems. No one would know how he'd threatened Joshua, how he'd tried to strangle the boy. No one would know how he'd sacrificed Kayla to save his own skin, how he'd failed to help Ben and Claire when they'd needed him most.

As if confirming her fears, she heard a dull metallic thud in the distance.

The helicopter's door closing.

"Oh God," she said as they burst into the moonlight and ran desperately across the castle lawn.

She hadn't heard the motor chug, the mechanical whir of the propeller, but she was certain at any moment she would.

Ben stopped running and the look on his face stopped her too.

Something was emerging from the trees near the beach.

This is madness, she thought but knew that wasn't right.

Whatever this was, it was worse than madness.

CHAPTER TWENTY-TWO

Eddie approached them.

Ben was about to speak to him, tell him they had to get to the helicopter, when he saw something that made his stomach clench spasmodically, his arms grasp Joshua tighter.

Eddie carried a child. Swaddled in a white blanket smeared with blood, the child was gathering something to its face. Eddie took another step toward them, and a woman appeared at his side. Like the child, the woman's features were all wrong, and he realized with sinking terror that both woman and child were badly burned, flesh scorched, hair sticky and clotted with gore. The black smell of violent death attended them; Ben thought of pagan ceremonies and innocent women burned at the stake, their charred bodies left hanging for the crows to peck clean.

Eddie was expressionless, and as the trio neared, Ben realized what the child in Eddie's arms was doing. Claire cried out and Ben longed to as well, but he no longer had the strength. Roughly Joshua's age, the little boy was smacking and chewing on something stringing out of Eddie's belly.

"*You happy now*?" Eddie asked, his voice a wet, brackish rumble. "*You happy, you fucking bitch*?" Eddie groped for Claire, who seemed too mesmerized to resist. Just as Ben was about to set Joshua on the ground so he could intercede, the burned woman seized a handful of Eddie's hair and dragged him down. "*No more!*" Eddie pleaded. "*No more!*" But her mouth was already battened on the flesh just below Eddie's armpit, the long, sicklelike teeth chewing into his rib cage. Eddie howled as the fangs crunched bone. The burned child continued to feast on Eddie's small intestine.

Making sure he had a good grip on Joshua, Ben swung Claire away from the ghoulish family and dragged her into a run. Casting a glance back, he saw them shambling after them. Ben pushed forward despite the loss of blood, despite the dizziness. He had to get them away from the monsters, had to reach the helicopter. They neared the solitary tower. He strained to see around the corner of Castle Blackwood, to spot the helicopter.

"*No*," Claire shouted as they passed the tower and heard the rumble of the helicopter's motor. Ben staggered forward as fast as he could, Joshua heavy in his arms. The motor grew louder as they passed the corner of Castle Blackwood and beheld the chopper. The blades began to spin.

Ryan was leaving without them.

Only fifty yards away, but Ben's breath was going. Though the pain in his side was excruciating, he managed to shout to Claire, who was a couple of feet ahead, "*You go first.*"

Though Claire was still running, her panicked face darkened in doubt.

He shouted, "*I'll hand him up to you!*"

The doubt vanished from her face and she dashed ahead. His vision dimmed and he stumbled, nearly went down. Recovering, he looked up and saw the interior lights of the chopper, Ryan pushing buttons. Ben's jaw clenched.

Ninety feet away. He couldn't stop now.

Getting closer. *Keep going*, he told himself. *Just keep moving, keep moving for your son.*

The propeller picked up speed, the motor an insectile drone.

Claire was almost there, but the helicopter was lifting, inching higher.

No!

Halfway there. He watched Claire rip open the door, scramble up into the chopper, but the landing runners kept rising, a foot in the air now. Two feet. Three. Higher. *Oh God.*

Ben heard Claire shouting, Ryan yelling a reply, but it was lost in the din. Then he glimpsed Claire swinging, slapping at Ryan's shocked face.

He cried aloud as the runners paused and began to move downward.

Ten feet away from the chopper he saw the door pushed wide, Claire's intense face and her waving, extended arms. Then her eyes swung up and grew huge. Ben whirled and spotted the beast following fast across the lawn, its movements an obscene combination of loping strides and panther-like bounds. It passed the tower.

The chopper hovered a couple of feet from the ground, Ryan screaming at them to *hurry goddammit.*

Ben lifted Joshua and thrust him into Claire's arms. She pivoted, placed the boy in the back seat. Ben lifted a foot and grabbed Claire's reaching arm just as something hit him with incredible force and slammed him face-first into the side of the chopper. Ben twisted as he fell and saw the creature climbing the runner, its hungry face leering at Claire.

Without thinking Ben pushed to his feet, reached between the creature's legs and seized it by the scrotum. It bellowed and reached down to knock his hand away, but Ben yanked with all his might and felt the leathery skin split. The beast howled in pain and tumbled off the runner. Ben screamed "*Go!*" as he stepped onto the runner and with Claire's help pulled himself into the chopper.

He climbed into the back seat with his son as Ryan guided the helicopter higher, higher, Claire staring down at Ben in amazement. Her mouth opened when she looked at his side, and when he noticed the rills of blood spilling onto the vinyl seat, he experienced another bout of dizziness.

Claire tore a strip from her tattered shirt and pressed it to his side. Leaning down, Ben touched the boy's cheek. For the second time in two nights, Joshua was unconscious. He was breathing, but it was harsh and erratic, the boy in some kind of nightmarish trance.

They had attained a height even with the fourth story of Castle Blackwood, and Ryan began to aim the helicopter east, the chopper still rising.

Movement from the corner of Ben's eye. He turned in time to see something that froze his blood.

Defying gravity as it moved rapidly across the bald face of the castle, the beast was following them, its progress unbelievably fast. Unable to look away, Ben watched in amazement, dimly appalled at the ease of its movements.

Claire had caught Ben's terror. "What?" she asked.

Instead of answering, he looked out the window as the beast ascended the face of a turret, climbed effortlessly to the roof.

The chopper rose ten feet above the roof and had almost reached the corner of the castle. The beast was gaining, but they would make it if they kept—

They screamed as the beast leapt.

Ben watched in horror as its demonic face hurtled nearer, nearer, and just when he was certain the beast would plummet harmlessly to the earth, the rear of the chopper dipped, the weight of the thing jerking them down.

Ryan was staring back in fright rather than concentrating on the trees looming ahead. "What the hell—" he began.

"*Watch out*," Ben yelled as the runners neared the dark tops of the evergreens. Ryan pulled on the controls, and they barely averted the forest. Under them, the black Pacific replaced dry land.

Ben spun around and glimpsed the beast crawling over the tail of the chopper, its head down to avoid the spinning blade. The back window was just large enough for Ben to see the creature reach out, latch on to the shell of the cabin.

For an insane moment he was reminded of that old *Twilight Zone* episode, the gremlin on the wing, and just when he expected the beast to rip off the propeller and send them crashing into the sea, the craft shuddered as it punched a hole in the door and ripped it open.

The beast appeared in the doorway and grinned at Ben.

Then its white eyes shifted to Joshua.

With a scream of fury Ben leapt forward and smashed the monster with a fist. Its head snapped backward at the impact, and when it looked at him, its face was livid with rage. Its talons whistled down and tore through Ben's face. He landed on his hands and knees, the blood gushing out of his forehead, his cheeks rent to ribbons. The beast climbed in, began to step over Ben's kneeling body. Its lustful, shit-tinged odor sent a charge through his flagging consciousness, made his teeth grind with desperate tenacity.

Ben summoned the final bit of his strength, grabbed the creature around the legs, and pushed to his feet. Bellowing in surprise, the beast tilted forward and clawed at Ben's back as he lifted its lower half up and out of the chopper, the feet drawing nearer and nearer the whirring blades until the cloven hooves disappeared in a pulpy spray.

The creature roared, reared back and as its head thumped the ceiling, Ben pushed forward, his upper body blasted by the wind, and drove the screaming beast through the open doorway. Its eyes flew wide as it realized it was falling, and at the last moment it grabbed Ben's shirt and pulled him through the opening. Ben hooked the corner of the doorway and felt his shirt torn away as the beast tumbled, screaming into the night. The blast of the wind threatened to break his tenuous hold on the doorway, but he felt Claire's arms around him, drawing him back inside. As he pulled himself weakly onto the bloody floor of the chopper, he cast one final look down as the beast splashed into the glittering sea.

CHAPTER TWENTY-THREE

Claire sat on the floor between the seats, Ben's unmoving head nestled in her lap. She caressed his bloody temples, wanting to say something to make it better, but knowing words were useless.

Ben was going to die.

His face had been slashed so deeply he didn't even look like the same man. The bullet wound in his side leaked. Through the hole in his cargo shorts she could see something pale in his hip, the bone showing. His entire body was a riot of gunshots and gashes. His breathing was labored, thin. Thank goodness Joshua wasn't awake to see him like this.

"Hard to believe we made it out of there," Ryan said.

"No thanks to you."

He gave her a hurt look. "You ever show any gratitude? Jesus, a guy risks his life for you and—"

"You tried to leave us," she said without heat.

He didn't reply.

The sound of Ben's breathing weakened.

"Hey, Claire," Ryan said, "I need you to get the map out of the glove box so we can find a place to land."

Not wanting to leave Ben, but anxious to touch down so they could get him and Joshua to a hospital, Claire eased Ben's head to the floor and rose. There wasn't much hope for Ben, but Joshua…if they hurried…

"It's over there," Ryan said.

She sat in the passenger's seat, opened the glove box. "Where is it?" she asked.

He grinned. "I lied, it's under my seat. Can you get it for me?"

"Get it yourself," she said and rose to rejoin Ben.

His fingers clamped on her arm. "I wouldn't do that."

She looked down at him.

"Sit," he said.

Wanting to punch his smug mouth but not wanting to cause a crash, she slumped into the passenger's seat and jerked her arm away.

"When I was laying on my belly back there in the forest," he said, "you kicked me in the ribs." He turned to her. "You remember that?"

She smiled. "Vaguely."

He nodded. "You also slapped the shit out of me when I tried to save our hides, get us the hell off the island."

"Because you would have left Ben and Joshua for dead."

He grinned and shook his head. "I remember you saying lots of things… how you wanted Ben to kill me, how I was a coward." His grin shrank, a hardness coming into his face. "I don't think I like you, Claire."

She opened her mouth as he raised Granderson's gun and aimed it at her heart. "Which is why I'm going to kill you first."

CHAPTER TWENTY-FOUR

Think, she told herself. *Think, damn you.*

If she made a grab for the gun it might go off and blow a hole in the gauges, destroy the sensitive equipment required to keep the chopper in the air. And even if she was able to overpower Ryan, disarm the creep, one of them could very well be mortally wounded in the struggle. If she died, Ben and Joshua were dead too. In the theater of her imagination she saw Ryan dragging their bodies to the opening and dropping them into the ocean.

If Ryan were killed, things wouldn't end any better. She could no more land a helicopter than she could run a four-minute mile, and even if she managed to get someone on the radio, she doubted it would happen like it did on TV, some steady, caring air traffic controller guiding her through it until they were safely on the ground.

Ryan's terrible grin had returned. "Where would you like it?" He gestured with the gun. "In the head or in the heart?"

Claire glanced down at her exposed white bra, her pale flesh where the shirt had been torn open.

Ryan's eyes went there too. "It's a shame," he said. "Three pretty girls like you, Eva, and Kayla all killed within a couple nights."

"You forgot your fiancé."

He shrugged. "Jenny was okay, but Kayla was better." He shook his head, a wistful look in his eyes, and her skin crawled at the thought of what memories he might be replaying. "I only saw a picture of Eva," he went on, "Lee had one at the funeral." He made a low whistling sound. "She was beautiful before that thing got to her."

Claire took a deep breath.

He turned to her. "So how should we—"

She dove across the seat and grabbed the gun with both hands. Under her she felt the controls depress. The helicopter shot downward. Ryan was screaming, struggling to wrench the gun from her. A vertiginous terror fluttering through her belly, she bit the heel of his hand as hard as she could.

He screamed and his hand flew open. She yanked the gun to her body and rammed an elbow into his stomach. Ryan doubled over, pushing her down as well, and the helicopter pitched toward the Pacific, Claire slamming the ceiling and tumbling to the back of the craft. She heard Ryan shouting something, aware that Ben and Joshua had been thrown to the back of the cabin as well, and just when she was sure they would crash she felt the helicopter straighten.

"*...you fucking cunt!*" Ryan was shouting. "*I oughta kill you for—*"

Shoving the gun in her pocket, she lifted Joshua and laid him on the back seat. She buckled him as well as she could and straightened Ben out so his body wasn't so crooked. She yearned to check on him, to make sure he hadn't broken his neck when the chopper plunged, but she didn't have time. Ryan could stop spouting his anger any moment, and then he'd realize he could defeat her by flying crazily again, send her catapulting against the interior of the cabin.

"*...and you tackle the fucking pilot...Jesus, you're a stupid—*"

She pressed the gun against the back of his head.

"Sit very still," she said. She sat in the passenger's seat and reached down to buckle her seatbelt. "If you try anything, I'll shoot you."

"You wouldn't shoot me," he said, trying to smile but making a poor job of it. "You did that, we'd all die."

"You want to take that chance?"

He didn't answer.

She said, "How far do we have to go?"

He paused. "That depends on where we're going."

"A hospital."

"I'm not landing at a hospital."

"Then somewhere close to one."

After a time, he glanced over at the gun, asked, "You know how to use that thing?"

"My dad was a policeman," she lied.

He seemed to believe her though. Several minutes later he said, "We're getting near the coast."

"What city's nearby?"

He shrugged. "Santa Rosa, I think. Maybe Petaluma. I'm not sure how far south we went."

Claire cast a worried glance back at Ben and Joshua, both lying unconscious. Ryan seemed to sense her indecision. "You know, I think we'll just land in the country somewhere. You can find someone else to drive you to the hospital."

Though his tone had been light, the undercurrent of cunning confirmed what she already knew. Ryan planned to touch down in a remote spot and take the gun away.

"You're not going to shoot me, Claire. We both know that. So I'm going to land where I goddamn well please, and you're not going to argue about it."

She was about to protest when Ben stirred. His groan didn't sound good, but at least it was a sign he still had some life in him. Though minutes counted and she was frantic to get Ben and Joshua to a hospital, she knew she couldn't stop Ryan from landing where he wanted. She couldn't shoot him and he knew it.

"Okay," she said.

He looked at her from the corners of his eyes. "And you'll let me go?"

"If you get us to the ground in one piece, I'll let you go."

"That's it?"

"As long as you promise to stay away from us for the rest of our lives."

"You've got a deal," he said.

He looked away, and in the window's reflection, she saw him smile.

CHAPTER TWENTY-FIVE

The sparse lights along the coast were replaced by the stronger glow of Sebastopol. Before they got there, though, he banked toward a large mountain forest.

Below, a road came into focus. Serpentining up the mountainside, it looked paved but deserted. Of course, she estimated, it was probably about two in the morning. Just about anywhere would be deserted at this hour.

She frowned. "Is it wide enough?"

"It's a tight fit, but we'll make it."

She didn't comment, her fear of perishing in a fiery crash returning. He brought the helicopter to a hover over the road. As they descended lower and lower, she had a fleeting image of a semi appearing out of nowhere and plowing into them, a final sick joke inflicted on them by fate.

They were thirty feet from landing when Ryan grabbed for the gun. Instinctively, she wrenched away from him, and though he seized her forearm, she switched the gun to her right hand just in time.

The chopper yawed toward the trees.

Gritting her teeth, she aimed the gun at his face. She held on to the seat as the chopper swayed frighteningly.

But he gave her an easy smile, righted the chopper as if nothing had happened.

"You bastard," she said.

He shrugged. "Worth a try."

When they touched down, he reached for the door.

"Wait," she said.

"Don't you want to make sure your boys are still alive?"

He was climbing out of the chopper as he spoke, acting for all the world like a child perpetrating some petty theft in front of his mother's eyes.

"*Stop*," she hissed.

He did, but his grin chilled her. "I thought your dad was a cop. Isn't *freeze* the right word?"

"Freeze then," she said, opening her door. "Wait there till I come around."

The road was dark, the scant breeze stifled by the trees lining the road. The rotor slowed, the silence of the mountain taking hold. The trees seemed to murmur derisively, as if they too were complicit in whatever wickedness Ryan still had in store.

His muscular body limned clearly by the woods, he said, "You want to kiss me good-bye?"

She thought of Joshua, his small bruised body in the helicopter. "Did you do what he said you did?" she asked.

He made a face. "The fuck are you talking about?"

"I want to know if what Joshua said was true."

He took a step toward her. "What did the little shit say?"

"He said you tried to strangle him after the crash."

He edged closer. "What do you think?"

She swallowed. "I saw the bruises."

Five feet away. "There's your answer."

"Don't make me," she said and he lunged for the gun.

Claire shot him in the face.

Ryan tumbled backward and lay without moving.

Claire held on to the gun – she'd seen too many horror movies to leave it where Ryan could get it should he somehow come back from the dead – and gazed down the winding road. Through the woods she glimpsed the twinkle of a security light. She set off at a brisk walk toward the light.

Soon she was running.

CHAPTER TWENTY-SIX

The smell told him he was in a hospital before he noticed the persistent beep. The pain came next – *damn, it was bad* – but with that came the knowledge he was alive. The hellish events on the island flooded back to him, and though the face of the beast kept replaying in his mind, the thought of Joshua rose above all else.

Ben opened his eyes.

The room was dim, but he could see well enough to know it was either dusk or early morning. He wanted to reach for the remote control dangling on the rail of the bed, but his arm wouldn't cooperate. He tested his fingers to make sure he wasn't paralyzed, and yes, they still moved. He tried again, his arm moving fitfully this time, and eventually his hand fell on the remote. His body buzzing with pain, he depressed the red button. After what seemed like hours, a nurse came in, gaped at him, and went out again. Moments later a doctor returned with her, and they both bent over him.

"Can you hear me?" the distinguished-looking man asked. Short white hair. Few wrinkles. Well preserved for a man who was probably nearing seventy.

"Yeah," Ben tried to say, but it came out a rattling croak.

"Are you in any pain?" the doctor asked.

"Joshua," Ben said in the same weak voice.

The doctor shook his head a moment before the nurse whispered something in his ear. Comprehension animated his handsome face and he said, "Your son is downstairs. He's anxious to see you."

The nurse went out, and the doctor frowned as if remembering something.

Ben's heart raced. "What's wrong?"

The doctor waved off the question. "It's not that...your son is fine, Mr. Shadeland. He was in shock when he was brought in, but now he's responding very well."

Ben was about to ask another question when the nurse opened the door and Claire came toward him. Her eyes were huge and full of tears. He smiled at her but grimaced as a withering pain scalded his body. He brought his hand up and touched the bandages.

She stood next to the doctor. "Can I…"

The doctor moved aside, said, "Of course. But be gentle with his left side. The bullet grazed his large intestine, but with proper care he should heal."

Claire nodded, moved around the bed.

"I'll leave you for a few minutes," the doctor said and went out.

Ben faced her. "How's Joshua?"

She glanced at the door. "I'll tell you about him in a minute…but Ben, I need to tell you something first."

He waited.

"Ryan shot you," she said.

"Huh?"

"The police will want to know. Ryan shot you twice, and he tried to kill me when we landed."

His mind reeled, struggled to process what she was saying, until he caught the frightened desperation in her eyes.

"You killed him," Ben whispered.

She didn't answer, but her eyes were enough.

"Exactly what he deserved," Ben said.

CHAPTER TWENTY-SEVEN

The police came and told Claire to leave. They weren't happy about her seeing Ben before they did, but after they talked to him for several minutes, they seemed to relax. He asked them when he could see his son. They told him they didn't know about that, there was some question about custody.

There's no question about custody, he said.

The boy's grandparents, they started to say.

Joshua's mine, he said and they didn't argue.

Claire came back as soon as they left.

"I want to see him," Ben said. "Now."

She nodded. A little while later the door opened and a nurse pushing a wheelchair entered.

Joshua looked tiny in the wheelchair, but his eyes grew large as he noticed how covered up with bandages Ben was.

"I look like a mummy, don't I?" Ben said.

Joshua nodded.

"It's Daddy," Ben said, raising his arms. "I know how bad I look, but I really need a hug."

The boy stared at him solemnly. He looked up at Claire, who nodded. Joshua climbed out of the chair and stepped closer to the bed. He made to climb up, but Claire lifted him and said, "This side." She carried him around the bed and deposited him on the blanket between Ben's right arm and his side.

Sitting on his knees, Joshua watched him with huge eyes.

Ben said, "Can Daddy have a hug?"

Joshua leaned forward, his beautiful face hovering over Ben's.

He kissed Ben on the lips and lay on his chest. Ben held the boy in his arms and began to weep. Ben held him and whispered how good their life would be, how much fun they'd have.

Joshua fell asleep within minutes. Ben joined him soon after that.

AFTER

The hospital didn't release Ben for two weeks. During that time Claire came to despise Jenny's parents, and she knew the feeling was mutual. Though they threatened to take matters into court, their lawyer must have finally gotten through to them. They ceased insisting they gain partial custody of Joshua, but for a short time they argued that the boy should be released to them until Ben improved enough to care for him. Perhaps because of this, Ben improved rapidly, and soon the grandparents went sulking away.

Ben's mother helped instead. When Ben was released, Claire and Ben's mom took him and Joshua back to his apartment. It was small and a trifle depressing, but it was quiet and a good place for Ben to rest. Claire took the time to get to know Joshua. The boy could be stubborn and he had a temper, but most of the time he was very sweet.

He was also very bright. When Claire told him one afternoon she thought they should get Indian food, the boy said, "Not necessarily." He used words like that all the time – *precisely*, *impressive*, *technology*, and her personal favorite, *recuperate*. He called her by her first name, and that was fine by her. She didn't want to force the issue, and so far the casual approach seemed to be working. He insisted that she read to him before naps – not before bed, though. That was Ben's job.

Joshua slept with his dad, and Ben's mother slept on a futon in the guest bedroom. Claire stayed on the couch.

Two months went by.

★ ★ ★

With some coaxing from Claire and Joshua, Ben finally agreed one day to go with them looking for houses. He was self-conscious about his face, which was still heavily bandaged from a series of surgeries, but when Claire changed his bandages she couldn't believe how much he was healing.

He called himself the Elephant Man. Claire said Frankenstein's monster was more like it, and he told her, when the doctor cleared him to engage in adult activities, he'd show her Frankenstein's monster.

They'd looked at three houses with the realtor, all of them in Sonoma County, when Ben said he didn't feel very well.

"One more," Joshua suggested, and of course Ben said *yes*.

The fourth house was a stucco ranch on three acres. It had been on the market a long time because its kitchen and bathrooms were sorely in need of updating, but it was on a big lot and the land behind it was preserved by the county and would never be developed.

Watching Joshua in the backyard, running around and trying to catch butterflies, Ben said, "We should probably put an offer on this place, huh?"

Her heart in her throat, Claire said, "We?"

He put an arm around her. "I suppose we should also get married to make the thing respectable."

She said, "I suppose," and they were engaged.

★ ★ ★

Two months later they were living out of boxes, but they were moved in, and the wedding date was set for the following spring. For a time they slept in separate beds, Ben not wanting to leave Joshua for even a moment. Eventually, Joshua talked Ben into letting Claire sleep with them. When Joshua napped, Claire and Ben spread a blanket in the yard and made love.

The movie was delayed, of course, but after Ben and Claire finally finished the score the producers were ecstatic about it, and a release date was set for the summer.

The night before Halloween they made a jack-o'-lantern and baked the seeds. Ben and Claire agreed they tasted like fingernails, but Joshua wolfed down a pile of them. When Ben put the candle in the carved-out pumpkin, Joshua nestled into Claire's side, his brown eyes huge.

"Don't you like it?" Ben asked.

Slowly, Joshua shook his head. "It's scary."

Ben took it to the backyard and smashed it with a baseball bat.

Claire could hear them in the backyard now. She was cleaning the pumpkin slop off the counter and enjoying the smell of the apple-spice candle Ben had bought her. She touched the growing swell of her belly, closed her eyes and listened to their voices.

That night Ben asked her something just before he turned off the lights.

Before answering, she glanced at the boy lying between them to make sure he was asleep. When she was, she said, "Of course I still think about what happened."

He frowned.

"Go ahead," she told him.

He said, "Do you think that..." He swallowed, took a deep breath. "Do you think, if it's still alive...could it ever leave the island?"

Claire felt a pressure in her chest. She wondered the same thing every night, but this was the first time either of them had spoken of the possibility. She had no idea if the beast was really dead. Or if it was alive, whether it could leave the island. She did know she would jump at shadows for a long time. Maybe the rest of her life.

But she said, "I don't think so."

He watched her and she saw in his eyes the same need she had for reassurance.

Claire said, "Whatever that thing was, I believe it was part of the island. If it somehow survived what happened, I think it went home."

"I think of it all the time," Ben said. "I picture it walking alone through the woods...moving through the castle at night...waiting."

She put a hand on his cheek. The scars were healing well. He looked very much the same as he had the night they'd met. Only now the sadness was gone, the haunted eyes. He had his son back, and he smiled a great deal. She hoped she had something to do with that too.

She said, "I don't know if it's alive, but I know we'll never see it again. We're safe now." She leaned over the sleeping boy and kissed Ben on the mouth. Lying back she said, "I know we're safe."

"All right," he said. He reached back, switched off the light.

In the darkness, he said, "Love you."

She said, "Love you too," and closed her eyes.

Soon, his breathing became slower, steadier. Claire tried to sleep a long time, but a dozen thoughts kept her awake. She worried Joshua might someday resent her the way Kayla had resented Ben. She hoped the boy would come to love her like a mother. She hoped she would be a good wife. She hoped *House of Skin* would be a success and that people would love their music.

Claire rolled over and stared out the window. The moon was full and bright. She watched it and gently massaged her belly.

And prayed the baby in her womb was Ben's.

ACKNOWLEDGMENTS

Thanks to my incredible wife and my three amazing children for supporting my writing. Thanks to Don D'Auria for being a fantastic editor and a patient guide. Thanks to my readers Clay, Tim, Melissa, Kimberly, and Tod for their honest feedback. And finally, thanks to Stephen King, Jack Ketchum, Brian Keene, Richard Matheson, Tim Waggoner, and Joe R. Lansdale for inspiring me and for showing me the way.

FLAME TREE PRESS

FICTION WITHOUT FRONTIERS

Award-Winning Authors & Original Voices

Flame Tree Press is the trade fiction imprint of Flame Tree Publishing, focusing on excellent writing in horror and the supernatural, crime and mystery, science fiction and fantasy. Our aim is to explore beyond the boundaries of the everyday, with tales from both award-winning authors and original voices.

•

Other titles available include:

Thirteen Days by Sunset Beach by Ramsey Campbell
Think Yourself Lucky by Ramsey Campbell
The House by the Cemetery by John Everson
The Toy Thief by D.W. Gillespie
The Siren and the Specter by Jonathan Janz
Kosmos by Adrian Laing
The Sky Woman by J.D. Moyer
Creature by Hunter Shea
The Bad Neighbor by David Tallerman
Ten Thousand Thunders by Brian Trent
Night Shift by Robin Triggs
The Mouth of the Dark by Tim Waggoner

•

Join our mailing list for free short stories, new release details, news about our authors and special promotions:

flametreepress.com